Leo's War

Based on the true story of Ireland's
secret World War II hero

PATRICIA MURPHY

Published 2018
by Poolbeg Press Ltd
123 Grange Hill, Baldoyle
Dublin 13, Ireland
E-mail: poolbeg@poolbeg.com

Typesetting, editing, layout, design, ebook © Poolbeg Press Ltd.

1

A catalogue record for this book is available from the British Library.

ISBN 978-1-78199-815-1

Typeset by Poolbeg Press Ltd

Cover illustrated by Derry Dillon

Printed and bound by CPI Group (UK) Ltd, Croydon, CR0 4YY

www.poolbeg.com

About the Author

Patricia Murphy is the bestselling children's author of a trilogy of novels about the Irish Revolution: *The Easter Rising 1916 – Molly's Diary*, *The War of Independence 1920-22 – Dan's Diary*, and *The Irish Civil War 1922-23 – Ava's Diary*.

She has also written the prize-winning *The Chingles* trilogy of children's Celtic fantasy novels. *Leo's War*, set in Italy during World War II, is her seventh novel for children.

Patricia is also an award-winning Producer/Director of documentaries including *Children of Helen House*, the BBC series on a children's hospice, and *Born to Be Different*, Channel 4's flagship series following children born with disabilities. Many of her groundbreaking programmes are about children's rights and topics such as growing up in care, crime and the criminal justice system. She has also made a number of history programmes including *Worst Jobs in History* with Tony Robinson for Channel 4 and has produced and directed films for the Open University.

Patricia grew up in Dublin. She is a graduate in English and History from Trinity College Dublin and holds M.A.'s in Journalism and Film Studies. She now lives in Oxford with her husband and young daughter.

ALSO BY PATRICIA MURPHY

The Chingles from the East

The Chingles Go West

The Chingles and the Vampire King

The Easter Rising 1916 – Molly's Diary

The War of Independence 1920-22 – Dan's Diary

The Irish Civil War 1922-23 – Ava's Diary

Published by Poolbeg

Dedication

For my Aunty Lillie – Sister Elizabeth Murphy of the
Sisters of Saint Francis, Philadelphia – with love

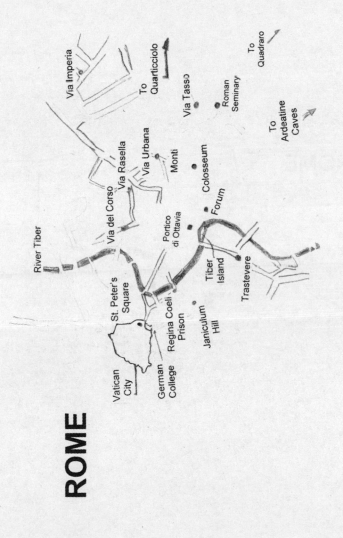

ROME

Vatican City

St. Peter's Square

German College

Regina Coeli Prison

Janiculum Hill

River Tiber

Via del Corso

Via Rasella

Via Urbana

Via Imperia

To Quarticciolo

Via Tasso

Roman Seminary

Monti

Portico di Ottavia

Colosseum

Forum

Tiber Island

Trastevere

To Ardeatine Caves

To Quadraro

Prologue

Italy 1943

Once upon a time there was this man who was a very bad artist in Germany. He couldn't grow a proper moustache. It looked like a slug on his upper lip. He was very shouty and spitty and they called him Spitler. When the Art School told him his paintings were rubbish, he decided to destroy the whole world. He really hated Jewish people. Nobody knows why. Maybe because, unlike him, they were really clever and talented. This made him shout until it looked like he would burst a blood vessel. He spat his hate all over the world.

Well, Spitler wasn't the only maniac in Europe. You've heard of Geppetto the carpenter who made Pinocchio, the little wooden puppet? Who wanted to be a real boy and whose nose grew longer when he told a lie? Well, Geppetto made another puppet with a big blockhead who wanted to be a real Emperor of Italy. His name was Muscle-weeny. When he told lies his chin jutted out even more. There was another one in Spain called Spanko and he was a real idiot too. And another one in Japan called The Emperor.

Unfortunately, lots of people believed their lies. At first the Germans wouldn't follow Spitler so he set up the Nasty Party to bully them all. He threw anyone who didn't agree with him in a camp. Muscle-weeny set up the Bashest party. They bashed in anyone's head who didn't do what he said. And he said a lot! The Italians got sick of him. But Spitler saved him and made him his puppet instead. Then the Nasties marched into Long-legged Italy and told them they were the kings. They marched in their jackboots all over Europe, planting their ugly red flag with the hooked cross everywhere.

The only ones who could stop them were an English fat man called The British Bulldog who chomped cigars, and another man in a wheelchair called FDR in the United States. They all spoke English.

There was another fellow in the East called Uncle Joe. He pretended there were no kings in his country, the USSR, and everyone was equal. But really he was the king. He changed sides a few times but now he was with the British and the United States. But it was taking them a long time to save the world. They needed a miracle fast before everyone died.

The End

I wrote this story for school. Luckily my mother read it first and laughed. She said it was very good. But I'd better not take it to school, as the nuns would have my guts for garters. They'd report me and I'd get into trouble with the Fascists who run Italy. So much for holy people. I can't afford to get into trouble because I am a mongrel who happens to live in Italy at the wrong time. My mother is an Irish-American, my father is a Jewish-English RAF pilot. My sister Ruby is seven and she is special and different. She didn't get enough air when she was born, so she has some problems with her muscles and things. But she is as kind as an angel and as clever as anything. She has russet-red hair like a pure flame – that's why they called her Ruby, my mother said. But I think my mama is just being fanciful when she says my hair looked like a lion's mane and that's why I'm called Leo.

I get called a lot of other not nice names in school. I am a moving target for every vicious little fascist bully in the playground who wants to look like a patriot. I get into a scrap at least once a day. Mostly because I barely speak in school and they all, including the teachers, think I'm a dunce. I've been held back two classes below and it's even worse that I'm taller than most Italian boys my age. I have to be honest – I don't care if they think my Italian is a bit rubbish. It lets me find out things and keep my head down. But I understand more than I let on.

We live in a ruined farmhouse on the edge of an abandoned village, Calcata, a huddle of ancient houses that are perched on top of a cliff. A few years ago, they thought it was going to collapse if there was an earthquake, so they made everyone move to a new village three kilometres away. Except us. We stayed put. So every day we have to trudge the weary miles downhill to the school. But we like being isolated. For in truth we are never alone.

My mother said to write my thoughts in a diary. Then at the end when this stinking war is all over, I will have a record. And maybe even a book. So that's what I'm doing. So meanies and Fascists and Nazis beware!

Chapter 1

Calcata
50 kilometres north of Rome
September 1943

"You're for it," Ruby said to me, looking up from the cart as I was pushing her up the hill back from school. She pointed to my black eye.

Sweat was trickling into it, making it sting, but I didn't want to rub it because that would make it even sorer.

The hot sun beat down on my shoulders, ready to scorch a pale Irish redhead like me. For the hell of it. I tried to make a face at her but I winced from the pain. I knew from past bruisings that my eye wouldn't be black yet. Just red. But no doubt I had another shiner, ready to blossom into a blue-black purplish flower in my face by the time my mother saw me.

"It's not my fault," I told Ruby sharply. "They started it."

It was true. It was that little scut from the village, Filippo, the pharmacist's son. They were throwing stones at us, calling Ruby names. *Idiota, storpio, deficiente.* Idiot, cripple, half-wit. They don't think I understand. They think I'm thick. But I know an insult when I hear it.

Ruby smiled her lopsided smile at me and giggled.

You see, Ruby has cerebral palsy and her muscles don't work so well – I think it means something like brain shakiness. And she's smart as a whip. She understands Italian and all. More than I do. And even some German. But when she tries to talk it comes out stuttery and wavery. But you can hear her cleverness, if you want to listen. You just have to flow with her words as if caught in a current in the river going downstream.

So, we'd been trudging up the hill when Filippo and his gang of toe-rags jumped out and started pelting us with rocks. I produced my big hurling stick that my Irish grandfather had sent me. I kept it with me at all times just for such an occasion.

"*Pomodoro!*" they taunted me. Tomato. "*Pelo di carota!*" Carrot-hair. And worst of all: "*Rosso mal-pelo!*" Red evil-hair.

"*Maiali fascisti!*" I roared back. Fascist pigs.

The little slimeball's father was a supporter of Mussolini, who was now back in power thanks to the invading Nazis. A puppet, as my mother said. And I could just see him jerking on a string to the Nazis' tune.

Then they called me another name.

"*Bastardo Inglese.*" English bastard.

That really got me going.

So I waved my hurley and they ran. I lit after them and they scattered behind the hill. I went back to Ruby in the cart and we trudged on.

Around the corner, they jumped me. Two of them pinned me down. And little Filippo, the vicious little article, punched me in the face. A direct hit in the eye that nearly made me black out.

Then they pulled down my trousers to look at my private parts.

"Dirty Jew," they said.

But they were disappointed. You see, I'm not circumcised.

"Told you he wasn't," said Guido, the cobbler's son.

I looked him hard in the eye. I used to think he was my friend. He looked away. Ashamed.

"The Nazis will get rid of you and the cripple," Filippo sneered at me, kicking me in the ribs.

I roared, "My dad and his RAF friends are going to come and bomb you to bits!"

He laughed in my face. "*Ha ha!* We all know you don't have a dad."

"And my mama, she's a –"

Ruby let out a screech.

"She's a what?" fat Filippo said, his second chin quivering like jelly.

I clammed up. I had said too much already.

"A dirty spy for Churchill?" He leered at me, spittle flying off his yellow buck teeth. Then he said a really mean word.

"Take that back!" I spat in his face and kicked out with all my might.

They ran off. But now I'd have to explain to my mother why I had a shiner. Again. But at least they left Ruby alone. Too busy hurting me.

I tried to think of some excuses. But I couldn't. My head was a bit woozy. At least there wasn't too much blood.

I sweated on up the hill, Ruby counting the last few cypress trees towards the top. I would have to think of an excuse. Quick. I was usually good at that. I was in trouble so often I got enough practice.

Chapter 2

As soon as we entered the driveway of our crumbling farmhouse just off the steep approach road of the volcanic cliff, my mother ran out, wiping her hands in her apron. She pushed a lock of her auburn hair behind her ear and smelled of lavender and rosewater. She smiled and it was like a second sun. My mother has this way of smiling that makes you feel warm from your head to your toes.

"Not again," she said, glancing at my eye, as she scooped Ruby up in her arms and carried her inside. "Leo, how many times do I have to tell you to stay out of trouble? Oh, my poor boy!"

I just shrugged and went to put the cart in the barn.

My mother, who trained as a nurse before we were born, immediately returned with a wet cloth to tend to my battered eye. It was beginning to swell a little bit.

"Guess who's here to see you!" she said.

I glanced over to the old garage at the other side of the house, wincing at the pain in my left eye. And there was a bright-green Bugatti – Aunt Delia's car!

Yaaay – no punishment for me today.

But let me explain a bit more. I'm Leo – Leo the Lionheart if you're me. Leo the Lost Cause to my teachers. Leo the Lovely, if you're Ruby. And my mother would say? Leo the loopy, lame-brained, lovable, larky lad. I think! I don't know what my father would say. He's off in the RAF fighting the Germans. And he really is a lionheart as he's Jewish. Not a holy one with ringlets. But Jewish enough for the Nazis to hate him. And if they catch him, they'll put him in a camp – well, I don't like to think about it. Well, actually, he may be dead. We don't know. The last anyone saw of him he was hovering between heaven and earth in his plane above the French coastline. There was a pea-souper, a dense fog over the Channel, and nobody's ever seen him since.

It's a long story how we came to live in Italy and got snared in this really big world war. But I'll tell it short.

We came here because my mother wanted to study at Maria Montessori's special school about how to help my sister. Maria is this really nice woman with a bun who loves little kids and lets them play. She says that's how they learn. I wish the nuns at our school listened. But fat chance of that because the Fascists kicked Maria out of the country (for not liking them at all).

But, anyway, you know about the nutter called Benito Mussolini, the Italian ruler. The one who nicknamed himself "Il Duce" – The Leader. The one I nicknamed Muscle-weeny. And his best friend the even bigger nutter Adolf Hitler who I call Spitler. Well, when Hitler started his big fighting, we kind of got stuck here. Particularly when the Italians rose up against Mussolini and tried to get rid of him. Anyway. Hitler, the shouty man with the stupid moustache and a big dream to kill us all, has invaded Italy.

Now that Muscle-weeny's best friends the Nazis have overrun Italy, we really can't get out. The Allies, that's the English and the Americans, have invaded Sicily and the south of Italy. They're working their way up the boot of Italy – very, very slowly. The Italian army fell apart and loads of Allied prisoners of war have escaped. Most everyone hates the Nazis. But there are a few sneaky Italians, the Fascists, who love them. They're also known as Blackshirts because of the black shirts they wear and they like to scowl so always look angry. So put the two together and you have the Nazi/Fascists – a super-concentrated evil force of the angriest people you ever met. The Nasty-Bashests.

I've just turned twelve – so, if the war is still going on, when I grow up I'm going to punch Hitler the Spitler's nose, so I am. And give him the biggest black eye you ever saw!

But, now, Aunt Delia was here and she always made all our hearts skip.

There she was with Ruby when I came into the kitchen – dressed all in yellow, her dark hair all pretty. The weather was hot even though autumn was on the way. I knew she'd have presents for us all! She wasn't really our aunty, just a distant cousin of my mother's. They grew up together as children in Ireland.

She came to see us at Calcata when she could. You see, her husband was Irish ambassador at the Vatican where the Pope lives. And our little village was about fifty kilometres to the north of Rome. She always had loads of goodies. Quite a miracle when there was a war on.

"How's the singing coming on, Leo?" she asked me in her strong Irish accent full of music and storm clouds. She was a brilliant singer. Had made records and all.

I looked down at my shoes.

"He won't go to the choir," my mother tutted. "He's a divil. Says he can't learn the words."

But the truth was I got into too many fights. And the priest who ran it was a creep. Came too close with his garlic breath.

Delia's dark eyes grew wide. "But, Leo, your voice is a gift from God! You should sing, a boy soprano like you, before your voice breaks."

Ruby said something in her halting way that we can all understand. "He sings me to sleep every night."

My mother melted then and gave me a big kiss. "He's a good boy really. Leo, my little lion. Now come here and I'll see to that eye!"

Well, soon we were all tucking into a big tea, with

chocolate cake, fresh plums and ham sandwiches like I remembered from back home in Ireland. Even though we hadn't visited in about five years.

We even had a singsong around the piano. My mother played and we sang some old Irish songs: "Danny Boy," "The Blackbird", "The Spinning Wheel". Delia had learned her songs from the Irish gypsies.

Delia and Mother talked about the old days. Them and all their millions of cousins. My mother grew up on an ordinary farm after the family came back from America where she was born. But Delia grew up in a mansion! Her father was really rich. He had struck lucky in the gold rush in the Klondike in Alaska.

"Do you remember, Eily, when we used to run around barefoot with the gypsies?" Delia said, her eyes going all misty with the memory.

My mother laughed. "Your father was always so kind to let them camp on his land."

"Tell us the story," Ruby said in her wonky way and crawled onto Delia's lap.

Delia smiled. "Well, when we were about the same age as you are now," she began, "the gypsies had a wedding on our land. Oh, it was a great day! Rabbits were skinned and boiled in stews. Big lard cakes were cooked over open fires. People came from miles away. Your mother and I wove garlands of flowers. Beautiful they were – lilies, roses from the garden, mixed with peonies and wild woodruff. The air was filled with their scent."

Ruby and I sniffed and almost believed we could catch it.

"Well, then the gypsies began to arrive from miles around in their caravans, travelling from all over Ireland. Some even from England and the Continent. Others who were wealthy arrived in motor cars – Fords and even a Rolls Royce."

"But some of the local people weren't too pleased." My mother picked up the story. "Oh no. They didn't want those people coming to their village. They called them names. Dirty, smelly, filthy thieves."

Ruby raised her skittering hands and put them to her ears. "Oh!" she said, her face wearing an expression of mock horror. It was a familiar story and we knew our parts.

"Well, the day before the wedding," continued Delia, "some men arrived with pitchforks. They weren't our locals, who knew and respected the gypsies and travellers, but from outside our parish. They were angry, so they were." She set Ruby on the table and stood up on the stool with the sweeping brush. *"Away with these filthy thieves!"* she shouted, her eyes darting out black hatred. *"We don't want them polluting us!"*

"The cheek of them!" I said. "Weren't the gypsies just the same as them? Just people who had no land and liked their own travelling way of life?"

"That's right," said my mother. "Well, Delia's father Tom heard all the noise. 'What's this commotion?' he demanded. They looked at him, fit to be tied."

"We've come to help you drive the vermin off your land!"
Delia shouted, acting the part of the baddies.

My mother pretended to be Tom. "'Well, there is vermin
here but it's your very selves!' She clambered up on the other
stool and stood nose to nose with Delia in mock aggression.
'The divil take you!'"

I took up the story. "Now, meanwhile, young Eily and
young Delia had been watching all this, their eyes big with
fear. So what did they do?"

Eily and Delia jumped down and pretended to be little
girls now – holding hands, drawing back.

"What will we do, Delia?" asked my mother in her little
girl voice.

"Sing!" said Delia.

So Delia, halting at first as if she were still a little girl, then
her voice sweeping and rich, sang "Phil the Fluter's Ball".

"Have you heard of Phil the Fluter
From the town of Ballymuck?
The times was growin' hard for him
In fact the man was bruck.
So he sent an invitation,
To his neighbours one and all,
As how he'd like their company,
That evening at a ball!"

My mother joined in. I joined in. Ruby beat time with a
wooden spoon.

"Well, by the end of the song everyone was laughing and
dancing!" said Delia.

"And you know what happened then?" my mother asked.

"I know, I know!" I jumped up and down. "Big Tom invited all of them to the wedding and there was feasting and drinking for three days. And then ever after he held a festival on his land once a year."

"And that's when we learned Delia had a voice to tame wild beasts!" said my mam, proud of her cousin.

Delia blushed.

"Maybe you could sing at Hitler!" I suggested.

Delia shook her head. "He's rounded up all the gypsies, you know . . ." But she stopped. "Whisht, let's not spoil our lovely day."

But it was as if a dark cloud had come over. I knew already. Hitler had imprisoned all the gypsies in camps.

Then we were shooed away and my mother and Delia settled down for a long talk. I came in and out a few times to listen.

They were speaking in hushed voices.

"There's a lot of rumours flying about," Delia said. "Kappler the new Nazi commandant is going to round everyone up. He's going to move against the Jews."

"I think we're safe here for now," my mother said. "No one suspects us or comes near this place for fear of earthquakes! They've accepted my stated reasons for being here, to learn about Montessori methods and help with translations for old Professor Fratelli. You remember, my husband's old tutor, who rents us the house?"

I gulped, suddenly remembering how I had let slip about my dad earlier. And nearly revealed my mother's secret but stopped just in time. Aunt Delia's presence had driven all that out of my head. I hoped Filippo hadn't listened to my boasting about my dad and was just fishing about my mother being a spy – because the bum-head was closer to the truth than he realised.

My mother didn't know that I knew about that radio. And that I knew she was part of the Resistance. And so was Delia. I'm good at playing dumb when it suits me.

"It's very tense now," Delia said. "There are a lot of Allied prisoners of war released since Mussolini fell. We're trying to get them all hidden so the Nazis can't recapture them. Monsignor Hugh O'Flaherty's network is doing a great job. He's got a whole team now."

Monsignor Hugh O'Flaherty? A priest taking on the Nazis? Monsignor is the fancy name for a high-up priest, like a big chief. I longed to know more. But, a holy man in a long black dress – how much use was he going to be? All the ones round our way were Holy Joes, sucking up to the Fascists. I wasn't convinced. It was a long time since I'd seen my dad. But one thing I remembered was he didn't really believe in God and religion and all that. I didn't know what I believed in but it wasn't a man in a long black dress.

I dropped my hurley, I was concentrating so hard on earwigging.

My mother jumped up. "Leo! I told you to play outside. How long have you been there?"

I could tell she was flustered by the way she wiped her hands on her apron.

"Just now. Me and Ruby are hungry," I said.

"Ruby and I are hungry," she corrected me. "But you've just eaten! Okay, go to the kitchen and I'll get you some bread and lemonade."

I saw that she had some papers concealed in her apron pocket. Messages, I guessed.

My mam had secrets – oh, yes, she did.

Just before she left, Delia called me to one side. "Well, have you considered my offer?" she asked.

Delia had asked me before if I would come and audition for the Vatican choir to sing for the Pope. He was the man in a white dress with a funny little round skullcap hat. He was really holy and all, and head of all the billions of Catholics in the world.

"The answer is still nope!" I said. "I don't want to wear a nightdress."

She looked at me with her deep eyes like two pools. "It's Ruby, isn't it? You don't want to leave her."

I bit my lip. Of course it was. I didn't have to say it. Who would protect her if the Nazis came to get her?

She mussed my hair. "Leo the Loyal," she said. "She's lucky to have you." She took a brown envelope from her bag and pushed it into my pocket. "Keep this safe," she said, "and keep it secret. It's your emergency fund. These are dangerous times. If anything ever happens, get yourself to the Vatican. Find Monsignor Hugh O'Flaherty, tall with glasses and hair that stands up on his head like a brush. He's usually at the steps in Saint Peter's Square around 6pm. Whistle a few bars of the oul' 'Blackbird', so he knows I sent you. If that fails, his address is on the envelope, though that's a bit more risky."

She meant the song but I filled my lungs and thrilled my blackbird impression and she laughed heartily, fit to burst. Then she gave me a hug like she might squash me to death.

That night I took the envelope out and opened it. Ten one-hundred lira notes, a thousand altogether! A lot of money. And inside was an address – *Monsignor Hugh O'Flaherty, Collegio Teutonico. The Vatican*. Then her own address.

It was alarming that Delia thought such a fund was necessary.

But just then Ruby and I had other things to think about. Organising our own midnight feast!

Chapter 3

"*Shushhh!*" Ruby gave me her familiar lopsided smile as I carried her down the stairs. I felt her little birdlike body tucked into mine as I balanced the rucksack on my back, packed with food for our midnight feast and other bits and bobs..

"You're getting heavier."

She giggled, thrashing her skinny limbs. "*Shushhh!*"

We made it to the barn outside, giggling in the moonlight, and I put her down on a pile of straw. Asinello the old donkey brayed lightly but settled back to sleep. I patted my pockets which were full of sweets that Delia had brought us, and Ruby rubbed her tummy.

After listening to Aunty Delia and Mam gassing about dancing in the moonlight, we were determined to have our own midnight adventure. It didn't matter that we were under a purple inky Italian sky, with the sharp smell of cypress trees and the sound of cicadas beating their wings in gnarled olive trees. It was still the same old moon glimmering in the heavens.

The barn was empty at the moment. Often we had people staying there. Fellows turning up like tramps, in tattered old Italian uniforms. I was never told, but I knew they were deserters running away from the army. They all had the same haunted look, eyes hollow from hunger and seeing terrible things, flitting around the place like shadows. I didn't ask where they came from or where they were going and they didn't say. Sometimes it might be an old couple, I guessed Jewish, or refugees from areas of heavy fighting. My mother changed their clothing. Fed them. They did a few jobs around the place. And then they melted away to be replaced by more people. Sometimes a band of partisans turned up, looking like ruffians and a bit bashed up, but grateful for the chance of a hot meal and a bed for a few days. They were members of armed groups fighting secretly against the Germans. They kept their firearms hidden, but I often spied them behind the haystacks, polishing their guns as if they were precious jewels, nursing them like extensions of their own arms.

Sometimes they were phantoms, like smoke.

Ruby believed that if you left washing on the line overnight, ghosts would inhabit it at witching hour and haunt you during the day. My mother often hung men's clothing on the line, such as trousers, shirts, even caps and braces. It was never there in the mornings. Clothes for partisans, I knew, and escaped prisoners of war.

But tonight the barn was ours and we stuffed ourselves with the leftover ham sandwiches, and all thoughts of war were forgotten in the sugary, milky crunch of Galatine sweets.

Ring-a-ding-aling!

The ringing struck like an earthquake in the night. I jumped up, dazed, covered in straw. We had fallen asleep in the barn. Even in my dozy state, I knew something terrible was happening.

I told Ruby not to move and I crept outside the barn. Suddenly I was very awake, all my senses on high alert. That awful thing I had dreaded so long, the knock in the night, had happened. I crouched behind a bush and scanned my surroundings like an owl hunting for the slightest sign of a mouse or a rat.

A grey hulking lorry was outside the farmhouse gate. The one used by our local police, for transporting prisoners. It was a round-up. They had burst through the gate, setting off the bell.

I moved from the bush and climbed into a big olive tree, bent and whorled with age, in the grove near the house.

My mother ran out to the path as they came up from the gate. She glanced towards the olive grove as if she had seen or sensed I was there. I knew without her making the slightest gesture that she meant me to be quiet.

"*Signora!* We have come to search the house!" a local policeman shouted out. It was Riccardo Two-Bellies as we called him because he was so fat. He sounded almost apologetic.

"I have nothing to hide!"

Two other police officers strode up, one of them grabbing my mother roughly by the shoulder and pulling her inside the house. My stomach went cold with fear. I could tell from the racket inside that they were thrashing the place.

I was frozen in the branches of the tree. I became a part of the tree, too petrified to move. My legs wood, my arms branches, my fingers spindly twigs. I don't know for how long. But after a time I heard *crash, bash, boom!* Them leaving the house.

I dared to peep out. The police were on the path, pulling my mother roughly behind them.

"Nothing," they said. And again, "Nothing."

Their chief glared at her, angry now. "Where are your children?"

She said nothing. He shouted at her. And when again she didn't answer he smacked her across the face. I had to bite my fist to stop crying out.

She spat out the words. "They are visiting Ruby's godmother in Naples."

But she'd made a mistake. Delia lives in Rome, you ninny mama! But that was wrong information she was giving them. On purpose, I realised. I was such a gom.

"I have nothing to hide!" she shouted. "Where are you taking me?

Ta-thrum, ta-thrum. My heart leapt in my chest when they threw her into the back of the covered truck.

"The warrant for your arrest came from the Gestapo in Rome," said the police chief.

Oh no! The Nazi secret police wanted her. That was really bad.

"Is it Regina Coeli prison?" she called out, wanting me to hear, I was sure.

But there was no reply except for the crash of the truck doors closing.

There was a loose pile of old stones by the grove, the remains of an old wall. If I dropped down I could pick up a stone and throw it. I was ready to do it, could almost feel its heft in my hand. But there was a flutter by my left ear. A mosquito. Its drone seemed to say *"Ruby, Ruby!"* Foolish, I know. But, God's honest truth, that's what it said.

I had to get back to my sister and get the hell out of there. I had to stop being part of the tree. But I had turned to wood like Pinocchio. Then pins and needles shot up through my leg. Fizzy foot, Ruby called it. I was a real boy.

I dropped quietly from the gnarled branches and stumbled back to Ruby.

There she was, crouched under the loose straw littered inside the barn, like a little animal burrowing into the earth.

I told her what had happened and she began to sob gently. The tears glistened on her cheeks. I stroked her soft russet hair and the teardrops fell without noise. Just the heave of her breath and her hot tears running down her cheeks.

Then the sound of heavy boots driving into the ground came thundering towards the barn.

I picked Ruby up and ran out the little door at the side.

"The tree!" Ruby whispered.

I ran towards the old olive tree again. Inside its trunk was hollow. I stepped in with Ruby and we crouched.

We stilled every nerve in our bodies and we were now both made of wood. We could hear hot breath in the night, panting. I saw it was the fat one – Riccardo Two-Bellies – wheezing into the night. They must have sent him back to do a check.

The sound of the barn door banging. Riccardo Two-Bellies mustn't have looked very hard. Asinello brayed as if to warn us.

Thud, thud. The footsteps came closer! We were only a few feet away from him.

A long pause. I almost stopped breathing. His torch beam probed the darkness, the light raking the still air. I was sure he had caught our scent like a bloodhound.

The seconds ticked by.

"*Not here!*" he called.

The sound of footsteps retreating. I didn't dare raise my head.

The lorry pulled off. The roar of the engine driving through the night was a rip in the world.

How did he not see us? Perhaps he did but decided to let us be.

We stayed like that in our tree coffin for what seemed like hours. Hearing only the cicadas *ticking-tick-ticking* in the night air like so many demented clocks.

"*G-go!*" Ruby stuttered at last. She did that when she was frightened.

I stepped out of the tree, shaking free my numb legs and banging my arms to get the blood going again.

"The Monachicchio saved us – I saw his red hat," she whispered as I lifted her out.

A magic spirit. Ruby believed in every fairy that ever existed. She said all the woods were enchanted thereabouts.

"If you say so," I whispered back. "Come on. We're going to meet more fairy creatures."

She nodded, happy.

We crawled on all fours back into the barn and set up the donkey and cart, putting a layer of straw in it to rest on, and an old tarpaulin. Our game was now real, the rucksack with the remaining food would be used in earnest. By a stroke of luck, I'd tucked my diary and Delia's envelope inside. Just as well as I didn't dare go back into the house.

And as the moon fell in the sky towards morning we set off towards Rome.

Chapter 4

I wasn't sure the donkey would make it with the darkness settling around us like a cloak and the moon flitting in and out of the clouds like a wonky lamp. Asinello was a stubborn 'aul eejit of a yoke, with big ears, a shaggy coat and stumpy little ears. But his back was broad and Ruby had a way of cajoling him.

She rode him in the saddle specially adjusted for her use and I sat bumped and bruised in the cart behind. We swapped over every so often. When we came to a hill I had to get out and coax him in the moonlight, terrified someone would hear us.

A light breeze ruffled the night air and I suffered a thousand heart attacks even though there was no sign of anybody about. But when the bright moon chose to show itself, we could follow paths. We passed miles of blasted and abandoned vineyards and olive groves, where bombs had dropped – my guess was by mistake for there was no military reason to hit a farmer's crop. But perhaps the Germans had tried to bomb partisans hiding out there.

The going was rough underfoot on a crisscross route of dirt roads. I didn't dare take the main highways in case we met Nazis. But I knew to head south and my compass told me we were going in the right direction.

"Sure, isn't there a saying that all roads lead to Rome?" I tried to joke to Ruby at one stage. I could only hope that was true.

We used to go there quite a lot when we were younger but not since the war came. I only had a hazy picture of it in my mind, of a vast city all yellow and crumbly and the big greenish dome of Saint Peter's at the Vatican.

I put the worries about my mama, her crying out, hauled away in the dead of night, in a box in my head. That's what she had always told me to do with other worries. But I had to hold the lid down tight. There were so many worries in there now, jostling each other for elbowroom. My father hanging between heaven and earth, and now my mother. Once or twice I nearly burst into tears just thinking of her in that police lorry.

After the vineyards, we passed through a beech forest, the fallen nuts crunchy underfoot.

I pretended to Ruby it was enchanted and we had to wave to all the tree sprites. She smiled happily.

"They are the forest nymphs, the Dryads," she said.

"They take human shape sometimes. Or it might be a folletto, the fairy creature that travels on the wind and in fogs."

She pointed and in a beam of moonlight I saw ghostly shapes flitting through the boughs of the trees, threading through the branches. My heart gave a leap at the strangeness of it. But I looked closer. They were only large spiders' webs dancing on a current of air.

But Ruby was having none of it. She cocked her head.

"No, it is a folletto – look how it shimmers and shakes!"

Then she spoke about other creatures. I let her prattle on, fairly sure there was no one about. She told me about a mischievous elf who would make you lose your track in the forest if by some bad luck you managed to step in his footprints. In order to find the right path again, you would need to put your shoes back to front. He would also kidnap children and scare off the cows on moonless nights. Apparently he was partial to forest fruits, which would explain his red-stained face, she said. I shuddered. All this talk of creatures was giving me the creeps.

After trudging through the beech forest, we hit a rough patch of blackened heath, scorched by a bomb, with not a blade of grass growing on it. It was a dusty, rocky plain and I felt exposed. But I was glad to get out of the haunted forest. We hurried as fast as we could across it to the next patch of trees.

We ploughed on through the trees, following a rough path. My own breath was ragged in my throat. Ruby

Leo's War

mercifully curled up in the cart and slept under the tarpaulin, in the nest of straw. I had filled the water bags for the donkey but worried they would run out soon. His flanks heaved with the effort. Soon we came to another patch of open ground, stony underfoot.

Ahead was an olive grove, the trees even more bent and whorled than the ones in our garden, like strange creatures fashioned in wood. We made our way through it and then into another forest of tangled oak and other trees and thorny bushes.

Halfway in, we came upon a tiny clearing where there was a rough stone hut, the kind used by shepherds, underneath a canopy of branches. But apart from the remains of a recent fire, there was no sign of life. I wondered if it would be a good place to have a little rest. But as I hesitated there was a sudden whoosh in the trees. I sensed a darkness closing in behind.

And then a shape dropped from the tree in front.

"Fermati! Basta!" Halt! That's enough!

The donkey brayed and kicked up its legs. I lifted up my hurley.

Before me stood a youth by the slenderness of him, dressed in ragged clothes with a cloth over his face. He had a mass of black curly hair and his dark eyes bored into me. He was cradling a rifle in his arms.

"Don't hurt us!" I cried out in Italian.

But the youth tore off his kerchief and laughed. "Englishman! What are you doing here?'

30

Ruby popped her head out of the cart, her hair covered in straw. Two other equally ragged boys emerged out of the trees and burst into laughter.

"Roberto!" I cried. He was the older brother of Filippo, my sworn enemy. A Blackshirt. He joined up even though he was too young and was sent to the Russian front. He sang the songs in praise of Mussolini with such gusto I used to think his lungs would burst. But he didn't look like a Blackshirt now. He was the opposite – the spit of a bandit.

I stood stock still, staring hard at him.

"We are partisans now fighting for freedom from Mussolini!" he exclaimed proudly. "I am the leader of our band. 'Lucky' they call me. Because I got us all back from the Russian front." He puffed out his chest with pride even though his little band of fighters looked like ragamuffins or the Lost Boys from the story *Peter Pan* that my mother used to read. And there only seemed to be two of them. Some band!

"This is Carpo, our sharpshooter," he said. "And cook."

He nodded towards a skinny little boy of about fifteen with tufts of blond hair peeking out of a cap. He wore a rough burlap sack tied at the waist instead of a jacket and his trousers were in flitters. On his feet were two left boots with twine instead of laces. But at least he had shoes. The other one, a tall skinny boy with glasses called Primo, had pieces of leather on his feet tied with string like some peasants wore. Roberto referred to him grandly as their "munitions expert".

"Gigi is sleeping in the hut. She's a refugee from the

south and she's joined our partisan group," he said, swaggering as if he were a battle commander. "The rat we roasted last night didn't agree with her."

While I gaped at this, the others laughed and Carpo patted his belly, saying, *"Yum, yum!* More for us."

I pushed the image of the rat out of my head and eyed the group suspiciously. "I thought you loved Mussolini," I said to Roberto. "You beat me up when I sang that song about him and you didn't even know what it was about."

"I knew it was disrespectful with those farting noises you made at the end!" He laughed then. His face brightened. "Sing it for us, eh?"

So I did! I puffed out my chest and sang at the top of my voice.

"Oh Mussolini, what have you done?
You have a fat head like a baby's bum,
You are the Duce but you're just a fool,
Everyone knows you are Hitler's tool!
Oh Mussolini, with your face like a bum,
If ever I see you, I'll tell you you're scum!
Then away I will run, run, run, run, run!
And one of these days you'll be shot by a gun!"

They listened, grinning, and cheered when I translated for them as best I could.

"You sing well for an Englishman," the string-of-beans boy, Primo, said.

Roberto looked around at his little band and smiled like I was his long-lost brother. He winked at me and cuffed me around the head. "You were right, Englishman! We have seen what a mess he made of his lousy stinking army by following those other German fatheads and we fight for Italy now!"

Primo, who looked like a student despite his weird footwear, spat, "Mussolini sent us into battle like lambs for the slaughter! I want Stalin to win the war and turn us all into Soviets. *Up the Reds!*"

Joseph Stalin was the leader of Russia. The one nicknamed "Uncle Joe".

"My grandfather in England is a communist too. But he hates Stalin. Says he's a new Tsar without a fancy crown," I said. "But, the funny thing is, my grandfather wanted everyone to share but he made my grandmother do everything for him."

Roberto laughed and rolled his eyes. "Share and share alike, eh! I don't think Joe Stalin is getting his toes frozen in a trench! All leaders be damned. I am for life and for the living of it!"

"But your parents," I said. "They think you are dead."

A shadow passed over his face. "If they know I am a partisan, I am dead to them anyway." I remembered his father at a flag-blessing ceremony. I was surprised to see him in his black fascist uniform instead of his usual brown pharmacist's coat, the silly little fez hat with the tassel perched on his balding head, his fat stomach pulled in by a blue cummerbund. His little ferrety eyes darted around the room as he sucked at his disgusting grey moustache, yellowed from smoking. We all tittered at his big fine speech about Italy's return to glory and I knew in my heart most Italians weren't really Fascists. Or most children anyway. They just had to pretend in case they got punished real bad by the stupid grown-ups.

Roberto narrowed his eyes at me. "You are the boy with the good arm and eye! I saw you play that Irish game with that stick. We are expecting some Nazis. Would you like to come with us?"

Without thinking I nodded my head but then I looked at Ruby. Her eyes were wide with fright. She reached out and tugged my jumper like a small puppy.

"We have to get to Rome," I said. "I have a rendezvous."

"Maybe we can help you with that – after we deal with the Nazis," Roberto said.

I didn't hesitate in case he changed his mind. A bargain struck. I nodded. I didn't feel I had much choice. The truth was, I was totally lost and had no idea where I was going.

Ruby clenched her face shut, pursing her mouth and squeezing her eyes tight – a habit of hers when she's annoyed. But then she relaxed her features and cocked her head to one side, to show me she agreed even if she wasn't too happy about it.

"Ruby can wait here with Gigi," said Roberto, pointing towards the little stone shelter. "Primo, put the donkey in the olive grove. Carpo, you hide the cart."

I lifted Ruby out of the cart. Then Primo unhitched Asinello and led him away.

There was something decided in Roberto's manner that

made me want to obey him. He was like an arrow ready to shoot from a bow.

I followed Roberto into the hut.

Someone stirred on a pile of sacking in the corner and Robert called out, "It's okay, Gigi! Just us with a little girl for you to guard!"

An older girl with wild matted hair, her face ashen, her clothes in flitters, was lying on the pile of sacking. I noticed she held a hunting knife in one hand. She pushed herself up on an elbow and stared at us.

Roberto cleared some straw away with his foot and a trapdoor was revealed. Under it was a small underground cellar.

I hid Ruby down in the bowels of the earth. She didn't say a word, even though it was as cold and dark as a tomb. She never complained even when I covered her in the sacking they'd left down there, even though it must have itched like a hug from a bristly pig.

"I'm sorry, Ruby," I whispered, "but we need their help to get to Rome. I have to go with them. Gigi will guard you."

She nodded. I hugged her and left.

"What if the Germans come?" I asked Roberto when we went outside.

"They won't know about the cellar. We'll be back in no time and Gigi will keep her safe. She may have a delicate stomach but she's braver than any boy. You should see her if she smells a Nazi! They destroyed her village so she's out for revenge." He mimed slitting his own throat. Then he clapped his hands together. "Now we are going to perform some sabotage!"

In truth I was excited. "Will I get to fire a gun? I don't think I know how."

Roberto laughed heartily and clapped me on the back. "We have only two guns and one of them keeps jamming." He gestured to Primo. "But we have something just as special. When the time is right we will show you."

Primo tapped the side of his nose and grinned.

I had a funny feeling that I might even enjoy myself.

Chapter 5

We walked for a long time over rocky terrain, with only the moon to guide our path. The ground rose steeper underfoot and we passed through a pine forest of swaying trees, the sharp clean smell filling our nostrils.

Eventually, we climbed a steep bank where down below a paved road cut through a ravine. On both sides of the road were sheer rock faces.

"The Germans will be coming through sometime tonight. Now all we have to do is wait," said Roberto. He turned to the others. "Right, boys, you know what you have to do."

Primo and Carpo began to quickly pile up small rocks at the edge of the ravine, while Roberto placed some on top of a nearby overhanging rock.

"These are just an emergency measure," Primo said. "We probably won't use them."

I helped them, terrified and excited all at once, my pulse racing, my heart pounding in my chest.

The moon was playing hide and seek and the night air was cold. Luckily the beam from Primo's torch was a mini-sun illuminating the contents of a curious little leather drawstring bag he carried on a belt on his waist. Inside were objects wrapped in cotton rags. He took one out as if revealing treasure.

"With this object we can stop the Germans," he said pompously. He uncovered it, like a magician displaying an amazing trick.

I almost laughed at the simplicity of his "weapon". It was a four-pronged metal device with hooked ends, a bit like a tripod but with one extra spike pointing up. I could see that, whichever way you turned it, one pointed end would be sticking up.

"It's called a bobjack – it's made out of two extra-long nails twisted and fused together." He fondled the vicious-looking spikey thing like a holy object. "This is the new improved version after my design for four sides instead of three. I was inspired by medieval 'caltrops'." He sounded as pleased with himself as a professor. "You know the Borgate, Mussolini's ugly new housing projects in Rome that are already falling apart?"

I didn't but nodded anyway.

"There are lots of partisans there," he went on. "A blacksmith there made it for me – he's a friend of Gobbo. And everyone's adopted my design. They are universally admired."

Primo sure was full of himself.

"Who's Gobbo?" I asked.

"He's a partisan. He's like your English Robin Hood – he robs from the rich to give to the poor. Except in this case the rich are the Nazis, eh!" Roberto laughed.

I thought Gobbo sounded interesting if dangerous. Holy smoke! His name meant "hunchback".

Roberto handed me three little bundles.

"Now watch what I do," he instructed. "Your job will be to throw these little beauties with that strong arm of yours right under the Nazis' wheels."

Before I could ask any more questions, he swung himself over the edge of the rock face and climbed down onto the road. The moon came out and I could see what he was doing as if he were a silhouette in a shadow puppet theatre. There was some horse dung and he placed a bobjack among it. He was just bending down to do the next one when two, four, then six headlights suddenly raked the darkness. Vehicles were fast approaching from further down the ravine.

We flung ourselves onto the steep bank, hidden by ferns, pine cones sticking into us. Roberto dashed back to the rock face and scrambled up to us using toeholds he seemed to know by instinct. Three light trucks and a lorry were coming towards us, pennants with swastikas on the front of the trucks whipping in the air.

"Primo and Leo, wait until the last minute to throw," said Roberto. "If we burst the tyres of one of the trucks, it will have to brake. As soon as they get out, Carpo and I will open fire. As soon as you two, Primo and Leo, have thrown the bobjacks, run like hell! Carpo and I will hold them off for a few minutes."

The headlights closed the gap in seconds. Primo threw a bobjack. It scudded across the road. But the truck had begun to brake at the mysterious flying object and I took aim and scored a direct hit under its front left wheel.

In a screech of brakes, it crashed into the rock face opposite us, wheeling around in the road. The second vehicle drove past it at top speed, the driver dousing its headlights. But the third vehicle clipped the crashed one and, after skidding violently, turned over completely. The lorry went straight into it, braking like mad.

Suddenly there were wild confused roars. Shouting Germans jumped out, shooting haphazardly.

"*Schnell, schnell!*" they roared. "*Ein Hinterhalt!*" Quick, quick! An ambush!

I saw Roberto, atop the overhanging rock, in full view, his face covered by his kerchief, firing wildly. A few Germans crumpled to the ground. But then others, using the vehicles as cover, let out a volley of shots.

Carpo's gun must have jammed because he and Primo took off through the forest.

Then Roberto stopped firing. His gun was out of ammunition. With bullets ricocheting off the rock face, the shooting seemed to be coming from all directions.

I burrowed deep into the ferns, forgetting I was

supposed to run.

In the confusion, another vehicle approached, headlights beaming through the night. A sleek officer's car, Nazi flags with the swastika flying from the front.

It was beginning to slow when I saw my chance. I rose quickly and threw my bobjack.

I missed the front wheels but by some fluke caught the back right wheel, causing the car to swing around violently and come to rest against the bank on our side of the road. The driver and a senior officer in a long coat clambered out. The officer ran to the front of the car, staring in my direction.

The crack of gunfire. He had let off a volley of shots.

A shower of rocks rained down on him and the driver, forcing them back behind the car. I glanced up to see Roberto hurling rocks.

"*Viva Italia!*" roared Roberto, still throwing.

"*Schnell, schnell!*" shouted the senior German officer.

At that moment, the moon blazed out. The German officer had moved to the front of the car, gun in the firing position. I saw him, tall and erect. I could have sworn there was a big scar running down his cheek.

I glanced back at Roberto and my heart lurched when I saw that a single soldier had somehow climbed the rock face beyond him and was creeping up on his position on the overhanging rock.

Having managed to reload his gun, Roberto fired at the officer but missed.

41

I saw the soldier beyond him raise his gun and opened my mouth to roar a warning. But bizarrely, such was my fright, I let out a piercing whistle and thrilled like a blackbird. But loud and desperate, as if I was a ship's klaxon warning of an iceberg.

Hearing me, Roberto in an instant dropped down flat on the rock as the soldier fired. Rolling off the rock, he landed on all fours, then crouching he scrambled down the bank and began to run like blazes.

Blindly, I followed him as shots whipped over our heads.

Back at the shepherd's hut, we were relieved to see all of us had made it.

Inside, Primo and Carpo were slumped, quiet and watchful, but relaxed when they saw Roberto. Gigi was still curled up in the sacking and merely grunted when we came in.

My legs began to sting like hell – my shins were lacerated by thorns but I'd been too frightened to feel it at the time – but Primo's thigh was bleeding badly from where he had fallen on a root in the forest.

I looked around, gasping for breath. "Won't the Nazis follow us?" I asked Roberto.

Roberto laughed. "You have to be natives like us to track through the forest. And even we get lost sometimes! No chance anyway. They think the woods are full of partisans and that ambushes like ours are staged to tempt them in."

I supposed he knew what he was talking about. They were far more effective – and braver – than I'd credited.

I needed to fetch Ruby from that cold cellar.

She was fast asleep in the sacking down below and stirred dreamily when I lifted her. When she saw me she smiled lopsidedly and went straight back to sleep, nestling into my shoulder. I laid her down carefully on the straw in the hut and she continued sleeping like a fairy child.

I sat down with the others and we began to relive the ambush. Soon we relaxed and were grinning all over our faces. Battered and bruised we might be but we were alive! We laughed like crazy boys – delighted with our mayhem.

But after we stopped laughing and reliving it blow by blow, Roberto frowned. "I lost my gun in the escape," he said.

"And I'll have to find more nails for some new bobjacks," said Primo. "We'll have to go back to that blacksmith."

Carpo looked down at his weird attire. "But not until we have some decent shoes and clothes. We'd get picked up looking like this."

Roberto cuffed me roughly on the shoulder. "Just as well you can whistle like a bird," he said. "I thought, even if I live I will have ringing in my ears forever!"

But he smiled and I could tell he was impressed. I felt a little inward glow of pride.

"Hey, have you heard this joke?" he said. "Hitler and Mussolini meet in Rome and Hitler wants to demonstrate how obedient the Nazi army is. 'Look, Benito,' he says, 'I will put ten soldiers in this room. Then I'll drop a feather inside it and close the door. When the feather hits the floor,

they will all shoot each other.' Five seconds after shutting
the door, the sound of bullets firing tells them the feather
has hit the floor. They open the door to find ten dead
German soldiers. Mussolini then tells Hitler, 'Adolf! Italian
soldiers are just as disciplined. I will now do the same thing
with ten Italian soldiers!' Ten Italian soldiers enter the
room, a feather is dropped and the door is closed. Ten
seconds pass. Twenty seconds pass. Thirty seconds pass.
After a minute they open the door, to find ten Italian
soldiers taking turns to blow air under the feather."

We all laughed like our sides would burst.

Primo wiped his nose with his hand. "No wonder there
are no soldiers left in Mussolini's army. Apart from being a
terrible general, we know he is a lunatic and we Italians
want to live! Only a few stinking Fascists who like to torture
and kill for fun stick by him."

"Do you think we killed anybody?" I asked then, half
afraid of the answer.

"I don't know," Roberto said. "A bunch of them were
wounded alright – that might have been by ricochets. But I
reckon that commanding officer was Kappler, the new Nazi
big chief in Rome. Shame we didn't get him."

Soon, I was lying down beside Ruby with the lads and I
fell into a dead sleep.

Next morning, before the break of dawn, Roberto brought
Ruby and me to the side of the road. It must have been
around six o'clock in the morning.

As I didn't think I could bring a donkey into the Vatican, I had decided to leave Asinello with Roberto and his band, hoping vaguely that they wouldn't end up eating him! They didn't seem to have much food and Carpo told me they were living on squirrels, mushrooms, berries, chestnuts and even the occasional rat and frog. So no wonder Gigi was sick.

Ruby shed a tear as she scratched between Asinello's ears one last time. Even I was sad to say goodbye to the old sack of bones. He had, after all, aided our escape.

Roberto insisted we take a tattered old cloak and battered old hat. "There's a lot of Nazis watching in Saint Peter's Square. Two red-haired children will stand out," he said, glancing at our hair. "But a dirty old beggar won't. Carry Ruby on your back and she can become your hump."

I shrugged. "Sounds like a lot of trouble."

"It will be fun! And prevention is better than cure."

I grinned. "It will be a good game to outwit the Nazis."

Soon a cart stacked with cabbages and pulled by an old grey horse approached, driven by a peasant with a beaten old cap on his head.

Roberto went into the road and waved him down. After a brief chat he agreed to take us to Saint Peter's Square and help with our disguise for one hundred lire. Luigi his name was. I peeled a note off my stash and handed over the money. I gave a hundred lire to Roberto too though he hadn't asked for it, and he was grateful.

The old peasant moved a few crates and revealed two

45

empty wooden crates that formed a sort of cavity in the centre. He had obviously smuggled people this way before.

"I can't thank you enough," I said to Roberto as we settled down among the cabbages. "If I can ever do you a favour ..."

"Maybe someday you can get us some decent shoes," Roberto said with a laugh. "There is a café by the ancient ruin known as the Portico di Ottavia in the Jewish ghetto. The waiter there, Gianni, is one of us. If you ever need to get a message to me, go see him." Then he hesitated. "I hope your mother is okay. She was brave, you know."

I nodded. I didn't like the way he spoke about her in the past tense.

"Maybe someday you can help get her out of prison," I said.

"Maybe. If I'm still alive myself!"

We embraced then and he had tears in his eyes. I was surprised by his emotion. Almost as if we were brothers. But there was a war on. You don't know if you will see people again.

Luigi the old peasant stashed the cloak, hat and my hurley up near his driver's seat at the front of the cart. Then he stacked the other crates bursting with cabbages all around us.

Roberto arranged a few more cabbages in front of me, and I couldn't see much any more.

"*Leone Rosso*," he whispered. Red Lion. That was my nicest nickname yet.

Chapter 6

I peeped through the cabbages and the early morning was still shrouded in a swirling mist as we ground up yet another hill. We were on the west side of Rome. I knew the old part to the east was built on seven hills, but we seemed to have ascended and descended a whole mountain range, mile by bumping mile. Luigi stopped off in random places, taking a route I couldn't fathom. I figured it was to pick up and drop off stuff. There were odd huddled conversations in doorways. Money changing hands. He was smuggling, I supposed, and evading Nazi checkpoints. But I was completely disorientated. I hoped Ruby was okay in her crate. Occasionally I was able to touch her fingers to check she was still alive but the cart jostled us so much we were often wrenched apart.

But, finally, the cart juddered to a stop and we got out on

a large terrace overlooking the city.

We gulped the air and stretched our stiff limbs. Poor Ruby was in pain – I could see it in the strained smile she gave me. But she didn't complain once and just sighed when I massaged her legs and arms to get her circulation going.

When I asked Luigi where we were he grunted that we were on the Janiculum Hill. Not one of the Seven Hills of Rome, but an eighth on the other side of the Tiber. Nearby was a big statue of a man on a horse. Garibaldi. I remembered from one of our awful school lessons that he was one of the founders of modern Italy. Better known in my house for giving his name to an oblong biscuit stuffed with currants that my grandma in London loved to dunk into her tea. I normally found them sticky and gummy and didn't like how the currants stuck to my teeth but how I longed for a bite of one now!

I looked out over the city and it took my breath away in the early-morning haze. Domes and bell-towers and ruins rising to the sky. Rome, the ancient city built on seven hills, the River Tiber slashing through. It was a sprawling city packed with buildings and inside it I knew was the Colosseum where Christians were fed to the lions, the ancient burial tombs of the Catacombs and loads of antique monuments crumbling to dust. The city glowed golden in the early-morning light as the sun burnt off the mist.

Nearby was the Vatican, the independent city-state of the Pope. At its heart Monsignor Hugh O'Flaherty.

Somewhere below me were Delia and her husband. And my mother behind bars, held by the Nazis. I shuddered to think of it.

There were lots of benches around and I could have sat down and stayed there for a bit longer admiring the view. But Luigi was anxious to make his rounds, jiggling from one foot to the other while he smoked a clay pipe.

We had no choice but to stay in the cart. We couldn't meet the Monsignor until later in the afternoon. We had hours to go before heading to the Vatican.

Just as we settled back into our crates, a shower of golden birds took wing, rising from a small stand of nearby bushes.

"A ccch-charm of goldfinches." Ruby moved her hands as elegantly as a bird in flight. "It's good luck."

The last thing I saw before I was buried in cabbages was the ballet of those little red-faced birds, their black and yellow wings flapping in the dawn light.

Only Ruby, I thought, would find gold among the blackness of Nazi-occupied Rome.

Soon we were trudging down the hill, teetering in our crates. Then suddenly we were in the stream of life, noise pressing in on us from all sides.

The old driver took a twisty-turny route through every back street in Rome conducting his shady business. We bumped *whoosh-whoosh* over cobbles and potholes. I smelt every smell – the strong tang of cheese, the whiff of garlic and rosemary and drains and woodsmoke. The scent of yeasty bread wafted from bakeries as we went down narrow side streets. I heard a clatter of complaining voices as Luigi called out for people to get out of the way. All around I could feel the pulse and hubbub of the city – though passers-by all seemed in a rush and people weren't congregating on street corners, talking loudly as Italians like to do. It was as if somebody had died.

The traffic roared by on some of the main roads like a river in springtime. But they were heavy vehicles. Nazis, I guessed. But I was too hungry and too exhilarated to be frightened. My stomach grumbled and rumbled.

Funnily enough Luigi still didn't hand over many cabbages. I peeped out carefully now and then. He was smuggling all kinds of stuff. Bottles of murky wine and green olive oil. Flitches of bacon wrapped in paper that he'd hidden at the front of the cart. I knew by the greasy smell.

Suddenly, in the late afternoon, things became much quieter as if we had left the streets. I counted five strikes of a clock. Luigi turned his head slightly and said it was the clock at St Peter's Square.

We had arrived at the Vatican. Where we would find Monsignor Hugh O'Flaherty.

My stomach was gnawing on itself and making noises like a small animal. All we'd had to eat was a few bites of bread dipped in olive oil that the cart driver had pushed through to us. I hoped Ruby wasn't suffocating and I reached out to touch her fingers in the dim green cabbagey light. Her fingers were as light as a feather but electric too, as if lightning flashed through her.

We arrived at the entrance to the square. When I peeped out, I didn't see any Nazi checkpoints but saw it all like a jigsaw. Saint Peter's Square wasn't a square at all but shaped like an oval and, with the steps leading up to the church at the far side, it was shaped a bit like a keyhole. It was vast, a huge piazza – an area of smooth rectangular paving stones with an Egyptian obelisk, a tall erect column, in the centre and two fountains. The Basilica, the name for the big fancy church, was a gleaming palace of white. It had a large porch called a portico with three sets of steps leading up to it, then the huge dome of the Basilica towering above.

People milled about, taking photographs and blessing themselves. Surrounding the open area were two curved colonnades with massive pillars, like two arms hugging the crowds.

Black-clothed priests and nuns flapped about like giant flocks of crows, and scattered among them like exotic birds a few higher-ups in vivid scarlet. There were also a few Swiss Guards standing sentry by the Basilica and patrolling around the square. In their striped blue-and-yellow outfits they looked like jesters I'd seen in a carnival before the war came, but there was nothing funny about them. They were erect and wary, serious and watchful. I was almost knock-kneed with fright.

We got out near the left-hand colonnade. The long row of pillars holding up the covered walkways gave us cover. Ruby clung to my back and the old cart-driver threw the big cloak around us. I carried my hurley to use as a walking stick. Luigi shoved the battered hat on my head. And so we became an old hunchback, Ruby bunched up under the heavy cloak. It was baking hot and I hoped she could breathe. It wasn't the best disguise ever but, from a distance, we'd pass. And I smelt to high heaven. Like dung. No one was going to get too close.

As I made my first awkward steps into the square, I got a shock. For it was also full of German soldiers in their jackboots and steel helmets. Many were relaxed and laughing, gawping like sightseers. But curiously isolated too, as no one would come near them. I edged back into the cooler air and shadows of the colonnade. There were lots of beggars about so nobody paid an old hunchback much attention. I walked on until we reached the end of the curving colonnade which was quite close to the steps up to the Basilica. There we skulked behind a pillar.

There was no sign of a tall priest with glasses and a shock of curly hair on the steps of the Basilica. We waited for what seemed like ages, my back creaking from the weight of Ruby. Then the bells rang out for six o'clock and people continued to pour in and out of the Basilica. Women in mantillas clutching prayer books, students, nuns, priests and monks. Finding a priest among priests would be like finding a needle in a haystack.

But, sure enough, as the sun began to sink in the sky a very tall black-clothed figure came out and stood on the steps holding a prayer book. His head was occasionally bent in prayer but he also looked up to heaven a lot and then would sweep the square with his gaze. I got the impression he was taking everything in, including me.

I took my chance.

"Right, Ruby. Hang on."

Ruby gripped my back and I pulled the old cloak around us. I stepped out from behind the pillar and walked across to the steps, like I thought a hunchback might. I didn't have to pretend to stagger. Ruby was a dead weight.

As I got closer I began to whistle "If I Were a Blackbird" as Delia had instructed. Breathlessly, I have to admit, what with my heart pounding and the effort of carrying Ruby.

The tall priest raised his head from the prayer book with a smile of pure happiness like he'd just tasted a toffee apple. He gave a slight nod. I saw simple steel-rimmed glasses hovering before piercing blue eyes, and a wide, smiling mouth. He had one of those faces that made you instantly like him. His hair stood up from his head in a black shock of curls. His nose was a bit like a potato but his lively eyes twinkled behind his round glasses and his face was the kindest face I'd ever seen apart from my mother's.

I continued to whistle out a few bars of Delia's "auld blackbird".

And, next thing, he bounded down the steps towards us.

When he reached us I gazed up at him, panting, knees buckling under the weight of Ruby.

"Follow me, boy," he said quietly. "A short distance behind."

Just then a couple of Nazi soldiers walked by, their

helmets glinting in the slanting sun. They glared over at us but Monsignor Hugh smiled at them and, making the Sign of the Cross, said *"Veni, vidi, vici."* Even I knew that was *"I came, I saw, I conquered"* in Latin, said by Julius Caesar after some battle or other. They passed on, not interested at all in a priest spouting Latin and an ugly old misshapen beggar.

The Monsignor led us through the colonnade itself and stepped over a small barrier into the road on the other side. He then led us into a narrow side street. I followed on a little way behind as though I had no connection with him. I had to scuttle to keep up with his long legs as he strode ahead. Ruby was good as gold, clinging on with all her might.

After covering a couple of hundred yards we reached a large building dominating a corner, surrounded by a terracotta-coloured wall. I had the impression we'd walked the long way round because the building was close to the Basilica. It was almost as if we'd doubled back on ourselves – maybe the Monsignor wanted to make sure we weren't followed.

There were double doors at the front of the building with steps and a porch with columns. But he led us to a gate under a stone archway at the side near an unmanned porter's cabin. As we passed though the archway, I glanced upwards at the inscription above. It said *Collegio Teutonico*. I asked him quietly what it meant.

"The German College," he said.

I nearly fell out of my standing, Ruby almost slipping

from her perch. The German College! I hadn't realised that was what the address meant. Of course Delia wouldn't lead us into a trap. But why was the enemy of the Nazis working in a German College of all places? Was he a double agent?

My stomach went cold but I had no choice but to trust him.

Inside, we entered the hush of an internal courtyard garden with a few tall umbrella pine trees, palm trees and bougainvillea bushes. I was about to unload Ruby under the tall fronds of a palm tree when he gestured to me to be quiet and to follow him inside. I blanched. It was also a graveyard and a cold tingle ran up my spine, frosting my very soul.

The place seemed deserted. The building was cool and dark with high ceilings. He led the way to an office on the ground floor overlooking the garden. It was simply furnished with a desk and chair and some tables. He closed the large wooden door firmly.

Sighing loudly, I took off the cloak and Ruby slid off my shoulders. The Monsignor caught her and gently placed her on a chair.

"Well, aren't you a sight for sore eyes!" he exclaimed, pouring us both a drink of water from a little pitcher on a table.

We drank greedily.

"No need to explain who you are, Leo and Ruby," he said in his musical Irish voice. "Delia already told me about you. Leo, have you come for your audition?" He winked at

Ruby as if it was a great joke and they were the best of friends.

"My mother's been arrested," I blurted out. "They might have taken her to the Regina Coeli. The Nazis wanted her. She told them we were in Naples to mislead them."

He took off his glasses and frowned. "We'll talk later, boy." His voice was filled with concern. "Now we'll go up to my room."

He scooped Ruby up in his strong arms and I followed him into the main building and up two flights of stone steps and along a dim corridor. All was silent, the stone walls like a tomb, our footsteps echoing on the marble floor.

We entered his room, partitioned at one end by two long curtains where there was a bed. In the main part of the room there was a washbasin, a desk, a radio set in one corner, a sofa and some easy chairs. A couple of golf bags filled up with putting irons leaned casually against the desk. A crucifix was on one wall and a picture of the Virgin Mary.

Ruby and I flopped down on the sofa.

"You're okay now – we can talk here," he said, handing us a plate of shortbread biscuits he produced from a drawer in his desk.

We began to eat hungrily.

"I'm sorry to hear about Eily. I'll look into your mother's situation tomorrow. She's an Irish citizen, isn't she? From a neutral country. They shouldn't be taking her anywhere."

"She has dual nationality," I said, licking my fingers. "She was born in America."

He frowned at that. The United States was at war with Germany.

I told him, my mouth full of crumbs, about the radio and about my father in the RAF. How we didn't know where he was.

He took out a handkerchief to mop his forehead. "If they think you're in Naples, that's the way we'll leave it. We'll keep you hidden until I figure out what to do with ye."

A tear slid down Ruby's grubby face. "I want Mama." She spoke indistinctly from tiredness.

"I know," said the Monsignor, reaching over to catch her tears with the handkerchief. "You have a very brave mama. And her children are just as brave."

He had understood Ruby perfectly.

I scratched myself and the Monsignor looked at me intently.

"We'll talk more, me boy. But I'd be thinking you need a wash."

He took a large linen cloth from a wardrobe and walked with me to a small bathroom a short distance down the corridor from his own room. He handed me a large bowl from a cupboard under the sink and told me to bring it back filled with water for Ruby when I had finished.

I washed slowly, enjoying the sharp clean smell of lemon-scented soap and the silky lukewarm water. I even washed behind my ears.

But I was a bag of nerves walking back up that cold corridor, waiting for a Nazi to jump out at me. *Schnell! Raus!*

I nearly spilled half the water with fright.

The door was on the latch. All was as before. Ruby was curled up on the sofa like a cat. She stretched and yawned when I came in. She looked very much at home. I hoped her muscles weren't feeling too tight. That happens with her palsy. But she seemed fine.

The Monsignor threw back the curtains at the end of the room and beckoned us to come to him.

"This can be Ruby's room," he said.

There was nothing there but a simple narrow bed and a bedside table, where I placed the water. We left Ruby there to give herself a wash. She can do that. She spills it a bit. But she likes to do things for herself.

Monsignor Hugh excused himself and went outside.

I gazed around the room. There was a single large window behind the desk. Even in the murky half-light the view was unmistakably the vast bulk of Saint Peter's. And to the left were elegant stone buildings, one with a smaller dome, squares and gardens that linked to the side of the Basilica.

I felt nervous again. There had been no Vatican guards or sentries outside the college but maybe I was prisoner as much as guest. I went back in to see how Ruby was getting on. She needed help to put back on her tattered old dress.

Through the half-pulled curtains in the gauzy light, I spied the Monsignor enter the room with two nuns in drab brown carrying trays with steaming bowls of soup. They were respectful towards the Monsignor but murmured to each other – in German! Instantly Ruby and I shrank back into the shadows as if a jackboot had come into the room.

But they were almost genuflecting to the Monsignor and only spoke when directly addressed. He was clearly a "big man", the boss. They didn't even glance in our direction. The older one was called Sister Boniface and she was severe and skeletal. Sister Boney-face more like. I didn't hear what the other one was called but she was as meek as a mouse.

They left us barley soup with spaghetti floating in it like worms. Ruby and I slurped it down. The soup was the best meal I'd had since we left home. Plain but well flavoured with salt. I thought of Roberto and the boys back in the woods and hoped they weren't dining on Asinello. But my mind was racing. Was the Monsignor a double agent? A spy?

After we finished, the Monsignor leaned back in his chair and chuckled, his face beaming.

"Welcome to the German College!"

My chest squeezed tight with nerves. "But why are we not in the Vatican, Monsignor?"

He see-sawed on his chair. "You are – sort of. We can't all fit inside the Vatican, you understand. But the college is owned by His Holiness the Pope. So even though it is outside the Vatican and leads onto the streets of Rome, it's governed by Vatican rules. The Vatican is a neutral state, playing no part in this war. So the military can't come in here. We're safe. But not as secure as in the Vatican itself, because they have the Swiss Guards."

I nodded, though I didn't really take it all in. I was feeling very sleepy and beginning to nod off.

"You can take the sofa, Leo," he said. "Get yourselves to bed and we'll talk about your mother in the morning. Oh, and call me Hugh. And only speak to someone who uses my codename 'Golf'."

My head hit the sofa and I blacked out.

Chapter 7

Ding-dong! Ding-dong!

Bells ringing! Clanging inside my head. But no, they were outside. Where was I? I jumped up with a start. The early-morning sun was filtering though the half-opened shutters. The window curtains had been pulled back. I sat up in bed. I could see the dome of Saint Peter's, rising like a giant meringue cake out of a blanket of mist.

It all came flooding back to me – our escape – the partisans – Monsignor O'Flaherty. For a moment I wanted to call out to Mama. Tears sprang to my eyes. But I bashed them back in with the heel of my hand. We were on our own.

"Leo!" Ruby called me softly from the other side of the curtains at the end of the room.

I ran to her and helped her out of bed. Her little smiling

face, the big brown eyes of her, made me happy. But we both froze when a soft knock came to the door.

I pulled the curtains closed, leaving just a little gap to peep out.

A stocky dark-haired man in pinstriped trousers and a dark jacket entered, carrying a tray, with a leather briefcase under his arm. He flashed a cheeky grin in our direction.

"Morning. John May at your service. The Monsignor – Golf – said to bring you breakfast. He said he had a new pair of golf clubs." He had a trace of a cockney accent like the people where my grandparents lived.

I relaxed after he used Hugh's code name.

He put the tray on the desk and slipped the briefcase down beside it on the floor.

Ruby and I shyly emerged like snails out of a shell. He pulled the napkin off the tray. Boiled eggs and toast! My mouth began to water. I was starving!

The man smiled broadly. "Why, you must be Ruby and Leo. You're the spit of your dad," he said.

"You know our father!" I exclaimed.

"And your grandfather. Best cloth in London. He's famous, is your grandpa. Provided the cloth 'ere for me butler's uniform!"

My grandfather was in the "schmutter business" and sold cloth to all the tailors in Saville Row. Dressed royalty and lords, he liked to boast, even if he was a communist. And even butlers in the Vatican! I wished I could write a letter and tell him but it would never reach him during the war.

The butler laid our breakfast out on the desk and pulled up two chairs. "Get stuck in. We have a busy morning ahead."

We did just that. How I loved sticking the soldiers in the egg yolk. I didn't even care if it ran all down my face. It tasted like liquid gold. Ruby's bare feet curled with happiness. But what was going on? How did this Englishman know all about us – and our dad's family?

When we'd finished, he opened the briefcase. "There's some fresh clothes here," he said.

Inside was a pretty green dress for Ruby – even if the material looked like the curtains. Shorts and a polo shirt for me. With worn but clean shoes and socks for both of us – and clean underwear. Ordinary clothes, not worn or patched. Even a brush for Ruby's hair. I felt like it was Christmas!

But there were also long black trousers, a white shirt and some sort of big white smock thing with a black tabard bit, suspiciously like an altar boy's outfit, that John May laid out on a chair.

"What's that?" I poked at it.

"A disguise to get you into the Vatican," John May said. "His Excellency the British papal legate wants to talk to you. He's like the ambassador to the Pope."

"What does he want to talk about?"

"Suspicious little cove, aren't you?" he said. Then he winked. "I like that. Now turn yourself into an altar boy, and no more of your lip!" He gestured towards the disgusting white cover-all that would make me look like a giant baby. Worse than the rubbish smock I had to wear in school when I was the biggest in the class and they treated me like I was simple and kept me back two years.

"No," I said.

"Suit yourself. But we can't brief you if you don't."

"Ruby and I won't go anywhere unless the Monsignor says so," I insisted. "Where is he anyway?" Even though Hugh had told us to trust anyone who used his code name, I wasn't ready to just yet.

"Very important man, the Monsignor," John May said, tidying up our breakfast things. "He's doing God's business, I shouldn't wonder. He's very 'umble like. But he's very 'igh up in the Vatican. Speaks fluent German, English and Italian, and has three doctorates an' all. Even more amazin' he's an amateur golf champion."

"But why are we staying at a German College? Is he a double agent?" I persisted.

John May laughed at this. "He's a miracle is what he is. Best man in the world, if you ask me. Solid gold. Been in the Vatican service since 1922 and knows everybody in Rome. And what's more important, they all adore him."

"So who are you, apart from being a butler?' I asked.

It was a rude question but he didn't bat an eyelid.

"Well, since Britain is at war with Germany and Italy, we no longer have an embassy. But we do have a minister and we took refuge inside the Vatican, which Hitler won't touch because he don't want to offend all the Catholic Germans. I am in fact just Sir D'Arcy Osborne's butler. And completely at your service on account of your old grandfather, even if he's just as argumentative as you!" He bowed low then rose up and did a little dance.

I liked him. A lot.

I was halfway into the altar-boy outfit behind the curtains when the door swung open. Monsignor Hugh strode in, carrying a little box which was highly polished, the kind they keep holy stuff in. "Leo, when you're ready, me boy, you come with me."

I stuck my head out. "I'm not leaving Ruby behind."

Hugh and John May exchanged a look. "John here is going to get her in. We'll take different routes."

I was about to protest when Ruby gave her lopsided smile and held out her hand to John May.

"Don't worry, Leo," she lisped and patted her tummy. "I have a good fizzy feeling inside."

It was decided. I was used to trusting Ruby's gut feelings. John May scooped her up in his arms and Hugh helped to cover her in a large white sheet. She looked just like a bundle of laundry, which was exactly the idea. He was out the door in a flash. I felt a pang. Not just at her going but at how little she was, how she could be bundled up like old sheets and pillowcases.

The Monsignor handed me the little wooden box and a crisp white cloth to cover it. He showed me how to carry it – held carefully up against my chest like an altar boy would. He told me to take my rucksack too but didn't explain why.

Then it was Hugh's turn to disappear behind the curtain.

He emerged all dandied up, wearing a low-crowned black hat with a circular brim, a long scarlet robe over his cassock. A vivid scarlet sash and silver-buckled black shoes completed the outfit.

"My semi-formal get-up," he explained. He handed me some rosary beads to dangle from my hand. "Now follow me a pace behind and keep your head low. Keep your lips moving in prayer. If you don't know any prayers, just keep your lips moving."

I followed him slowly down the stairs, worried I might trip up in my gown. I felt a sudden pity for women as I tried to balance the little box and my rucksack without tripping over the hem.

A fine procession we made as we came into the burst of sunlight in the courtyard, and went through the archway and along the street towards Saint Peter's Square.

We turned left, stepping daintily over the little barrier between the street and the colonnade. Although I kept my head down, I stole the odd glance at the great columns. I remembered being told in school that from a point in the square near the fountains, it looked like there was only one row of columns, but up close you saw there were four. The colonnade was a place of light and shade, shadows and nooks, perfect for a game of hide and seek.

My skin prickled at the nearness of grey-uniformed German soldiers who hovered in little groups, laughing loudly and swaggering about like they owned the world.

I darted a look at the Swiss Guards. They weren't wearing their jesters' outfits today but were in plain dark war-service uniforms, carrying guns. In a few steps our little procession was in the small piazza right in front of the Basilica.

I wondered how Ruby was getting on. What if the Nazis had stopped her and John May? Hitler didn't like people who were different like Ruby, people they saw as crippled or retarded. What if they suspected what was bundled up with the laundry and snatched her? I began to pray in earnest.

At the entrance gate to the left of the Basilica the Vatican guards barely glanced at us. In fact, they almost scraped the ground bowing to the Monsignor. We crossed the inner square and went past the high wall of a building with a dome that Hugh said we could see from his room at the college. It was the Sacristy, he said, containing vestments and treasures, and was attached to the Basilica.

"We are approaching the inner sanctum, the core of the Vatican which no ordinary pilgrim gets to see," he whispered to me as he waited for me at a door.

We went through an ornate corridor with lots of holy statues, a whole army of them keeping watch, and then out a side door.

We approached a corner. There were a couple of more ordinary Vatican police dressed in blue uniforms and peaked caps, different to the Swiss guards. *De-dum, de-dum* went my heart so loudly I thought everyone could hear it. I was sweating under my big dress. It was extremely hot for the time of year, almost out of spite it felt to me. But the two police officers snapped to attention and saluted as if Hugh was a lord. He gave a slight nod of his head. Nobody asked us for identity passes.

Hugh swept through a maze of little squares and passages surrounding the great dome, very much at home, me trailing behind like a puppy. I was dazzled by all the glory and gilt, the marble and vaulting columns and felt I was little among the hush and majesty of everything.

Then we were heading out into the open spaces behind the main buildings.

"Let's stretch our legs and give you a bit more of a tour!" he called back as he powered onto the gravel paths.

Everywhere there were yellow-and-white flags, with the papal insignia, a sort of fancy popey crown with crossed keys. It was even painted onto paving stones. I liked that it was light and airy, the exact opposite of the ugly squat swastika brooding its hatred at us.

Rome was supposed to be an "open" city. A city where both sides had agreed there would be no fighting or tanks or guns. But that lasted only a few precious weeks before German jackboots echoed on the cobblestones and Allied bombs fell. But here in this city within the Eternal city, it was just about possible to believe in it.

Hugh pointed out a few things. "We're only a hundred odd acres, but we have our own railway, you know, bringing in supplies from the countryside. Libraries, a pharmacy, a small hospital, even our own post office. Everything you would expect in a small country."

He pointed out the Governor's Palace too, the Sistine Chapel and the Vatican museums.

About half of this tiny country was covered in gardens, perfectly manicured, with grottoes, arches and statues, plenty of them of Holy Mary. It all looked like a picture, perfect in every detail. Palm trees swaying in the breeze, tall stately cedars and straight cypresses standing like sentries.

Flitting through the shadows, careful not to be seen, were quite a few guards and police. As well as the Swiss Guard, and the ordinary Vatican police, they even had their own army – the Palatine Guard, Hugh told me. Normally they were about five hundred, he said, but since the war started the numbers had swelled to two and a half thousand. Half Italy applied to join! They looked splendid in their magenta berets caught up with a cockade in papal yellow, and swishy blue cloaks. But Hugh said that was their ceremonial wear. They normally patrolled in drab grey overalls, a black cloak and a red beret. There was also another exclusive elite corps of Noble Guards who were the Pope's special bodyguards, he said, whose dress uniform was red jackets, thigh-high boots and plumed helmets – they all had to be lords and dukes. The Pope sure had a lot of protection for a holy person!

The Vatican also had its own radio station, the tower rising to rival the dome of Saint Peter's. Marconi the inventor of the telegraph had installed it himself.

I never thought much about the Pope before but I could see he must be a big deal if even Hitler respected his independence.

In silence we headed back to the Sacristy but turned right and walked towards a plain four-storey brick building next to it. Hugh pointed over to a familiar-looking terracotta building, lush trees rising over its wall, swaying in the breeze.

"That's the German College," he said. "And that's its cemetery where the trees are."

I was surprised. "Then didn't we go a long way round?"

"We did so, me boy," the Monsignor agreed. "But the main thing is to be safe. There is a much shorter way but it means going through two or three security-guard posts. They are used to seeing me alone and would be suspicious of you at once." We entered the building. "So many people go in and out of the main entrance gates that there's far less risk of being questioned."

"But what about Ruby and John May?" I asked.

"Well, John May has his own ways through of course. He is well known to all the guards and they all owe him favours in more ways than one. And Ruby is hidden in a sheet!"

We crossed the hall to take a small passenger lift.

I was thrilled. I didn't often get a chance to go in a lift. Hugh pressed a button to the top floor. As the lift started to climb I felt a whoosh of excitement.

He turned to me. "Now that wasn't too bad, was it, me

boy? This is the Hospice of Santa Marta – Saint Martha. The Vatican still uses the ground floor for offices but the foreign embassies from Poland, France and England use the top floor. We are a place of refuge for them."

The lift came to a shuddering halt. Hugh pulled back the two steel doors and we emerged into a small passage. Then he led the way down a corridor to a door at the end. He pressed the bell.

The door was opened by a fancy footman with a stuck-up face who bowed low. I didn't like the way he looked me over as if I was a piece of dirt. Especially as I had washed.

We were now in a long corridor of an apartment. John May came towards us and ushered us into the first room on the right. He turned to the footman.

"That will be all, Livio. Can you run along and pick up the Legate's messages at the front gate?"

The footman frowned as if that was a task too lowly for him but then nodded and left.

We entered a comfortable drawing room, carpets underfoot. Ruby was already seated in a plump armchair eating chocolates and laughing with a tall older man who looked to me like a prince. He rose to greet me and bowed.

"Sir D'Arcy Osborne at your service, young sir. I have been hearing from your charming sister here that you are known as everything from Leo the Lazy to Leo the Long-jumper!"

"You can understand her!" I blurted out.

"Perfectly," he replied. He had kind eyes and a ready

smile. He patted the seat beside him. "Now sit you down and tell me all that has happened."

"Not until I've taken off this perishing dress!" I exclaimed.

He laughed and John May took me into another room where I transferred the altar boy's outfit into my rucksack.

All three of them listened intently to our adventures. Sir D'Arcy Osborne questioned me about my mother's radio equipment. I said I didn't know what had happened to it but she usually hid it very well. She had broken it into segments, hiding parts in her sewing machine and other parts were behind a removable brick in the wall so it would be very difficult to find. They seemed satisfied with that.

"But can you find my mother and rescue her from the Nazis?" I asked impatiently.

There was a silence. Hugh steepled his fingers and looked at Sir D'Arcy Osborne.

"We have already made some discreet enquiries," said Sir D'Arcy. "But it is a delicate matter. We don't know for sure where she is. She might be in the Regina Coeli prison. But she may have assumed an alias so it's difficult to check. You see, your mother was not just with the Resistance but was also working for us."

I gasped. "I-I d-don't understand," I stuttered. "Who is us?"

Hugh leaned forward. "We are the Rome Escape Line. We run a network helping Allied prisoners of war, partisans and Jewish people escape from the Nazis and the Fascists. We try to help anyone deemed an enemy of the state."

My mind reeled back to the frequent calls to our farmhouse by boys on bikes and motorbikes. The random arrival of strangers in the night that never stayed. I knew she was part of some big operation. I just never knew exactly what.

"Your mother transmitted messages for us," Sir D'Arcy Osborne continued. "You remember Professor Fratelli, who owned the villa where you stayed, your father's old tutor? He sent her the messages to transmit, disguised as research for his book on mythology."

I must admit I barely remembered the old professor who had lots of tufty hair. But it was like the last piece of a jigsaw, that translation she was supposed to be working on was messages.

"And Professor Fratelli?" I asked. My father's former tutor was Jewish and had retired back to Italy.

"Gone into hiding," Hugh explained. "It's got a bit hot at the moment what with all the uninvited Germans about."

A thousand questions leaped to my mouth but I listened intently as he explained about the Rome Escape Line.

The Monsignor had first come into contact with Allied prisoners of war when he was an interpreter visiting camps with the Papal Nuncio, another papal bigwig. He made sure a list of captured prisoners was broadcast on Vatican radio so their loved ones would know they were safe. But he also ensured they would get their Red Cross parcels. The

Fascists didn't like what he was doing so they forced his resignation. But all the prisoners knew he was on their side.

Back in the Vatican, he became a rallying point for the hunted and those on the run. Jews and anti-Fascists in danger turned to him for help. He hid them all over Rome, including some within these very walls. And even in a flat right beside the Gestapo Headquarters! Well, they weren't going to look under their noses, Hugh said!

But the top brass at the Vatican got worried and didn't want the Vatican to become a mecca for escapees and refugees in case the Nazis invaded the Pope's territory. So Monsignor Hugh found them other hiding places, including in convents and flats.

"Are there many prisoners of war on the run?" I asked.

"Thousands and thousands," Hugh laughed. "In some cases the guards let them out, thinking the Allies would be coming soon. Even some Italian guards deserted. And some of the POW's join up with the partisans."

"But Hitler put Mussolini back in power," said Sir D'Arcy Osborne. "The Allies are bogged down in the war and the prisoners are now swarming on Rome."

I briefly had a vision of horrible Hitler pulling the strings of fathead Mussolini.

Sir D'Arcy nodded. "So we secretly run this big operation, protecting thousands on the run on a wing and a prayer. Monsignor Hugh has a big network of priests and nuns and ordinary Italians, finding food and places to stay."

"We also have the Man Upstairs on our side," twinkled

Hugh, gazing up at the ceiling.

I whistled. And I had thought most of the priests and nuns were just Holy Joes, turning their eyes up to heaven and ignoring the hell on earth under their holy noses. I would treat them with more respect in future. Now I knew they could be part of Hugh's network!

"Count Sarsfield Salazar from the Swiss legation, another neutral country," Sir D'Arcy Osborne continued, "handles approaches through the former embassies and tries to arrange safe passage to Switzerland for some of them. He also tries to coordinate those hiding outside Rome in the countryside. And John May here is my eyes and ears. He has contacts all over Rome. High and low. And he knows how to lay his hands on everything from trousers to tea."

My jaw must have dropped to the floor because they started to laugh.

"But how do you do it without the Nazis seeing you? Are nuns and priests smuggling stuff under their habits?"

"That's Hugh's department," said Sir D'Arcy. "He's not known as the Scarlet Pimpernel of the Vatican for nothing! He leads a double life, just like that famous English aristocrat Sir Percy in the story set in the French Revolution. *'They seek him here, They seek him there, Those Nazis seek him everywhere!'*"

"They don't even suspect John May, he's that good," Hugh said with a smile. "He gets all our food, he's our expert on the black market – the most magnificent scrounger you ever met. He has a genius for it."

John May blinked modestly. I could see the three men were very close – like the Three Musketeers.

"They don't suspect Hugh either," said John. "They think he's anti-British on account of 'im being Oirish!"

I was wondering why they were telling me all this.

"For reasons beyond our control, we cannot move Ruby and you for a few days," Sir D'Arcy Osborne said.

"I'm not going anywhere without seeing my mother." I bit my knuckles, a habit my mother hated. "I'll only do what she says." Thinking of her made me stop gnawing my hand. I could almost hear her say with the laugh in her voice: *You gom! Quit that!*"

"We will continue to find out what we can," said Monsignor Hugh kindly. "She might not be at that prison."

Sir D'Arcy turned to the Monsignor. "And, dear Monsignor, you too must be more careful. Kappler is moving closer."

The name made my blood run cold. That commandant Roberto thought we had ambushed on that road. I didn't say anything. Just in case I got Roberto's band into trouble. And I knew instinctively that the Monsignor wouldn't get mixed up with the Resistance, only the saving people side of things.

Hugh shook his head like he didn't care about Kappler. "I place my faith in a higher power." He turned to me. "Kappler is the Nazi chief in the city," he explained.

"But still we have to be more careful," said Sir D'Arcy.

"With everyone converging on you, the Vatican authorities might clamp down on you."

Hugh nodded to John May. "I'll have to leave soon. We'd better sort ourselves out." They went into another room, leaving Ruby and me alone with Sir D'Arcy.

"Does the Pope not know what you're doing?" I asked.

"Officially no. The Pope has to be neutral. Otherwise the Nazis might occupy the Vatican." Sir D'Arcy gazed out the window. "Let's just say he cannot be held responsible for what he doesn't know about."

I remembered the trim, angry man at the head of the convoy we ambushed. His cruel voice. "And Kappler? The Nazi chief?"

"He's a vicious character. Likes to follow orders to impress Hitler. But don't worry. We shall prevail."

"Why can't we stay with Delia?" I asked.

Sir D'Arcy looked thoughtful. "It's too risky. Her husband is the ambassador and Ireland is neutral. With your mother in prison it could jeopardise certain arrangements. It's better for all of us that he maintains cordial relations with the Nazis."

"You mean they entertain the Nazis!" I must have spoken very loudly because Ruby told me to shush. "But Hitler and Mussolini are horrible! Everyone should be joining together to fight them!"

Hugh had re-entered the room. He was very quiet on his feet for such a big man.

"It's complicated," he said. "People do their bit in their

own way. Only God himself knows the big picture. It's like when I play golf. To hit the ball with maximum force, it must balance on a little tee."

He went behind the ambassador's desk and took out a set of golf clubs and balls and set up a wastepaper basket as a target. He balanced one on a special tee for indoor use.

He gave the ball a whack and it landed perfectly in the basket.

He held up the tee and his golf club. "So what helped put the ball in the basket? Was it the putt or the tee? No, it was both working together."

"It was your crafty eye and strong arms too," piped in John May. "Even though you hold the darn club like it was a hurley from that game of yours. I don't know whether it's the devil or the Man Upstairs helps you but I've yet to better you."

"The luck of the Irish," Hugh winked. "And don't say anything bad about hurley. Leo here is mighty!"

Suddenly he looked at his watch and, excusing himself, dashed out of the room.

Sir D'Arcy Osborne laughed. "Prayers. With all the hugger-mugger going on, I forget he's a priest! He says Mass all over the place too!"

John May led us to a large circular table in an adjoining dining room set with linen, sparkling silver and gleaming crystal glasses.

Ruby and I looked at each other and grinned. We felt like a prince and a princess. We didn't even have to go out to wash our hands because the sneaky-looking footman, Livio, brought us a bowl and a napkin with small bars of soap that smelled of lavender.

Around us were portraits of the British royal family and maps of the war in Europe and around the world. There were little flags with stars on them for the Allies' positions. Horrible swastika ones for the Germans. I didn't like to see so many swastikas in Italy and all over Europe.

John May then served us with grapefruit, tender steak with mushrooms, grilled tomatoes and panna cotta dessert. I was afraid I was eating like a little pig. But both Sir D'Arcy and John May encouraged me, heaping up my plate and applauding me when I managed an extra steak. The juices ran down the back of my throat and I mopped my plate up with bread.

John May looked after Ruby, making her napkin into a little bib, and cutting her food up small for her. Whatever lay ahead, we were having a little bit of heaven on earth.

After lunch, Ruby and I were so full that we both had a little nap on the large sofa. I awoke when I heard Hugh who must have come back from prayers, chatting to Sir D'Arcy. When they mentioned my mother's name, I pretended to be asleep.

"She might already be at the Regina Coeli prison," I heard Sir D'Arcy say.

My heart lifted a little in hope. Did he have some information?

"Or being questioned," he went on.

"I pray it doesn't come to that. Even if she talks, she hasn't much to say," said Hugh.

I didn't like the sound of that. My hope plummeted like a tiny bird shot down. I was nearly about to interrupt them when Hugh spoke again.

"I have to make a call to Mrs. M at Via Imperia and Prince Doria at the palazzo. I might just drop by the prison. It's only about fifteen minutes from here along the Tiber. Sure isn't it practically on the way!"

The little bird of hope took wing again.

"The two youngsters can stay here. It's lovely to have children about the place," said Sir D'Arcy. "We'll say they are your nephew and niece for now. But we'll have to find a safe place, especially for Ruby."

"Maybe Mother Mary Saint Luke can help," Hugh said.

All these plans worried me. A nun! A flipping nun! There was no way I was going near a nun if I could help it. But I decided not to say anything. If Monsignor Hugh was going to see my mother, I was going too. And I wasn't going to ask anyone's permission!

Chapter 8

"*Alice* – my favorite!" lisped Ruby when Sir D'Arcy took down a big illustrated volume from a shelf with a large collection of children's books.

Ruby pointed to John May who was looking at his fob watch and she and I broke into laughter.

"The White Rabbit!" she whispered, pointing to the illustration.

"All he needs is a tail!" I muttered.

Ruby broke into squeals of delight.

You might say Ruby wobbles when she moves. But to me she shimmers. Like a dragonfly dancing on water or a cyclist adjusting to stay on a bicycle. She has to move to hold her balance.

I noticed Sir D'Arcy watching her with a kind eye when he joined us. He was already growing fond of her, I could tell. He smiled at her with warmth. And I loved him because he didn't seem to mind that she mussed the pages of his expensive book. Or that she drooled a bit. He just gently dabbed her mouth with a handkerchief, a proper gent.

Sir D'Arcy disappeared, leaving Ruby with the book. Hugh and John May busied themselves in another corner of the library. I wandered over and saw they were stuffing papers into a bible with a secret compartment. Hugh also put packets of cigars and cigarettes in various pockets in his habit. He sure was a funny priest.

Then he ran his hands through his shock of curly hair, bid us good day smiling like a good-natured bear, and headed out the door. I reckoned he'd be easy to keep up with. It was hard to miss him.

Without being noticed by John May who was still sorting out papers, I picked up the rucksack with the altar-boy outfit. On tiptoe, I snuck towards the door like a burglar. Ruby blew me a kiss and then, making an "O" with her index finger and her thumb, blew through it. It was her way of sending me one of her angels. Ruby thinks there is magic everywhere. That she can drink silver moonlight and eat golden sunshine. Even in this stinking war.

I was in the hall of the apartment now. Within seconds I took my chance. I slipped out the main door into the corridor.

But when I got outside I was unsure of my bearings. I remembered the lift at the end of the corridor. Opposite was another door. I tried it, and found myself on a staircase.

I dashed down the stair, three at a time, nearly breaking my neck.

All was quiet with that churchy hush one would expect in the city of the Pope.

Outside, I hugged the walls as I followed Hugh at a distance, retracing the way we'd come in or so I thought. But I was soon confused, so maybe it was a different route.

The large looming buildings, the heavy air of holiness, pressed down on me. I felt a sudden stab of fear when I remembered the guards at the exit. I hadn't thought about how I was going to get past them. But I remembered Hugh had said that they were less worried about people leaving than getting in, so I hoped they wouldn't notice me.

Just before I reached the inner courtyard near the main gate, I spotted the Monsignor in deep conversation with a tall thin-faced priest wearing a short purple cloak, who handed him some letters. I ducked behind a pillar.

But when I peeked out again, the thin important-looking priest was walking hurriedly across the courtyard, his cloak swishing behind him, and Hugh had disappeared.

I checked round the corner but there was no sign of him. Could he really disappear into thin air? Had God given him special powers? I dashed forward towards the exit, which lay somewhere across the courtyard. My heart went *pitter-patter*. My breath *heave, heave*.

I was close to tears, panting with the exertion. But a little voice in my head said: don't be a crybaby.

But something was wrong. I was being followed. I stiffened. There was a presence looming behind me. I started to shake.

"Whisht, boy," came the unmistakable soft voice. "'Tis only myself."

Monsignor Hugh put his hand on my shoulder and I heaved a sigh of relief.

"Well, boy, if you're determined to get yourself into trouble, you might as well learn it from a master." He chuckled softly to himself. "Come along with me. Now same drill as before, a respectful few paces behind me. If anyone asks me who you are, I'll explain you're a new altar boy. Get your disguise back on." He handed me an identity card: **Leonardo Rossi. Aged 11**. A blurry photo of a boy who could have been anyone. Close enough. **Race: Aryan**, it said. A bit unnecessary as Jews didn't get identity passes.

"But my Italian's not very good," I said as I dressed.

"I'm sure it's better than you think," he said. "But we'll speak in English and, if anyone questions it, I'll explain I'm teaching you."

He strode off on his long legs, his arms swinging as if he were just crossing a field in Ireland to inspect a cow. I'd underestimated him. As Sir D'Arcy had said, Hugh wasn't known as the Scarlet Pimpernel for nothing!

The guards let us through, bowing and scraping to the Monsignor. Soon we were outside in the great square of Saint Peter's again, nipping through the colonnades back towards the German College.

At the porter's cabin of the college, Hugh ditched the letters, his hat and the scarlet robe and sash.

"Time for your tour of the capital," he said. "*O Roma Felix!* O Happy Rome! Someday I will write a book about it but this is the alternative guide."

He smiled and I caught that smile and it sang through my whole being. I would have followed him anywhere.

Chapter 9

We walked and walked, Hugh slicing through the streets on his long legs, me scuttling like a beetle behind. Hurry, hurry, don't dawdle, I told myself. No time to gawp at the grand buildings, the flash of a painted door here, the stone columns, the windowpanes glistening in the sun. All the life crowded into the streets. Posters in German and Italian all over the walls, bossing everyone about.

Everyone was in a hurry. The housewife with the straw bag, the workmen in overalls carrying ladders, the newspaper sellers crying in the street: "*Another victory for the Axis Allies! Hitler victorious against the Russians!*"

"I see they've lost no time painting the post-boxes black," noted Hugh as we passed a workman slapping paint on with distaste for his task.

I felt the bigness of the place. The grand tall buildings,

the paved streets. The colours of gold, terracotta, buttercup yellow. The black cobbles beneath our feet. Everything was gold and silver and red and deep blue. Crumbling villas jostling with ancient ruins, grand fascist streets scything through neighbourhoods where alleys and crooked buildings crowded in on top of one another. We could walk forever and never see the end. It was like a storybook come to life.

"*All roads lead to Rome,*" we learned in school. And here were all the people led to this city of stone and light and noise.

We crossed the fast-flowing Tiber that cuts Rome in half, avoiding the main thoroughfares where the Nazis forbade other traffic, Hugh said. There were so many priests and nuns about, nobody paid much attention to us. More streets, getting narrower and a bit shabbier now. A few German patrols. But they were stopping workmen not clergy so we strode on by.

We took a zigzag route down side streets with tall thin houses and crumbling facades with balconies. We cut down a few narrow alleys. At one point we went through a building and came out the other side onto a small square. Hugh never hesitated, finding his way as if by instinct.

At Piazza Salerno, we walked around a corner then went through an archway between a grocer's shop and a butcher's. Slowly we climbed three flights of steps. We were in a narrow street, Via Imperia. There were numbers on all the doors. And we stopped at one.

Across the street, I saw the flicker of a curtain. "Are we being watched?" I hissed.

"Always behave as if you are." Hugh boldly waved at the window. The curtains stopped twitching.

Someone peeked through a window beside the door we stood at. The concierge. He opened the door, a small wizened man with white hair sticking out of his head.

"Welcome, Monsignor," he said, smiling.

The door opened. Inside it was as a cool as a tomb. We were led up to the first floor.

The Monsignor rapped on the door. A series of three knocks, then two sharp raps. A pre-arranged signal.

The door opened a crack. A dark head and two big eyes peeked out. It was a young girl.

"Ah Monsignor, my mother is expecting you." She spoke in English with the trace of an accent.

"How are you, Mary?" he said with a grin. "Tell Mrs. M I've brought a friend."

Inside, the flat was tiny. We were in a little parlour and a record was playing on the gramophone. The song was English – something about blue birds and white cliffs.

On the other side, I glimpsed a kitchen with three girls seated around the table. There was also a wizened old lady rocking on a chair crooning to herself. She gave me a toothless grin.

A small dark woman with a smiling face came out, pearls around her neck.

"*Ah, it is just you!*" she shouted in English above the noise of the record.

She threw her arms around the tall Monsignor, reaching

somewhere around his chest she was so small. Then she pinched my cheek and kissed me on the top of the head.

"Gemma, you can turn it off now!" she shouted. She turned to the Monsignor. "It disguises any noises they make if they have to escape! But I keep telling her to play Italian songs!"

"Maybe you should play something from Malta to completely throw them!" joked the Monsignor. Then he explained to me that Mrs. M was originally from the tiny island in the Mediterranean near Sicily, which was a British colony – and that was why her English was so good.

Gemma, a pretty girl with a lively smile, came out of the kitchen and took the record off. The other girls around the table tittered.

The wizened old grandmother ambushed first Hugh and then me in an embrace. Then she grabbed my hand and kissed it, and shot back into the kitchen before I had a chance to react.

Beyond was a balcony. To my surprise, three other men came into the kitchen! But no one was alarmed. They were wearing the ill-assorted clothing of those on the run, so they must have been partisans or escaped prisoners.

I followed the Monsignor and Mrs. M to a side bedroom. She smiled and threw back the covers. Five men were hidden under the heavy blankets, fully clothed.

"Cor, Monsignor, you didn't half give us the shivers!" said a tall skinny man in English, leaping out of bed.

So there were eight people hidden in this tiny apartment! All of them escaped British prisoners of war. I chatted to two of them, called Pip and Tug, two lively sailors in the British navy.

"The worst thing is being cooped up, Pip said. "But it's fun here with Mrs. M. She's like a mum to us. And the old grandmother bakes bread like you wouldn't believe!"

Tug winked. "And her daughters ain't 'alf good dancers."

Hugh told Mrs. M about the curtain-twitch opposite.

"I think Fascists have moved into that house," she said. "It is very possible we are being monitored."

"You will need to be even more careful," Hugh said. "I will move some of the men on."

"Ah, my boys," Mrs. M said, "I love them all. They light up our life and God will provide."

"We'll give him a helping hand." Hugh handed her an envelope.

Mrs. M. smiled as she opened it and saw that it was full of money. "The Nazis have come three times and each time they see me and my six children and old mother. They never believe we can all fit!"

As we left, one of the POW's put the English record on again. They told me it was Vera Lynn singing a song called "The White Cliffs of Dover".

Mrs. M's daughter Gemma started dancing with him. Round and round they whirled, closer and closer. I thought they would fall through the floor.

I wanted to stay but Hugh whispered it was time to leave. He led me through the kitchen out the door onto the balcony. It looked onto an inner courtyard.

There was a ladder leaning against the wall. He put it across to the neighbouring balcony and indicated that I crawl across.

I looked at all the windows, staring at us like eyes. "Won't someone see us?" I whispered.

"There are only friends here," he said with a smile.

I glanced down and immediately started to shake. The ground swam beneath me like I was in a boat. Washing strung across lines from balcony to balcony flapped like sails.

I took off the altar-boy smock and stuffed it in my rucksack. Hugh removed his clerical robe and put it in a rucksack that Mrs. M produced. Underneath he was dressed in a polo shirt and trousers. He had even put on sandals.

I climbed across, keeping my eyes straight ahead. Hugh pulled the ladder in as I reached the next balcony. His legs were so long all he did was climb up on the balustrade and heave himself across.

In the next flat was a little old lady knitting at her kitchen table. Hugh made the Sign of the Cross at her and she gave him a gummy smile. It clearly wasn't the first time he'd come this way.

Then it was out the door and down a back stairs of crumbling stone.

We emerged into a busy narrow back street and joined the passers-by, most of them workmen and office girls.

Hugh took me by the elbow and propelled me around

the corner onto a wide street full of shops. He produced a cap from his trouser pocket and squashed it down on his unruly mop of hair.

I caught a glimpse of us in a shop window with nothing on display. We looked like father and son out for a walk. Or maybe out-of-town tourists sightseeing. Somehow the tall priest had become an ordinary man with his young son. I thought about it. It was clever. The Nazis would be looking for a priest not a dad.

A good hour's walk back towards the Tiber brought us to the ghetto – the cramped place where the Jewish people lived.

I was very thirsty and, as we rounded the corner into a square called Piazza Mattei, I was overjoyed to see a fountain – an amazing fountain where four boys holding dolphins by the tails reached out their hands to catch turtles teetering on the edge of the bowl above.

I splashed my face and drank.

"Ah, the *Fontane delle Tartarughe*, the turtle fountain," said Hugh. "The turtles were added by the famous sculptor Bernini in the Renaissance. Some say it was to honour the Jews, who historically carried their belongings on their back as they didn't have a homeland."

We plunged further into the ghetto. The streets here were much shabbier and more crowded. The buildings were tall and many-storeyed, the alleys narrow and shaded. Hugh told me that as the Jews weren't allowed expand the ghetto out, instead they built up. He pointed to the thin rectangle of sky above.

Thousands of people it seemed to me were crammed into the crowded alleys. There were old ladies selling what looked like rags at street corners, the strong smell of kosher butchers and a few gnarled vegetables outside a boarded-up window that must have been the greengrocer's.

I told Hugh I was nearly fainting with the hunger, so we stopped at a baker's. Even though there was a long queue, we were ushered to the top and Hugh bought me a round bun called a "bagel". It was delicious, warm and moist inside with a toasty crust. We were lucky to get it, the baker said. He now only had enough flour for one more day.

Nearby a ruin loomed out of a hole in the ground – the Portico di Ottavia, meaning Octavia's Gate. It's where the old Roman fish market used to be, Hugh said. I sniffed but there was no pong of fish today. There was an ugly building near the gate that was a museum.

I looked at all the people. It reminded me of Shepherd's Bush where my father's people lived. My grandfather travelled everywhere with his bolts of cloth, all over markets in the south of England, but he had a little shop near the market above a delicatessen run by a man with a long beard. Once I saw a big rat run between the huge barrels of pickles. There was a big picture of Karl Marx under a red flag on the wall. Usually, I could barely remember my grandfather but standing here in the ghetto I could hear him railing against "that criminal Uncle Joe", meaning Stalin, and picking lint off his immaculate well-cut suit.

My grandmother Yerma was small and hunchbacked,

her dark hair under a scarf. She would roll her eyes, black as raisins. "You tell him," she'd say. "I bet he's trembling there in the Kremlin at the wrath of Josiah Cohen the cloth-seller in Shepherd's Bush." She was good at selling things herself. Sold so much china and plates from Stoke-on-Trent she was able to support her son at Oxford.

My father had fallen out with my grandfather when he joined the RAF instead of taking a job in the university. My dad said the Nazis hated the Jews. He was going to fight them. It wasn't the right time to be a scholar. He changed the spelling of his name too to Coyne – my mother's maiden name, Irish, meaning barnacle goose. *Cohen. Coyne.* Two sides of the same "coin", my father said. A good a name as any. He'd change it back if we won the war. A precaution, he said, in case he was captured by the Germans. But my grandfather felt that he'd been disowned. Cohen meant "Holy Priest of the Temple". Even though my grandfather didn't believe in God but only Karl Marx, he couldn't forgive my father for betraying his name. Adults were weird.

What was happening to them all now? Was London still standing? Was Papa Cohen still hunched over his bolts of cloth, whipping them out like billowing waves, shouting about politics with his friends? My grandmother scurrying off to the synagogue for her lonely prayers. And what about my father? He wasn't alive. He wasn't dead. Missing in action. Suspended in some no-man's-land. I pictured him hanging above the clouds. Just stuck there.

Now here in the Roman ghetto were these my people? The men with the skullcaps and long beards. The children with dark eyes in thin faces. The women in worn clothes. And others, smart and business-like. Rich-looking. How could so many people live in these narrow streets, packed together like rabbits in a warren?

"I love it here," Hugh said. "The Jews are a mighty people."

We stopped at another Jewish pastry shop on a corner of the Porta di Ottavia, called the "Boccione", behind an unmarked double wooden door that Hugh said was a local landmark for two centuries. It was locked. He knocked a special knock, another signal.

The owner of the bakery, her hands floury, came out. She was old with a big flabby face. She pinched my cheeks. Her name was Bianca and she explained she only opened every other day because she didn't have the ingredients.

She led us in even though they were closed and cut me an extra-large slice of *pizza ebraica*, a special Jewish pizza that she had in a special cabinet. Not the familiar doughy pizza with tomatoes at all but a dense nutty-fruity coffeecake, a brick of sweet dough bursting with whole almonds, pine nuts, raisins and chunks of candied fruit, burnt almost to a crisp on top. Bianca told me proudly that the Boccione had been her family's business for generations and that her mother devised the recipe for Torta della Ricotta, a sweet and lemony cheesecake topped with pine nuts and icing sugar.

"That is my last cake for a while," she said sadly. "I cannot get ingredients for love nor money."

Hugh ate his with relish and Bianca refused to allow him to pay. "Put it in the box for the orphans," she said. "Ah, how I wish I could give you a slice of your favourite *mandora e visciole crostada*! But the Nazis have stolen all the cherries."

Hugh's eyes lit up. "Ah, the wild cherry and almond-paste tart! A taste of heaven. And the chocolate one too. Paradise dancing on your tongue."

His face was so expressive I could almost taste it myself.

But Bianca frowned. "Chocolate is rarer than gold now. The greedy Nazis have eaten it all, *pah!*"

They were making me mad with the hunger!

"The Nazis have demanded 50 kilos of gold from us, you know, to save ourselves," she said, mopping her face with her apron. "A ransom. Kappler says if we pay it we will not be rounded up and deported to the workcamps."

"I know," said Hugh. "The Pope has offered help with a loan but the Jewish people are raising it all themselves. Quite impressive to gather so much in such a short time."

The woman shrugged. "It should save us. I think. I have given them my second-best candelabra. My wedding ring. The Nazis are *rashanim* – evildoers. But they are men of honour."

I puzzled over her words, how could they be opposites – evil and honourable? But I thought maybe she meant they would keep their promises.

Hugh looked grim and not too convinced either. "I pray to God they are. If you are worried, Bianca, I can arrange a place for you."

But she shook her old head. "Aren't we the oldest Romans? Here since the second century before you Christians turned up. This is my home, why should I run?"

Hugh patted her on the arm and she held his hand for a moment, like old friends.

Out on the street, people were talking in their own dialect, a mixture of Italian and Hebrew. It sounded throaty and clotted. Like the people were feeling a lot and put it all into the words.

"Why does Hitler hate the Jews so much?" I asked Hugh as we continued our walk.

"They are scapegoats," he said. "You understand what that means? When you don't want to lay the blame on the real cause, you invent an enemy. Then you don't have to own up to the truth. So Hitler can blame all that is wrong on a people who cannot fight back." He frowned.

"But the Pope won't let the Nazis hurt the Jewish people, will he?" I asked.

Hugh furrowed his brow again. "We will do everything in our power to save them."

He explained to me that Rome's Jewish community was the oldest in all of Europe. "As Roman as the Pope with as much right to be here. Maybe more since they came here well over a hundred years before Christ was even born, as Bianca said."

As we walked he pointed to boarded-up shops, delicatessens and restaurants and shook his head sadly.

"These places used to have the best food in Rome. Now they are closed because they can't get the ingredients. How I miss the couscous, hummus and falafel. Baccala – the salty fish, zucchini flowers, goulash, planked and fried artichokes, grilled tuna, oxtail, tripe, the sweetest lamb!" He went on and on.

My stomach was growling even louder now!

We walked back down to the Via Portico di Ottavia and found a charity box embedded in a wall adjacent to a bar. It said, in Italian and Hebrew: *"Give to the orphans."* Hugh popped some money in the box as Bianca had asked him to do.

We walked on and I looked up and saw the name on a nearby bar: *Gianni's*. Roberto's friend! The owner was stacking chairs outside. He was sandy-haired, mid-thirties. Hugh gave him a wave and he smiled back and beckoned us over for a drink. He was a gentle fellow, not Jewish, and there was nothing to make you suspect that he was up to his neck in the Resistance. He had a hushed conversation with Hugh as he downed his espresso. I sipped the most gorgeous sharp lemonade, bubbles dancing on my tongue.

As we left I said that Roberto said to say hello.

Gianni smiled. "Any friend of Roberto's is a friend of mine. A good kid. Wild as a mountain goat but his heart is in the right place."

Hugh led us outside the ghetto, and across the river we jumped on a crowded tram.

The tram driver did a double take. Then he winked. "Free," he said. "See you at Mass in the German College at six tomorrow."

We took a seat towards the back. I watched Hugh scan the seats. No sign of Nazis. But you never knew who might be a snitch or have a loose mouth. Around us housewives with baskets on their knees chatted in the musical Italian that always sounded to me like the twitter of birds. Some workmen in old clothes dozed.

The city rushed by, a parade of colour and life unfolding.

A few stops later we jumped out with a friendly wave from the driver.

"All the tram drivers come to the early Mass in the college chapel so I never have to pay a fare," grinned Hugh.

"Is there anyone in Rome you don't know?" I asked him.

He screwed up his face, as if racking his brains. "Well, you know what they say in Ireland about strangers being friends you haven't met yet? I'm only a nodding acquaintance of Kappler's."

"That stinking Nazi. I wouldn't spit on him if he was on fire." I nearly spat too.

"We are all brothers and sisters under God," he said. "You never know. Some day he might have a change of heart. And we'll become friends."

"You'd never!"

"Well, never say never is my motto. I wasn't too fond of the British when I was a lad, and now we're the best of pals!"

I said nothing but bunched my fists. All I could feel was

black hatred towards Kappler and his gang. Then Hugh smiled his special smile and I could only wonder at his big heart.

We were at last headed to the Regina Coeli on the west side of the Tiber. I crossed my fingers, hoping to see my mother.

As we walked along, we passed a group of Nazis putting up a roadblock, using their little white fences. My hands fisted into balls again and I shrank into the side of the building.

"Walk tall, Leo," Hugh said quietly to me. "If we don't look guilty, they won't suspect anything."

"They don't need an excuse," I said. "I hate them."

He shook his head. "But we'll never fight hate with hate," he said. "We have to fight the evil they represent, without hating the person. I know it's hard."

I felt tears spring to my eyes. "It's impossible. And there are so many of them."

"It only takes one candle to put out the darkness," he said. "Be the candle, Leo."

Chapter 10

The Regina Coeli loomed like a fortress near the Tiber. The area of narrow streets around it looked shabby. Hugh said it was the working-class neighbourhood called Trastevere. The same one we'd clattered around in Luigi's cart. But the people were solid gold and anti-fascist. And partial to a bit of smuggled bacon, I thought.

The prison's yellow stone was warm in the afternoon sun. But its bars and bolted doors made it cold and forbidding. Its name meant "Queen of Heaven" and it used to be a convent, Hugh said. There were several guards at the entrance – Italian Fascists, and some SS.

The women's prison was next to it and was called the Mantellate. It was down a side street.

"This used to be a convent too for Carmelite nuns."

There were bars now on the many small windows of the cells.

Then Hugh said a little poem.

"They're nuns are Mantellate
But in Rome they're just dark cells.
And there's no Christ inside these walls,
Despite the hourly bells."

Down an alley he put his clerical garb back on over his tourist clothes.

"It might be better if you stay outside, Leo," he said. "We don't want the Fascists to link you to your mother."

I felt a volcano in my tummy. *"No!"* I said. "You can't stop me!"

But then a breeze ruffled my hair. Maybe it was one of Ruby's angels. I immediately began to think better of my defiance.

"All right. I agree. But if she's there can you pass her a note?"

He nodded and pulled out his journal. He tore a page from it and handed me a pen.

I had a brainwave. I wrote the note in Ruby's Snowish. It was her secret language of some Irish my mother taught us, mingled with English and words of her own invention. Only we knew it. It wouldn't make sense to anyone else even if they found it.

What I said was: *We are well. With Mon H in the Vat. There are partisans in the forest near the old Roman road led by Roberto in case you escape. We love you. I am making sure Ruby eats her vegetables. We heard goldfinches on our way here. Ruby said the collective name was a charm. xxLeo.*

I had so much to say to my mother. But all I could manage was these few things. I hoped she could read between the lines.

I waited for Hugh at the Tiber. I crouched near the water's edge, skimming stones on the water near the Ponte Giuseppe Mazzini. *Flusso di Roma*. I thought. The flow of Rome.

I skimmed a stone. Another stone skimmed near mine. I looked across.

It was a young boy with a cheeky grin. Hair black as shining coals.

Under the bridge, beside the embankment wall, a couple stood huddled in conversation. Nervous, glancing around, dressed in shabby clothes, too hot for this weather, so unusually warm for this time of year that people were calling the heat wave "Lucifer". The boy came and sat beside me.

"My parents think we are going to be deported," he said. "I am making a wish."

I took a guess. They looked Jewish.

"We fled here from Germany," he said. "But now we don't know where to go. My parents are arguing about whether to give our gold watch and chain to the Nazis. Or use it to try to escape."

"I know someone who can help you," I said.

He just shrugged.

"Monsignor O'Flaherty will save you," I said eagerly. "He stands at the steps of Saint Peter's every evening at six. Tell your parents."

The boy just shrugged again.

We stayed skimming stones for a while.

"*Ethan!*" his father called. A Jewish name.

"My cat is about to have kittens," Ethan said. "We live near the Portico di Ottavia in the ghetto."

"I know it," I said. "Do you like Bianca's pies?"

"I love them! I don't want to leave."

A black Nazi car, swastika pennants flying, went by on the bridge. I shrank back. It was like the car we'd ambushed with Kappler, the tall sleek officer with the cruel face.

Ethan's parents called him again.

"The Nazis have a list, you know," he said. Even if you're a bit Jewish they record it all in a big book. My parents say they take you away and put you in a camp. No one ever comes back. They take partisans too. And disabled people."

He skimmed the stone and smiled when it skipped three times.

"Children too?" I said. My heart tightened when I thought of Ruby. I remembered that look between Sir D'Arcy Osborne and Hugh, not wanting her to be out on the street.

"Especially children," he said. "They think we're vermin. Like rats. And disabled Jewish children are worst of all. They torture you too."

I shuddered.

His parents called him again, more urgent now.

"I'm half Jewish," I whispered. "Though I'm not circumcised. Which half of me will they take? My legs or my head?"

Ethan smiled.

"Make sure to tell your parents about the Monsignor," I said.

The boy nodded thoughtfully and got up and went back to them. I noticed that he walked with a limp.

I skimmed another stone. When I turned around again the little family had disappeared.

I felt curiously lighter. It was the first time I'd ever told anyone about being half Jewish.

Moments later, Hugh returned. He smiled his smile like an angel and sat beside me.

"Good news – I think that –"

"Have you seen her?" I interrupted him.

He shook his head. "Now, it's early days. I made a few enquiries. I'm not supposed to visit prisons any more, so I had to be discreet. Nobody answering to the name of Signora Eileen Coyne has been taken. But a prison warder who is friendly told me that there is a lady who is a nurse inside about your mother's age, who came in from the Calcata district. She wears a headscarf. She is kept in a special area for political prisoners inside the women's prison. But they allow her to work in the hospital."

My heart leaped inside my chest, wildly like a trapped bird in a cage.

"Have they tortured her? I want to kill them!"

I felt hot and cold at the same time, my head pounding. I had a sudden urge to throw myself into the Tiber.

Monsignor put his arm around my shoulders. "I don't

think she has been hurt. If it is her, she is working alongside the nuns. I gave the Head Sister your note. And the female doctor there is on our side. Your mother is very smart. Somehow she must have managed to take on another identity. For now she's useful to them."

"But is it really her?" I asked. "I won't believe it until I see her with my own eyes."

Hugh smiled. "I'm praying it is."

I felt a slight lifting of the pain. Somehow it was a comfort to know that she might be in the same city as us.

I looked up at the bridge. Ethan was passing over, dragging his foot behind him as he hurried after his parents. He gave me a wave. I wondered if I'd ever see him again.

Chapter 11

We took the tram to our last stop, Palazzo Doria Pamphilj on Via del Corso. There were no cars, only Nazi lorries flying by. No other traffic was allowed. We were to visit a prince. Through the windows I saw a kaleidoscope of images crashing together as we rattled along. A mound of artichokes. A flash of black-shirted Fascists, ruins, piazzas, people rushing by. Ruins everywhere. Some of them ancient, some of them made by the allies bombing the city.

I noticed the initials SPQR everywhere, strong and forceful, so I guessed they had something to do with the Roman Empire.

"It means *Senatus Populus Que Romanus* or 'The Senate and People of Rome'," Hugh told me. "But children make fun of it and say *Sono Porci Questi Romani* – these Romans are pigs!"

"Romans are definitely crazy!" I smiled but then I frowned. "But the Nazis and the Fascists are pigs."

I was expecting the palazzo to be a fancy house. But when we walked up the Via del Corso, it had a grimy grey exterior. Hugh said it kept its charms hidden. How I longed for Ruby to see a palazzo. I resolved to try to remember as much as I could to tell her. Hugh enjoyed telling me about it.

"What you are going to see is one of the finest palaces of Rome inhabited by one of the finest men. Prince Filippo Doria Pamphilj is descended from Pope Innocent X but his mother was English. That pope supported the Irish against Cromwell – you know, back in the 17th century."

My eyes darted around. No black shirts or Nazi sludge-green. But any moment I expected jackboots to come upon me.

"The Prince is one of our biggest supporters. And even though he is one of the richest men in Rome with another even bigger fancy palace surrounded by parkland, he would never kowtow to the Fascists.," continued Hugh. "Mussolini hated him because he would never fly the fascist flag. His daughter couldn't even go to school because she doesn't have a fascist card."

Hugh strode down the street. He obviously knew his way around. We didn't go through the imposing main entrance but slipped around the corner to a simple wooden doorway nestled in a wall. I thought I saw someone on the corner of the building opposite as Hugh produced a key and unlocked the door. He was clearly used to coming and going here. I tugged at his sleeve and flicked my eyes across the road but now there was nothing to be seen.

We entered into a neat courtyard heady with the sharp scent of lemon trees, the shush of gravel underfoot, a circular fountain in the centre.

"Now wait for your eyes to fall out," said Hugh.

We went through double glass doors and the swish of heavy red curtains and were greeted by a dapper elderly man, the secretary of the prince.

My eyes didn't fall out but my mouth dropped to the floor. Inside was a picture gallery full of huge gilded mirrors dripping with gold! And there were another three Hugh told me, all around the courtyard. The floors were covered in fancy parquet tiles polished like honey and the ceilings were full of pictures that Hugh told me were called frescoes. Between the many windows were mirrors and candelabras, also lavishly gold-painted sofas and spindly chairs. And statues! A whole army of them! Some with no heads, no arms, busts without bodies. How I wished Ruby could see it! She'd think she was in a fairyland.

A sprightly man with swept-back hair bounded into the room.

"Welcome, welcome!" he said in perfect English. "Ah, I see you are impressed, young man! Do you know I have a thousand rooms? Buckingham Palace has only seven hundred and seventy-five!" He was a tall man, slightly stooped, in an elegant suit. But there was fire in him. You could tell.

109

"Your English is very good," I said.

"I went to Cambridge University, you know. Badly injured in a sculling accident. So I married a Scots nurse, who brought me back to health. She's still looking after me after my spell in a concentration camp courtesy of Il Duce."

"Kappler likes to pretend to be an Anglophile, you know," said Hugh. "He also collects Etruscan pottery and loves dogs."

The Prince nearly spat. "He is a barbarian. And you must be careful, Hugh. He knows you are the ringleader of our Rome Escape Line and will stop at nothing to get you."

Hugh merely smiled and pointed up the roof. "He'll have to contend with the Man Upstairs." Then he winked at me. "And the luck of the Irish! As I said, it's useful that the Germans think the Irish and the English hate each other! So they imagine I couldn't be in league with the British."

The Prince then insisted I come to admire the famous painting of Pope Innocent X.

"It's by Velasquez, don't you know," the Prince said. "Look at him, my wily old ancestor. How would he feel if he knew that at this very moment I am planning to blow him sky high?"

Hugh and I gasped.

"The German high command of the Waffen SS wants to take this palazzo over. I will bomb it first," he said matter-of-factly. But his eyes were burning. "There isn't one painting here worth the freedom of our land, or one hair on the head of one of our honest citizens."

"You might have to go into hiding," said Hugh.

"I will dress like a tradesman and disappear among the working people in Travestere," he said. "No one will see me. My daughter who is fair has already dyed her hair black." He glanced over at me. "You might think about that too. Red hair is too noticeable."

We walked through to another gallery, and he pointed to a table where the cardinals used to leave their hats.

We walked on, viewing the paintings. My head swimming with all the chandeliers, holy scenes, devils and angels.

"The tide will turn, Hugh," the Prince said, rubbing his hands together. "Thousands of Italian soldiers are deserting the army and joining the Partisans. They don't want to fight for the Nazis. There are also thousands of women running messages, organising supplies. We will not let these monsters join our homegrown fascist monsters and destroy our country. The Resistance grows stronger every day."

We trudged through what felt like miles of ornate corridors. I was feeling a bit bored. I know it's bad but I soon got sick of gold paint and swishy curtains and big dark paintings. Though there were scenes of paradise too. Fat little tanned angels fighting pale ones. Loads of old people in olden dress. A big scary one of devils with horrible teeth that made me think of the Nazi torturers. They all looked amazing and all. But I wanted to be outside.

When we got to the end of one gallery, the Prince smiled and took out a set of golf clubs.

111

"Monsignor, will you join me?" He set up a wastepaper basket at the bottom end and a wedge to use as a tee down the length of the gallery.

They invited me to join their game. But I was happy to keep score. Hugh won even with his terrible grip. He sure was very light on his feet for a big man. I imagined he'd be handy in a fight and would have a good left hook.

Afterwards the Prince went to an elaborate desk and took out thousands of lire. He wrapped the money in an embroidered cloth with a crest on it and put it in a leather wallet. He handed it to Hugh and as he did the secretary ran in, his face red, his tailcoat flapping.

"It's Kappler! He's here with troops to storm the palazzo!"

I peeked out a window. The Nazis had blocked off the street and stormtroopers were fast approaching. Across the piazza I could see Kappler in a leather coat getting out of his car. And it was the very man we had seen on the road to Rome. I knew by the cut of him. Angry, cold, precise even at this distance.

"Go and stall them at the door," the Prince instructed his secretary. "Hugh, it's you they are after. I urge you to hand yourself in. They might shoot you if they think you are resisting arrest. The game's up."

"If they don't find me and the money, they have no proof of anything. I'm away!"

Hugh was already across the room, his hand on the doorknob. He had grabbed his rucksack and stuffed the cash into one of the inner pockets in his cassock.

"I'll make a run for it. Or hide in one of your thousand rooms. Leo, stay with the Prince!"

But I was having none of it and was on his tail. He shrugged and let me follow him.

We ran blindly down a corridor, away from the front door. There was a short flight of stairs leading to the cellars. Hugh stopped for a moment and ran down the stairs with me close behind him.

Down in the bowels of the house, the cellars were cold and musty. We heard a strange rushing noise from one cellar and looked in. Coal was pouring down a chute, a rumbling black waterfall.

Hugh and I ran in. I wondered if he was thinking of hiding in the coal. The acrid dust was already hitting the back of my throat and making my eyes sting.

"They're getting coal in for the winter," Hugh whispered to me. "And where there's coal, there are coalmen."

There was a break in the coal pouring in. Hugh risked a look up through the trapdoor.

Two grimy coalmen were above us, worriedly watching something – no doubt the SS men. Then they moved away.

Hugh climbed up the mound of coal and grabbed a coal sack from a pile at the top of the chute. I could see by the mischievous look on his face that he'd had an idea. He took off his robe and cassock and stripped down to his vest and trousers, stuffing the clothes in the sack together with his rucksack. I did the same and handed him my clothes and rucksack to hide with his own. Then he smeared his face with coal and so did I. I enjoyed that bit.

Just as one of the coalmen was bending to throw in the next bag, Hugh called up, his voice little more than a breath. *"In nomine Patris et Fillii et Spiritus Sancti!"* In the name of the Father, the Son and the Holy Spirit.

The coalman started when he heard the sound coming from the cellar. He looked like he'd seen a ghost! But his face softened, recognising the Monsignor.

"You'll be doing God's work if you let us through," Hugh said softly in Italian.

The coalman nodded and called to his companion. They whispered to each other and then dropped down into the cellar. Without exchanging a word, Hugh and I climbed up.

We saw a line of SS men, grimly focused on blocking the side entrance and other doorways of the palazzo. Hugh strode by them toward the coal lorry, carrying the bag of "coal" on his back, the rucksacks hidden inside. I cursed myself as I suddenly remembered my little diary hidden within, betraying my true feelings about their filthy leader. I followed close behind him, my heart hammering so hard I thought it would give me away. I had that strange feeling I get when I'm nervous, like the whole world is frozen in time. The SS men barely glanced at us. In fact, they backed off as if they were worried their uniforms would get dirty. But there wasn't the blackest coal that was as dirty as those SS men.

We got to the coal lorry and hid in the back of the vehicle under a mound of dirty coal sacks.

"*Suche das Dach!*" one of the SS men called out.

"They think we might be on the roof of the building," Hugh breathed to me.

The crunch of heavy boots on gravel as if they were grinding the world underfoot.

I curled into a ball, terrified they'd look in the lorry.

The coalmen came back and got back into the lorry. The engine started up and the lorry pulled out of the courtyard and slowed. It must have been a roadblock. Hugh's calm presence stopped me from panicking.

"*Gehen!*" the SS officer shouted. Go! He didn't even bother to look in.

The lorry drove on a few streets. It slowed again as we turned a corner. Hugh and I jumped out and the lorry went on its way.

I followed Hugh into a piazza. There was a small church and we ducked inside. The priest was on the altar. He looked startled when a big coalman and his little assistant loomed in the doorway. But didn't seem bothered at all that we'd get some of the altar cloths dirty. Hugh explained quickly what had happened and the priest ushered us into the vestry.

Hugh quickly washed his hands and face at a sink, drying them with a white towel which still came away black from the coal-dust.

He then shook the priest's hand vigorously. "Don Pietro, we've met a couple of times before."

"Yes, indeed," said the priest who was a medium-sized man with a big warm presence and a kind face. "Most people remember me because of my surname – Pappagallo." He laughed softly as I grinned.

Pappagallo means "parrot"!

"Leo, Don Pietro does God's work with identity cards."

Don Pietro laughed. "Yes, I have a stamp from Naples that helps many a traveller get past the Nazis," he said.

"Take care. The Nazis will send spies to catch you out," Hugh warned.

But the priest smiled. "I'll take as much care as you evidently do."

They both laughed.

Then Don Pietro went to the front of the church to keep watch.

I took my turn at the sink and washed my face and hands quickly.

Hugh had put his cassock back on. I changed back into my shirt. My shorts were filthy. But I was a boy after all and boys are often dirty.

We slipped back outside. I chased after Hugh as he took one of his long twisty-turny journeys down side streets and back alleys, heading gradually towards the German College.

Back in his ground-floor office in the safety of the college, Hugh, with a huge smile, took the money out of the wallet. It was a huge amount – at least five thousand lire. More money than I'd ever seen. He hid it inside a large prayer book with a hollowed-out centre and placed it in a briefcase.

Then he telephoned the Prince. I put my ear close to the receiver.

"I'm back home," he said.

I could hear the sigh of relief from the other end.

The Prince explained how the SS had combed the palace.

"I am afraid Colonel Kappler is a very angry man. He put a lot of effort into trying to arrest you," the Prince said. "He spent two hours here, and he asked me to pass on a message that one of these days he will be entertaining you in Via Tasso! Using their famous interrogation methods, I have no doubt.'

Via Tasso! Their torture chambers! My blood turned to ice.

"You will have to be careful too, Prince. I will get identity cards made up for you and your wife and daughter," Hugh said.

"He said he's going to paint a white line defining the Vatican territory, Hugh, and you're not going to be allowed out," the Prince said. "He'll arrest you if you do."

"Is he now? I'll have to send messengers from now on," Hugh agreed. But he winked at me. "Or find another way to cross over it."

"My sources tell me Kappler is also planning to move against the Jews," Prince Doria said. "You know he asked them to pay him gold and he won't send them to camps in Germany? Would you trust him?"

"About as far as I could throw him," said Hugh.

He turned to me with a big smile when he put the

receiver down. But he must have seen the troubled look on my face. "You'll be safe here, Leo. And Ruby too."

I touched my rucksack, thinking of my diary.

Once more Hugh read my mind. He rose and went to his desk. Opening one of the large drawers, he fished out an armful of papers. He dumped them on the desk and beckoned me over as he pressed down on the bottom of the drawer. Through some ingenious device, the wood slid back to reveal a hidden drawer under the false bottom.

"Keep anything you want in here, me boy," he said with a wink, showing me how to re-set the secret compartment.

When he left the room, I hid my diary and the money Delia had given me, and put the mess of papers back in.

I was very relieved to see Ruby back at Sir D'Arcy Osborne's apartment when we slipped in later in the evening. I felt more scared now, fearing a sniper on every building corner, a Nazi around every bend. But Hugh seemed unconcerned.

Ruby hugged me tight when she saw me.

Hugh and the Sir D'Arcy huddled together to talk about Kappler's attempt to arrest Hugh. There was a lot of worried shaking of heads and tutting.

"We'll need to delay moving you both for a few days," Hugh said.

Ruby's eyes went huge with alarm.

"Where?" I asked.

"I have to confirm it in the morning," Hugh said. "But I

promise you'll like her."

"Her?"

He began to whistle and didn't answer. I recognised the lively tune. It was "Phil the Fluter's Ball" that my mother and Aunt Delia had sung back at Calcata.

We spent the night in the luxury of the Santa Marta Hospice. John May brought us cocoa and we slept in adjoining bedrooms with feather beds!

As he came to collect our cups, real Doulton china like my grandmother sold back in the East End, I risked asking him some questions about our likely hiding place.

"I reckon he'll take you to Mother Mary Saint Luke – she's this really nice Canadian –"

"Not on your nelly!" I shouted before he had a chance to say "nun".

He raised an eyebrow at me.

"There's no way I'm living with a bunch of nuns," I said.

"You won't have to wear the 'abit," he said. "If you were a nun there'd be none of them left."

But I shook my head vehemently, snorting with annoyance like an angry bull.

"I reckon it's got to be better than being shot at by Kappler," he said. "He a real mean one. He has it in for the Monsignor. Knows he's runnin' rings round Hitler's finest."

"Why can't we stay here?" I said.

John smiled kindly. "We've loved having you youngsters around the place. But we got to be practical. We 'ave to keep the beds for all the prisoners of war and partisans who need refuge. And even though we're supposed to be safe there's always the risk of being raided."

I wasn't sure I wanted to leave the safety of Hugh and the Vatican. Particularly as I still wasn't completely convinced it was my mother in the prison. But what choice did I have? But I made a plan. I wasn't leaving Rome until I had a chance to see for myself.

Chapter 12

"Good news!"

Hugh came to see us at breakfast as we feasted on hot buttered toast and marmalade. It tasted like Oxford in England where my father had studied. New College where he read Classics as a scholarship boy. It was called New College even though it was one of the oldest. We visited his old tutors every time we went to England. Old white-haired men in flowing robes like old Professor Fratelli. One of them always had crumbs down his front and drank a lot of sherry. They wanted my father to come back and be a "fellow". I didn't know what a fellow was but it sounded like a fine thing to be. My father told me you get lots of free dinners in fancy colleges. But my mother said you had to be really clever and study lots of things. "Maybe after we've defeated the Nazis," my father said. That was even before war was declared. My dad hated the Nazis way before everyone else. Him and Churchill.

For a moment it felt like the war was far away until there was the scream of a plane outside our window. But it was just a Nazi reconnaissance plane. They'd been flying over a bit more frequently recently. I wondered if they planned to bomb the Vatican.

"Mother Mary Saint Luke says she has room for two more," Hugh went on. "The convent is on the outskirts of the city. There's less chance of being raided." He sounded as if he was selling me something I didn't want to buy.

"I don't want to go," I said.

Hugh smiled at me sadly. "It's this divil of a war. I could just about explain your presence here as an altar boy. But it will be safer for Ruby with the nuns. That way you can stay together like you want."

I knew he was right but that didn't make it feel any better.

Hugh said he'd come for us later in the afternoon, after he'd said his prayers on the Vatican steps. We knew what that meant: in case anyone came to see him. He slipped off again as was his habit. Then John May disappeared and Sir D'Arcy went to his office and we were left to play in the grand staterooms.

It was a fine warm day. Ruby wanted me to read *Alice In Wonder*land with her. But I had other ideas.

The coast was clear and I knew my way. I wasn't leaving Rome without finding out for definite if my mother was there in that horrible prison. I explained to Ruby to say that I'd just nipped out to look at planes. We both looked out for RAF planes all the time, thinking maybe our father might be in one of them. But she gave me that look that said, "I know you are up to something, Leo." So I told her I was going to the prison. She nodded seriously and gave me an extra tight hug.

I wore my altar-boy outfit. Just another boy making his way to choir practice. I wasn't even nervous when I passed a few priests and an important one in a big pointy hat – a bishop, I guess. The guards didn't even look at me as I went through the main gates, just as Hugh said.

Once in the piazza I went behind a pillar in the colonnade and removed my altar-boy outfit. I was just a schoolboy now with a satchel. I saw a strange sight at the entrance leading into the streets of Rome. A team of Nazis on their knees painting a white line, while an overseer consulted a map and pegged out its direction with markers and string. Kappler was serious. What an idiot if he thought that would restrain Hugh!

I felt a tiny flutter crossing over the white line, knowing Hugh could be captured if he did that.

Soon I was hurrying along the banks of the Tiber, making my way to the Mantellate women's prison.

Even though it was a warm day, I felt a chill approaching the building. I walked around and there was another block of buildings that backed onto the high walls of the prison. I reckoned I could see into the prison courtyard from their flat roofs.

On one of the buildings, I noticed there was a plaque on a wall for a boy's boarding school. I reckoned that I would see the prison and the inner courtyard from the back of the school. This was a stroke of luck. Even better, a line of boys was coming back into the building.

I tagged onto the end of the line and nobody noticed. Or at least not the teachers.

A couple of boys at the end poked each other when they saw me. But I winked at them and put my finger to my lips.

"I'm new," I whispered. "I don't know where I'm going."

They were on their way to class.

"Funny being near a prison," I said to the nearest small boy who had a gentle moon-shaped face.

He shuddered. "We hear them moan and cry every night."

We reached a long corridor leading on to classrooms.

"I'm playing a trick on a friend in my class," I said. "Can I get out on the roof?"

The two boys giggled and pointed to a staircase at the end of the corridor. I gave them a thumbs-up and darted away.

I climbed the stairs two at a time and went through a little trapdoor. There I was on the roof, which was surrounded by a low wall. Below was the prison courtyard, bounded by barbed wire and covered in cross-wires lest anyone try to scale the walls. The unyielding walls of the prison were rust-stained and pockmarked, and the small windows barred. There were daytime noises, crashing sounds like kitchen utensils. But underneath I could hear some moans and cries.

I crept to a corner of the roof as the light began to dim towards late afternoon.

I crouched down, hidden below the parapet. Before I knew it, I was singing like the blackbird itself, full-throated.

I moved from corner to corner. I didn't care when people shouted out. I knew that I only wanted to sing "If I Were A Blackbird" for my mother, a sound from home.

"If I were a blackbird I'd whistle and sing . . ."

I whistled and cajoled, my lungs a bellows, my heart a pump. I willed my music into that prison.

"And I'd follow the ship that my true love sails in . . ."

I was going to bring those walls crashing down. So I sang and sang.

My breath was ragged in my throat, my voice hoarse. But I kept it up.

After a while I heard it, a faint note but then it came louder.

"And on the top rigging, I'd there build my nest . . ."

I wanted to catch that sound in my heart and take it back to Ruby. But I didn't need to. There was every feeling I ever felt in that short snatch of song.

"And I'd pillow my head on his lily-white breast!"

It was like a piece of her heart coming into my ear. There was only one person inside those walls who could sing it like that. My mother. Alive. For now.

I slipped back down the stairs and through the school. I passed a hooded monk who gave me a startled look. He knew I was an interloper. But he said nothing

I headed back to the Vatican, slinking against buildings like a cat. I saw patrol cars, a few Nazi roadblocks. But I felt strong. My mother in answering my song had given me back some of my fire.

I slipped back into the college and called into the chapel as that was where Hugh was saying Mass that evening. Light flooded in through the stained-glass windows, pooling rainbow colours on the marble floor.

Monsignor Hugh was saying Mass in his strong, rumbling voice. Even if you weren't holy, it gave you a holy feeling.

Ruby was there with one of the German nuns. I went and knelt down beside her. She smiled and whispered to me that when Hugh prayed it was like being touched by an angel's wings.

Hugh saw me when he raised the host. And there was something in the way he made the Sign of the Cross in my direction that made me think he knew where I'd been. He was blessing my discovery, the precious secret I was hugging in my heart. My mother and I were in the same city. We were breathing the same air, near the banks of the Tiber.

"Mama is in the city," I whispered to my sister.

Ruby hugged me tight, as always happier the closer to my heartbeat she gets. She gave me a butterfly kiss on my cheek with her long lashes.

"I think Hugh needs you straight after Mass – on the steps – to help somebody important," she said.

I was puzzled. Why would she say that? Or maybe she was just guessing. But I followed Ruby's advice. She had a sixth sense, like my mother always said.

So after Mass I joined Hugh on the steps of St. Peter's, at a respectful distance. We didn't talk. There were more soldiers about than usual. It felt tense today. A crackle in the air. The cry of a bird startled me. Hairs pricked on the back of my neck. Like there were marksmen posted at every corner, waiting for Hugh to cross the line.

Then I spied them – a shabby couple lurking behind one of the pillars in the colonnade. I'd seen them before. Ethan's parents. I knew without having to see him that Ethan was behind the pillar.

Hugh was engrossed in his breviary, praying fervently. A few SS patrolled by the line, taut as springs. Then a large group of excited and noisy schoolgirls came with nuns frowning at them, worrying them like sheepdogs.

Ethan's father took his chance. He came up to Hugh. In his hand was a little leather bag.

"Monsignor, we are German Jews. The Nazis have asked for our gold to protect us from the camps. But we do not trust them. We have already fled from our home. Can you take our gold and ensure our boy is kept safe until the madness ends? It does not matter if they take us once he survives."

I looked at the man, the pleading in his eyes, the desperate energy of his words.

I stepped closer to Hugh. "Ethan is my friend," I said to him.

Hugh scanned the square and smiled. "We can do better than that. I will take the boy and give you fake identities."

Tears sprang to the man's eyes and he thrust the bag into Hugh's hands. "Please take this as payment for his care."

Hugh smiled sweetly. "I tell you what. I'll keep it safe for you. You can collect it after the war is over."

I thought the man would dissolve into sobs. But he pulled himself together, his creased face quivering with emotion.

Hugh put his hand on his shoulder and smiled kindly. "You won't be offended if I dress young Ethan as an altar boy!"

The man laughed then.

Hugh gave him an address in the Trastavere area, which he said was a safe flat. The concierge was one of the Rome Escape Line and would give them a room. Then he told him to wait.

Ethan's father let the crowd of schoolgirls sweep by again and slipped back behind the pillar.

Then Hugh instructed me to go back to the German College and fetch two suitable fake passes from the bottom drawer in his desk and an extra altar-boy's outfit.

I felt ten feet tall carrying out my instructions. Even though I darted by Nazis they barely looked at me. Once inside the college I quickly selected two passes, a Signor and Senora Centazzo. I guessed they were about the same age as Ethan's parents.

I had to be mindful not to run, carefully carrying the prayer book in which the passes were hidden. The day was darkening into night. We didn't have much time.

I darted behind the colonnade. Ethan was hidden in the folds of his mother's coat and peeped out when he heard me approach.

"Leo!" he said eagerly.

I quickly helped him put the altar-boy outfit on, which drowned him.

His mother was dark-haired and pretty and was trying desperately not to cry. I knew that look from my own mother. Once he was dressed, she bent down to kiss him on the cheek. She spoke to him in German but it sounded soft and kind, not like the harsh language used by the soldiers. "*Liebling*," she called him. I knew that meant "darling".

"You are a kind boy," she said to me. "You will protect him."

"I will." I handed them the passes.

His father shook my hand. "After the war we will all go for ice cream," he said. But with a sad nod of the head as if he didn't believe it.

"With my parents too," I said. "And my sister Ruby. You'd like Ruby."

They smiled at me and, after final embraces with Ethan, they left.

I glanced around the colonnade. Hugh was approaching.

"Just do as I do," I told Ethan.

As Hugh passed by, wrapped in prayer, we slipped in

behind him, heading towards the German College.

Ruby was delighted to have a new playmate. Soon they were laughing and joking like they'd known each other all their lives. I felt a tiny twist in my heart. Jealousy. But then I was happy that they both had a friend.

Ruby listened wide-eyed as Ethan told her about the Nachzehrer – a horrible German demon of the night. How it chewed and spat out the bones of dead people. And could only be killed by putting a coin in its mouth and cutting off its head. Then she told him that there were lots of good creatures too, like the folletti wind and fog fairies, who would help his parents.

"And Hugh too of course," she smiled. "He is as good as a Fairy Godfather."

As the darkness settled and it got near time for bed, Ethan cried a little. But without asking he got into the bottom of Ruby's bed. They slept head to toe.

In the morning, Sister Boney Face as usual brought us breakfast – some bread and cheese. She made no comment on our new arrival and scarcely glanced at Ethan.

But as we ate, another nun arrived. Tall and brisk in her movements and with a broad smiling face, she was more like a doctor or a teacher than a nun.

"This is Mother Mary Saint Luke," Hugh said. "She is from Brooklyn and works in the Vatican Information Bureau."

"Pleased to meet you all. But, hey, my parents are Irish,

my real name's Jessica Lynch, so I'm practically one of the family! And any friend of the Monsignor is a friend of mine." She had a laugh in her voice but she was precise and sharp with a crisp American accent, not someone to mess with.

But she looked a bit worried when she saw that we were three. "We only really have room for two more," she said to Hugh, not realising I was in earshot.

I didn't hesitate. "Take Ethan instead of me. I can stay here and maybe join the choir. Can't I, Hugh?"

Ruby looked at me, all eyes. But she hugged me. "You could come and visit?" She held my hand tight. She was thinking of Ethan, I knew, but also our mother – she was wanting me to stay near her even if she couldn't.

Hugh smiled. "Well, it's not a bad idea. He's a smart lad, our Leo."

"I'll just keep running away if you take me," I said to the nun.

Mother Mary Saint Luke looked thoughtful. She glanced at the two passes that she'd had made up to escort Ruby and me across the city to the convent, not realising I already had the "Leonardo Rossi" pass. "Ethan's a better age for this ID," she said.

And just like that, it was decided. Hugh left to sort out the transport.

As Ethan packed his bag, he beckoned me over.

"My cat is about to have kittens in our flat near the Portico di Ottavia," he said. "She has a star on her head. I don't want to Nazis to kill our cat."

131

I shrugged but tears came to his eyes and he grabbed my sleeve. He said nothing but his eyes were big with pleading.

There was a loud knock and then this big hefty nun burst through the door. She had a fresh open face, a potato nose and little round glasses. She beamed like a cherub and looked like Hugh's twin. He made a comical nun, smiling out from his wimple, plain-faced and good-humoured.

"I've come to accompany the wee one," he said. His voice was surprisingly female.

"That's the worst disguise I've ever seen!" I laughed.

Hugh laughed too. "Well, you see, they are trained to follow orders, those SS boys. They are fierce literal. And they'll be looking for a priest not a six-foot-two-inch nun." He looked up to heaven, like the holiest nun who ever lived.

Mother Mary Saint Luke handed him his pass. "You have a point, Sister Assumpta of the Virgin Mary, our dear sister from the Emerald Isle."

"But Ruby can't walk very far," I protested.

"She doesn't have to," said Hugh. "Our good friend the ambassador's wife Delia Murphy is waiting outside in her car to bring her nun friends back to their convent with their two charges."

Delia! My heart lifted.

"She can say the children have been vaccinated against tuberculosis in town if there are any checkpoints," Hugh continued. "Besides, our Delia's very keen to visit the nuns who've been trying to help her lay hands on a pig. We won't reveal that last bit if we're stopped."

"But how can the nuns help with that?" I asked.

"They've been praying for black-market bargains," Mother Mary Saint Luke said with a laugh.

I relaxed then. Delia could charm the birds from the trees, as my mother always said. And she'd do anything for sausages and bacon!

"Sister Assumpta" scooped Ruby up.

As she said goodbye, Ruby clung to me tight, but then she blew a halo around me and tweaked both my earlobes. It was her way of "making me magic", she said.

Ethan too hugged me tight around the waist. "My cat's called Sonno," he whispered. "She's a tabby and likes to curl up in the hot press in the laundry room."

I didn't look as they went out the door. But my eyes stung. I wasn't going to cry. Not when I had to worry about rescuing a cat.

Chapter 13

After Ruby left in October there was a hole in my heart. The air whooshed about me in the autumn chill where she should have been. In the following days when I found a little stone shaped like a heart, or one with a hole that Ruby said you could make wishes through or saw a dancing bird, I wanted to rush to tell her. But there was no one to tell. If I had felt like the heart was ripped out of me when they took my mother, this felt like it was dying a little day by day. When I lost my mother, at least I had Ruby. Now I was alone.

So Hugh kept me busy, traipsing around every sight there was to see. A blur of alleys and ruins, jostling crowds and then empty parks. All the columns and cobblestones, piazzas and palazzos. The Colosseum, the Pantheon, the Trevi Fountain, the Spanish Steps, the Catacombs. I lost track. They jumbled together like a scattered jigsaw. Ruins everywhere and marble and always the menace of Nazi patrols. The war felt very big and I felt very small.

I remember the people. The crowds of young men with nowhere to go, sitting on the Spanish steps, slouching into the shadows, fearful of the next Nazi round-up. Celeste, the mad cat lady at the ruined pillars of the Colosseum forlornly calling for the stray cats, "Here, Pelo! Here, Zitti!" scratching her bird's-nest hair. The massive woman selling postcards near the Trevi fountain perched on a little camping stool.

But Hugh and I weren't just sightseers. There were jobs to do too. I was glad to be busy. Dropping off a prisoner's clothes here. A batch of food there. I saw men unravel a jumper and knit hats for themselves in backrooms of tiny flats. Men playing football with a stuffed sock in a basement of an ironmonger's shop. Men huddled together in the attics of convents and monasteries, trying to be invisible. Russian men. Englishmen. Americans and Poles. Even a couple of Irish. Thin men, tall men. Short men. Hairy men. Bald men. Even a few women. Jewish and partisans. All with the same pallor of being stuck inside. The same hollow eyes and haunted faces of hungry people far away from home.

I scanned all their faces, even hoping one was my dad. Though I knew he was either bombing somewhere or dead. Killed or killing. That's what it was all about. I couldn't really remember a time when we weren't at war or talking about going to war. Seemed like normal now. I wondered what German boys thought. Guess they just wanted to play like me. *Achtung! Schnell!* Did they shout, *"Danger! Quick!"* pretending to be English? And miss their dads. Except we were the good guys. I think. Well, mostly anyhow. Hugh said war at its worst also showed people at their best. I hoped he was right.

But it also meant making compromises, Hugh told me. I could see that. Having to play the devil at his own game like Delia and Dr Kirwan having to entertain Nazis. I saw it too with others who had to mix with the Nazis but turned it to other uses.

One day Hugh took me to a fancy hair salon on the Via Veneto. He was dressed as a painter, with me as his young assistant. We carried a pot of black paint and our cover was that we were painting street-signs and post-boxes Nazi black. The surrounding area was thronged with high-ranking officers. I almost shivered. They swaggered and strutted in this part of town, as if they owned it.

We went past a hotel and then the hair salon where some very high-class Roman ladies and German women in clicky heels and fur stoles were having their hair done. I shrunk into myself.

Hugh directed me around to the back entrance where a girl was mixing dyes in a small room and making coffee. He asked her to fetch René, and said something about golf. She left with a tray of coffee that she spat into, giving me a big wink.

A neat man with a trimmed moustache and thinning hair, and wearing a white coat like a doctor, joined us. He embraced Hugh and ruffled his hair.

"Best hair in Rome," he said. "Would you like me to trim it for you?"

Hugh laughed. "Sure better leave it the way it is. Nobody would know me otherwise."

René winked and ran his fingers through my carrot-red hair, fingering it professionally. "Irish hair," he said and then kissed his hand. "Beautiful!"

"You should see my sister Ruby," I said. "Her hair is like a fiery sunset."

"I think he needs to become a little less memorable," Hugh said.

"No," I said emphatically. "You are not dying my hair."

René smiled. "Hugh, I can tell you that the Nazis do plan to save the treasures in the monastery of Monte Cassino and bring them to the Vatican."

"That's a relief. Those papal documents and art works are priceless," said Hugh.

"They also plan to take over the Hotel Regina. And a battalion of Germans will pass through Rome. They are on their way to the front and do not need to come this way but the Nazi high command wants everyone to know who is boss."

Hugh nodded, digesting the information.

Then René turned to me and took out his scissors. "And how do I know all these things? Because every day I cut the hair of fine Nazi wives." He made a cut of imaginary hair.

"*Snip, snip, snip!* And they talk, these women. To each other. Not realising I understand German. And the ones who speak Italian tell me things. Where their husbands are going. When new troops are arriving. *Snip, snip!* And each little tidbit of tittle-tattle is another snip in their defenses." He clenched his hand. "Young boy, I hate those wolves. I would love to use my scissors in a different way. But in my own small way, I do what I can do to help the Allied war effort – one snip at a time."

I uncrossed my arms. "Well, I suppose if it means the Nazis won't notice me."

So that's how I now had brown hair. Like a mouse. They put this smelly stinky dye on me. René gave me chocolates to eat while it was setting and next thing gone was the tufty red hair to be replaced by the short brown crop. He was right. He showed me a mirror and I recoiled at my own reflection. I looked like everybody and nobody now. Smaller and younger somehow. Just another boy. He also gave Hugh some liquid to put on when it started to grow out.

"Or come back," he smiled. "Maybe you will grow to like it."

I shook my head. I never much cared for my red hair. Too easily the butt of jokes. But I really missed it when it was gone.

Hugh said I could shave it all off too for another disguise. He ran his hands through his own glossy shock of curls. Lucky him!

About a couple of weeks after Ruby and Ethan left, Hugh

was extra-busy flitting about like a black shadow. Over and back to the Vatican like a golf ball he putted from his tee. He went to dinner in the Vatican most nights. One night he told me he would stay over at the Hospice because he was working with Vatican radio, the one installed by Marconi. The one that German reconnaissance planes were always flying over.

I know what Hugh was doing. Helping to give the names of people who were safe. They have a system. *Thrum-thrum* go the wires. *Dial-dial* go the family at home. *schh-schh* goes the radio finding the right station. Then a voice, a rich posh voice, starts broadcasting about picnics or something. And names start popping up. So say it's Sam Brown from Scunthorpe: then they broadcast something like "And Sam Brown from Scunthorpe is very close to realising his dream of visiting Roman antiquities". Then his family know he is still alive and probably in Rome. I wondered would I ever hear my dad's name. But he was MIA, missing in action. Maybe shot down somewhere over a French beach. But in my dreams he still hovered in the sky. Caught between the earth and the sky. Life and death. Between heaven and hell.

I bided my time. Hugh would be back by seven o'clock in the morning, after he said Mass. This was my chance to see about Ethan's cat. But then something else occurred to me. It was also the time of the Sabbath. As the light faded into dark, there would be a hush over the ghetto. Jewish people would be staying at home. Lighting their candles, saying their special prayers and eating the strong-smelling gefilte fish. There would be cinnamon buns and crispy matzoth, maybe. People greeting each other with *"Shabat shalom."*

The memory of the spicy smell wafting from my grandmother's kitchen made my toes curl with pleasure. Even my grandfather would relax into the Shabbat to please my grandmother. Moaning and grumbling all the time. Not praying. I thought he was once, but he told me he was actually humming the *Internationale* – the song of the communists. But he still stayed home. Passing around the Kiddush cup filled with wine. Eating the plaited challah bread. But he was reading a book by his own God called Marx. He said that was his bible. I loved the sweet spongy taste of the plaited challah bread as I bit into it, the snap of the matzoth crackers. Observing the quiet and family time. My father too would become the good son to please his mother. Putting on the little cap, his yarmulke. Saying the prayers. I liked it too. The warmth like a big hug.

Except without my mother. She was a *shiksa* – a non-Jewish woman – an outsider. She stayed away.

But the rest of us snuggled in, having nowhere else to be, nothing else we had to do. My grandfather would tell stories and we'd play games – Snap and dominoes. Every time his tales got taller.

The rain was falling. Ethan had given me an address near the Portico di Ottavia in the ghetto. People were rushing about, getting ready for the Sabbath. When the first star appeared in the sky, it would begin.

I skirted the doorways, sticking to the shadows. Near to the gate was a hole in the ground – an excavation of some ancient monument. I watched closely as a cat jumped over a small barrier fence. But it was a scrawny black cat, not a tabby.

A group of old women and men, including a couple of holy men, rabbis with ringlets and skull caps, huddled together chatting just at the doorway entrance to Ethan's flat. I waited, my nerves on edge, for them to move off. I dug my nails into my palms, willing them to go away. Stupid people! Couldn't they hurry up!

The evening darkened. Curfew was approaching.

Just as they looked like they'd run out of conversation, an old lady dressed in rags ran up. It was Celeste the cat lady from the Colosseum, looking more dishevelled than usual.

"Flee! Run away!" she cried. *"They are coming for you all!"* She paused to catch her breath.

The old people looked at her in annoyance, just glancing at her.

"I have run all the way from Trastevere on the other side of the Tiber. Just a few hours ago I heard it at the home of a woman I clean for. The wife of a policeman told me her husband had run into a German. He has a list of two hundred Jewish heads of households. They are going to send everyone in the ghetto away!"

The old woman who sold clothes laughed. "But we have just given them all our gold. Even the Vatican wanted to help us."

Celeste's eyes bulged out of her head and she grabbed the arm of one of the rabbis. "You must believe me! It's God's truth!"

The rabbi just shook his head. "Go in peace, Celeste. The German Nazis are *rashanim* but they are men of honour."

Rashanim. Evildoers. Old Bianca at the bakery had said the same thing. Again I found it hard to understand. Could those who did evil ever be trusted?

"They will be too busy counting all our gold," said the old clothes-seller.

A large crowd had gathered.

"She's crazy," someone near me said. "Look at her with her bird's-nest hair! Everyone knows her whole family is touched."

Celeste's eyes grew wilder. Her arms flailed around like a windmill, disturbing the air.

People laughed. But this enraged Celeste even more and she started to shout and swear, spittle flying from her mouth. *"They have a list! You will all be taken away! The 16th of October 1943! You are doomed!"* She grabbed the rabbi's arm again.

The rabbi shook himself free of her grasp. "Go back to your place, Celeste, and leave us be. Sabbath is drawing near. Trust our good leaders. They have saved us with the ransom. We paid up all the 50 kilograms of gold."

"You'll be sorry! If I were a fancy lady you would believe me! You think I'm lying because I am dressed in rags." She started to pull at her clothes in a fury, tearing them even more.

The rabbi saw his chance and scuttled off deeper into the ghetto towards Temple Square.

Celeste stood for a moment, howling. *"I swear! On my children's heads! The ransom was a trick!"*

The crowd began to drift away. Then she ran off.

The clothes-seller put her hand to her head. "Touched," she said to an old man.

But Celeste's words had shaken me and I followed her, wanting to know more.

As she headed towards Trastevere, she stopped at a bin and started to scrummage around. She found a bone with some raw meat on it and gnawed at it. She looked like what they said. A madwoman. I felt foolish for believing her even for a second.

But I was uneasy. I plucked up my courage and headed towards the synagogue in Temple Square. Maybe the rabbi had proof it was all fine and he would reassure me.

As darkness fell and the first star appeared in the sky, people were heading to the temple. Soon they would see all the lights blazing inside. So many shining shimmering lights glinting off the Stars of David, Solomon knots and Jubilee trumpets in the glowing vessels of worship. It would be as if little flames flashed from the golden brocaded curtain hung before the Holy Ark, the Ark of the

Covenant of the Lord. It would have been even more golden if they hadn't already given up all their precious candlesticks.

The organ sounded out and there was a chorus of young voices. *"Lekhah dodi, librat Kallah!"* they sang. *Come to meet the Sabbath!*

That was the song my grandmother tried to teach me, hoping maybe I would be a cantor too.

Now mothers would be lighting candles in the Sabbath candlesticks. Not the best ones. They had been hidden since the Germans came or given up to pay the ransom. Old men like my grandfather, with prayer books in their laps, would be reciting the blessings and shouting at their noisy grandchildren.

All was well. But it was too dangerous now to hang about with curfew approaching. I needed to get back to the Vatican before nightfall. I decided I would try again in the morning, at first light. The ghetto would be even quieter and it would be easier to sneak into Ethan's old flat.

Back at the college, I fell into a deep uneasy sleep. I dreamed I was pushed into a cellar and beaten with candlesticks. And then drums were sounded in my ears. I didn't wake until nearly 5 o'clock in the morning. I was drenched in sweat. It was still pitch black. I reckoned I had an hour and a half. So I snuck out of the Vatican, my heart in my mouth.

It was raining hard. Rain plashing on the cobblestones,

on the terracotta buildings, on the awnings of cafes. I took shelter in a doorway as a troop of seven Nazis marched by, their boots like nails in a coffin on the cobblestones.

As I neared the ghetto, I began to shiver. The sight of the Nazis had unsettled me. It was early, even for them to be on patrol. But I was close to the Portico di Ottavia, near the small café owned by Gianni, the friend of Roberto's. I wasn't going to turn back without at least having a look for Sonno the tabby.

The light was on but Gianni hadn't yet opened up. I saw with relief, through the shutters, that he was pressurising the espresso machine. I tiptoed past.

"Leo!"

The sound of my name was like a smack to the head. I turned round. It was Gianni, frantically waving at me.

"Come here immediately, boy!"

I hesitated but he came towards me and ushered me inside, firmly closing the door. There was an almighty racket of boots crashing on the ground. Gianni opened a shutter partly and we looked out.

Two columns of German soldiers came down the street in their grey-green uniforms. Helmets slick with rain. Maybe a hundred of them. Officers standing in the middle of the street stationed armed guards at every intersection. Neither of us spoke, shocked by the sheer number of soldiers in these narrow streets.

A few passers-by gathered outside Gianni's window and stopped to watch.

"They are taking away all the Jews!" a woman said.

"Are they not just taking the men for labour duty? To take to the camps in Germany?" an old croaky voice shouted out.

"They are taking them all," I heard a woman say. "All the Jews in the ghetto and the city."

I felt I'd been struck by lightning. All the Jews? So Celeste had been right!

But where were they being taken? What about me? I cursed myself. I had left my identity card in the pocket of my other shorts.

Two guards were posted across the way from us in front of an alley.

I heard someone shout in Italian. *"The Germans are taking everyone away!"*

A woman ran out of the alley, limping, dragging her leg in a plaster cast. A coat over her nightie, her shopping bag in her hand. She handed the sentries cigarettes. They accepted and she asked them what was happening

"Taking away all the Jews," the older soldier answered in faltering Italian. He seemed kind.

The woman slapped her hand against the plaster cast. "But I cannot go. I have a broken leg. I am going with my children to the hospital."

"*Ja, ja,*" the older soldier said, his accent soft.

"Austrians," Gianni whispered to me. Gianni wasn't Jewish. He would be safe.

The Austrian gestured with his hand out of the ghetto

and nodded. He was going to let her slip away with her family. "Where are the children?" he asked.

The woman went back up the alley and started to call to an upstairs window. "*Sterina, Sterina my friend, come! They are coming to take us away!*"

"*In a minute! I'll dress the baby and be right down!*" her friend called back.

But then our view of what happened to the injured woman was blocked. Captured families straggled more or less in single file down the middle of the street. SS troopers at the head and tail of each little band, prodding them with the butts of their machine guns to keep them in line. Mothers and fathers carried babies and toddlers in their arms, holding the older ones by hand. A father still in his dressing gown kept his hand on his child's head. An old woman with one shoe limped along, drooling from the mouth. I even saw the clothes-seller who earlier refused to believe mad Celeste's warnings. Tears were streaming down her face as she clung to her bundle of rags.

Gianni turned pale and put his arm around my shoulder. We watched a paralyzed man carried in a chair. An old grandmother, deaf and blind, stumbling over her long skirts. A mother with a tiny baby clasped in her arms.

A woman grasped the hand of a German officer, weeping and kissing it. Perhaps she hoped to soften his heart. But he shouted at her and cuffed her across the head.

Stunned passers-by gathered on corners. Rigid. Like us. Too frightened to do anything.

The woman with the broken leg came out of the alley with four children. The Austrians let her pass. But at that moment a German Nazi officer and two soldiers came down the street.

"*Juda? Juda?*" the officer shouted at her. He was holding a card.

The woman, fearless, grabbed it off him. "*You, your family and other Jews in your household are being moved. Take with you food to last eight days,*" she read. "*Ration and identification cards. Pack a small suitcase. Lock up your apartment. The sick cannot under any circumstances remain behind. You and your family have 20 minutes after the receipt of this card.*" She flung it back at him. "But we not Jewish!" She clutched the children to her.

The officer asked her name and consulted a list. She told him. He shook his head. Her name was not there. The woman staggered away with the children. As soon as the Germans backs were turned the children fled down side streets. The woman fainted. Several passers-by came to her rescue and carried her away. I hoped she'd make it, this fearless woman who had pretended not to be Jewish.

A short while later, German soldiers dragged the injured woman's friend with a baby in her arms out of the alleyway, then the rest of her family. "I should have listened!" she cried. Dressing the baby had proved to be fatal.

I realised for the first time there was a smell of smoke from a small woodburning stove at the back of the café. Gianni had been burning papers. Of course, it struck me. He was a partisan – he had to get rid of incriminating papers.

There was a loud knocking at the café door.

Gianni came out of his trance. He looked at me with pleading eyes.

I ran to the sink, filled a jug with water and rushed to the stove. The last of the papers had burnt to ashes. I doused the flames.

There was only time to hide under the counter as Gianni opened the door.

"I have permission to obtain a cup of coffee," a young man said, his voice tremulous. "An Austrian soldier took pity on me when I said I wanted to say goodbye to the old place." Without speaking, Gianni poured a cup from the espresso machine. I could hear the man sipping it noisily, the tremble of the cup against the saucer in his hands. I froze, worried the Nazis would come in.

"What are they going to do with us?" the man said. "Will I ever play cards here again?'

"*Schnell!*" came a guttural shout.

The man left. Gianni bolted up the door again.

"You have to leave," he whispered to me. "Go out the back entrance – it will lead you out to an alley by the church of Sant'Angelo in Pescheria."

"The cat," I said. "Ethan's cat. Has it had kittens?"

Gianni looked at me helplessly. "I don't know. But cats can look after themselves. You have to go. Tell the Monsignor he must stay inside the line and not leave the Vatican. It is not safe for him."

There was another sound of shouts in the street. So I slipped out the back entrance, through a backyard full of old discarded tables and junk.

Then I heard a *miaow* from the neighbouring yard. I looked over in time to see a tabby cat, scrawny and covered in sores. In her mouth she carried a tiny furball. A kitten. It looked barely alive.

The cat ran out the back and I was about to follow when I heard more shouting and the sound of trucks. I paused. Then followed in the direction of the cat.

But I had made a mistake. I saw I was near the ugly little museum. There was a small excavated area, cluttered with ruins. The Portico di Ottavia. I had blindly gone around in a circle, too busy looking at the cat.

To my astonishment, the Germans had gathered all the rounded-up Jews into this pit. They were arranged in lines, some with coats over their pyjamas, others in hats and with suitcases as if going on a voyage. I frantically scanned their faces, checking for old Bianca from the bakery. But she wasn't there. I hoped she'd got away.

One woman was combing her daughter's glossy black hair. The girl was about twenty and she clutched a tin can of food in her hand. She must have grabbed it from the kitchen as she left.

"Don't worry, Settimia," her mother coaxed. "It will be like a holiday camp. We will have food all the time."

But her daughter closed her eyes and shouted out, "*I do not believe it! They will kill us all!*" But then she opened her eyes and they were burning. "But I will survive wherever they take us so I can come back and tell what I see. I swear to God!"

Two trucks covered in tarpaulin, their brakes screeching, came to a halt at the Portico di Ottavia, almost running over Ethan's cat that had scampered across the road. The trucks were the murky colours of German military vehicles. The right sideboards were lowered by shouting soldiers. The loading began. People were shoved up with insults, blows from guns. Children were snatched up and thrown after their mothers. The disabled man was flung on board like a piece of rubbish. People wailed and cried out. *"But they said they wouldn't send us away! They promised. They took our gold!"*

A truck left. Another one arrived and began the work of loading the people.

A young man argued loudly with an SS officer in German, gesturing towards a pregnant woman. I think he was saying she was his wife. Another woman with a little girl, who was watching with a group of passers-by, looked at the pregnant woman with anguish. The officer ordered soldiers to grab her and her daughter. The two women looked like sisters. But they left the man who had blond hair. He must have been non-Jewish. He screamed as they grabbed the women and the little girl by the wrists and hurtled them into a truck.

A truck screeched off just as the tabby crossed the road again. I nearly cried out as it disappeared under the wheels. Seconds later the tabby cat lay dead in the roadside, its half-starved brown-and-black striped body streaked with red.

I don't know why I did it but I ran out and scooped up the little furball it had dropped from its mouth. There were shouts and cries. A shot ran out. But I ran and ran, down by the river. My legs flying under me. Slipping and sliding on the wet cobblestones. I ran till my heart felt like a stone in my chest.

I reached the Ponte Garibaldi and ran blindly on. A truck screeched past. As it turned, someone threw a child out of the back and he or she was rescued by a group of workmen.

I got to the other side of the bridge and collapsed.

I don't know how I got back to the Vatican. But I woke up in my bed. Nestled beside me on the pillow was a tiny tiny kitten. I fell back into an exhausted sleep.

Chapter 14

I dreamed and dreamed of things I had seen and wanted to not see. The drool of the old woman with one shoe. The shocked face of the mother dragged onto the truck. The eyes of the clothes-seller. I even saw Celeste's angry mouth and dreamed she was trying to swallow me. I was lying in a hole in the ground. Then angry men in black threw earth on me. The soil clogged my mouth and I was choking. Then I would wake and fall dead asleep again.

"Well, that's one way to avoid auditioning for the choir!" Hugh's face swam before my eyes, coming in and out of focus as if I was looking at him from the bottom of a deep well.

I sat up in the bed. Hugh was stroking the little kitten that wriggled from his huge hands and scampered across the covers to lick my face.

"I'm starving!" I said.

"You've been in a fever nearly two days," Hugh explained. "Sister Boniface has been minding you."

I snuggled the kitten and decided to name her Lulu because that's how Ruby first said my name when she was learning to talk. And I guessed it was a girl.

The nun appeared in the doorway carrying a tray with a bowl of soup. "*Bitte,*" she said.

I shuddered. "*The Jews!*" I cried out. "They took them all, Hugh. They lied to them about the gold!"

"I know." Hugh's face took on a look of anger. But it passed. "May God forgive them. I know I struggle."

"But why didn't the Pope save them?" I pleaded.

"The Pope was tricked as much as the rest of us," he said. "We must dry our tears and keep up the battle in their honour."

"*I hate the Germans!*" I looked daggers at the nun.

She flinched. She might not have understood what I said but she couldn't mistake my hostile glare. She hurried off, head down.

"The Germans are people too," Hugh tried to soothe me. "They have been enslaved by an evil regime. Hitler waged war on his own people first. By all means hate the evil that people do. But never hate the people."

The nun came back in again and I dived under the bedclothes.

"Relax, Leo," Hugh said. "Sister Boniface is a good person. Though she said you tried to strangle her as she

154

mopped your brow! You were in a terrible fever, so you were."

But German nun or not, I was starving and wolfed down the thin watery gruel.

It all came back to me. I had dreamed I was in a burning pit, an ancient colosseum and all the pillars tumbled down. I had a hazy memory of a black SS guard shaking me. But now I realised it was the poor nun.

"What's happened to the Jews?" I asked Hugh.

He shook his head. "Over a thousand of them were deported," he said. "To the camps."

I didn't say anything for a long while. "The Pope must have known!" I cried. "He must have known! The Jews thought the Vatican would protect them. Why didn't you do more!"

A shadow passed over Hugh's face. "None of us are safe with Kappler. None of us knew. We believed they'd ransomed their freedom. I wish I could have done more."

I felt bad then. Hugh was in danger of death if he passed that white line. Kappler was like a fox trying to catch a chicken. One wrong move and Hugh was gone and the safety of all those hidden with him.

I jumped out of bed. I had to get out of there. Get some air.

It was only then I became aware there was another presence in the room. A tall, well-built man stood up. He was about the same size as Hugh but dressed in peculiar clothes – cut-down desert boots, ill-fitting trousers and a too-small coat. But his bearing wouldn't have looked out of place on a parade ground. He smiled. Before he even opened his mouth I knew he was a British military man.

Hugh's face brightened. "This is the boyo who is going to make sure Kappler doesn't get the better of us."

The officer saluted. "Major Sam Derry. Delighted to meet you."

He spoke in the clipped tones of the British officer class. Like some of my father's friends from university. No nonsense but kind with it.

He smiled. "Now the Monsignor and I are going to get this Rome Escape Line on a regular footing, all shipshape and Bristol fashion," he said.

I stood to attention. "I want to help."

The Major and Hugh exchanged a look. I knew what was coming. You are too young. We can't take the risk. The war is no place for children. *Blah, blah, blah!* But before Hugh could say anything the Major surprised me.

"We might take you up on that."

I jumped up, eager now. "My father is in the RAF, you know, or was. My mother is in Regina Coeli prison – Mantellate, the women's section. It's in my blood."

"Good, good," said the Major. "So let's get started."

Hugh shook his head, smiling as if it was a joke. But I was excited now. Eager to get my hands on a gun.

But instead of giving me a gun, the Major took out a big ledger and a whole pile of notebooks.

"Our first task is to get all the records in order. You can

help Hugh and me to get it all down on paper. Every last prisoner of war, Jewish refugee and partisan. Where they are. Where they came from. How much they eat. How much we spend on them. The price of every last piece of bread and smidgen of olive oil. The dangers. Our collaborators and helpers. And our enemies."

My face fell. Instead of being a secret agent I was to be an office clerk. *Boring. Boring. Boring.*

But I cheered up when Major Sam explained it was "Top Secret" work and a lot of it would be in code. That was something. Though I couldn't tell anyone.

"The British government will someday pay out for every penny spent. We have to keep good records," said the Major cheerfully as if it was really exciting.

Hugh went to his desk and took out sheaves of papers from several hidden drawers and hiding places including where my diary was tucked away. There were a pile of screwed-up papers, bits of notes on old pieces of manuscript. Some of it looked like it had been dug up.

The Major groaned. "Let's get cracking, Leo. We have our work cut out for us."

So for hours I became Bob Cratchit, the poor hardworking clerk in *A Christmas Carol* by Charles Dickens. But I soon found it strangely comforting. And it was awe-inspiring. There were *thousands* of names! English, Soviet, Americans, French, Belgian. There were Jewish professors and Italian partisans. English top brass and sons of generals. Irish guards and Italian opera singers. Even

German deserters. Mostly men. But some women and children like Ethan. Many had jobs in the Vatican. Some were in monasteries. Even the Pope's summer residence!

I thought about how hard it was to get food for them all and clothing.

They gave me a great job too. Thinking up codes names for us all. He told us to assume all the phones were bugged.

I decided to call Major Sam, "Patrick" and Sir D'Arcy Osborne "Mount" because he was at the summit of command.

Major Derry said to Hugh, "You are already 'Golf' so we'll keep that."

"Count Sarsfield can be 'Emma', to throw everyone off the scent," joked Hugh. "And we'll call the prisoners 'dispatches' and 'parcels' and 'clubs' too."

"What about me?" I asked.

"Do you play golf too? Or cricket?' Major Sam AKA Patrick, asked me.

"He's a great man with the hurley," said Hugh. "It's an Irish game like hockey only miles better!"

"We could call you Hurley?" suggested Major Sam.

"No – why don't we call him Setanta?" Hugh said. "He was a legendary Irish warrior who killed the fierce hound of a man called Culann with a sliotar – the leather ball they use to play the game. And after that he volunteered to stand in for the guard-dog and was called Cú Chulainn – the Hound of Culainn."

"Setanta it is!" proclaimed Major Sam.

I was quite pleased with that.

"And if you ever get into trouble with the Nazis and the Fascists and have to pass us a message, just mention the Hound of Culann," Hugh added.

Chapter 15

I was a spy! Well, sort of, I suppose. A small link in the chain of people fighting Hitler the Spitler. I was glad Major Sam Derry had joined our gang. He was nice. When an Allied plane flew over, I whispered into the fresh air, "I'm one of you." I wished I could tell my dad.

Sam, now rechristened Patrick Derry with a new identity pass, was supposed to be an Irishman working at the Vatican. I hope none of the Nazis could recognise an Irish accent because he certainly didn't have one!

For my first big assignment, Major Sam made us dress in rough clothes.

He tapped the side of his nose. "We have some hush-hush business to conduct in the Vatican garden – a rendezvous," he whispered.

I was so excited! Maybe I was going to get a gun or

special stuff for smuggling documents.

We used our passes to get into the Vatican garden, Sam carrying a sack filled with yellow biscuit tins.

In the rose garden, near the statue of the Good Shepherd, an elderly gardener with a lined tanned face was shovelling compost from a wheelbarrow. A smile spread across his grimy face when he saw us and he nodded towards a pile of garden implements beside some sacks. Major Sam took a pick and handed me a shovel. I looked at it like he'd handed me a bunch of flowers or something useless.

"What am I supposed to do with this?" I asked.

"Dig," he laughed.

"But I thought it was spy work," I groaned.

"It is. We have to bury these documents. The routine and boring work is just as important as the heroics. It's not all jumping from planes behind enemy lines."

The elderly gardener laughed as I huffed and puffed, cursing the hot sun under my breath. But we soon got into a rhythm with Sam turning over the sods and me shovelling the soil away.

I was so engrossed in the work I only noticed at the last minute some people approaching. I shaded my eyes with my hands in the noonday sun and saw a strange group. A man with a film camera, two clerics dressed in black and a few paces behind them a tall thin man dressed all in white so blinding it was as if he was lit from within. His Holiness the Pope!

"*Quick, quick!*" the gardener hissed. "*Behind a bush!*"

I was surprised when the gardener joined us, crouching down behind the large hedge.

I peered through a hole in the hedge. So this was the famous Pope Pius XII. Hitler's Pope some called him because he never condemned the Nazis straight out. The Good Shepherd others called him.

His skin even at this distance was extremely pale, like he never went outside. He sort of glowed like a white flame in the sunshine. He hung back, looking up at the statue while the camera crew set up. They had a tripod and put the camera on it. He brought his hands together in prayer, his fingers long and tapering.

The sight of him made me tremble for some reason. He radiated some sort of power. I glanced over at the gardener. But he had his eyes lowered. Major Sam, however, looked as transfixed as I was.

The Pope stood for a moment and then the camera moved to the statue. Then without anyone saying anything, the Pope moved on, the camera crew scurrying behind. I was disappointed. I wanted to talk to the film crew.

"We have to hide from him every day," the gardener said. "He does not like to see us when he takes his daily walk to talk to God outdoors."

"What!" I exclaimed. "I thought it was only in case we ruined the picture for the camera." I translated for Major Sam, who scratched his head.

"He's the top holy man," he said. "What he doesn't see he can't know about. He's got to keep on the right side of the Nazis to keep them out if you know what I mean."

"Where are his Noble Guards?" I asked, expecting to see the red-jacketed men in thigh-high boots that Hugh had told me about lurking behind the rose bushes and the tall cypresses.

The gardener shook his head. "The Holy Father prefers to walk without them in the garden."

But it made me wonder. What did the Pope know about all the people hiding under his nose? The Jews kidnapped from the ghetto? I guess he had a lot on his mind, having to pray to God and all most of the time. But he must have known some of the stuff going on under his holy nose.

The old gardener scratched his head. "He is very holy and very important. Even his secretaries have to be on their knees when they speak to him."

Even though the Vatican had its own railway bringing in supplies, there were so many more mouths to feed with all the people hiding in convents and monasteries. Rations were terrible. Food was getting to be in short supply and we had a lot of electricity blackouts. But I was glad of the distractions from that box in my head full of my worries. And little did I know that a very convincing cover was being cooked up for my spywork.

A few days after we saw the Pope, Major Sam had a bombshell to drop on me. Instead of going back with him to the German College, he told me I was due at the Sistine Chapel. I smelled a rat.

"You don't mean I have to be a choirboy?" My voice nearly became a shriek.

"'Leonardo Rossi' alias Setanta, you have no choice. It's our best cover story," the Major said with a wink. "You have an audition, so don't muck it up! Now go meet Hugh at the main entrance."

Hugh and I passed through miles of corridors and magnificent halls, Hugh striding along very much at home. A few times he pointed out paintings and statues that he said the popes had ordered to celebrate the victory over Martin Luther. That fellow who started his own religion, the Protestants, really got under their skin, and I was beginning to share Luther's annoyance at all the holy flummery and gold.

"Prepare to be dazzled," said Hugh. "That boyo Michelangelo painted the chapel for years on his back. It's a miracle."

I just shrugged. So many things in Rome had that effect.

Then a huge door opened, a man in a dark suit stepped aside and I gasped at the scale of the Sistine Chapel, craning my neck to look upwards at the sheer teeming wonder of it all.

There was God reaching out to Adam, who extended his hand a bit casually, as if he really wasn't that bothered about becoming the first human being – or else he was scared witless! But this was just one panel on a vast ceiling. There was the Garden of Eden, the Flood – I listened to Hugh blather on with half an ear. Because the one thing that amazed me was they were nearly all buck-naked! I'm not telling a word of a lie. As naked as newborns, here in a holy church. And not just any auld one but the Pope's chapel!

My eye quickly fell down past the plummeting sinners of The Last Judgment. Michelangelo's giant mural certainly put a lot of other holy paintings and statues and stuff in the shade.

Standing before the altar was a smallish priest with snow-white hair. When he turned round, I could see an intense look in his eye.

"This is Don Perosi, the Maestro of the Sistine chapel, the leader and genius of the choir," Hugh introduced us in English.

He was a roundy man, portly under his habit, hunched around the shoulders.

"So you wish to join my choir?" he said in heavily accented English that looped and soared like birdsong. He was warm and modest, not frightening at all.

"Yes," I answered.

He smiled at me and asked me to open my mouth. Then he looked at my tonsils.

He bid me go stand in front of the altar. He beckoned to Hugh to join him and walked down to the back of the church.

"Can you sing the 'Ave Maria'?" Don Perosi asked.

I was a bit ropey on the words, and croaky when I first started.

165

Don Perosi conducted me with slow awkward gestures that I could barely see. With his white hair and stoop, he was like an old monk from a fresco. But he wasn't that old. Maybe fifty.

Then he stopped me.

"Can you sing it like this?" he asked. He sang the same words, but with a different, gentler tune.

I copied him. After two attempts he seemed satisfied. He was intensely focused when he directed me but a bit on edge.

Then he turned to Hugh and whispered.

I walked up to join them and sat in an adjoining pew. They were deep in conversation and didn't take much notice of me.

"Times are hard. It's difficult to get boys," Don Perosi said. "But he will do fine. His voice is beginning to turn. But we will work with what we have."

Hugh asked him how many he had in the choir now and he grinned.

"About two hundred," he said with a laugh. "But some of them are rather old for choirboys and have voices like foghorns! At least young Leo here can sing and he is young!"

Hugh looked around for me and was startled that I was so close.

Don Perosi turned to me and beamed. "Welcome to my Singing School, young Leo!" He bowed to me. "You are now a member of the oldest choir in the world. The music you will sing is the soul of prayer. Music I have composed or arranged specifically for this space. The emphasis is on the melodic sweep and phrasing. You are God's instrument now. I will require you to come to rehearsals five days a week in the mornings."

Hugh nodded. But I must have looked horrified.

"When you can," added Don Perosi. "I understand the Lord has other uses for your talents."

So it was official. My mother's dream had come true. I was a Vatican choirboy, even if it took the Second World War to make me one!

I would have to break my vow and wear a dress, a dark-wine one with a white surplice on top, like a smock, and not just as a disguise. I have to admit I did feel a tiny bit proud!

Chapter 16

The Choirmaster kept us late most evenings, practising hard for Christmas. Major Sam was pleased because being a proper choirboy put me beyond suspicion and meant I was in the Vatican at the crack of dawn and last thing at night, smuggling in documents.

I kept myself separate from the other boys, partly out of habit. I wasn't used to mixing with boys who didn't want to kick my head in. But they all knew each other a long time. And they didn't want to talk much either. You never knew who to trust. Sometimes we played football. But to them I was a shadow flitting in and out of practice.

It was also hard work and Don Perosi was a strict taskmaster. He was kind but exact and again and again we had to go over the same phrases, the same high notes.

But sometimes when we got it right, the fluting voices

sounded like they might go up to heaven, up to the beautiful frescoes and live among the gold and silver and all the colours of the rainbow.

But one night as I went back after burying some documents, shining a torch in the darkness, a screaming came from the sky. I was inside the Vatican, just between Saint Peter's Basilica and the Vatican railway station when I heard the thrum of an engine. A plane was circling several times overhead. Hard to see if it was Allied or German in the dark. I was just squinting up into the inky sky to work out where the low drone was coming from, when *Boom!*

A plane flew low about a hundred metres overhead.

The Vatican was being bombed! All around was the tinkle of glass. It was raining glass!

I dived under a bush and curled into a ball.

The first explosion was by the city wall, a little way away. It hit a cardinal's house, I heard later.

But the second was right beside me. A direct hit on the roof of the mosaic studio, where they stored the thousands of mosaic cubes used for repair and decoration. I shone my torch and all around lay shattered pieces of coloured glass as if a giant kaleidoscope had exploded.

The third bomb was behind the imposing building that Hugh had told me was made up of three buildings joined together and was called the Governor's Palace. Windows and doors were blown out as if a hurricane had swept through the building.

I crouched low again in among the greenery but grew stiff with fright.

I forced myself to get up and run towards the radio station where Hugh was broadcasting names of escaped prisoners of war.

But as I ran the fourth bomb fell ahead of me. My heart! There was a massive boom! My ears rang. I was covered in plaster. But the radio station still stood. There were shouts from the Palatine Guards.

Hugh flew out and grabbed me by the arm. "Let's get back quickly," he said. "Thanks be to God, only one Palatine guard is slightly wounded."

We ran then, shards of coloured glass littering our path like a giant vase had been smashed.

It was a miracle no one was killed or the Pope harmed.

We found out what had happened the next morning. They were cluster bombs, designed to hurt property. The Nazis were blaming the Allies. It was too dark to see the markings of the plane but everyone knew it was the Germans. Millions of lire worth of glass had been destroyed. Saint Peter's was shut all day Saturday to sweep it up.

The next day, Sunday, was a dull rainy morning. But that did not stop the crowds from every parish in Rome teeming into Saint Peter's to check that the Pope was still among us. Unharmed: the White Dove of Peace. Black umbrellas aloft, the crowd must have looked like giant beetles from the air.

Large groups gathered, all the faces leaning towards the

window of the Pope's study, on the third floor in the great block of the Apostolic Palace. With one voice they shouted "*Evviva il Papa!*" Long live the Pope!

The rain fell down but under their umbrellas the crowd paid no attention to the weather.

The Pope's secretary, dressed in his black soutane, looked out from the study window. He popped back in. Seconds later, the Pope all in white appeared at the window. All the umbrellas closed as if by magic and all the faces were raised towards him with a roar of cheering.

As he held up his hands in blessing, a sudden silence fell and the words, "*Benedictat vos omnipotens Deus Pater et Filius et Spiritus Sanctus*," could be heard distinctly. *May the Almighty God bless you, the Father, Son and Holy Spirit.* The cheering broke out again.

Hugh wore a beatific smile on his face, as if he'd seen an angel. I too was touched by the Pope's holy power. But then a little bitter fist of doubt twisted inside.

"Hugh, why doesn't the Pope lead the people in an uprising?"

Hugh shook his head. "The Pope is our spiritual leader. He has to keep his eyes on heaven."

My face fell and then I felt the volcano of anger in my tummy. "Heaven is not much use to people with Nazis trying to kill them."

Hugh scratched his head. "It's hard to explain and the Lord knows I don't know what's in the Pope's mind. But he has to think of things we don't have to worry about. He's not a military general but a holy man."

But I was having none of it. "Well, I live on the earth and there's Nazis thinking they can own every country."

Hugh gazed at a cross, as if looking for inspiration. "For the Pope, his job is to serve the Eternal Church, handed down to him from the time of Saint Peter and to be handed on until the end of time. He is between heaven and earth. Come on – I'll show you something."

He led me to the Basilica, striding ahead vigorously. I followed, full of curiosity. Inside, we went in the main door and straight up the centre to the main altar with the big bronze canopy. Then turned left into a side aisle.

The aisle was vaulted, with a gold roof and a geometric pattern on the floor, light streaming in from the high windows.

"Would you believe me if I told you we might be walking on top of the bones of Saint Peter, the chief apostle of Jesus and the founder of Christianity in Rome? They crucified him too, you know." Hugh spoke in the hushed voice priests often used in the Vatican.

I looked down at the floor, not understanding a thing. "Is there a grave under here?"

"Let me show you," he whispered.

Hugh then led me into one of the little chapels on the left before the main altar, called the Clementine Chapel. It was named after some old medieval pope called Clement. There was a large builders' sheet covering one wall. Hugh pulled it back to disclose the remains of a brick wall and a marble

172

wall. He took a flashlight from a box at the entrance to what looked like excavations below and led me through.

Inside was a short tunnel then two flights of steps.

"We are descending fourteen hundred years into history," Hugh said. "To the beginnings of the Church in Rome."

We were soon deep in the bowels of the Vatican, directly under the main altar, Hugh told me. The smell was earthy and pungent. Hugh's flickering torchlight revealed a series of passages.

"This is a big secret project," Hugh said. "They usually only work at night so as not to disturb Mass during the day. But as the church is shut today, they will be taking advantage of that to get work done."

There was something enchanting about being under the Basilica. A crackle in the air. Even for a half-Jewish doubter like me. I felt like I was in a time machine.

"By popular accounts, Saint Peter was crucified in Rome," Hugh told me. "But upside down because he said he wasn't worthy to be crucified the same as Christ. He was buried down here and, in the fourth century AD, the Emperor Constantine ordered Saint Peter's Basilica to be built over his grave to honour the founder of our Holy Church."

We entered into a stone chamber, dark with some pools of light.

"Excavations have been going on for some time," Hugh said. "The present pope ordered them to see if we could find the actual remains of Saint Peter. But when war broke out it was also decided to dig a secret tunnel so the Pope could get to safety if there was an attack on the Vatican."

"Do you mean there is a network of secret tunnels under the Vatican?" I asked, incredulous.

"They wouldn't be secret if I told you." Hugh's voice was humorous.

I knew better than to question him further. My mind was reeling. Was that how Hugh was able to come and go under the nose of Kappler? Is that how he stayed one step ahead of that bloodhound?

There were a series of arches and stone walls, many of them red, some held up by temporary scaffolding. It was difficult to make out what was hidden in the shadows, but it was some sort of crypt.

Then I heard clinking sounds. We rounded a stone pillar and there by candlelight were workmen digging into the earth with pickaxes and scraping the soil with spades.

In a clutter of bones and artefacts, a workman was examining an ancient archway. He nodded to Hugh but continued with his task of examining the brickwork. Nearby was a stone table with bone fragments.

"Are they them?" I asked pointing to the bones.

"No, the potentially Saint Peter ones are already in a lead box in a special place. The bones were found beneath the red wall, near Saint Peter's grave. The pope's private physician says they belonged to a man in his seventies. We have high hopes they could have belonged to Saint Peter himself. There are some lavishly decorated pagan tombs down here but some early Christian symbols have been found nearby, a palm and a dove. And an engraving was found saying *Petros Eni* – Greek for 'Peter is here'! Now isn't that the best detective work you ever heard!"

In another nook a workman was cleaning an inscription on a wall with a large pumice stone, carefully polishing so as not to damage whatever the inscriptions were underneath. He smiled at us and spoke to Hugh in rapid Italian, too fast for me to understand.

"This is Giovanni, one of the foremen of the *Sampietrini*, the 'little Saint Peters' – the artisans who take care of the Basilica and who have been brought in to work on the excavations. This is the grafitti wall, as they call it, with a jumble of etched symbols and letters."

Set into the wall was what Hugh called a marble receptacle, that was shaped like a little marble post-box. Giovanni burst into a stream of rapid Italian again, shining his candle at the opening and pointing vigorously.

"Giovanni says he widened the hole in the plaster there under orders of the Vatican head of the excavations and found another pile of bones with some reddish cloth fragments. They are in a box somewhere too. He was the one who found the fragment of the red wall that said '*Petros Eni*' – 'Peter is here'."

"Maybe they are his bones too," I said.

"Maybe," said Hugh. "That's for the archaeologists to work out."

I thought, what a grizzly job archaeologists have, working through piles of old bones!

We bid goodbye to Giovanni in his black hat and brown overall and went out through a different tunnel.

We were in the secret underground world of the Vatican and proceeded along a tunnel where Hugh had to crouch.

We emerged into a cave where there were faint shafts of light.

Hugh turned to me and said: "So now you can see why the Pope at all costs will not let the Nazis come in here. He is terrified that they would desecrate the grave of the founder of our sacred Church. He doesn't even want them to know that we have found the grave. There's a real risk too that the Nazis will kidnap him and dishonour the Church."

I frowned. "I still can't see why a pile of old bones is so important, even if they did belong to Saint Peter."

Hugh smiled. "Well, sometimes it's a question of faith. I'd like to be able to tell you that you'll understand when you grow up. But these things are fierce complicated even for a grown-up. Or a priest. And there may be more going on than we know about. The Pope doesn't discuss what's going on with the likes of me."

"Maybe God's working through you," I said. "You are standing up to the Nazis. Why are you doing it?"

Even in the poor light, I saw that his eyes blazed. "I can't bear to see injustice, Leo. We all do what's right for our own conscience. I would do it for anybody in need. God has no country."

"Will we get rid of them, the Nazis, do you think?'

Hugh's face looked resolute. "It won't be for want of

trying. Rome has had to deal with waves of barbarians. We will see off this lot too!"

The air was cold in the small cave and I had lost my bearings.

Hugh held the torch up and I saw that there were rough steps set into the side of the cave. He tilted his head upwards. "Just above there is a manhole that comes out in a side street on the edge of Saint Peter's."

My eyes adjusted to the dim light and I could make out a square cut into the roof of the cave.

"So that's how you come and go!"

Hugh tapped the side of his nose with his other hand. "I told you the Lord worked in mysterious ways. It's only for emergencies, mind. Come on, I want to show you something else."

There was yet another tunnel leading off the cave. We trudged for what felt like miles but probably was less than a few hundred metres.

Then we came to a steel door. There was a concealed locking mechanism that Hugh worked and we emerged into another short tunnel, a concrete structure. Hugh told me it led into a big tunnel built for an underground road.

I heard a babble of sounds, human sounds. To my astonishment, as we came into the main tunnel I saw it was full of people! Like a shanty town of refugees.

"This tunnel goes under Gianicolo Hill – the Janiculum Hill," Hugh said. "It leads to an embankment on the Tiber. Here's where lots of Rome's poor people have taken shelter.

Mussolini called them the "popolini" – little people. It's his fault they have to live like mice under the floorboards!"

It was a curious sight. In some places sections were partitioned and whole families had taken up residence. There was the smell of frying onions, a whiff of drains, old decrepit ladies asleep on beds of sacking, dirty-faced children with no shoes, filthy feet clambering over piles of old furniture. Scrawny mothers fed tiny babies at their breasts, their faces strained and tender at the same time.

Here and there sick people lay on beds of straw, groaning and sweating. One old man had constructed a whole house out of books, ancient bound volumes stacked like bricks and covered in an old canvas as a roof. Hugh told me he was an old Jewish pedlar, who used to sell rare books at a stand in Saint Peter's Square.

It was another world away from the gleaming palace of the Pope dressed all in white, the hushed voices of prayer in the Vatican, the fine ladies in their black mantillas who prayed in the churches. The nuns' scrubbed faces, their hands wrung in prayer.

I thought of Ruby reading *Alice in Wonderland* in Sir D'Arcy Osborne's quarters, of how Alice disappeared down the hole into another world. That was us as we picked our way through the broken furniture, the piles of canvas and straw beds. People either nodded their heads at Hugh or ignored us, as if they were used to the sight of him.

I was glad to get back to daylight when we emerged from the entrance to the tunnel between Porta Cavalleggeri and the railway station, just minutes away from Saint Peter's Square.

Hugh dusted himself down and we walked back to the German College as if we'd been out for a stroll.

"Handy little route," Hugh said matter-of-factly. "And it can take you down to the river too. But you have to be careful as sometimes the Gestapo secret police post sentries."

But that night as I lay in the little camp bed I was sleeping on since Major Derry had joined us, I tossed and turned. I didn't feel as optimistic as Hugh. Not while my mother was still in prison. I burned to see her, to tell her the good news about me being made a choirboy, singing *"Ave Maria"*, even if it was because singers were in short supply. But we were all on a knife-edge. The bombing of the Vatican had made it worse. What if something happened to me before I could rescue her? There was nowhere safe when murder could fall out of the sky.

The next day and the next, I retraced my visit to the boy's boarding school next to the prison, first thing in the morning. But on neither occasion did my mother respond to my call.

I cried and cried each night on that little camp bed. I didn't mean to. I tried to write things in my diary but the tears just slipped out, like my eyes were leaking.

Perhaps Hugh had heard me, for a few days later he announced we were going to visit the prison. He smiled as he told me. "I hope you'll feel comfortable in our disguise."

Chapter 17

I dearly hoped the guards at the Mantellate prison had bad
eyesight because Hugh and I were a right pair of ugly nuns.
He towered over me. But he reckoned I would pass as a
young novice, a trainee nun. We were dressed in the drab
brown of the German sisters at the college with a wimple, a
piece of stiff cloth covering our heads and neck like a
bandage, topped off with an overhanging veil, brown for
Hugh and white for me. But the wimple was a godsend – it
was as good as being mummified. And as we proceeded
with bowed heads, the veil shielded our faces from closer
inspection.

As we walked through Rome carrying our Red Cross
cases with medical supplies, our alibi for entering the
prison, and took the tram, I discovered that people didn't
scrutinise us too closely. Wearing a habit was almost a cloak

of invisibility. My idiotic expression came in handy too. We didn't converse. Just looked holy. I guess Hugh was praying, clutching his rosary beads. He was convincing enough. Somehow he managed to change his big stride so he sort of glided across the cobblestones and dusty streets. I still had to scurry after him, but he was more elegant somehow.

Hugh told me we were to call in to see Gianni for a special cake.

I was wary approaching the ghetto. There was an eerie feeling as we approached the café, the streets much quieter than normal. I kept my head down, so I didn't have to look at the Portico di Ottavia where they'd lined up all the Jewish people.

Gianni did a double take when he saw us. But refrained from laughing as he beckoned me inside with a cautious glance up and down the street. Hugh stayed outside to keep an eye.

"Tell your mother to take only little bites," Gianni said to me in a low voice. "This is a nourishing cake. It will have a little of what she needs. If she, for example, needed to take a trip."

I was puzzled by his words. But then it hit me. If she managed to make an escape. Perhaps there was a file inside. I asked him and he nodded.

"Tell Roberto I will try to sort out some shoes," I said.

"There is a woman in Turin called Ada Gobetti who is leader of the Resistance there," he said. "She can organise for people to go over the mountains into France or

181

Switzerland. I will make contact with her in the event your mother gets out."

There was an armed guard on the gate but, when Hugh gestured to the medical supplies in the cases with the Red Cross, he barely glanced at us and opened the big iron gate without asking any questions. We went through into the building, my habit swishing against the cold stone floor. The cold seemed to rise up through the bowels of the earth. There were several niches with statues in them, left over from its convent days.

A female warder with a large bunch of keys tinkling at her waist came out of a side room and led us through endless grimy corridors to the hospital wing. *Clang, clang,* went the keys as she opened each set of doors at the beginning and end of each corridor. She banged each set of doors after us.

I grasped the handle of my Red Cross case tight. Inside were the lint, bandages, iodine and medicines that could mean life or death for an inmate.

There was a horrible smell inside the prison. Old cabbage, rotting rubbish, a manure odour like the drains didn't work too well. Damp oozed from the walls. Here and there I saw suspicious stains like dried blood.

We passed cells with iron doors. We didn't see any inmates but could hear them moaning and crying. Some called out to us, *"Get me some water!" "Warder, my prison mate has thrown up!"*

It was a zone of the living dead. The air was cold and thin.

Finally we came to a large set of double doors that led out into a central courtyard. Across the way was the hospital wing. There were barred windows but they were all high up. It was strange seeing the inner courtyard and the walls, which I'd gazed at with such fury and longing, from the inside. Breathing the same air as my mother.

The warder rang the bell and put her hand out to take the medical supplies. I saw she had a big mole on her upper lip and her skin was pitted and rough.

But Hugh told her in a voice of pure sweetness, "My instructions were to hand them to the doctor. From military command."

He spoke Italian with a German accent. Clever. He was making her believe he was German. But she was reluctant to let us through with our supplies. Probably wants to filch some of them, I thought unkindly.

"The prison governor is one of our patrons," Hugh persisted. "He has many Masses said at our convent for his dear departed parents. I'm sure he would be interested to know that the warders here helped us carry out our mission."

Then he reached inside his habit and took out a packet of cigarettes. The face of the warder changed.

"*Sulima!* What all the top-ranking SS officers smoke!" she exclaimed, trying to snatch them from Hugh's hand.

But Hugh held them aloft.

"Perhaps you will grant us five minutes alone with Frau Doctor?"

The warder agreed gruffly and ushered us in. Only then did Hugh hand over the packet.

Inside the ward, the smell of antiseptic was oppressive but there was calm order here even if the conditions were cramped. There were at least thirty beds crammed into the narrow room. Some of the patients just lay on their beds moaning. Others wore bandages and casts. Several of the women had black eyes and bruised faces. A couple had their hands wreathed in bandages.

I scanned the faces, anxiously searching for my mother.

An older woman doctor in a white coat, her untidy grey hair pushed behind her ears, came toward us. Her frown instantaneously changed to a smile when she saw the case that Hugh held.

"Sister! What a lovely surprise!" she said, reaching out eagerly to take the case.

"You're very welcome," Hugh said as he handed it over.

She smiled at me. "And I see today you have company on your charitable rounds."

"Well, doctor, my young novice here was hoping to see a friend of her aunt who I believe is a nurse here. But we cannot recall her name."

A look of understanding passed over the doctor's face. "Ah, she is tending to prisoners in the isolation ward. We have a couple of suspected cases here of Syndrome K. They need to be evacuated to the Tiber Island hospital."

At that moment, a woman burst through the double doors at the end of the ward. I swear to God, I smelt her before I saw her. A waft of lavender and rosewater. How she still managed it in here, I would never know. My mother! But she was thinner and had aged. A scarf covered her hair and her eyes were big in her face. Her abundant springy auburn hair was gone. Now it was close-cropped under the scarf, and almost totally grey. But she still had that quick energy about her, that warmth that made me want to hug her. I just wanted her to blanket me in her arms and make the war go away.

"*Mama!*" I blurted out. But then I pulled myself together and said, "My mama wants to send her greetings."

I don't know whether my mother was more surprised that her son was dressed as a nun or that I was there in the first place. She burst into merry laughter, so infectious everyone laughed along. Then she threw open her arms but before she could embrace me Hugh caught my arm and the doctor indicated that he should usher me and my mother into a nearby office.

"You have the length of time it takes to smoke a German cigarette," Hugh said, closing the door and leaving us alone.

I fell into my mother's arms for a hug. She kissed my forehead and I felt something come back to life in me. Quickly she explained how when she was at the police station near our village, she was mixed up with a batch of other prisoners. She had managed to hack off her hair so that she wouldn't be recognised. And then it had gone grey overnight all by itself! The village police turned a blind eye when she said she had no papers. She was grateful for that. So when she was transported to Mantellate, she gave a false name. Signora Marianna Salvanaio. Said she was Italian Swiss, a nurse, and had lost all her papers. She had asked to see the Swiss legate, Count Salazar, but so far had been refused. She had quickly volunteered for nurse duty and the doctor, a sympathetic Italian woman, had been only too happy to have her.

The doctor and Hugh joined us in the office. "We don't have much longer," Hugh said.

My mother looked gratefully at the doctor and told me she had protected her from Kappler.

The doctor smiled. "I was lucky to find someone so skilled in caring for my Syndrome K patients. She runs a high risk of getting it herself."

"That's an uncommonly useful diagnosis," said Hugh. "And what are the symptoms?"

"It's highly infectious and patients have to stay in special isolation wards. They have to cough any time there are Nazi-Fascists about."

Puzzled, I looked to Hugh for an explanation.

He then explained to me that the Vatican had a hospital on an island in the Tiber near the Jewish ghetto. It was often used as an isolation hospital for people with infectious diseases and therefore shunned by the Nazis and the Fascists. That was where the doctors had come up with "Syndrome K". The perfect cover for protecting Jews as no Nazi would risk the disease. "K" for Kappler was their little joke.

"But we have to be careful," my mother said. "The Fascists have placed ordinary prisoners as spies amongst us. We don't always know who to trust."

"Ah, so my mother is close to getting infected," I said, realising their plan.

"We must get you false identity papers first," said Hugh to my mother. "And lean on Salazar to get you out. But the Swiss have to be careful. They can't be seen to work with us."

"Some friends in the Resistance are trying to find ways to have you taken to safety," I said. "They are contacting Ada Gobetti in Turin."

My mother's eyes lit up! "Ada is amazing. She has practically invented the Resistance networks!" She gazed at me with hungry eyes. "And Ruby? Where is my baby?'

"She is safe at the mother house," said Hugh.

"I am in the Sistine choir now," I said to my mother.

"What!"

"Truly I am. Ask Hugh."

Her eyes shone with pride.

"They don't have much choice these days," I muttered.

"You have a beautiful voice, my dear," she almost crooned, tears in her eyes. Then she wagged her finger at me. "But I don't want to be disturbed by blackbirds anymore – for your own safety."

I smiled at her.

She mussed my new brown hair hair. "Soon you will be my Leo the Red Lion again. Look how you've grown! I hope you're brushing your teeth? And washing behind your ears?"

There was a flurry of activity outside the door, patients moving about, nurses banging on a trolley.

One of the nurses called out to the doctor. "The warder has finished her cigarette."

"We don't have much time," Hugh said.

I opened the case and took out the cake. "Mama, this cake is just for you. Keep it for a good opportunity and take only little bites. Some of the contents might be harder than you think." I gazed into her eyes and nodded my head in the direction of outside. Away from this stinking prison.

We heard the warder's hacking cough nearby.

"Doctor, we will rely on you to be ready for when your top nurse, 'Marianna' here, comes down with the dread symptoms," Hugh said. "Especially if there are Nazi germs about."

"I will be ready for when the Vatican doctors come here to confirm," said the doctor. She looked intently at my mother. "Signora, I am worried about you."

My mother smiled. "I am okay for now, especially as I can see my children are in safe hands. Let the older women go first. They are suffering. I like to be of use to the patients. But, you never know, I might get struck by it soon." She gave a little cough and winked at me.

"Particularly if you ever have to speak to someone nasty whose name begins with the same letter as the disease," I said.

The doctor took the cake and hid it among a pile of paper records in a locked drawer appropriately marked "*Files*".

"It's always good to have a nourishing cake with iron in it," she said. "We'll keep it as a back-up."

As I left, Mama slipped something into my pocket. It was an embroidered handkerchief, the one she'd used to dab her tears, with the letters "R" and "L" intertwined.

The warder was at the door. "We need to go, Sisters," she said gruffly. "Next time bring me Lucky Strikes. Not these stinking German cigarettes."

"We'll put our faith in God," said Hugh to the doctor. "And our own good actions."

"And Lucky Strikes," I said.

"Amen."

As we walked through the ward, women thrust notes into our hands. Messages for loved ones. One woman even gave us an embroidered sock with an address inside on a tiny piece of paper – "*Love always to my family*" it said. I thrust it into my habit and didn't catch the woman's eye in case I cried.

I decided I was going to make contact with Roberto then through Gianni. Just in case they could ever organise a prison escape.

Chapter 18

"I've ordered the fake Swiss identity cards for your mother. In the hope we can get her out," said Monsignor Hugh. "I've spoken to Count Salazar about interceding with the prison authorities but he's nervous that he could jeopardise the whole operation if he's seen to take too close an interest in her."

My heart fell. She was in limbo.

But I wasn't going to wait. If the Rome Escape Line couldn't help her, maybe the Resistance could. I was going to get word to Roberto via Gianni to see if he could spring her. Maybe they had already made contact with Ada Gobetti in Turin. I didn't know where that was except that it was further north and close to the mountains.

The kitten mewled against my chest as I started out. It made me feel a little less nervous. I knew it was stupid bringing Lulu, the little furball. But she began to cry as I left and I thought it might give me courage to look after something smaller than me.

The early-morning mist swirled in ghostly shapes around the dome of Saint Peter's. It made me think of all the poor people wrenched from their homes in the ghetto. But also of Ruby and her funny stories about fog creatures. It made me shiver but I had to be brave. I was on a mission.

There was hardly anyone about. I saw a few workmen in their overalls carrying a ladder on the opposite side of the road. But they barely glanced in my direction. I didn't like the idea of revisiting the ghetto on my own and kept my eyes down as I approached Gianni's café at Portico di Ottavia.

I dashed the last bit, relieved to see the light shining through the glass front. I gave the *rat-tat-a-tat* knock.

Gianni greeted me warmly when I entered and gave me some warm chicory coffee with a dash of milk. It was slightly bitter but the heat going down the back of my throat revived me.

Gianni smiled sadly as I told him my plan about wanting Roberto to organise the Resistance to release my mother from the prison. I knew that smile, the "you're just a kid but I'm going to pretend to listen to you" smile that adults give children when they have no interest whatsoever in helping them.

"So they can all dress as nuns and have a habit for my mother. Then they can make a dash for it and shoot everybody in the way," I said.

He looked down – shamefaced. "Look, I gave you the cake. But I did it out of friendship for the Monsignor and you. There is no plan to release your mother. We can only help if the Monsignor gets her out."

I felt my stomach lurch. I suddenly felt like I couldn't breathe.

"But I thought you were setting up an escape!" I was close to tears.

"But you said yourself your mother feels it more important to stay where she is," he protested.

I shook my head. "Of *course* she wants to be with Ruby and me! Hugh can find her a job inside the Vatican."

"Have you not seen what a fortress that prison is!" he said. "You have no chance."

"But the Resistance have guns," I persisted.

He shook his head as he wiped down tables and put out little jam jars with little flowers in them. "Listen, Leo. You're a smart kid so this is why I'm going to tell you this. The Resistance is planning some special operations. They involve lots of planning. Lots of risks. They don't just spring people from prison. It's not how they work."

I bit my bottom lip, feeling I might cry.

Gianni gave Lulu a little saucer of milk. She lapped it up with her tiny pink tongue.

"Look, Leo, even if they wanted to, Roberto and his band cannot really come into the city. They don't even have proper clothes and shoes. They'd be arrested on sight."

I remembered the strange footwear of Roberto's ragged

band, the sacks for jackets. The broken boots and shepherd's leather.

"I'm sorry if I gave you false hope," Gianni said, "but there won't be any back-up if the Monsignor fails. If your mother takes a chance she is alone."

Hot tears stung my eyes. I wanted to punch him. The air was heavy with tension between us, like a storm about to break.

"Shoes are a big problem," Gianni said, trying to change the subject. "Even worse since they got rid of the Jewish cobblers. There's no one to repair the shoes."

"Well, I'll get them some," I said fiercely.

With that I picked the kitten up and ran out of the café.

I ran and ran blindly, not thinking where I was going.

The sun was rising now but there were still threads of mist around, trailing over the still streets. Somehow, breathless, I found myself at a piazza. It should have felt like the sacred core of the world. A deserted square reached by two narrow alleyways, dimly lit, with a fountain, two umbrella pines and an old church. There were sounds from inside the buildings of people stirring.

But I felt utterly, utterly alone, with only the kitten in the world. How sad I felt. I stood up but, as I did, a dog barked and the little kitten took fright and jumped from my jacket. *Oh no!* A snarling dog took after her, its lead trailing in the gutter. I plunged headlong down the street trying to keep pace with them, dimly aware that another figure was also following.

Lulu dodged down an alley and with good cat-sense ran up a tree in the centre of a small dusty garden, the only living thing there. I leapt past the dog and quickly climbed up to retrieve her. I scooped up the trembling kitten and stuffed her back in my jacket. The dog was up against the tree, pawing at it, snarling up at us. I reckoned I could make a run for it, down the opposite alley between two tall houses. I threw myself down on the other side of the tree. But then everything happened at once.

The dog tore around the tree and jumped towards me just as I threw myself to the ground. I sprawled badly and rolled into a ball, terrified the dog would attack me or kill Lulu. But I was lying against something hard. My heart thumped so fast I thought it would break through my chest. It was a jackboot polished like a mirror.

I looked up.

A Nazi officer was standing there erect, a swastika armband around his arm, a peaked cap with an insignia of the eagle, a skull embroidered on the neckband of his jacket.

He shouted at the dog, which immediately backed off and sat.

I was slightly embarrassed to see it wasn't a German Shepherd that they used for round-ups but a dachshund, an oblong sausage dog, waddling and comical on its short legs.

The officer had one hand on his hip. He poked me with his gleaming jackboot and put out his gloved hand. I flinched, thinking he was going to strike me. But he laughed. And helped me to my feet.

I backed away from him, my head down.

"You and your cat have had a lucky escape," he said. He spoke good Italian with a strong German accent. "But you don't need to be afraid of Winston, my pet dachshund. He is a big pussycat."

Winston – the name of the British prime minister. Must have been his little joke.

He called the dog over and encouraged me to stoke him. But I stayed away, anxious that the dog might still pounce at my kitten.

"Up early, boy, aren't you?" he said.

I glanced at him nervously.

Kappler my mortal enemy.

He had a long pointy nose and his sandy hair was sparse under his cap. Apart from the visible scar on his left cheek, he looked like a shopkeeper or a minor official in an office, as exact as a watch. Not the brute I knew he was.

My throat constricted. I didn't know what to say. Couldn't say anything. He looked at me intently.

"Have we met before, boy?" he said. "You look familiar."

"I am from Travestere," I said, trying to imitate the thick Roman accent.

"I hope you are not a partisan?"

He said this as a joke, I think. For he chuckled in a forced way, like his face wasn't used to laughing and smiling.

I shook my head.

He stepped closer and looked into my face. Then he did something strange. He tugged at my hair.

I felt all the blood drain from my face. Did he recognise me from the attack, even though I had dyed my hair? I thought he was going to ask to see my identity card. But his stupid dog came to my help. At that moment, it took off down a side street. Kappler cursed under his breath. He took off after it, glancing back at me.

I didn't hesitate. I plunged back down the opposite side street and ran with all my might back up by the Tiber towards the Vatican. Like I was in the Olympics. Like the dog, now a snarling hound of hell, was at my heels. My breath was ragged in my throat, my heart a beating drum. This was what it was like living in the world's largest and most deadly game of hide and seek.

Church bells rang out for 7 o'clock. I tore back into the German College and got there just before Hugh returned from Mass.

When he came in the door, he sneezed. I saw the look on his face.

"It's Lulu, isn't it?" I said.

"Yerra, one of us will have to go. She makes me sneeze. And I don't think she'd be any good at saying Mass!"

"I don't want to lose her," I said stubbornly.

"We'll think of something," he said. Then he crinkled his eyes as if remembering something important. "One of our favourite persons has invited us to lunch and was most insistent you join us."

Well, wasn't I only too delighted to find myself later that

day at the Irish Embassy! Delia greeted me as warmly as if she hadn't seen me for a thousand years. She played the piano for us and asked me to sing. I was a little bit wobbly on the high notes.

"I'm only too thrilled that you are now a choirboy," she said. "Just in the nick of time! Your voice is maturing and that's all for the good too. You don't want to be like one of those poor old castrati they used to have at the Sistine. Well, I won't say what they used to cut off them to keep them at the high notes!"

I winced – I had heard about the castrati – but Delia laughed, as only she could. Not like Kappler's constipated sound, halfway between a bark and a cough.

Most of the plates and food came up on the dumb waiter. I loved that "dumb waiter", a funny name for a little lift that brought food up from the kitchen. The door went *ping* and out came bread and some kind of cheese. The cook came in with soup in a massive tureen that was too big for the dumb waiter.

"I hope it's not cat meat again," Delia said with a wink.

The cook didn't react at all so obviously didn't speak English.

Delia shook her head. "I'm not kidding you – nearly all our cats have disappeared. Including Mayo, my favourite Persian."

"We have a little tabby looking for a new home," Hugh said.

I glared at him. But he rolled his eyes and smiled like an angel.

But she shook her head. "I'd love it. But they get catnapped here in the city. Particularly by my cook." Then a gleam came into her eye. "I have it! You know I'm in league with the nuns to get a pig on the black market?" She looked at Hugh. "Now you don't be makin' any judgments with your sharp clerical eye. Ambassador's wives have to eat too and what am I going to feed all them waifs and strays you keep sendin' to me?"

"I was just thinking you could give me the hindquarters," he said.

Delia laughed. "Okay, it's a deal. If you lend me Leo as an accomplice. But I've just had a great idea. Why don't we give the kitten to the nuns? They need one to chase all the mice."

I shook hands with her before Hugh could refuse. "It's a deal! And I can see Ruby too when we take it there. Please, Hugh!"

He closed his eyes and then smiled his holy smile. "Isn't that a great idea altogether? Kills more than a few birds with one stone."

So it was all arranged. We would collect the kitten and deliver it to the nuns after lunch. And see Ruby!

I was a bit sad. I liked the kitten. But I liked her enough to want her to have a long life and not end up in soup!

We dropped Hugh back in Delia's diplomatic car to pick up the kitten.

When he left, I asked Delia if she knew how I could get my hands on some pairs of shoes. I needed them for friends of mine.

She laughed good and proper. "Well, you've come to the right woman. I have another scheme going too. But I don't want to get Hugh into trouble. It involves a little bit of ducking and diving as John May would say – and, believe it or not, shoes!"

My eyes lit up. "If you give me a fair few pairs I'm your man."

She laughed. "Bedad, there's no flies on you!"

Hugh came back with the kitten in a basket and Delia said to him that, as we were going on a drive the next day, it would be better if I spent the night with her.

Hugh narrowed his eyes suspiciously. "A drive tomorrow as well as the nuns? Well, what I don't know I can't talk about. But be careful, the pair of you."

He handed me something in an envelope for Ethan and told me to be very careful of it.

We set off to see Ruby. I was sorry I was going to lose Lulu. But glad she was getting away from this beautiful, maddening but stinking, dangerous city.

Chapter 19

The convent was situated on the outskirts of Rome among olive groves. The journey was fun as Delia sang as we went and improvised funny words sending up the Germans. She taught me another popular song:

"Hitler has only got one ball,
Goering has two but very small,
Himmler has something similar,
But poor old Goebbels has no balls at all!"

There were a few military checkpoints. But when they saw the green, white and orange of the Irish flag on the front and the driver showed the diplomatic pass, we were waved through without any questions asked. Delia beamed and waved to them all, as if she was a royal princess.

I felt safe with Delia. Her warmth and kindness wrapped around me like a warm, snuggly blanket. I knew she was brave too. Hadn't she continued singing in Belfast once when there were bombs going off outside! My mother had told me it was in the newspaper and all.

When we reached the convent, Delia was delighted to discover that Mother Mary Saint Luke was there too – visiting her religious order's HQ. While they went off together, laughing like schoolgirls to see about the pig, I was able to catch up with Ruby and Ethan.

A young novice showed me the way. She was from Quebec in Canada and had a French accent. I felt relaxed with her. She told me how she loved having so many children about the place. They were all God's children. That was the teaching of our Lord. She asked me if it was dangerous in the city.

"Nowhere's safe in this stupid war," I said, looking up. "You could be in a palace and a bomb could fall out of the sky."

She cast her eyes up and made the Sign of the Cross. "I shall pray for the Lord to protect us all and turn the evil from men's hearts."

I will pray for the bombs to fall on the stinking Nazis, I thought, but didn't say anything, her being a holy nun and all.

She led me to an apple orchard where birds were singing mixed with the sound of children's laughter. I hadn't heard that in a long time. There among the boughs, a group of children were playing and singing nursery rhymes.

Among them I saw my sister's glorious red hair, Ethan's dark mop at her side.

"*Ruby!*" I called out and ran to her, Lulu in the basket.

She turned and dashed into my arms. "*Leo!*"

I hugged her tightly, until a miserable mewling little *miaow* came from the basket in my hand.

Ruby broke away and looked in. "Ethan!" she called.

He came, shyly at first. Then he ran to see what was in the basket.

I was so pleased to see him. They both looked well. More filled out than when I'd last seen them. Colour in their cheeks. Almost glossy. The nuns had been taking good care of them.

I took Lulu out and Ethan knew at once it was poor Sonno's kitten. He was so happy I felt bad that I would have to tell him that Sonno was dead. Then I gave Ruby Mama's embroidered handkerchief.

"A-a present!" She traced the lovingly embroidered R and L. Tears fell from her eyes and she sniffed the handkerchief. "I can smell Mama's tears too."

"Is my cat safe too?" Ethan asked me.

I couldn't lie to him, his big eyes looking so trusting in his open face.

"She's gone to cat heaven," I said. "She's with Delia's cats and they are all playing with the angels."

His head dropped and big fat tears fell from his eyes.

"It was a truck accident," I said. "It was quick. She didn't suffer at all."

Ruby wiped his eyes with the handkerchief and that cheered him up. She squeezed the hankie into a ball and shook it out, flying it like a sail catching a breeze. "This is a magical hankie. It takes your tears and sends them away."

Ethan asked me if I knew anything of his parents. I handed him the envelope Hugh had given me. Inside was a photograph of his parents dressed as a nun and a monk. He was so happy and gazed at it with joy. He kissed the photograph lightly.

"You have made him so happy," Ruby said. "Sometimes he cries himself to sleep. Now he can send them magical thoughts of love."

Then for the next few hours I forgot about the war. We played with the kitten. Ethan showed us a complicated game of stones he'd invented. It was really clever.

We had afternoon tea with Mother Mary Saint Luke and Delia. Delia sang for the "orphans" and distributed some biscuits her cook had made for them. I didn't like to think what might be in them. Delia's old canary maybe.

The children also sang for Delia, including Ruby and Ethan. I was so proud of them.

"They're not trying to make you be a Catholic, are they?" I asked Ethan.

He shook his head. "No. But I am learning the words and hymns so I can pass as a Catholic if the Nasties come," he said.

He told me that Ruby had had a dream about a raid on a monastery. There was a bad monk with the Nazis and they caught out some of the Jewish men and the partisans because they didn't know the words of the *"Ave Maria"*.

"If that happened for real they would take them away and send them to the camps. Or shoot them," Ruby said. "That's why we must call Ethan 'Sebastian' like on his identity card so he doesn't slip up."

"But I'm not really Sebastian," Ethan said solemnly. "That's just pretend."

"It's like we're all in a play," Ruby said brightly. "We change our characters and learn a part so that we can continue to play again."

So I spent some time tutoring them in the words of the "*Ave Maria*".

"Ruby has been telling me about the fairies," Ethan said. "She tells me stories every night to keep away the bad thoughts. And how the little monk fairy with the red cloak saved you in the tree and how he is keeping us safe."

I shook my head. "Ruby tells pretty stories."

She gave me her stern look. "Leo doesn't believe in anything. But I know the folletti fog fairies helped you recently save Lulu, when that dog was chasing you!"

"What!" I exclaimed. "What do you know about that?"

"So it did happen," she said smugly. "I dreamed it."

"I bet Delia told you," I said. I didn't want to entertain her wild notions. But I must admit it spooked me a bit.

Then she began to prattle to Ethan again. "There are also the ones who live in the woods. They are helping the partisans. Like Roberto. They will help them find shoes. But maybe lots of left feet!"

I was startled. How come Ruby was so good at guessing

all the plots I was trying to weave?

Ethan and Ruby looked at each other, heavy with a secret. Ethan whispered in Ruby's ear and she nodded. They were going to tell me.

"We have been telling each other stories about the Blackshirts and Nazis and who they really are. Why they are so mean." Ethan's voice was hushed.

They looked at each other as if they'd done something really naughty.

Ruby's voice was a rustle on a breeze. "W-well, the Blackshirts – do they howl at the moon? Do you think they are werewolves?"

I laughed but Ethan nodded seriously.

"And – do you remember, Leo," he said, "those nightmare Nachzehrer creatures I told you about at the German College that chew on people's bones? I made a story where the Nazis are Nachzehrer."

"And other creatures too. Bad ones," Ruby said. "Like vampires and devils."

I laughed again. But they both frowned. Ruby's bottom lip stuck out. They were cross with me for making fun of them. Ruby hit me lightly with her fist.

"But, do you think – maybe – it might be real?" she insisted.

I hugged them both tight. "They are behaving like beasts. But I'm afraid they are humans just like us. They have become bad or are made to do bad things. But they aren't creatures out of a story."

Ruby looked at Ethan. "I told you Leo doesn't believe in anything."

I smiled at her and chucked her under the chin. "Come on, let's not spoil our day. Tell me about the nice fairies."

Ruby smiled then and picked up a dandelion clock and blew it. "There. Little baby fairies will be born from the seeds and travel all the way to Rome to guard our parents."

She spoke with such faith I could almost see the tiny little creatures flit away with their gossamer wings.

"That's more like it. Think about the nice things, you two, eh?"

They smiled and nodded.

But it was time to go. Mother Mary Saint Luke came to take me back to Delia.

Ruby's prattle used to annoy me. But how I longed to stay in that garden in the mild afternoon sunshine talking of fairies with little red cloaks.

Mother Mary Saint Luke led me to a barn at the side. "The generous amount Delia has paid us for getting the pig will be great for bargains on the black market," she said. "The current rations are terrible. Perhaps you could pass on a message to Hugh to ask the Pope to help us. Hugh knows the right strings to pull."

I nodded. "I'll pass on the message."

"We don't want the children to see the pig leaving," she said as we entered the barn, which smelled of apples. "They've been feeding it tidbits. They'll be heartbroken tomorrow when they find it's gone. Thank goodness the

Lord brought us the kitten."

I wanted to say it wasn't the Lord but Leo, and I'd also rescued him from a Nazi dog. But there was no point. The nuns would just say God was working through me. If that was the case, it was time he started to do a bit more work in earnest and give the devil a run for his money.

Delia was standing by a pen, surveying a pig. I nearly died when I saw the size of it. It was large and pink with stiff hairs, a wet nose and a cunning look in its piggy eye. I was due to share a back seat with the horrible smelly creature all the way back to Rome.

"No way!" I told Delia.

"But, sure, haven't I just paid forty-five pounds for him!" she insisted.

So with much huffing and puffing, we pushed the creature into the back seat, as it was way too big to fit in the boot which was filled with apples and vegetables the nuns had given Delia as a gift. Mother Mary Saint Luke gave us chamomile flowers to feed it, saying they would make it calm.

Franco the driver was swearing. He was a neat dapper fellow, with his hair slicked back like an American movie star. "Here I am, I have driven through bombs and curfews – just so I can get pig-shit all over my lovely car!"

"Well, Leo, would you rather lie in the boot among the apples and the turnips?" Delia asked.

But I couldn't stand the idea of being locked in a boot. So I gave up.

We put lots of sacking on the back seat and a sort of harness on the pig. Then Delia laughed and said I could sit between her and Franco. "If we're stopped at any checkpoint, we'll say the ambassador's Uncle Herbert has had a bit too much to drink!"

We drove all the way with the windows down. The funny thing was Delia started singing and soon we heard massive snores from the back.

Delia snorted with laughter herself. "Well, that's the first time in my life I'm delighted to send the audience to sleep!"

When we got back to the embassy, I was glad to see the back of that pig as it was handed over to the cook.

We had a sparse supper of anonymous soup. When the cook brought it in, Delia clapped her hands and said in Italian. "And has another of my favourite cats gone missing?"

The cook gave her a dirty look.

But Delia just laughed. "My cook is famed for her sauces. As we say in Ireland, hunger is the best sauce! Eat up. *Miaow!*"

I tried not to think there were bits of cat meat floating around in the soup. But she was right. My mouth was lonely for food. I wanted to breathe in the aroma of basil and garlic. I fell on it like a wolf on a lamb. I finished every last mouthful, even licking the bowl.

Delia packed me off to bed early. I didn't even get to play with the dumb waiter or with her children who were all staying at their schools, which they often did during the week. Blon, her older daughter, was staying with a friend who lived closer to the university.

"You've heard the story of the elves and the shoemaker," Delia said as she showed me to my room. "Well, tomorrow we're going to play out the Roman version!"

Chapter 20

We set out in the middle of the morning. Delia told me to wash well, behind my ears and all. I somehow expected we were going to scale a wall and dress all in black like cat burglars stealing diamonds in a film I once saw. But I was surprised when Delia came down in her respectable tweed suit and summoned the car. It was the official limousine with the Irish tricolour streaming from the bonnet, usually reserved for special occasions.

"It's daylight robbery, so it is!" she joked as we got in. "On you go, Franco – you know where we're headed."

We set off.

"Now let me explain the plan to you," Delia said.

"Once there are no pigs, I do not mind what we do," said Franco.

Delia laughed and thumped him on the shoulder.

"You're a caution! We are going to call on my dear old pal, Nonno the shoemaker, with a pair of my husband's old shoes." She held up a pair of brogues that were a bit down at heel. She pretended to make them dance. "You see, Nonno has a new job. Repairing shoes for the Third Reich."

That was the *Third Realm*, meaning the third German Empire. That's what Hitler called his nasty regime. The first one was in the Middle Ages and the second in the 19th century. I thought of all those Nazi shoes and boots, thinking Hitler just wanted to grind us all into the ground with them.

"Now, Nonno is going to leave a pile of shoes near the doorway of his workshop," Delia went on. "The Nazis have grabbed most of the shoes in Italy, so they won't miss a few. While I'm distracting the office staff, your job is to pile them in the boot. As many as you can cram in."

"What if something goes wrong and they catch me?" I asked.

"We'll pretend you're a bit simple and you thought that's what we asked you to do."

I made a vacant face, the face of a simpleton that I'd used to great effect all through school in Italy.

Delia laughed.

"But what if they ask to search the car?"

She pinched my cheek. "Don't be bothering your head with if's and but's. They probably won't even have a guard."

"And what about Nonno? Will he get into trouble when the shoes go missing?"

"Not a bit! There's so many pairs they're coming out of his ears!"

"Does it bother you it's stealing?" I asked her as we slowed in front of a large red- brick building behind a fence.

"I consider it 'liberating' the shoes. The Germans shouldn't have been so selfish as to grab them all in the first place."

That settled the matter for me. If it didn't bother Delia I wasn't going to let it trouble my conscience.

The shoe depot was a plain, nondescript warehouse building set back from a row of terraced houses. There was a gate to drive in and some offices in a separate building off to the left of the main building. There was no guard, nor sign of any checkpoint. But why would there be? The Germans would never expect anyone, least of all an ambassador's wife, to steal shoes!

As the car pulled in, an official ran out from the office buildings. Delia put her head out the window.

She explained her visit and the official, a fat balding Italian with an old-fashioned courtly manner, smiled and bowed as if she were the queen.

"Nonno does all our shoes," she explained to him in Italian. "Would you mind if we popped in to see him?"

The official explained he would have to ask the manager, who was German. The way he said it with a roll of his eyes suggested he wasn't overly fond of his new boss. Delia asked where Nonno was based and he gestured vaguely over towards the main warehouse building as he went back into his office.

She got out of the car and told us to park at the side entrance of the warehouse beside Nonno's workshop on the left.

"I'll distract them for a bit and you get loading!" she laughed, dismissing us with a wave of her hand.

So we did as she bid us. As we drove round the corner, the sharp tang of leather filled my lungs. The side entrance was open and a little old man with a long beard came out. He looked just like an elfin shoemaker from a fairy story in his long leather apron filled with tools. Ruby would have loved him.

Inside the open doorway I caught a glimpse of his worktable with a shoemaker's lathe. And all around the walls boots and shoes in every size stood to attention on shelves. There was a row of wooden models of the foot. There were also piles of different kinds of leather and a small table with threads. Along the top row of shelves were gleaming jackboots, enough to march all over Europe, terrorising everyone with the click of their heels. On the middle rows were army boots. And on the bottom, mixed shoes of different sizes.

By the side of the doorway was a big pile of random boots and shoes, a small mountain of shoe leather. The top teetered with boots in shocking disrepair. Ones that couldn't be reused.

There was a sign by them, saying "leather for recycling," in Italian.

I wondered why Delia thought they would be of any use to anyone.

Franco opened the boot and without further ado we piled them in in armfuls. I inhaled the deep smell. There was something comforting about it. Luxurious. And I realised it was only the top layer that were falling apart. The rubbish shoes and boots concealed hundreds of brand-new or well-repaired pairs. There were even rubber boots and smart Italian dress shoes and women's lace-ups.

The shoemaker scurried back and forth, whisking pairs of shoes off the shelves at random and adding them to the pile. Shuffling the remaining pairs together, careful not to leave too many gaps.

"I am very particular," he chuckled. "I discard many, many pairs. And they never check." Then he spat. "Filthy swine. They killed my only son, hauling him off to a work camp in a round-up even though he had a delicate chest. His mamma cries every night for him."

We worked fast and feverishly. When the car boot was near to bursting, we heard Delia's warm voice, screaming with laughter. She was letting us know she was near. I threw the last few in and the driver rammed down the boot. We leaned against the car, as if we were just taking some air.

Just in time. Delia rounded the corner accompanied by the manager, a tall beaky-nosed German in civilian clothes, and the grovelling Italian official. There was also a pinched-faced woman, carrying a file.

"Would you mind if I had a little look at the workshop?" Delia asked in Italian, all wide-eyed.

The officials nodded in unison, heads bobbing up and

214

down like ducks in a pond.

The shoemaker was now seated at his lathe, diligently tapping a new sole onto a pair of stout boots. Delia peered at them intently.

"So, Nonno, will you have time to do His Excellency's shoes?" she asked him, all dimples and wide smile.

The shoemaker scratched his head. "Come back tomorrow. They should be ready."

"Maybe you'd throw in a new pair of jackboots. They'd be great for country walks," she said. "Not that we have much time for walking these days."

Everyone laughed. The officials were fawning over her, eating out of her hand. I was terrified they'd smell all the shoe leather from the boot. But they were too busy peering inside the stretch limousine.

"Why don't you get inside for a ride?" she said as she ushered me into the car. "Jump in here beside my boy."

The officials laughed. But the next thing I knew, they lumbered in beside me and sat opposite, composing themselves with great dignity, like they'd suddenly been transformed into ambassadors themselves. I sat rigid and unsmiling. But they just nodded in my direction. They clearly assumed I was her son.

We drove to the gate and they clambered out, delighted with themselves.

But I didn't breathe easy until we turned the corner.

Delia turned around to me. "Well, just as well they didn't suspect the booty in the boot!"

We turned into a small side street on our way back. The car slowed at an intersection. Delia turned to me again. "That was like taking candy off a baby."

But just then, to my horror, there was a shout and out of the corner of my eye I saw someone loom in front of the windscreen. A German soldier had run out and stood in front of the limousine!

Chapter 21

Delia's eyes looked wild in her face. But she instructed us to stay calm and stuck her head out the car window as the soldier came around the side.

But to our surprise, he didn't challenge or speak to her. Instead he collapsed in a heap by the car door!

"Quick, there's smelling salts in the front compartment," she instructed.

We all got out of the car. Franco turned him over onto his back and I handed the salts to Delia who held them under the soldier's nose. The paleness of his face was heightened by his sandy hair and delicate features.

Within seconds he came to.

"Please, I am a conscript in the German army but I am a priest," he said in halting English. "They said I had to be a medical orderly and not be a chaplain. I saw your Irish flag on the car." He coughed. "I have been fasting since midnight from food and drink in the hope of finding a way to say Mass. God has sent you to me. I do not want to be sent to the front as a soldier."

"Let's get him into the car," said Delia. "He's falling apart!"

So together the three of us helped him to his feet. We put him into the front of the car and he slumped against the seat.

As the car moved on, he lapsed into a doze.

"What are we going to do?" I asked. "If any other Germans see him, they'll think we've kidnapped him."

"I'll take him to Hugh of course." She gave me a big wink. "If anyone stops us and looks in the boot, we'll say he's our escort for the 'booty'."

Delia thought it was all great gas. But I wasn't so sure.

"What if he's a spy? It could be trap."

Delia shook her head. "You're getting very cynical for a gossoon. Let's leave it up to Hugh to decide. If he's a priest as he says, the German College will be the best place for him."

So we headed back to the Vatican. None of the checkpoints stopped the diplomatic car.

As we went down Via del Corso we saw a line of Nazi troops led by an outrider with a red sign for them to follow. I willed them to move on quickly and not glance in our car. They were obedient and kept their eyes on the sign.

I saw a newspaper headline. The volcano Mount

Vesuvius in Sicily was smoking. That's all we need, I thought. God had great timing.

We were in luck. Major Sam and Hugh were both at the College.

The young priest was very weak and was put to lie on Hugh's bed. Hugh asked him a few priestly questions in fluent German and seemed very happy with the answers. He embraced him and called him Father Benedict.

Then he turned to Delia. "I'll organise someone to take Father Benedict to Father Palazzini at the seminary. As Koch's gang doesn't suspect it, it's fairly safe at the moment."

Delia nodded in agreement. And put on a meek face, as though she was a child who had done something wrong but knew she'd be forgiven.

"I have a confession to make. My boot is full of a merciful bounty of shoes. Hundreds."

Hugh shook his head but he was only pretending to be annoyed, for the next moment he looked up to heaven and smiled. "Well, truly the ways of the Lord are mysterious. Wasn't I just praying for the very same thing, as our boys are practically walking around barefoot."

Delia smiled. "And you need a good stout pair of boots if you're runnin' away from Nazis."

"Would you mind taking some up to Don Pietro in Monti?" Hugh continued. "He will help hide and distribute some shoes. Say about a hundred pairs."

Delia nodded and I was happy I would get to see Father Don Pietro again.

"What will we do with the remaining shoes?' Delia asked. "Should we bring them in?"

"No. We might be seen. There's a visiting delegation of German priests inside. Listen, there's a spot at the back of the Vatican where there's an overgrown thicket. Get Leo to throw the remaining pairs over the boundary wall and I'll sort out someone to gather them up."

The telephone rang and Delia answered it.

It was Sir D'Arcy Osborne. Delia hummed and hawed on the phone in the way adults do when they don't want to reveal the subject of a conversation to listeners. Then the conversation seemed to become more relaxed and less confidential. "My dear esteemed friend, I need to ask John May to pull some Vatican strings to get me a wood-burning stove. Meself and His Excellency are half frozen to death." She continued laughing and joking with Sir D'Arcy for a while and then put the phone down.

She turned to me. "Leo, there's something I need to deal with urgently here. You go to Don Pietro with Franco in the car – he knows the way. No one will bother you. You look like a nice respectable boy. And it's better anyway if I'm not caught delivering shoes."

Hugh then gave me a large volume on church architecture that he said was to be put in the hands of Don Pietro. "John May just dropped this off a few hours ago for him. Sure aren't you saving me a job? It's great timing altogether!"

I was secretly thrilled to be driving around Rome in a

diplomatic limousine. So after I got to exercise my hurley arms lobbing shoes over the Vatican wall, we headed down to Via Urbana. I would once more get to see the priest who had helped Hugh and me transform from coalmen.

Chapter 22

Don Pietro lived up near the Forum, a sprawling load of old ruins that people came to gawp at because it used to be the old Roman marketplace and centre of Roman life. Monti on the hillside was where the poor people lived – a jumbly warren of orangey, peachy houses and cobblestone lanes. We took a roundabout route and after the car climbed a steep lane we made a stop in Piazza de Grillo and got a view of the Forum. But also a palazzo with a medieval tower and an old abbey built into the ruins of the Forum. People still rushed through the streets but many of the shop fronts were boarded up and the few that remained open had almost nothing in them. But there was something beautiful about it all, the buildings with a glowing peachy colour, the crumbling stones.

Don Pietro's address was at Number 2, Via Urbana, in a

small upstairs room with a terrace. His housekeeper, a dark-haired woman, came to the door. She looked me up and down but when I said "Golf" sent me she smiled broadly and wiped her floury hands in her apron. She pointed down the road and told me he was at the church of the convent of the Little Sisters where he was chaplain.

I found him in the sacristy of the convent while Franco waited in the car. Don Pietro had this special air about him. A mischievous face, like Hugh's. And a kindness that filled the room. Not holy but special.

A shabbily dressed fellow who said his name was Oscar was with him, shifty-looking and nosing around as he waited while Don Pietro filled out a new identity pass for him. He looked me up and down in a way I didn't like.

When he left, Don Pietro beckoned me closer. I handed him the book sent to him by John May. His face lit up. He opened it carefully and I saw that papers were concealed inside. He held one of the sheets of paper up to the light, admiring the Vatican watermark.

At that moment, a woman in tears came into the sacristy, clutching a photograph. Her black hair was streaked with grey and she was dressed all in black, like she was a widow, her eyes red-rimmed and desperate, like she had been crying for days.

She glanced at me but Don Pietro nodded and she could contain herself no longer, breaking into loud sobs. "It's my son," she said. "He needs forged papers. He is an army deserter and he needs to go south. There are rumours of round-ups in our area. There are spies on our street. Nasty stinking cowards, the devil take them! I am sure one of them has betrayed him." She paused here and looked guiltily at the priest. "Forgive me, Father, but I know I can't forgive them if anything happens to my son."

The priest patted her back sympathetically. "Dear Donna Liliana, we are human and we feel as humans. God looks at us with kind eyes if we strive to be better. Help is at hand." He beckoned to her to hand him the photograph.

He rummaged in the back of his desk and took out a stamp. Then he affixed the photograph to one of the pieces of paper sent to him by Hugh. The pot of glue was hidden in a small box that looked like a bible.

He signed the paper and handed it to the woman. "Your son is now Orlando Licata, a former employee of the Neapolitan diocese sent to the Vatican. He is now trying to get home to Naples to visit a sick family member. God speed him on his errand of mercy."

The woman collapsed into sobs again but these were sobs of relief. When she recovered, she said, "But he is dressed in rags. His shoes are falling apart."

The good priest disappeared into the sacristy and came out with some trousers and a jacket. "Here, take my spare suit. I am sure he is thinner than I am, but he can say he lost weight." He laughed then, so warmly we all joined in.

"I think I can help with shoes," I said.

Don Pietro's face lit up.

All three of us went outside. The woman hung back at

the porch while I led Don Pietro out to the car. I asked Franco to open the boot.

Don Pietro gave me a big hug and smiled happily when we displayed our "booty".

"The Good Shepherd attends to his flock," he chuckled. His smile was like sunshine on a cold day in winter.

Don Pietro took out a stout pair of brown shoes, not too new, not too worn, and took them back to the lady.

She looked at them as if they were magical and might transform at any minute into a pair of birds and take flight. "But these are perfect," she said softly. "His size. How did you know? Wide too, like his feet."

"May he walk many safe miles, as if his feet had wings," said the priest, blessing them.

The woman smiled then, radiant, so different to when she walked in.

She tried to give the priest some money but he put it in the shoe. "For the voyage," he said.

She embraced him and hurried off with a light step and a smile on her face.

"So many unfortunates, subject to the whirlwinds of persecution," he said. "Thankfully the Lord has provided me with a mysterious Neapolitan stamp and I am in his hands."

"Monsignor Hugh has sent these shoes to you," I said.

"Blessed are the shoemakers! And the Monsignor!" He looked up to heaven and clapped his hands. "The Good Lord is merciful. But we have to be practical." He disappeared back into the sacristy and came out with three sacks.

We drove to his apartment a few blocks away.

We filled the sacks with boots and shoes. There were more left over even after I put aside quite a few pairs for Roberto and his merry little band of partisans, including a pair of jackboots I thought Primo might like and a pair of lace-ups for Gigi. But Don Pietro refused to take all of them and said he might have an idea for using the rest.

Then he led us to his room on the second floor of the small apartment building and out onto the terrace. A breeze was blowing and the air was fragrant with the scent of the many pots of basil growing there. We sat at a small table.

"Maria Teresa, bring us that coffee you've just made!" he called in to his housekeeper. "My housekeeper is from Terlizzi in the province of Bari in the south like me."

Maria Teresa came out, expertly balancing a tray of coffee and cake in one hand.

The coffee was ground barley but warm and sweetened with a drop of milk, and the cake was dark and dense but surprisingly sweet and tasty.

As Teresa wiped her hands in her apron, I saw that her left hand was badly burned. She held it up.

"Best thing that ever happened to me!" She laughed a deep throaty laugh. "You are amazed I say that, boy. But, you see, I was a migrant labourer from the south. Little more than a slave. I burned my hand in the chemicals of that stinking Viscose factory on Via Prenestina near San

Lorenzo goods yard. And Don Pietro rescued me from being a beggar in the streets."

"That factory was a hellhole," said Don Pietro. "I was their spiritual advisor. But how can you care for the soul if you ignore the body that is its house? There were thousands of workers living in sheds, forced to work long hours for little pay. But Mussolini wanted the country to be self-sufficient. He didn't care at what cost. I wrote to the Vatican about it. But it was I who was dismissed from my post."

"But luckily the Sisters of the Child Jesus here took him as their chaplain," Maria Teresa told us. "And I didn't even have to become a nun!"

Don Pietro breathed in the deep smell of basil growing in the pots around. "Ah, reminds me of home in the south!" he said. Then he rubbed his hands together. "If you are willing, I know some people in the suburbs who need some shoes."

"I am at your disposal," said Franco.

"Go to the Borgate on the outskirts of the city and ask for Gobbo – the Hunchback of Quarticciolo," Don Pietro said. "He is a good boy, Giuseppe Albano. A little wild. He thinks he is like your English champion 'Robin Hood' – robs from the rich to give to the poor. But he will know who to give the shoes to."

"I have heard of him!" I said. "He is a friend of my friend the partisan Roberto the Lucky."

There was a sudden knock on the door leading out from the terrace. I froze, nervous. But Don Pietro raised a finger to reassure me. "That is our secret knock."

The door flew open and framed in the doorway was a man with jet-black hair and a moustache, with a strong intense face. He carried a suitcase in one hand and raised his other fist in a salute.

"Greetings, comrades," he said.

Don Pietro rose to embrace him. "My dear old friend!" He turned to us. "Leo and Franco, my new friends, meet one of my oldest friends from Terlizzi. The astonishing Gio, professor of philosophy at the Cavour High School. Join us for coffee, Gio! Friends, I must warn you, Gio is a communist. We spend all our time arguing. Christ versus Lenin. But I always try to tell him anyone who is on the side of humanity plays for the same team."

Gio's dark intense eyes flashed with merriment. "You have heard of Lenin, Leo? From the Russian revolution?" He spoke with great urgency and excitement as if the revolution had just happened yesterday.

I smiled. "Heard of him! I've had him rammed down my throat since I was tiny. My grandfather in London is a communist. He had a picture of him on his wall. And Marx too, but not Stalin."

Gio smiled widely.

"My grandfather says he is no better than the Tsars," I said, "and just wants to be king himself. I think he's a big Russian eejit."

"Another time I would like to engage you in discussion," Gio said with a laugh.

But he was tense and paced around the terrace.

"I need to get to the Quarticciolo for a meeting," he said. "But there is a checkpoint down the street."

"We could take you," I said without thinking.

"We have already agreed to take shoes there," Franco said.

"But will it be safe for the boy?" Don Pietro worried.

But I was desperate to go there. I thought I might be able to reach Roberto who I knew went there to get bobjacks.

Franco smiled. "I have just improvised a simple secret compartment in the boot. No Nazi has ever searched the Irish diplomatic car. We are neutral. But, just in case, I now have a new design."

I went into the kitchen to help Maria Teresa with the cups.

"Gio is very brave," she said. "He writes an illegal newspaper and is a supporter of the partisans. He will take that case of newspapers with him. He is watched all the time and if caught with them he could be executed. Make sure no one sees him get in your car. For all your sakes."

I nodded my head. "I will tell Franco to go around the corner. Gio can jump in there."

"It is dangerous for you and Franco too."

"I want to do whatever I can. My mother is in prison for helping the Resistance. She worked for Monsignor O'Flaherty's Escape Line too. In fact, she helps anyone who is against the Fascists. And I am the same. It's in my blood!"

She gave me a sad smile. "Our homegrown Fascists think they are the big people, now that the stinking Nazis are here to back them. But there are more of us than them! And they'll see. Love is stronger than hate. But I fear for us all."

We went back to the terrace where Don Pietro produced a coil of rope, well made and sturdy.

"This is for Hugh," he said. "I know he keeps a coil of rope under his bed. My father made this. He had a workshop in Bari and wove ropes of jute and flax for all the fishermen. Hugh is the best fisher of men I know. Please give it to him."

I felt the rope, its twisted fibre surprisingly smooth to the touch.

Don Pietro embraced Gio. "Who knows how this will end?"

Gio, with confidence, smiling, replied, "With the victory of reason, of justice, of peace."

"With our deaths," Maria Teresa said ominously.

But Don Pietro just laughed. "I will be going to the Heavenly Father. And you too, Gio – even if you deny His existence. I will be happy to see the surprise on your face when the Angel Gabriel takes you for a guided tour!"

They laughed together then – two old friends.

Gio walked to the door, then turned, fist raised and clenched, and proclaimed, *"We will emerge from darkness into light!"*

Don Pietro raised his right hand and made the Sign of the Cross. "Amen, my friends! Go safely in the care of the Lord."

By the time Franco and I got downstairs there was no sign of Gio but, when we drove around the corner and stopped, he emerged from the shadows. Maria Teresa followed, carrying the case full of newspapers. She handed it to Gio and kept lookout.

Franco opened the boot and helped Gio to hide inside.

We drove off. Maria Teresa didn't wave to us as I looked back at her.

I was terrified but strangely exhilarated. Now we didn't only have stolen shoes but a fugitive from the Nazis in our boot!

Chapter 23

We drove away from the city towards the east.

"When Mussolini decided to restore Rome to its former Imperial glory," Franco explained, "he cleared away all the poor people from around the Colosseum and Ancient Roman buildings and dumped them in twelve new districts called the Borgate on the outskirts of Rome."

This was a part of Rome I had never seen before. We drove through teeming mudflats with filthy children playing football. It looked like there had already been a war here. There were half finished blocks of flats that people were already living in, surrounded by some shack-like houses. Garbage was strewn everywhere. I saw rats run across the road in broad daylight. In the distance I could see long blocks of buildings, with balconies. But already they looked like they were falling apart

"The Nazis don't come here very often," said Franco. "They think it's a wasps' nest, full of partisans and bandits. And they are right!"

We drove further into the abandoned building site of Mussolini's half-finished idiot grand plans. Soon they would look worse than old Roman ruins.

Then I shrank into the seat when, to my horror, I saw a rough band of boys jump out on the road and flag down the car.

They were carrying guns and looked like bandits. Even more menacing than Roberto's little gang of outlaws.

But Franco didn't seem too worried and drew to a halt. A couple of rough boys shoved their faces against the windscreen. One of them mimed slitting my throat.

Franco rolled down the window. "I will only speak to Gobbo. And back off from my car. Gobbo won't be best pleased."

The large boy who had forced a gun in through the window pulled back.

"Ah, you are Franco from Gobbo's old neighbourhood?" Then he stood to attention and roared at his army of boy bandits. "Stand back. He is a friend."

They formed a ragged armed guard as we slowly drove on, Franco avoiding the potholes as we went. Mostly boys, filthy, dressed in plundered German uniforms and old Italian army cast-offs. One of them was even wearing cowboy boots.

I was glad when Franco pulled up the window again.

The stink of drains was overpowering.

"We can relax here. It's run by the partisans," he said.

"Are they armed resistance or armed robbers?" I asked Franco, glancing at our filthy escort.

He smiled. "Gobbo's army is notorious. The Germans have a price on his head. They rob the food shipped to the front for the German army and redistribute it to the poor. Some of it also finds its way onto the black market."

I looked out the window. There were no roads, and there were piles of rubble and rubbish everywhere. The terracotta paint on the concrete of some of the buildings was already peeling, making them look horribly dilapidated. Who could blame Gobbo for robbing and stealing from the Germans when they had so little?

We stopped at Gobbo's encampment which was surrounded by a sort of wooden fence made up of German helmets on poles, like heads from a medieval city.

The chief bandit, the big boy, blew a whistle.

A moment later Gobbo came out.

He was shorter than me, handsome with gleaming white teeth and flowing black hair, like a Musketeer. He wore a red chequered shirt and a kind of cloak around his shoulders, a black Stetson hat perched on his head at a jaunty angle. I thought he was playing up to being a Robin Hood. But when he drew closer, I was reminded that his back was crooked, so he was perhaps trying to hide his deformity. He was maybe about seventeen but he walked like a general.

His face lit up with the smile of a happy boy when he saw Franco.

"My friend!" he said and shook his hand warmly. Then he bowed low. "To what do we owe this honour?"

Franco went around the back of the car but, before he opened the boot, I stood in front of it.

"Do you know a partisan by the name of Roberto? Code name Lucky?" I asked Gobbo. "Some of our booty is for him. You must promise me you will keep it safe for him."

He looked at me intently as if sizing me up. "I can do better than that." He whistled, a long wolf whistle that made the hairs on the back of my neck stand up.

To my great delight, first Primo and then Roberto himself bounded out of the shack. They looked even thinner and more ragged than before, harder and older. But they wreathed me in hugs as if I was their long-lost brother.

"Leo! This is a wonderful!" said Roberto. "But no more the Red Lion, no?" He tugged at my mousy hair.

I grinned. "A red rag to the Nazi bulls. It had to go. I hoped you might be here."

"You were right to hope! We are here to collect a new consignment of bobjacks and ammunition."

"And anything else we can get our hands on," said Primo. His lips were chapped and his skin was raw and red from being outdoors all the time. But he looked stronger, less bookish. More like a fighter.

"We have a few more recruits now, you know," said Roberto. "We're a thriving unit!"

"Then you'll have even more need of what you asked me to get you," I said.

Franco opened the boot and took out the sacks filled with shoes. Well, about twenty pairs of eyes nearly fell out of their heads!

Gobbo let out a long whistle and bowed low to Franco and me. Some of the boys immediately grabbed shoes. But Gobbo blew a whistle and they stopped.

"*Attention, boys!*" he roared. "Anyone would think we were an uncouth army of bandits. We will do this in an orderly fashion."

"Roberto and Primo go first," I said. "I've put aside some pairs for them."

Primo immediately fell on the long pair of jackboots I held out to him and, tearing off his shepherd's footwear, thrust his feet into them. Then proceeded to do a quick march.

Roberto chose a gleaming pair of brogues, stout and stylish. He also scooped up a bunch of extra pairs for other members who had joined his band. And took the lace-ups for Gigi who had stayed behind with Asinello.

Then all hell broke loose as the others dived into the sacks. Fighting nearly broke out over a couple of pairs. Some people managed to end up with two left feet. But Gobbo shooed them all over to the side of the shack to sort it out.

I was glad because I didn't want to let Gio out into that madness.

"We have one more piece of contraband for you," said Franco, opening the secret compartment.

Gobbo bowed low when he saw Gio emerge, stiff and crumpled but glad to be back in the fresh air.

"I am honoured," said Gobbo. "The famous Gio from GAP. We will escort you to your comrades after you enjoy our hospitality."

GAP was one of the most famous partisan groups.

He led us inside where a young girl made us surprisingly good coffee and gave us German apple strudel.

"We have liberated some good food," said Gobbo. "Please enjoy. Forgive us if we don't toast the Wermarcht, our generous patrons."

We laughed.

"This is an ugly duckling part of Rome," Gobbo said. "But we are free and there are many partisans hiding out here. We are an underground army."

"Don't get too cocky," said Gio. "They are increasing the number of Nazi police in Rome. The Blackshirt Fascists are setting up murder gangs. So the Nazis use them to do their real dirty work. Things are going to get hotter. Those vile dogs, Caruso the Fascist police chief and Koch the torturer, are in charge of the fascist crackdown. They are only too happy to be the attack dogs of their Nazi masters."

Gobbo smiled. "I heard a funny story – that fat fool Caruso got arrested by his Nazi friends in a round-up – they thought he was acting suspiciously! Now he has his own little gang of SS to keep him safe."

Gio let out a grim laugh. "He will make us all suffer. And Koch, who is half-German half-Italian, is under the protection of Kappler. He has his own torture chambers and makes it his business to hunt down and kill partisans."

"But we are ready," said Gobbo. "We want an uprising! Kick out the dirty Fascists and their Nazi overlords. Kill them all, I say!"

Roberto and Primo cheered. But Gio frowned in thought.

"Patience," he said. "Things are happening. Try not to do anything rash."

"The Americans and British are stuck down the heel of the boot of Italy," said Gobbo. "They are making no progress. Meanwhile the most I can do is attack the German supply lines. We can't sit around waiting for liberation that might never come."

Gio took out the newspapers. "You can help me distribute these."

I looked at the front page. Pictures of troops. Stories about massacres.

"Sure," said Gobbo with a big smile. "But you know a lot of the people here can't read?"

"Then you can read to them," said Gio, his eyes flaming. "We must use the time we have to prepare the Italian people for a new tomorrow."

"Let's put food in their bellies first," said Gobbo.

"At least you can refrain from carrying out any unauthorised operations while we plan our strategy," warned Gio.

I saw his stern side. He must have been a tough teacher.

As they continued to argue I called Roberto over to one side and told him about my mother.

"Now that you have shoes, perhaps you could rescue her," I said.

He scratched his head. "We need more than shoes. Guns too. Vehicles. We don't know Rome either."

"Please, maybe I could ask Gobbo," I said, my eyes pleading.

Gobbo must have heard me. He stopped arguing with Gio and came over to me.

"Ask me what?" he said.

He listened to what I had to say about my mother and how I hoped the partisans would help me free her.

He shook his head when I'd finished. "That's a suicide mission," he said.

"Please help me. I have a sister – she's like you, Gobbo – she's not a hunchback but is disabled. The Nazis would like to kill her. But I think her imperfections are perfect."

His eyes filled with tears but he was unmoved by my pleas.

"I do owe you a favour for the shoes," he said. "So, one word of advice. Stay away from the Cinema Barberini and the Hotel Flora coming up to Christmas."

I laughed. "I'm under cover as a twelve-year-old choirboy in the Sistine Chapel. I don't usually go to cinemas and hotels frequented by Nazis."

Roberto put his arms around me. "It's too big a job for any of us," he said.

I told him about Ada Gobetti in Turin. He didn't know much about her but said he'd try to learn more.

"If you spring your mother, we will hide her and escort her to safety," he said.

But I felt he didn't really mean it.

I was crushed. But tried not to show it. "What will you do now, Roberto?"

"Go back to our work with our new shoes," he said. Then he patted something which was hidden under his jacket. "And our bobjacks. There are Nazis to catch."

I was annoyed though and walked off. But Roberto called me back.

"Let's part on good terms, eh? In this war you never know when you will see someone again."

I felt bad about myself then. I was small-minded, as my mother would say.

We embraced.

Roberto ruffled my hair. "Say hello to Ruby for me too."

I was thankful then, for his kindness. "Say hello to Gigi too. And scratch Asinello behind the ears for us. The way he likes it."

Roberto gave me his big wide smile.

But, as I sat in the front of the limousine, I brooded. If my mother was to escape, I was going to have to organise it myself.

Chapter 24

Hugh was delighted with the length of rope from Don Pietro, showing it off proudly to Major Sam.

He formed it into a lasso and swung it wildly around the room. "This is what I'll do to any of those Nazi boyos who dare come in here!"

Major Sam ducked. "I see your lassoing is just as wild as your golf swing," he said.

But Hugh deftly lassoed him. "Now that will teach you to be so smart! I'll only release you if you agree that we're going to give all our escapees the best Christmas ever."

Major Sam nodded. Hugh clapped him on the back and laughed his big uproarious laugh.

"Now Leo here is going to be Santa's helper," he pronounced.

"But, Hugh, we can't even have Christmas trees –

Mussolini banned them, remember?" I said.

"Well, unless he's planning to come to the German College, he'll be none the wiser."

So for the next few weeks I was caught up in "Operation Christmas".

It was a massive undertaking being a little elf for Father Christmas. Hugh got out the ledgers. There were over 4,000 prisoners on the books. Getting a gift organised for all of them was a military operation.

John May came into his own and turned up with decks of cards and a batch of liqueur chocolates wrapped in colourful tin foil. When I asked him where he got them, he winked and said, "Never you mind. But don't taste them, you little beggar. They're alcohol."

Of course I did taste one on the sly when he went outside to get another box. On my first bite I thought I had gone to heaven. The warm, sweet chocolatey taste filled my mouth. But then this bitter, disgusting liquid like sour cherries and rust squirted out, trickling down my throat. I coughed and spat the whole thing out, just as John May came back into the room.

He laughed and cuffed me good-naturedly on the head. "What did I tell you! Hope that keeps you away from liqueurs for loife!"

The nuns unravelled old jumpers and knitted many pairs of socks. I remembered some of the escapees knitting and suggested knitting needles and wool for some. Some fancy society lady friends of Hugh's arrived with bundles of red ribbon and old silk scarves to wrap presents in. And unwanted silk socks that their husbands no longer needed. I knew why for some – they were on the run.

I was especially happy though because an Italian princess brought me a bike! It was a beaut – an English Raleigh with a basket on the front. It was going to be great for delivering all the presents. Hugh had the brainwave of painting it with the Vatican colours of white and yellow and sticking a Vatican insignia on it of the cross keys.

"You are now an official Vatican messenger!" he said.

I was pleased as punch. But there was a downside. It might get me past the Nazis – but it also made me more conspicuous, a big yellow-and-white target. But it was the "least worst" option as the Major said.

It was Sister Mary Saint Luke who suggested we give soap as a present. But it was in such short supply! Delia's cook came to the rescue. She made it herself the old-fashioned way from lye, which came from ashes from the fire, and added the comforting scent of lavender and lime. Blon, Delia's daughter, delivered it in the limousine. And laughed to tell us that at least the new woodburning stove that Delia had somehow wangled with the help of John May was earning its keep!

"The officials back in Dublin were cross at Dad at the cost of it," she said. "But sure isn't it being put to great use!"

I asked her how her medical studies were going. "Well, I'm having a terrible time following the lectures in Italian," she groaned. "But I'm getting there."

She and Hugh concentrated on sorting out the ribbons and the paper. I got busy wrapping some of the soap, so soft and slippery in my hands. I'd never been a great one for the soap but it was so fragrant I was almost tempted to have a wash! John May read my mind and told me to keep some. I put a bar in my pocket. I was thinking of my mother and the prisoners in Mantellate.

A few other priests and nuns and then some of Major Sam's escapees dropped in to help. Two of them I liked very much – John Furman, short and wiry and fluent in German and Italian, a redhead like me. And Bill Simpson who was tall and thin and could play the double bass. They were his old pals from his time in prison and a great laugh. They were planning to deliver turkey, whiskey and rum hidden in suitcases to safe houses.

"It would be almost worth getting searched to see a Nazi's face when he saw a turkey!" joked Simpson in his Scottish accent.

"He'd have it quick as a flash," said Furman. "Make a change from German sausage."

Hugh and Blon were talking about war stuff. I wasn't earwigging exactly. But I couldn't help overhearing in that small room.

"There's a rumour flying about that the Germans want to kidnap the Pope and remove him to Lichtenstein," Hugh said.

Blon shook her head. "Oh, the poor Holy Father! The German ambassador Von Weizsäcker isn't a Nazi, though, is he?"

"No, but he'll do their bidding. He was powerless to stop the Jews being deported from the ghetto," said Hugh.

"There are rumours too of plots to depose Hitler. But no one can get near him in his heavily fortified battle headquarters deep in the forest in Prussia. It's not called the Wolf's Lair for nothing."

Blon shook her head. "Oh, when will the Allies be here!"

Hugh looked thoughtful. "It's slow going. They have crossed over from Sicily but the Apennine Mountains and the geography of Italy are against them. The Germans are digging in. If the Allies hope to come up the boot of Italy from the south they have their work cut out for them. It's full of jagged mountains and marshlands. It's not an easy route to Rome."

I thought about the length of Italy, just like a boot, kicking Sicily down to the Mediterranean Sea. I recited the rhyme.

"Long legged Italy,
Kicked poor Sicily,
Into the middle
Of the Mediterranean Sea.
Austria got Hungary
And took a bit of Turkey,
Dipped it in Greece
And fried it in Japan!"

"Except it's Hitler doing the kicking and the Nazis marching all over Europe in their jackboots. With the Japanese helping them in Asia," said Blon, shaking her dark hair. She looked like a film star, her face so beautiful it was almost hard to look at.

Hugh looked thoughtful. "It would be good to know

what the Germans might do if the Allies ever manage to take Rome. Do you know Prince von Bismarck? German envoy, one of those Prussian aristocrats. Handsome fellow, even if he is a Nazi . . ."

Blon burst out laughing. "Sure my mother has great gas altogether saying how he's trying to gate-crash Roman society. He is a prince, after all, descended from the famous German chancellor. But a lot of the upper crust here are fiercely loyal to the Pope and are anti-Fascists. He's up against it, no matter how charming and handsome."

"Well, it might be an idea to get yourself invited to lunch and see what he thinks the Germans might do if they have to withdraw," said Hugh. "Will they respect its open city status and leave it for posterity? Or bomb it like they did Naples?"

Blon smiled wickedly. "Are you turning me into a spy! Only if I can go and get my hair done at René's."

"Sure he's one of our own," said Hugh. "Gets us all the gossip from the Nazi ladies."

"Don't go to the Barberini or the cinema or the Hotel Flora near Christmas!" I blurted out.

They all looked at me with surprise. I told them what Gobbo had told me.

I thought Hugh would scold me and tell me not to be minding the word of a bandit. But he took it all in.

"We will take all due care. Some of our POW's take risks going out on the town and stray into the badlands. You never know where the dangers will come from these days!"

Chapter 25

A couple of days later on the 20th December, we found out that Gobbo's warnings unfortunately came true. Major Sam ran in from one of his walks, clutching an underground newspaper.

"The Italian Resistance has struck! They've bombed a cinema and killed eight German soldiers. The same in a restaurant. And attacked the Hotel Flora, the headquarters of the German High Command. It's rumoured one German and a woman have been killed. A lot more soldiers have been injured, the Germans won't say how many. A spy was attacked too. Leo's intelligence was sound."

I felt a little stab of pride, even as I felt terrible about all that death and explosion. Even if they were Germans. Even though they did terrible things.

"God have mercy on their souls," said Hugh. "They are

Hitler's victims too."

I looked at him, incredulous. "But they do his bidding. They deserve no mercy."

Hugh shook his head. "Think of how we have all had to obey the Nazi regime. Tyrants don't just control us with guns but by sowing terror in men's souls. The Nazi blackguards have cowed the German people. Do you know they can be executed for even telling a joke about Hitler?"

"The worse thing is the curfew now starts even earlier – at seven o'clock in the evening rather than half eleven at night. We won't be able to go anywhere," said Major Sam drily. "Now that really is no laughing matter."

"Ah, but that won't apply to the clergy. We will still be able to go about doing our religious duty," Hugh said. "You might have to dress as a Monsignor again and revisit your vocation, Sam."

"I thought I made rather a good one." Major Sam made the Sign of the Cross. "But there's worse yet. There's a ban coming on bicycles because the Resistance have been using them for their attacks. Someone threw a bomb from a bike. There's a rumour that it was at the Regina Coeli guards outside the prison. Several were killed – they wouldn't say how many. Now anyone using bicycles will be shot."

I shuddered, thinking of my mother, how it would be doubly dangerous for me to go near the prison or attempt to get her out. They were bound to increase security. But I was also upset about my new bike. I was really looking forward to using it and I was due to deliver a batch of presents to Mrs M, including a big bag of Vatican flour for Christmas baking.

"Those Nazi blackguards!" I yelled. It was like all the air had been let out of my tyres.

But John May told me not to worry. He had an idea and said to give him an hour. He nipped out for a bit and then came back and led me to the courtyard. There was a wheel from a pram affixed to the back axle. It didn't even touch the ground.

"Here's your new Vatican 'tricycle'," he said, bowing to it as if unveiling a new invention. "The regulations said 'bicycle' and that means *two* wheels. Everyone's doing it, so I think you'll get away with it. Crazy Romans!"

I laughed. "I will be like Gino Bartali – if he changed to a tricycle!" I worshipped Bartali. He had won the Giro d'Italia twice and even the Tour de France. He was the best and, even better, he had refused to dedicate his win to Il Duce. He was very brave.

John looked at me intently. "You can be like Bartali in more ways than one." He bent down and unscrewed the cross bar. "See this hollow tube. It can be used for smuggling documents. Nobody knows this, but Bartali has smuggled thousands of documents with false papers that have saved Jews from one end of Italy to the other."

"Wow! I'll do it," I said without hesitation.

John winked at me and stuffed a roll of papers inside. "Drop these at the seminary beside the Basilica di San Giovanni, after you've been to Mrs M. It's one of the properties outside the Vatican but part of our territory," he said. "And keep your wits about you. Koch's gang are bound to be looking for revenge after the bombings. He hates partisans with a black fury."

I headed off before he could change his mind and say it was too dangerous. I felt just like Bartali now, bumping over the cobblestones, the air rushing around me.

I wasn't the only one riding a "tricycle". The street was thronged with bizarre three and four-wheeled contraptions. The Romans weren't going to let a little thing like a Nazi rule stop them in their tracks.

All the Italian families were getting ready for Christmas. People might not have put up Christmas trees but there were plenty of *presepi* – Nativity crib scenes in churches and in some shop fronts too. Baby Jesus lying in the straw surrounded by Mary, Joseph and the animals. Including the nearly life-size one in Saint Peter's Square beside the obelisk. I supposed the Nazis couldn't really ban Christ. But in Rome presents wouldn't come until the 6th of January when the Wise Men brought gifts to the Baby Jesus. Then the Befana, the old woman, would come and check first and you would either get a sweet or a lump of coal in your sock. She is the Christmas witch, streaked with soot from all the chimneys. In the past I got little sewn dolls and sweets. And even though I was naughty I never got garlic or lumps of coal. Ruby and I always sang the song that goes something like this in English:

La Befana comes at night
In tattered shoes
Dressed in the Roman style

Long live la Befana!!
She brings cinders and coals
To the naughty children
To the good children
She brings sweets and lots of toys and gifts.

Ruby said that was because even if my deeds were black, my heart was gold. And I was the best brother who ever pulled a pigtail! Then we would eat panettone, the sweet yeasty cake light as air. But not many people would have panettone this year. Mrs M would, though, because John May had got her some of the Vatican flour. Her crazy old mother could make it and I was about to deliver it.

It was bitter cold. My icy breath hung in the air. But as I neared Mrs M's house, I sensed something was wrong. I saw her son Paul hurry around a corner and I chased him. He worked at the Swiss Legation, so he was in the know and protected.

"There's been a raid!" he said. "Luckily, I got to warn them in time and the escapees are all out walking the streets. But it was close. They were looking for someone near here with a radio. But it's too close for comfort. Maybe come back tomorrow."

"But I have too many other journeys," I said. "Surely now is the safest time. Even if they're going to come back, it will take at least half an hour."

He flicked his eyes in the direction of a café opposite their apartment where a few people sat drinking coffee sitting at the tables and chairs outside.

"Go up quickly if you have to," he said. "Koch's men are posted permanently on the street now. They haven't quite worked out what my mother is up to. But they know something's going on around here. They think they blend in better because they are Italian but we can see through to their black hearts. He's the one in the trench coat and the trilby wearing a blue scarf. Be careful!"

Turning his back casually on the café, he slipped me his key.

I was determined to leave the presents. So I decided on a plan.

I parked the bicycle across the road down an alleyway and, without being seen, watched the spy. He was pretending to read his morning newspaper. I went and took the bag of flour which was wrapped in a bigger brown-paper bag out of the bicycle basket. I hesitated. It was precious stuff, I knew. And holy flour, used to make the host in the Vatican, the purest milled white brought in from the countryside on the private Vatican railway. But this was a good cause surely. I made up my mind. Those fellows deserved their presents. I transferred some of the flour into the brown-paper bag used for carrying it. Half a loaf was better than none.

Then I watched him carefully. Like all people, he thought he was thorough. But he looked down one side of the street more than another. I darted across the road with the flour and flew up to the first floor of the house next to the café. I was in luck: as I had hoped, there was an open window over the stairwell.

At the window, I lobbed the flour right on the spy's head. It exploded like a sudden snowstorm.

"What the hell!" he shouted, knocking over his cup.

I bounded down the stairs and darted back across the road to the alleyway where I had stowed the bicycle. I peeped over at the kerfuffle. The spy was too busy wiping the flour out of his eyes to see me, and the other people were all craning their necks, trying to figure out where the flour had come from. I chuckled to myself.

With fumbling fingers I opened the door and raced up the stairs. There was the sound of raised voices on the other side of the door. But I gave the secret knock.

Mrs. M came to the door, smoothing her apron. She threw her arms around me. "Mother of God! So nice to see a welcome visitor! We've had a few undesirables drop in!"

Inside, I saw Mrs M's old mother and three of her daughters, Gemma, Mary and Rosie, rushing around clearing up. Drawers were upended, clothes cascading out of them like crazy waterfalls. Books and papers were strewn all over the floor.

"We were saved by the Nazis' lack of imagination once again. They couldn't believe even six of us lived here. Let alone our posse of soldiers!"

"But isn't it getting too hot now to have POW's?" I asked. I knew she could be executed if caught.

Mrs M shook her head and dismissed all fear. "It was a general search. They still don't suspect the nice respectable widow woman with too many children in a tiny flat!"

Gemma was on her hands and knees, putting the records back in their sleeves.

"Vera Lynn's 'White Cliffs of Dover' was right beside the gramophone but by a stroke of luck they didn't notice it," she said. "I distracted them by humming 'Lily Marlene', their favourite song, while they were here. That gave Mary enough time to sidle over and shove Vera Lynn under the record player."

I gave Mrs M the presents and she was so happy she gave me another of her great, breath-squeezing hugs.

I guiltily told them about my flour bomb. But Gemma was delighted.

"I hate the way that traitor sits there day in day out," she said. "Now at least he might have to change that filthy trench coat!"

Mrs M's crazy old mother was thrilled with the flour. "I will make the best panettone ever. Blessed by the Pope himself!"

I went back the way I came. There was no sign of the spy.

Chapter 26

I pedalled furiously towards the south of the city. It began to rain, furiously, heavily, leaping off the stone streets. As if the rain was strafe-bombing the city, pounding it with water into the ground.

I was soaked to the skin. But the downpour emptied the streets and I made good progress.

My destination was the Seminario Romano – the place where they trained all the priests in Rome. It was just by the Basilica di San Giovanni, by the city walls. I'd been there before with Hugh on his grand tour. He'd told me it was the most important church in Rome, even more so than St. Peter's, as it's the official church of the Pope, even if he rarely visits. It even has his throne and the altar contains a cedar table that was supposed to have been used for the Jesus's Last Supper. So it's the holiest of holies. I can't believe I'm remembering all this stuff he told me. It must be catching!

I rang the bell on the huge wooden door. There was a notice on the door in both Italian and German, the usual one placed on Vatican properties outside the city. It said, **"This property is part of the Vatican. It is used for religious purposes. All searches and entrances for such purposes are prohibited."** It had been issued by the Nazis themselves.

But there was something in the air that made me twitchy. I was glad when a young priest opened the door. He bid me enter and merely raised his eyebrows when I said I needed to bring my bicycle inside.

Hugh's friend, Father Palazzini, one of the head priests, arrived just then, a youngish large loose-limbed man like a big bear. The younger priest disappeared back inside the building. I dismantled the crossbar of my bicycle and took out the documents.

"Mamma mia!" Father Palazzini exclaimed. He glanced quickly at the papers. "These identity documents are most welcome."

He led me along a corridor, bare except for a few holy pictures. There were several seminarians about. They glanced at me furtively and looked as if they were uncomfortable in their habits. Father Palazzini slipped some of them an identity pass and their faces lit up like Christmas trees.

One of them raised his left hand to bless me. "It's your

right hand," Father Palazzini corrected him in Italian. He quickly swapped over.

So they were hiding prisoners here too!

"I'll take you by the scenic route," Father Palazzini said. "I'll drop some of these papers as we go."

We passed through a chapel where a few nuns dressed in blue habits were foostering about, putting flowers and Christmas wreaths on the altar. One of them with rosy cheeks gave me a big smile. In a side chapel, a nun was placing candles alongside an open coffin. But there was nobody in it, which seemed odd.

Father Palazzini tucked some of the papers into folded hymn sheets and handed them to one of the nuns with a whispered instruction. "That will answer some prayers tonight," he said to me with a chuckle.

Then he led me along two more corridors and down into the cellars. There were several seminarians lolling about on beds. Some of them looked suspiciously old to have a calling to the priesthood.

We continued down a corridor and walked right up to a wall with a big full-length picture of an old pope. I glanced at Father Palazzini who took down the pope's picture. Behind it was a concealed door. It was covered in plaster and only a careful examination would reveal its existence.

Father Palazzini unlocked it and knocked *rat-a-tat, tat-tat-tat*.

We inched open the door. And to my surprise there was Hugh and a few chaps, a couple of them priests, or dressed

257

as priests, I couldn't be sure. On the table were five loaves of bread.

"Well, fancy meeting you here," said Hugh jovially. "Tumiati here," he pointed to a man in a threadbare suit, "is about to make a special visit to Bari. I was called here for a last-minute meeting. And it's great that you have brought the identity papers."

I shook the hands of the men.

"John May had these loaves of bread made specially and they each contain a microfilm with a list of everyone in our care," said Hugh. "Tumiati is going to smuggle them out. So let's hope he doesn't get hungry on the way to Bari!"

They all smiled. I felt a little rush of pride. They were the lists I'd helped Major Sam compile.

I told Hugh about the raid on Mrs M's. They all laughed when I told them about the flour bomb. But Hugh looked grave, wrinkling his brow. He shook his head at me.

"It's getting late now and there's a lot of activity on the streets tonight," said Father Palazzini to me. "It might be best if you stay the night."

Hugh nodded. "It would."

"Come on," said Father Palazzini. "We'll store your bike at the back and I'll take you for a special supper in the refectory. We eat surprisingly well by the grace of God. "

So Father Palazzini and I trooped back the way we came to retrieve my bicycle.

"We have about 200 extra seminarians here," Father Palazzini told me in a confidential whisper. "Including 55

Jews. There may be a raid any day now and even though we have several secret passages and escape routes, it's wise to have identity passes for everyone. You are a good boy, Leo."

He led me to an interior garden and pointed to a shed for my bicycle on the opposite side that was tucked into a building opposite the seminary. There was an exit to a back street nearby. There was also a covered bridge above that linked the buildings at the fourth floor.

Father Palazzini pointed to the link bridge. "See, we can move from one building to the other if necessary." He left me to sort myself out and rushed back into the main building.

After I stowed my bike, I went back through the garden and returned to the refectory. There were a few other seminarians dining, talking in clusters. Another odd bunch of new priests. But I really enjoyed my dish of stracciacella – chicken broth with eggs and Parmesan cheese, a traditional Christmas dish in Rome, the cook told me. I savoured the smell rising up in steam. It slipped down my throat like velvet.

I was just draining the bowl when there was a loud banging noise and raised voices.

A young priest dashed in, habit flying. *"Quick, hide, everyone! There's a raid! There are fifty of Koch's men circling the building!"*

I flew up out of my seat, my first thought Hugh. But Father Palazzini grabbed me at the refectory door and told me there was another passage leading from the secret room that led out to the baptistry and Hugh would take that. It would be better if I headed across the bridge into the adjoining building. From there I could get to the shed where my bike was.

He shooed me towards the flight of stairs that led to the bridge and ran off. I darted back to pick up the slice of pangiallo, the dried fruit cake that the cook had left just for me.

Everywhere trainee priests flew around like a flock of disturbed starlings, black gowns flying behind them like wings. I panicked, forgetting which way Father Palazzini had pointed.

I could hear a priest arguing at the main entrance. "No, you have no right to come here!"

The bark of a gun almost stopped my heartbeat. Then someone shouted and swore in Italian. *"The next bullet will be in your head if you don't let me through!"*

Rough voices could be heard at the door. More shouting.

Father Palazzini came back and was surprised to see me still there. He pulled me by the scruff of the neck. "Quick, through here, there's no time."

We fell through a doorway, just ahead of the black-shirted Fascists. They were led by a man in a suit, his jet-black hair plastered into his head, a black moustache across his upper lip like an ugly slug. Koch, I guessed.

I was back in the church.

I saw a man jump into the coffin. A priest was at the altar, saying prayers, several kneeling in the back row.

I panicked. Frozen.

"Over here!"

It was the nun with the rosy cheeks. She lifted up her ample skirts and beckoned me over. I dived at the same time as Father Palazzini was shrouded by the skirts of the elderly nun next to her.

The rosy-cheek nun fanned out the cloth and all was darkness for me at I lay curled at her feet, a frightened kitten fleeing from a pack of wolves.

My heart was a hammer pounding in my chest in time to their prayers. Threatening to skitter out of my body. The blood thrumming in my ears.

"Have some respect in the house of God!" the priest called out.

There were thumps and gasps and the sound of heavy feet on the marble floor.

Loud harsh voices shouting, *"Come out, you communist pigs!"*

"Jew-lovers!"

Then the sound of nuns singing over the angry voices. A bell ringing, ringing.

I was so frightened I almost blacked out.

I lay there for what felt like hours but may have only been minutes. The many layers of skirts made me feel like a mummy in a tomb.

And then skirts rising, a dim light filtering into my eyes. I scrambled to my feet. Dazed. The rosy-cheeked nun took me by the shoulders and held me in a hug. The heavy smell of incense filled the air. A broken statue of Christ lay on the ground, severed in half, shards everywhere. Bibles and hymn sheets scattered on the ground, torn and trodden on. But on the bench was another pile of rumpled hymn sheets concealing the identity passes. The quick-thinking nun must have sat on them. She quickly scooped them up and, blessing herself, stuffed them inside the front of her habit.

Father Palazzini grabbed me. "They've gone for now. You must head over the bridge. No time to lose."

My legs were giddy. But I ran then, up the stairs. *Pant, pant!* Over the bridge. I had one thought. Get to my bicycle and get the hell out of there.

My bicycle was still in the shed, untouched. I took the exit that led onto a side street and, jumping on my bike, pedalled furiously into the dark night, praying Koch's gang of thugs and the Nazis were somewhere else.

I could only pray that Hugh too had had a lucky escape.

Chapter 27

Hugh was putting the telephone down as I crashed through the heavy door that led into his room in the German College. I almost wept with relief.

"They picked up eighteen. Including the poor fellow pretending to be dead in the coffin. A traitor priest smoked them out by making them recite the '*Ave Maria*'. Those who couldn't do it were taken away."

I gasped. It was just what Ruby and Ethan had feared. I wondered sometimes if Ruby really did have special powers.

Hugh's brow creased like it did when he was puzzled and annoyed. "They also raided a couple of other Vatican properties. It's a worrying sign, so it is. They no longer respect our neutrality."

I looked around our room. We were only a stone's throw

from the Vatican, but they were on the rampage.

"Are we safe?"

Hugh looked around and smiled. "I have my rope to escape with, you have your hurley. Let them try is all I can say. But the only way we'll be truly safe is if they are defeated."

"You don't think they would really kidnap the Pope?' I said. I pictured him with his thin white wrists, his huge brown eyes and his white clothes, as frail as a baby bird. He was a holy man. It was wrong to treat him like a chess pawn.

Hugh shook his head. "They won't move yet. But I don't like the way they are closing in. I don't like that cur Koch having free rein." He looked keenly at me. "I'm thinking we should move Ethan and Ruby anyway, just to be on the safe side. Even deeper into the countryside."

I nodded. I was sad at the thought of them leaving that beautiful orchard full of birdsong in the convent, but I knew he was right.

I still ventured out over the next few days to deliver some more presents. But I was careful, always on the lookout for spies and raiders. I was glad of the distraction for what was really spooking me was the fact I had to sing at Midnight Mass in the Sistine Chapel!

And then on Christmas Eve morning, we had a call from Prince Doria. He needed to get away.

Hugh arranged for him to change into a Swiss Guard uniform that John May had got hold of. At the changing of the guard at 6pm, as they passed by they acquired a new recruit. Off he marched into the sanctuary of the Holy City.

My footfall echoed on the corridor as I joined the other choristers at 11 o'clock on our way into the Sistine Chapel for Midnight Mass. The gold paint up above us and in the side walls glowed in the light of a thousand candles. High up above us, Adam reached across and God gave him life. Did Adam hesitate for a moment, perhaps in fear of all that being human, the good and the bad, would mean?

Only the clergy came to this Mass and some honoured guests, among them Sir D'Arcy Osborne and Major Sam.

A parade of cardinals in their red hats took their seats facing the altar, their footsteps echoing around the church. I couldn't help noticing their delicate leather shoes. Then the bells rang out and, in a magnificent embroidered robe, the Pope swept onto the altar.

I knew I was only there because better singers had been evacuated. But I sang my heart out as we offered up Palestrina's Madrigal with cries of joy.

"O magnum mysterium!"

O great mystery!

Our voices soared up towards Michelangelo's fresco of the birth of the world.

"Ut animalia viderent Dominum natum, iacentem in praesepio!"

That animals should see the newborn Lord, lying in a manger.

265

"Beata Virgo, cujus viscera meruerunt portare ..."

Blessed is the Virgin whose womb was worthy to bear ...

And then up through the roof to the sky and the stars and the heavens. I sang for Hugh and the Rome Escape Line, for Ruby and Ethan in the convent. For my mother and all the other prisoners in Mantellate and Regina Coeli.

"Dominum Iesum Christum. Alleluia!"

Our Lord, Jesus Christ. Alleluia!

I sang for my grandparents in London, hoping they were still alive and not troubled by bombing at least for this one night. I even sang for my father, wherever he was, dead or alive. I sang for Gobbo and Roberto and his partisans. For all those poor Jews transported from Rome.

"Alleluia!"

With every fibre in my body, I prayed to a God I wasn't sure I believed in. Please let the war end soon. Please let this be the last Christmas under the Nazis.

And as I looked around at all the faces, elderly cardinals, holy noble ladies, choir boys just like me, I guessed they were all praying for the same thing. When will it end? When will the Allies come?

Chapter 28

Saint Nicolas somehow found me in the Vatican, for my stocking bulged with gifts. A Swiss army pocketknife engraved with my initials. Sweets, an orange, the skin fragrant and knobbly. The German nuns had knitted me some woolly socks and a new red jumper, the wool soft and smelling of beeswax, so unlike the green prickly one I had been wearing. Sister Boniface must have knitted it by candlelight alone in her cell.

While Hugh said Mass in the chapel at six o'clock, I took my chance. I ran all the way to the Mantellate prison. I clambered up on the rooftop of the boarding school at the back and climbed up.

Then I sang with all my might the *"Magisterium"*, sending the notes across the courtyard and through the prison walls, into my mother's heart. I didn't care if I would be caught. Or if they had increased the number of guards since the bombing. It was my Christmas gift to my mother.

As I finished with *"Alleluia!"* something wonderful happened. The sound of clapping and cheering rose like a crescendo, breaching the windows, rushing through the nooks and crannies in the walls. The cry rang out – *"Alleluia!"* – and was taken up and repeated like a wave breaking on a shore.

"Alleluia! Alleluia!"

You can imprison our bodies but you won't break our spirit, they seemed to sing. *Alleluia!* For in our hearts we are free.

The sky was cold and leaden. But the sound escaped even if the people couldn't.

Soon there were rough voices, shouts of *"Quiet! You will be put in solitary!"*

But for that brief moment, we had defied them, the enemies of all that was good and kind and human. I hoped my mother had heard me. I hoped that, even if she was cross with me, she was also a little bit proud.

I cycled back on my Vatican "tricycle", whistling, chuckling to myself, as the bells rang out for Christmas morning. Many, many people had gathered in Saint Peter's Square to visit the manger, the life-size figures near the obelisk. But there would be no public Mass said by the Pope today. Too dangerous for the Nazis and the Fascists to have so many Romans gathered together in the Vatican.

The nuns served Christmas dinner as normal in the

German College and Major Sam dined with us. I resolved
not to be so surly with the nuns. It was not their fault they
were Germans. And they had knit me woolly socks and a
jumper. We had duck with apple stuffing. And Sister
Boniface was so proud when she served us a whole stollen
– a pastry cake stuffed with fruits and nuts. I wondered if it
was made with some of the Vatican flour John May had
"liberated".

"Well, Sister, that's the best damn Christmas cake I've
ever tasted," said Major Sam.

"See, Baby Jesus. Inside his blanket, *ja!*" Her old bony
face blushed with modesty, as she pointed to the ridge
down the centre and the tapering at both ends.

I couldn't quite see it myself but laughed to see the
powdered icing sugar all over Hugh and Major Sam's faces,
giving them moustaches and beards like Saint Nicolas. I
licked my own with relish. And oh! The sweet taste of the
candied peel, and the raisins, the crunch of the almonds.
And the spices on my tongue. Sister Boniface explained
they were cardamom and cinnamon.

"My family are from Dresden," she said in German, with
Hugh translating. "It is my grandmother's recipe. But I
added almonds in honour of this great country and the
Pope. I added a splash of English spiced rum and a mere
whisper of Irish whiskey to add harmony to the flavours."

I'd never heard her talk so much!

So there we were in Rome. An English major, an Irish
priest, and a half-Jewish boy enjoying a cake made by a

German nun with international ingredients. The whole world was in that cake.

I ran after her and gave her one of my chocolates. Her plain old face lit up and I could have sworn a tear came to her eye. She clutched it like it was real gold and put it in her pocket. Then with a sudden rush, she embraced me.

"Peace," she said in heavily accented Italian, "to all men in this season of goodwill!" She released me and beamed at me. And I knew then that Sister Boniface and me were friends for life.

And if we could be friends – a skinny old nun from Bavaria and a ragamuffin half-Jewish, English, Irish-American mongrel – then maybe someday our countries could be too.

Chapter 29

If Christmas Day had been quiet, the next day, the 26th of December – Saint Stephen's Day as Hugh and I called it, Boxing Day to Major Sam – was a riot!

Early in the afternoon a stream of priests and escaped POW's arrived. Even Delia and her husband and Blon and Nuala her younger sister came. Her other children had colds and were at home with the cook. John Furman and Bill Simpson too. And Pip and Tug from Mrs M's.

"Your Father Christmas deeds are a legend, Leo," Pip told me. He held up his new pipe. "Pleased as Punch I am with this."

Another lively Irish priest called Father Spike Buckley, who looked after all the escapees who were ill, came too. En route from some medical mission of mercy. His pockets were stuffed with lint and ointments and medicines.

"Hey, give Father Spike a drink," John Furman winked. "And he'll sing us a song!"

So after a glass of whiskey he gave us his rendition of "Mother Machree".

"Oh, I love the dear silver that shines in your hair,
And the brow that's all furrowed and wrinkled with care,
I kiss the dear fingers so toil worn for me.
Oh, God bless you and keep you, Mother Machree!"

Spike capered around the bed and went down on his knees to Sister Boniface as she came into the room with a tray of Irish whiskeys. She smiled and everyone laughed uproariously.

Then Delia was persuaded, not that she ever needed much persuading, to sing her famous song, "The Spinning Wheel".

"Merrily, merrily, noiselessly whirring,
Swings the wheel, spins the wheel, while the foot's stirring.
Spritely and brightly and airily ringing,
Thrills the sweet voice of the young maiden singing."

There was something in the way she rolled her "r's" and sang so naturally, conjuring up the picture of Eileen spinning, spinning in her cottage, that stirred everyone's heart. I thought I saw Hugh wipe a tear from his eye. And I thought of my own mother Eileen, locked in that stinking hellhole.

But amid all the gaiety, dark rumours entered the door.

"The Germans have taken a census of the population," I heard Dr Kiernan the ambassador say to Hugh. "Only those on the list will get food tickets. They are trying to force all the escapees from their hiding places. There's an estimated one hundred thousand Italian soldier deserters, over three thousand POW's and hundreds of Jews."

"The food situation is tight enough already," said Hugh. "No butter, sugar or rice has arrived in Rome this month. And there are more and more refugees fleeing from the war in the south pouring in every day. The Nazis are tightening up the ration books." He turned to Major Sam. "We'll have to dig deep in our pockets to get food on the black market. John May will be busy."

"And we have to stop the escapees coming into Rome," said Major Sam. "We just won't be able to feed any more. We need to be more careful. Kappler is stepping up efforts to break us. The numbers of Gestapo police has gone up from 400 to 2,000."

Hugh shook his head. "Well, maybe. But I'll never refuse anyone who needs my help."

"I think you'd better stay close to base," said Major Sam. "With Koch's gang on the rampage, they could scoop you up and you'll end up 'down there' in the place whose name we dare not speak."

But Hugh just grinned, as if to say: you try stopping me.

While they chatted, I spoke to Father Spike. "If a person was dangerously sick in prison, would they take them out to hospital?"

"Unlikely," he said. "The only way a sick person would leave would be in a coffin."

Nuala, who was a few years older than me, nearly a young lady, was kind enough to play a game of tag with me all over the German College.

"Are you going to be a priest when you grow up?" she asked me.

I looked at her like she was a madwoman, the eyes falling out of my head.

"Are you cracked! I'm half-Jewish! Some priest I'd be."

"Which half?" she joked, sizing me up. "The left or the right? Or the top or the bottom?"

"It's shot through me like threads in a tapestry. That's what my mother says."

But I must have looked a bit sad at the mention of my mother because she punched me gently on the side of the arm and said, "Sure every bit of you is grand!"

It gave me a warm fuzzy feeling inside when she said that.

"Hey, have you been in the Pope's room?" she asked. "He has two telephones and all. One has a golden handle for all the important people. Isn't that gas!"

I told her it was impossible to get near the Pope these days what with his eleven Noble Guards around him at all times. All lords and dukes but you wouldn't want to mess with them. They were all crack shots.

When we got back to Hugh's room, dusty and panting, dying for a drink of water, everyone was gathered around the wireless, listening to the BBC.

The announcer was going through a big long list of names of people who were guests at a party.

"Michael Hughes and Brian Smith from Hackney, both 5th division, were there. And Francis O'Mahony and Bill Davis from Hull ..."

On and on the list of names went.

Hugh had a happy smile on his face. The BBC was broadcasting all the names of the prisoners of war Hugh was keeping safe in Rome and the surrounding countryside. All over Britain, some mother at a fireside in Kent or a doctor and his wife in the Yorkshire Dales would heave a sigh at the sound of their son's name. And maybe they would sleep well at least for tonight, knowing their loved one still breathed on the earth. Even if it was far away in Italy under a Roman sky.

That night I lay in my bed wondering. My mother had been a link in a chain communicating news like this, before she had been captured. Nobody was reading her name out.

I needed a plan to get my mother out of the prison. And I was thinking, would it work to get her out in a coffin?

Chapter 30

The New Year – 1944 – was only a few days old when a porter arrived at Hugh's desk on the ground floor with a crisp white envelope.

It was a gold-embossed invitation to a reception at the Hungarian Embassy.

"You won't go, will you?" I asked. "Major Sam warned you it's not safe."

"The devil I won't!" he said. "The Hungarians are in the Germans' pockets and there's always something to learn. I'll go and find out what I can."

Remarkably, Major Sam thought it was a good idea and that I should go with Hugh as a messenger to sound the alarm if anything fishy happened. Hugh thought he was turning into a fussy old woman. But he reluctantly gave in.

So we set off to the reception. Hugh in his Monsignor

finery, the red cloak and sash, and the pinky-purple dress that he called his cassock. It had about a million buttons up the front. Perched on his bush of curls was his square biretta hat with a tuft like a big pink geranium. I wore my dark-wine altar-boy dress with the white smock over it. I was to pretend I had been collected from the dentist and was nursing a toothache, so not able to talk.

We travelled in the German College's car.

The embassy was on Via dei Villini to the east of the city across the Tiber where there were loads of big posh mansions.

Inside, the grand palace was stuffed with bigwigs. Ambassadors wearing sashes, their wives dolled up in gowns and earrings. I even spotted an African prince in a headdress woven with gold thread. There were a few Nazis too, who I eyed warily: a couple that looked like generals and a nasty-looking SS officer in a black uniform.

I stayed in the hall entrance sitting on a chair near the coats, while Hugh strode in, confident as you please. A ripple went through the room as if a dolphin had just somersaulted into a tank of sharks.

I got bored after a while, sitting feigning a toothache. Nobody had noticed me at all. Not the servants too busy kow-towing to the big-wigs. Not the important people, too busy admiring each other. The Nazis weren't interested in small fry like me. So I peeped in the door of the main reception room and spotted a table groaning with sugared fruit, cakes and biscuits. A giant chandelier caught the light as waiters circulated with trays of drinks. Surely nobody would mind if I had a bite to eat?

I sidled over to the table. Nobody noticed me as I took a couple of napkins, filled them up with cakes and biscuits and stuffed them in my pockets. I was well pleased with my little hoard and slid back around the room again.

Then, as I passed a little recess, I noticed Hugh towering over a grand-looking old man, medium-sized with white hair and piercing blue eyes. It was Von Weizsäcker, the German Ambassador. He was talking intently to Hugh, leaning in close, but almost standing on tiptoe.

I crept nearer, straining my ears.

"We know you are involved in the Escape Line," he said to Hugh. "Don't deny it. It has gone on for too long and it has got to stop."

Hugh looked at him with a polite smile on his lips, as if listening to an unfunny joke. "Are you asking me or telling me?"

The ambassador leaned in closer. "In future you will stay where you belong. If you leave the Vatican City, you will be arrested on sight. This is a final warning. Think carefully about what I have said."

I looked around desperately. There was an open patio door. If needed we could make a run for it.

But Hugh just smiled all the more and, walking back towards the main room, said very loudly, "Your Excellency is too considerate. I will certainly think about what you've said," and then he paused, knowing full well the whole room was listening. "Sometimes!"

The ambassador looked red in the face as Hugh strode off.

I ran back out to the hallway and Hugh joined me shortly afterwards.

As Hugh swept out the door in his red cloak, bobbled biretta in his hand, I trailed behind him. I glanced up as heels clicked on the path.

A Nazi officer rushed up the path, his grey coat over his shoulders, his peaked cap down low. Kappler.

The Monsignor wished him a good evening in German. I shrank into myself and averted my face so Kappler wouldn't look at me.

Kappler merely nodded and continued towards the door. The air crackled as the two mortal enemies passed so close by.

I scuttled after Hugh into the waiting car.

"That was Kappler!" I said.

Hugh merely smiled. "I told you we were just nodding acquaintances." But then he turned to me. "Well, you heard the Ambassador threaten me."

"I wanted to thump him," I said.

"Von Weizäcker isn't the worst. He's not even a Nazi. But he has a job to do."

"And Kappler was there to make sure he did his bidding," I said. "I certainly would like to do more than thump him."

My stomach was still somersaulting. But I knew I was all

talk. I couldn't even look him in the face.

But if that wasn't bad enough, next morning Hugh was summoned to a meeting with his boss, Cardinal Montini, in the Vatican.

He met Major Sam and me back in his room afterwards.

"Well, that was a very hard rap on the knuckles," said Hugh. "My boss has repeated to me the ambassador's warning. Or should I say threat. I've had a right telling-off."

Major Sam looked down in the dumps. "So does that mean the end of your involvement with the Escape Line?"

Hugh gazed out the window at the dome of Saint Peter's. He steepled his fingers and paused for a second as if in prayer. "He told me to be more cautious. But he didn't give me a direct order to stop. I'm not being sent away from the Vatican. So, I guess, I'll just have to be more careful." He winked at me.

Major Sam shook his head. "You wily old cardinals and priests! I thought only the devil spoke with a forked tongue?"

But there was more bad news the next day. The rector of the German College had found out about Major Sam – that far from being Patrick Derry, an Irish Vatican worker, he was harbouring a British major under his roof! The rector told Hugh he had to give Sam his marching orders to stop the Nazis tearing the place apart. Major Sam would have to go and live within the walls of the Santa Maria Hospice with Sir D'Arcy Osborne. He was crushed.

"What about me?" I asked. I had grown fond of my camp bed and didn't want to leave.

They both looked at me.

"I need to stay with Hugh," I argued. "I am allowed in to sing at the Sistine Chapel. You need me more than ever to run messages. And, besides, bombs can fall on the Vatican too as we know."

To my surprise, they agreed.

"But at the first sign of trouble, you are coming inside the walls," said Major Sam.

A phone call interrupted our discussion.

Hugh put the receiver down, the blood drained from his face.

"Kappler is closing in on us. They've arrested Joe Pollak, one of our boys. And Pip and Tug and another one of our helpers, Nebolante. He's a big chap in the Resistance."

Major Sam pumped his fist into his hand and swore. *"God damn it!"*

I was worried about Pip and Tug who I'd met at Mrs M's and at Christmas. But Hugh tried to reassure me that they'd just be sent to a prison camp.

There was a loud knock to the door. Bill Simpson ran into the room, sweating.

"Six armed SS men charged our flat on Via Chelini! Nebolante's cook fell apart and revealed our whereabouts. They've got Bruno the Yugoslav and Herta the young Austrian girl that helps us. And they've got John Furman."

Major Sam groaned and paced the flat. "Our

organisation is falling apart!"

Hugh coolly took out his golf club. Balancing a ball on a book, he set up his shoe as a target on the other side of the room and took a shot. If it was anyone else you'd think he was being a great eejit altogether. But we knew Hugh was thinking.

"Okay," he said at last. "Kappler has some of the pieces of the puzzle but not all. Let's warn all the safe houses and move anyone who is known to the people they've arrested."

Major Sam agreed. "But we need to streamline the organisation. It's too leaky. We have to assume anyone captured can be tortured for information."

Hugh took another shot. "When the Irish were fighting the British, they used a cell structure. Each person knew only the identity of the three or four people in their cell. The lead person is the only one who knows the identity of the overall team leader. It worked to bring down the British Empire. It might just help against the Nazis!"

Major Sam gave him a sideways look. "You know a lot about it for a priest!"

"I was a seminarian during the War of Independence in Ireland back in the 1920's. Sure, I was never involved. But that didn't stop me getting arrested on my way to a funeral and spending a night in a prison cell at his majesty's pleasure, until my superiors had me released." Hugh teed the ball expertly into his shoe.

"You're a man of many talents. And surprises!" said Derry. "I can see why you're so sympathetic to prisoners."

Hugh smiled and soon after hit the phone to warn people to abandon their lodgings.

All over Rome, American soldiers and English former prisoners of war had to change locations. I was sent off to dispatch monks' and priests' cassocks so they could safely move around the streets before the curfew which got earlier and earlier.

That evening Major Sam put on Hugh's clerical habit, the black biretta and the red robe and set off for his new home with Sir D'Arcy Osborne at the Santa Maria inside the Vatican walls. I would of course see him all the time. But it wouldn't be the same.

But Sam was lucky to have Vatican protection.

A few days later Hugh came off the phone and thrust his head in his hands.

"You remember our two helpers, Bruno and Herta the Austrian who they arrested the other day? Herta was sent to Austria to spend five years in prison."

Hugh got down on his knees and prayed. There were tears in his eyes.

"They executed Bruno this morning," he said, rising to his feet. "That was a message from a friendly prison guard. Bruno asked the guard to let me know that even though they tortured him, he didn't talk. May God have mercy on his good soul."

I felt a hollow feeling in my stomach. And then I was red-hot with anger as if lava was coming up inside me.

I kicked the chair. *"I wish they were dead instead! If I had a gun I'd shoot Kappler dead too!"*

Hugh held me gently by the shoulders. "If we behave like them, then they've really won. They've trampled not just on us but on all that is good and human and dignified. Let God decide what to do with them."

Tears spilled from my eyes. I couldn't stop them. I sniffed back the snot. Hugh handed me his handkerchief.

"We will win by being better than them. Don't worry. They can't win in the long run. They can't kill everybody. They win for a short time. But inevitably the goodness of people bubbles up. Take that anger, Leo. Sit with it. Now let's figure out what we can do to stop the cat pouncing on us mice again."

He stamped his foot then, the big priest in his black cassock. His eyes gleamed out of his steel-rimmed glasses. But there was steel too in his eyes.

I blew my nose and put the hankie in my pocket.

"I'll deliver as many messages as you want," I said. "What about Don Pietro in Via Urbana? Won't he be at risk in this crackdown?"

Hugh nodded. "I've tried calling a few times but can't get through. There's been some problems with the phone lines."

Hugh dialled Don Pietro's number again but there was no answer.

Without speaking, he wrote a note.

"Take this to the good man," he said. "Tell him to head

to the Vatican. I'll find a place for him and any others he's protecting."

I smiled then. "So you're obviously not heeding the warnings of the German ambassador or the Cardinal!"

Hugh scratched his curly head. "Well, you see, I only promised to think about his message." He stood up straight and blinked, smiling his comical smile. "And there you go. I have thought about it. And do you know what? I don't think I'll be thinking about them much again!" He grabbed a golf club, pretended it was a walking stick and tottered from side to side, codding that he was Charlie Chaplin. "And that's what you call a Kerry answer!"

I laughed and grabbed the note. But Hugh insisted on sewing it into my jacket.

I set off on foot. Hugh thought it was better I leave the bicycle so as not to attract notice.

As I cut through Saint Peter's Square, I saw a team of Nazis on bended knee touching up the white line across the entrance to the square, the line that defined the boundary of Vatican City.

To keep Hugh in, I thought, an animal in his pen. And then, striding past the obelisk in the centre of the square, his soutane swishing about his long legs, there was Hugh. He walked as if to break through the line. The Nazis tensed. Their overseer shouted an order. Two of the soldiers stood up and fumbled a bit – they looked ridiculous, fussing about where to put down their paintbrushes. They braced their rifles.

Hugh, with a beaming smile on his broad face, stopped

short at the line.

"*Guten Tag*," I heard him say loudly in perfect German. Good day. And then he pointed at the line and said something else in German, all good nature and jollity. Before they could respond he laughed, turned on his heels and headed back across the square. I bet he was saying they'd missed a bit.

But, as I headed across the Tiber and risked a tram journey, I kept my eyes peeled. There was no doubt about it. With two thousand police to call on, Kappler was closing in on Hugh.

Chapter 31

I had a strange feeling as I ran through Rome to Monti, the note hidden in the lining sewn into my jacket like an unexploded bomb. The last time I'd come to visit Don Pietro I'd been in a fancy limousine with Franco. Riding like a little prince. Now I was just another ragged boy on the street.

On the street leading to Via Urbana, a horrible sight: a ragged line of grey/green uniforms and screaming mouths. A roadblock down the end of the street. I saw their grey/green uniforms, the colour of sludge, and their angry movements, like mad puppets. They were jumpy, that was clear. They had put up a barrier and were wielding their guns and pulling people aside for questioning. Most of the "rebels" looked like old beggars and housewives, anxiously clutching their bags, probably full of black-market goods they'd paid a fortune for. The *popolini* – the little people – Mussolini called them as if they were ants nobody cared about. Except for Hugh.

I darted down an alleyway and came up the Via Urbana from the other direction. When I reached Don Pietro's house, I ran full pelt up the stairs. *Heave, heave*, went my chest. *Ba-boom* went my heart. There was a sick, heavy feeling like a stone in my stomach, I didn't know why. That dread. What worse thing than all the other worse things I'd seen waited for me around the next corner? Like one of Ruby's demons stalking my nightmares.

As I climbed the stairs, voices rose and fell out on the terrace like the sound of a river coursing in spring.

A man hurtled out of Don Pietro's flat as if on fire, pinning me to the wall.

I ran into the kitchen. Maria Teresa looked at me in alarm, her arms full of documents and papers, feeding them into the wood-burning stove.

"That was Colonel Rendina who ran out – he's high up in the Resistance," she said.

The Resistance newspapers crinkled in the flames, their print turning to ash. Words too powerful for the Nazis to hear.

"We have been betrayed!" Maria Teresa cried. "I know who it was too. That stinking two-faced dog Oscar. That was his alias but he's a Nazi informer! May he burn in hell!"

I remembered that slinking cur at the convent chapel, a

mangy good-for-nothing if I'd even seen one.

Don Pietro stood in the doorway. "Do not condemn the poor man. He knows no better." Over his shoulder I saw Gio his Communist friend from Bari, hunched in a chair.

"You need to go," I gasped. "Hurry, the Nazis are down the street!"

The screech of brakes!

"Schnell!"

The thunder of jackboots up the street.

Maria Teresa ran onto the terrace, her face white with terror.

"Run for it. I will distract them," she said as she came back in.

I glanced down the street through the window. Troops were marching towards us, fanning out around the house. There was no escape.

Maria Teresa grabbed hold of my arm and pointed towards the roof. Overhead was a wide beam, criss-crossed by another, just wide enough to take a skinny boy. She put a chair on a table and with her help I hoisted myself onto the beam. I lay like Christ on the cross, my arms laid out on the cross beam. My head to one side.

I was just in time. I heard what sounded like an avalanche tear through the door. Maria Teresa's raised voice. Boots grinding into the ground as if to smash it out.

"What do you want? This is the home of a man of God!"

Shouts in guttural German.

Then one spoke in heavy accented Italian. "Where is that

forger, that partisan priest? We found his equipment at the convent."

Teresa screamed at them. A stream of Italian words hurled like air-bombs at them. But they barely registered against the hail of German shouts and commands.

I lay like a dead thing. Terrified I would topple down on them. That I would wet myself and my piss would trickle down. I could see their helmets, not far below me. Smell their stinking sweat like animals. They tore around the room, breaking things up. I scrunched my eyes shut. But not seeing was worse.

I opened my eyes. On the wall above the sink was a small cracked mirror. In it I saw three Don Pietros come into the room, hands up.

"I will come quietly," he said. "No need to harm Maria Teresa."

There was a triumphant shout in Italian. *We have that filthy Communist too!* There must have been Blackshirt Fascists hunting with their Nazi friends.

They had captured Gio.

More shouts. *We caught that Resistance pig Rendina in an alley!*

The fleeing man hadn't made it.

I heard Teresa remonstrate with them in rapid Italian, too quick for me to make out the words. But I knew that tone. The sound of desperation. The sound of hope leaving the room.

Two soldiers grabbed Don Pietro as he made the Sign of

the Cross. Another couple dragged Gio. His dark hair, his defiant face. He pulled away from them to the doorway, spat at them and was slapped in the face.

I just wanted them to go. I just wanted it to be over. Praying they wouldn't look up.

"May God have mercy on all our souls," said Don Pietro. "I will cooperate. Tell me what you need to do. Please do not harm anyone else in my name."

They took him from the room.

The sound of receding footsteps. Maria Teresa still crying and arguing. A door banged shut. I closed my eyes and the whole world went spinning.

I don't know how long I lay there on the cross. I felt like I would never move again.

But I couldn't move. I was stiff with fear.

There was the sound of banging below. As if they were tearing the house apart.

Then quietness.

"Leo, come down, they have gone."

It was Maria Teresa's voice. There was the sound of scraping below, a bang against the gable wall.

"Inch yourself along and you can come down by this ladder."

Mechanically, like a wind-up toy, I did what she asked. Slowly, painfully, splinters in the wood catching in my skin. I reached the ladder and, shaking the pins and needles out of my hands and legs, descended. Maria Teresa was holding it firmly.

I almost fell into her arms. She gave me a drink of water. It cascaded down my parched throat. I collapsed on a chair.

"Where are they?"

"They've taken them 'down there'," she said. Her normally neat hair was all over the place, her eyes wild in her head.

Laggiù – "down there" – as they referred to Via Tasso, the torture chambers, not daring to say its name.

"Don Pietro went quickly to save me, didn't he?" I said. "They would have fought if I hadn't been there."

She patted me on the head with a kind smile. "Dearest child, Don Pietro would never have fought. He is a gentle as a lamb even if he has the heart of a lion."

She gave me a piece of bread to eat.

"Now you must go back to the Vatican and tell them what has happened."

I brightened. "I'll get Hugh to tell the Pope and he won't let them kill a priest."

She smiled at me. "You do that." But her eyes, scorched with anger and worry, told a different story. She almost spat. "The Pope does not know what is going on outside his palace. His eyes are looking a different way! To the God in heaven who has turned his back on Rome!"

As we got outside the door, an old man rumbled by in a cart. Maria Teresa had a quick word with him and he agreed to take me into the city and drop me close to the Vatican.

I confess I didn't take anything in during the whole journey – the streets a blur of columns, crumbling ruins, flashes of red and yellow and people scuttling like mice on the cobbled streets. It was all rectangles, triangles, cubes and squares, like the broken coloured glass bombed to pieces in the Vatican.

Everything was taking place inside my head. How the helmets of the Nazis made them look like cockroaches. And how Don Pietro among them, even though he was a normal size, looked like a giant of a man.

Chapter 32

The cart driver let me out a few streets away from the Vatican. I wondered if it would be safe to walk right in. Hugh had said we had to be careful. They were watching him now all the time, every day more Nazis patrolling along the white line at the entrance to the square, all around the boundary wall surrounding the Vatican. And yet I knew he would be there on the steps outside the Basilica like every day, whatever the weather, standing with his breviary, praying, scanning the square, a beacon for people looking for help.

I was almost in tears, fearful to see so many Nazis patrols on foot, in vehicles. The note! I suddenly thought. It was still sewn into the lining of my jacket. If I was stopped and searched and they found it, they would have something on Hugh.

I froze. I needed to evade them. I needed to think like Hugh. How did he do it day after day? It was a game of cat and mouse or as if he had magic powers. People swirled around him and somehow the ones who needed to found him. And in the moments when the guards turned or changed, he had vanished and led them to somewhere safe, behind a colonnade, through a mysterious door, down a manhole, leading them to safety. The Pimpernel of the Vatican. But to me he was a magician.

That was it! A disappearing trick.

I was relieved to see I was near the entrance to the tunnel near the Porta Cavalleggeri and the railway station, where Hugh and I had emerged after he'd shown me Saint Peter's bones. Maybe I too could be a magician and sneak into the Vatican. Surely this was a special emergency. At least I could hide down there and get rid of the note.

I watched the mouth of the entrance. There were no Nazi guards, no Gestapo secret police smoking cigarettes in plain clothes pretending to be ordinary Italians. So I dashed into the tunnel where the *popolini* lived like mice – the forgotten people – and through them I flitted, like a ghost on my way to Hugh. Through the whiff of drains, the dirty children, the families bedded down on sacking.

I was thinking of my mother and Ruby as I walked by sick old people and painfully thin mothers. I was thinking of them, with every in and out breath and every heartbeat. And even of my dad in the sky, suspended between heaven and earth. He still hovered there in my dreams, caught between the devil and the deep blue sea, the Nazis and little French seaside towns. All the good and the bad in this world, neither in it nor out of it. And I wondered if he had ever dropped a bomb on a boy like me. A boy just walking about. Not expecting death to fall out of the sky.

My heart was breaking because of the loss of Don Pietro but I couldn't think about that now. Into the box in my head it went. But I couldn't think straight at all. I wanted to hide, burrow into the earth and get rid of the note. But I couldn't get away from people, so many huddled underground. Couldn't breathe among the smell of frying food and human waste down there in the tunnel. My head hurt. I felt oppressed underground, as if the whole world was pressing down on me.

I slipped down to the little recess that led to the cave under the Vatican. I took off my jacket and scrabbled at the stitching around the lining, then pulled out the note and ripped it to tiny pieces. Then I worked the secret latch in the steel door and went into the cave under the manhole.

But the torch that was left in the box failed. I got confused and couldn't find the entrance to the tunnel that led to the excavations and then back to the heart of the Vatican. Shafts of shimmering light came down through the manhole. I decided to risk coming out into the street. I was desperate now to get back to daylight and felt braver without the note. I clambered up the rough steps and emerged out of the manhole in the street near Saint Peter's Square. It was silent and empty as I kicked the manhole back into place.

Saint Peter's Square, however, was teeming with Nazis, black stains on the gleaming white of the Pope's home. And there was quite a few of them standing guard right on the white line across the entrance.

My heart leapt to see Hugh on the steps, standing firm like a lighthouse. I hung back near a pillar, watching anxiously.

Hugh bounded across the square, almost danced across it. So light and quick for such a big man. He walked down to the line facing his enemies, looking the Nazi soldiers in the eye. Almost taunting them to grab him across the line. But the black cordon of soldiers shrank back, as if he was protected by some white light, some special power that shielded him.

I didn't dare approach Hugh. Worried that maybe Kappler, having seen us together at the Hungarian Embassy, would link me to him. I was on edge and confused. SS men in plain clothes lurked in the shadows and behind the pillars of the colonnades. I tried not to remember their shouts as they stormed Don Pietro's. Their joy at finding Gio. But the crashes and harsh voices rang in my ears, taunting me, making me tremble.

All I wanted now was to hide and get inside. I decided to go back to the German College. But Nazi soldiers were swaggering all around the boundary of the Vatican territory. Making a show of strength.

I sweated and panicked, woozy with fear. Every window might conceal the watchful eye of an enemy. Every doorway, a Nazi ready to pounce or strike. I shrunk into myself. Forced myself to calm down.

There were a few Nazis patrolling on foot. But I reckoned if I did a loop of the side streets off the boundary path, I could then make a run for it and slip back into the German College unseen.

The coast was clear as I came near the College. I streaked across the road, narrowly missed by a motorbike that roared by out of nowhere. The driver cursed me and I turned to roar back. But I lost my footing and tripped on a cobblestone. I lay sprawled on the ground, dazed from the fall. But even before I looked up, I saw the gleaming boot leather, winced as it connected with my head in a rough kick like I was some dog in its way. A rough hand grabbed me by the scruff of the neck.

The grey-clothed arm held me at arm's length. I tried to focus, dazed from the fall.

"Why if it isn't the songbird of Regina Coeli?" The voice was mocking, ironic, cold. "I too once heard a blackbird's whistle ring out in the night during an ambush. We know more about you than you think. Let me guess. Out running errands for the Monsignor."

My eyes came into focus. I saw the pale-blue eyes, the thinning hair, the smile playing on his hateful lips. Kappler. I had fallen straight into the hands of my mortal enemy!

Chapter 33

"For the last time! Will you cooperate?" It was Captain Priebke, Kappler's deputy, screaming in my face in Italian.

I was in a cold dark basement – "down there". Via Tasso. On the outside it was a smudged yellow apartment block. On the inside the rooms were blacked-out torture chambers and windowless cells. So cold it felt like hell had frozen over.

They had tied me to a chair with rough rope. Each leg bound to a leg of the chair, my hands tied behind my back. Done with care, precise knots. Priebke knew what he was doing. Damp oozed down the stained wall. Blood-stained. There was the sharp smell of disinfectant that they'd used to wash away the bloodstains. But the sickly smell of blood still lingered. Nearby was a table covered in instruments of torture, a hammer, a whip. I tried not to look at it.

Priebke leaned in. "We know your mother is a partisan and you run messages between the partisans and that Irish priest O'Flaherty. Where is she hiding out?"

I know it seems strange but I nearly fainted with relief. At least they hadn't worked out my mother was in the Mantellate prison. Hugh was right. They were literal-minded. They were looking for an auburn-haired Irishwoman. Not a grey-haired Italian from the Swiss border.

"We know she is with the partisans in the mountains," he said. "And Hugh O'Flaherty is the link. She is leading that band in the hills."

I almost laughed. They thought my mother was with Roberto rather than under their noses. It was such a funny idea it gave me a brief moment of hope.

"Hitler visits a lunatic asylum," I spoke rapidly in Italian. "The patients give the Hitler salute. As he passes down the line he comes across a man who isn't saluting."

Priebke listened despite himself, puzzled.

"'Why aren't you saluting like the others?' Hitler barks. 'My Leader, I'm the nurse,' comes the answer. 'I'm not crazy!'"

Priebke leaned in. The sour smell of the onions from his lunch on his breath made me gag. I could see the bristles up his nose.

He paused, like the sadist he was. He walked away. But then he suddenly reeled back around at me and slapped me hard in the mouth.

"There's your joke, you little shit!" he roared. "You stupid little fool! People have been executed for less. It's an offence to insult our supreme leader."

I didn't mind the pain. The fascist bullies had trained me in withstanding pain in my school for so many years that it was second nature for me now to shut down.

I sang a song inside my head. "The Blackbird" whistling and singing away.

But I must have sung out loud for Priebke rounded on my again and struck me on the side of my head.

"Did you know your precious Monsignor is a British spy? But his puny little army of priests and nuns won't stop us winning the war."

I nearly laughed out loud again that they thought Hugh was a spy.

"We know where you went to school, where you lived. We will harm your family," he sneered. This time he picked up the whip and cracked it hard across my legs.

I let out a yowl of pain. But I squeezed my eyes shut, determined not to cry.

"Go look for them there," I managed to say back.

I tasted something in my mouth. Blood. Something was loose. A tooth. My swollen tongue felt for the gap. But it was at the side, a baby tooth anyway. So I didn't care. But what if I swallowed it? But my throat was too swollen.

"Where?"

He loomed in closer. I saw bits of food in his teeth, white spittle at the side of the mouth. Large pores on his nose.

"My school. We had a picture of Mussolini and Hitler on the wall," I muttered through my bleeding lips. "The teacher asked us to suggest who we should put between them. 'Jesus,' I said. Because we all know that Jesus was crucified between two criminals."

Priebke just shook with fury and cracked the whip beside my chair. I flinched but didn't say a thing.

"A white line at the Vatican means nothing to us," he sneered. "Kappler is the leader of Rome not the Pope!"

"So you win and Hitler and Goring his general are standing atop the dome of Saint Peter's church," I went on. "Hitler says he wants to do something to put a smile on the Romans' faces. So Goring says: 'Why don't you jump?'"

This time it was Priebke's fist that connected with my stomach. Winding me, making me splutter.

"You will cooperate with us," he said. He smacked me hard across the face with his open palm. And again and again, pausing in between for different lengths to catch me by surprise.

I moaned in pain. I must have passed out because the next thing I felt was a cold splash of water in my face. My lips were so parched, and caked with dried blood, I was nearly glad of it.

My eyes were seriously bad now though in the harsh light I was seeing quadruple. It was like surfacing from the bottom of a well. But as the four faces swam into focus, I realised it was two people bearing over me. Kappler had joined Priebke.

"You have gone too far. We need the boy alive."

Kappler spoke in German and I was surprised I knew that much of the language. I must have picked it up from listening to Hugh speak to the nuns.

I opened my eyes.

"Oh yes, we know all about the Monsignor and his Escape organisation," Kappler said, switching to English. "We have spies everywhere, you see. It is only a matter of time before we close the whole thing down."

I tried to keep my face neutral, not betray any emotion. I stared at a place over his left ear on the wall. I tried to remember some of the things I'd seen when they dragged me in. So there was someone left to remember them. I'd seen this on one cell they were clearing out "*Addio, piccola mia – non serbarmi rancore un bacio,*" one prisoner wrote – "Goodbye, my little one – don't hold any bitterness on my account, a kiss."

I looked around. The windows were blacked up. It was no longer 'laggiù', the torture chamber "down there". I was here now.

I went through all that had happened since my capture in my head so I would remember everything. I had spent the night in an empty cell beside several prisoners. Colonel Montezemolo, a lion of a man, who'd had all his teeth and nails pulled out but still didn't talk, Simoni the old general, and Stame an opera singer. Last night he'd sung to calm us all in his soaring tenor voice. They said they were only allowed rations of two oranges that they shared between

303

five cellmates. Montezemolo could hardly speak his face was so badly bruised from beatings. But he hadn't said a word.

And then, as a guard brought in the food rations, a cell door swung open across the corridor and I saw Don Pietro praying with a thin tall young man with fair hair. An Austrian deserter, someone said, name of Joseph Reider.

"Don Pietro!" I'd called out.

But the door swung back. A guard banged the door and told me in rough Italian to be quiet. I heard them pull someone out who screamed he didn't want to be interrogated. I barely slept a wink. Knowing it would soon be my turn.

Now here I was in the heart of my fear. I received another smack across the head from Priebke bringing me reeling back into the torture chamber of Via Tasso.

"We know where your English and American escapees are hiding out." Kappler's voice was thin and cold. "We know the addresses of all those apartments where the Monsignor keeps his troops. Luigi the smuggler has told us everything."

I started to sing, my voice cracked. "The Blackbird". Luigi, I thought. That old vegetable seller that brought Ruby and me to the Vatican? I sang again. And then I laughed. But what would he know? I had spoken my thoughts out loud.

"Shut up, you stupid pig!" Kappler shouted, angry now. "In twenty-four hours I will have closed down all the

Monsignor's operation. All those escaped prisoners will be back behind bars. Or worse!"

Was he bluffing? Surely the vegetable seller didn't know so much. But, as if reading my thoughts, Kappler preened himself and took out a notebook.

"Our intelligence operation has paid off. We have all the names and addresses. Do you really think a *priest*," he almost spat the word, "could take on the might of the Third Reich!"

I spat out my bloody tooth. It landed on his uniform. He recoiled as if I'd shot him.

He brushed it away with a glowing white handkerchief.

"Everybody else talks. Why not you, little runt?" Kappler paused.

"Do you know what I call your Tweedle-Dum and Tweedle-Dee?" My voice was high and cracking. "Spitler and his puppet Muscle-weeny."

Kappler lost his patience and hit me hard on the shoulder. I noticed he was wearing black gloves. Like he didn't want to get his hands dirty with this work.

Priebke said something in German and pointed to his head. "*So ein Idiot!*"

They thought I was touched. An idiot.

"We know where your sister is," Kappler said in his heavy accented English, his voice rising in anger.

My tongue was thick in my head but I managed to speak. "She's far away from here!"

Something inside me dissolved. I thought I might wet or

soil myself. And if they found Ruby, they would find Ethan.
They would send them both to a camp to die. Two
misshapes. Mistakes to the Nazis.

I was about to speak but he interrupted me.

"All I have to do is lift up the phone on the table and the
convent will be raided," he said.

My attention snapped back. But Ruby and Ethan were
no longer at the convent! Hugh had moved them after the
raid on the seminary! They were deep in the countryside
now at a new secret location. Kappler clearly was in the
dark for all his secret agents and informers skulking around
Rome.

But at that moment, a knock came to the door. Priebke
opened the door and it was another officer, an Italian Fascist
Blackshirt, with a prisoner. A great hulking shape,
snivelling like a baby. It was Luigi the vegetable dealer. My
blood froze. Koch was with him, with his miserable little
moustache and black hair greased onto his head. He
grinned like he'd won the lottery. Poor Luigi must have
been tortured.

"This idiot has agreed to lure the Monsignor over the
line," he crowed.

I stared over at Luigi. He caught my eye but only began
blubbering again, staring at the floor.

"My wife and children, I have to think of them," he
pleaded. He was addressing me.

Kappler smiled at me with his evil gleam. "We don't
need you now, you little fool. You had your chance." Then

he turned to Priebke and spoke in German. He gestured towards the phone so I assumed they were planning to get Luigi to call the Monsignor.

What were they going to do to me? Kill me?

"I am a choirboy at the Vatican," I pleaded then, afraid. "I sing for the Pope."

Kappler once more read my mind.

"And what did the Pope say when we cleared out the Jewish ghetto? Nothing!"

My mind reeled back to that day I'd rather have forgotten. The children snatched from their mothers. The crippled boy tossed on the lorry like a carcass of meat.

"Another boy at the bottom of the Tiber. The fish will eat the evidence," he said. "The Pope is too busy mumbling his prayers and being nice to Hitler so that he won't destroy the Cradle of Civilisation." Kappler's voice dripped with contempt.

My brain whirred into action and I spoke without having a plan.

"Hugh won't be fooled by an old cart-driver," I blurted. "I'll do it. He'll believe me if I speak to him on the telephone. But you must promise to let me go."

Kappler nodded. Priebke untied me from the chair. But my legs were too unsteady. Together, Kappler and Priebke hauled me and threw me on the chair at the desk.

"You say one wrong thing and I will kill you," Kappler breathed as he handed me the receiver.

He ran his gloved hand casually across my neck. I

shivered at his loathsome touch.

"Tell him you and Luigi will wait for him in the cart at the entrance to Saint Peter's Square. That he needs to visit a group of escaped prisoners in the countryside near the Ardeatine Caves. Get him to cross the line."

I dialled the number. Tears came to my eyes when I heard Hugh's voice at the other end of the phone.

"Hugh," I said.

"Praise the Good Lord!" he exclaimed. "I was worried sick about you. There's been a series of –"

"I'm safe but you'll have to come with us," I interrupted. "I'm with Luigi and there is a group of prisoners near the Ardeatine Caves that need your help. It's to be raided. They will only move if you tell them in person. We'll wait for you by the end of the colonnade at the German College side. We can all travel by cart."

"Right," he said. "I'll meet you after noonday Mass at the Basilica. I'll straggle out after the last of the Mass-goers." He knew what I was asking him. To cross the line into the territory ruled by the Nazis. But he didn't care for his own safety. "But are you alright?"

Kappler gestured to me to lay the phone down.

"Just me and Luigi, with the cart," I responded. "No, Cú Chulainn is busy this time."

Kappler snatched the phone off me but I'd managed to mention Cú Chulainn and what's more in answer to an unasked question. It would be enough to alert Hugh. Cú Chulainn – the Hound of Culann.

And Kappler didn't suspect anything. I was just an idiot boy after all.

Less than an hour. I hoped it would be enough time for Hugh to activate a plan and warn all the others. Otherwise I was luring Hugh and the whole Rome Escape Line into a trap!

Chapter 34

I sat up beside Luigi as he drove the horse and it seemed to me the whole cart trembled. But it was just me shaking as we made our way to Saint Peter's from Via Tasso.

Crawling along behind us was a black car containing SS officers dressed in civilian clothes and carrying concealed weapons. This was to be a covert arrest. They were going to pretend to be Mass-goers visiting the church. They didn't want to alarm the crowds visiting Saint Peter's Square. Then some way behind them was another black car containing Kappler and Priebke and several other SS officers in uniform. There were also two motorbike outriders on standby. They were taking no chances.

The idea was that I was going to rush up to Hugh in Saint Peter's Square and bustle him along to join us immediately after he came out of Mass in the Basilica. Luigi would stay with the cart. Guns would be trained on him in case I tried anything stupid. On me too, I didn't doubt. Then as soon as Hugh crossed the line he would be seized and put under arrest for disobeying the order to stay on Vatican territory. For conspiring to rescue enemies of the Third Reich.

As we passed by the Colosseum on our way to the Vatican City, I thought about how the gladiators must have felt before going out to risk being pulled to pieces by the lions. But the thought oddly gave me courage. A little bit. That box of worries inside my head was jammed full now.

And I thought about Cú Chulainn. How he had used the very strength of the hound against him, his big ungainly size and anger, to find his weak spot, his big braying throat that couldn't stop proclaiming his power.

I had to get a grip and work out a plan. Kappler was cocky. But no matter what he said, no matter how much he despised the Pope, he still had to observe Vatican neutrality. That was their weak spot. As long as we stopped Hugh going over the line, they couldn't touch him.

But I was gambling too that Hugh forewarned was Hugh forearmed. That he would have some plan in place.

Luigi was almost comatose with shock, driving as if in a trance. But as we passed the Forum I said, "That's where the Romans once ruled, Hugh told me," and something seemed to stir inside him. His back straightened a little and he seemed more alert.

I had to try to talk to him. I said, "Listen. You can't trust them. They'll still kill us. If you get the chance you must dash to safety – Hugh and the Church will protect you."

"But my family. My wife is sick. I need money to pay for her doctors. Even if I die the Nazis will give her that," he said. "They said so."

I looked at his rough hands. Worker's hands. And I felt bad for thinking meanly about him. Even though he was betraying us, he was thinking of his wife.

"But why would the Nazis help your wife? If you are dead, they don't need to do anything at all. Once they have Hugh, they won't care about you or your family one little bit. You need to stay alive and you know you can trust Hugh to help anyone in need."

He nodded his big slow head, digesting what I said.

"But the Nazis will stay with me near the cart," he said.

"If there's a chance, I'll try to distract them and you can make a run for it. We can get you into the Vatican and Hugh will get someone to pick up your family and bring them somewhere safe. Have you really ever seen anything that makes you trust the Nazis? Look what they did to the Jews in the ghetto!"

We came to a roadblock. It gave Luigi a moment to think as his large hands fumbled with the reins.

A German officer on a motorbike rode up and waved some papers at the soldiers manning the roadblock. They clicked their heels to attention and let us through. But not before the officer had shouted at me and hit me lightly over the head with a rifle butt. I guessed he meant I wasn't to talk to Luigi.

It was a bright clear day. *Giornata de B17,* the Italians called it – a good day for American planes to bomb,. And at that moment a buzz of planes flew low overhead. Their black shapes streaked across the sky. I almost wished they'd strafed us there and then. Reduced this place to rubble and even more ruins and swallow us all up whole. Almost. They would hit the wrong targets and all the children would be hurt for nothing. Just like at Monte Casino where in February a host of Allied bombers had flattened the monastery. No Germans killed. Only about 230 refugees who'd fled there. War was a mess.

We skirted the Trevi Fountain with its aquamarine water fed by an aqueduct and its fussy statues. Rococo, Hugh told me. I remembered the name! It reminded me of the cocoa that Mama made us before it got scarce.

We went up the wide expanse of Corso Vittorio Emanuele and crossed the Tiber at the bridge. Named after the first king of Italy. He had gone too. They all went eventually, the tyrants and the kings. But so did we, the little people caught up in their grand schemes.

And then we were in the bustle in front of Saint Peter's Square. We pulled the horse and cart up on the street close to the colonnade on our left-hand side. We were outside the line in Italian territory.

That white line stretching from one colonnade to the other right across the entrance to the square separated the Pope's territory from Rome's normal streets and meant nothing to most people. For Hugh it was life or death.

313

Luigi and I got out of the cart and waited. In my hand was a walking stick that had been in the cart – Luigi's, I supposed.

Nearby was Kappler's car, parked behind the colonnade on the other side.

Kappler had timed it deliberately to coincide with people coming out of midday Mass. It made it easier for the disguised SS officers to mingle among the Mass-goers. If I failed to lure him over the line, or Hugh smelled a rat as he got up close, they would be ready to surround him and hustle him over.

People milled around the square – there were even German soldiers on holiday taking photographs – there among the nuns hurrying from Mass, the holy old ladies clutching their prayer books, the out-of-towners with their mouths open like flies, gazing at the most historic site in Christendom.

Kappler was tense. I could see it through the windscreen, even at a distance. Too used to wielding brute force. That was his weak spot.

And then across the expanse of square on the Vatican side of the line, there was Hugh on the steps. Tall, commanding, his black soutane sweeping down to the ground, the still spot in the buzzing square that wasn't a square. It was as if a cord between us grew taut. I sensed that he knew we had arrived.

Flicking at the corner of my eye, I noticed more than the usual number of Swiss Guards patrolling in their plainer blue uniforms, their guns on their shoulders.

The panic was threatening to jump out of the box in my head. But I clamped it down. Nailed it down tight.

I left Luigi at the cart, knowing SS men had him in their sights and I set out to cross the square. The plainclothes officers in their trench coats were already across the line, pretending to be tourists as the Mass-goers streamed by. My legs felt like lead walking across the expanse of the square. I was sure Hugh had clocked me but he stood looking at his breviary, waiting for me. But was it my imagination or was that John May hovering by the guardroom close to the steps?

I glanced back. Kappler's car behind the colonnade had moved forward. It was more visible than he must have realised.

As I neared the steps, I beckoned to Hugh to come, as I'd been briefed to do by Kappler. He walked boldly across the square with that big stride of his. As devil-may-care as if out walking the country boreens in Kerry.

We were quite close to each other now and I could see the smile playing on his lips, the glasses hovering in front of his eyes. He held out his arms as if to greet me. But I realised he was delaying as he neared me and that the Swiss Guards in their plainer outfits were close by. I thought I saw a couple move through the colonnades but I couldn't be sure. Hugh glanced across the square to where Luigi waited with the cart. I suddenly realised that Hugh had a plan up his sleeve. It was Luigi and I who were going to be grabbed and hustled inside the safety of Saint Peter's.

He embraced me when he reached me and whispered, "Don't worry".

I caught him by the sleeve and pretended to be coaxing him towards the exit, gesturing towards the cart, acting out my part, meanwhile telling him he needed to come with me but hoping he could read the truth in my eyes. I was afraid some lurking plainclothes might be able to hear what I was saying.

Hugh nodded and said, "I understand" and we walked back through the square in silence, heading for Luigi who was standing beside his cart, tending to his horse.

We drew closer, just a few feet from the line. Plainclothes SS officers were hovering nearby, pretending to take a photograph. In a few steps, we would be across the line and Kappler would have his prize.

But as we neared, it was Luigi who gave us a surprise.

"Father, forgive me!" he shouted and dashed between the SS officers and Hugh.

His large bulk took flight along the side of the colonnade. Two other SS officers in plainclothes by the pillars, who I hadn't noticed before, took after him. It was hard to believe he could run so fast. But he was running for his life. Before they could catch him, I saw in the distance Swiss Guards grab hold of him and hustle him away. Two more Guards, their guns bristling, stood in front of the SS officers to stop them from following.

Frustrated, the other two SS men lurched at Hugh and tried to rugby-tackle him across the line. But Hugh stood firm, strong as an ox. Three more Swiss Guards followed by John May flew across the square. But then more Nazi uniformed officers appeared out of nowhere and came to help their comrades in the scrum.

Four of them were dragging Hugh now as if he was a bull being dragged into a pen. But he became a dead weight.

"*Setanta!*" he roared.

I awoke from my stupor.

I launched myself at them, kicking the back of their knees, jabbing them with the stick I'd found on the cart. It worked! Two of them let go of Hugh to swipe at me.

To my huge surprise, a group of the German nuns from the Teutonic college rushed over and surrounded the hustling group. They were led by Sister Boniface, determined and energised, like I'd never seen her. As if a flame burned within. "*Heilige Mutter Gottes, rette und beschütze uns!*" she shouted in German. Holy Mother of God, save and protect us!

"*Im Namen des Vaters und des Sohnes und des Heiligen Geistes. Amen!*" chorused the other nuns. In the Name of the Father, the Son and the Holy Spirit. Amen!

This had a strange effect on the officers. They dropped Hugh, who immediately was grabbed by John May and a group of Swiss Guards who pulled him back towards Saint Peter's.

I looked across to the white line. Kappler was standing there cursing, throwing his black gloves down in frustration. I grinned to myself.

But my delight was short-lived. Priebke, in plain clothes, was somehow alongside me and had grabbed me by the ear. His hands tightened their grip. He didn't seem to care that he was defying the neutrality of the Vatican. I was just a boy after all. I resisted and pulled against him but I couldn't free myself. I knew that in less than a minute, I would be pulled across the line and bundled into their black car to sleep with the fishes in the Tiber.

But then a strange thing happened. Priebke recoiled as if blinded. He pushed me and I lay sprawled on the cobblestones. I looked up. A window had been flung open on the third floor of the Apostolic Palace to the right of Saint Peter's. It had bounced the midday sun straight into his eyes. There, in gleaming white, stood the Pope. He seemed to look down on us for what felt like an eternity. Priebke was frozen. A sound went up around the square.

"*Il Papa! Il Papa!*"

People fell to their knees, praying. The sound of prayer rose up to heaven.

Priebke scuttled off and disappeared.

A pair of strong arms pulled me up. It was John May.

"Blimey O'Reilly! That was close. I reckon Hugh O'Flaherty has more than nine loives!"

He led me back to St. Peter's.

Inside the church, all was quiet and hushed. I gave thanks that we had lived to fight another day.

Hugh was seated at a pew. "You hit the Hound of Culann straight in the mouth there," he said, pleased as punch. "And Luigi is right inside the Vatican walls. No more black-market deliveries for him."

"His wife and family?" I asked.

"Our local Salesian Fathers are arranging for them to be spirited away," he said. "As soon as you said his name, we acted. It was only a matter of time before they rumbled poor Luigi."

"He told them all he knew," I said.

He bowed his head. "It's understandable. None of us know if we would have the strength to last out. But he doesn't know much of anything anyway."

"But I said nothing. They think I'm a moron."

He laughed. "After the war you might be able to go on the stage." But then he looked at my battered face. "You're a brave lad. And a smart one. We live to fight another day. You are truly Cú Chulainn now."

"More like Cú Hugh," I said. "How did you stop them dragging you across the line?"

"'Twas no worse than what I used to face on the Gaelic football pitches every Saturday back in Killarney." He stood up immediately, laughing lightly. "Come on. We have work to do to move all our guests before they round up the lot of us!"

Chapter 35

I was now lodged within the walls of the Vatican with Major Derry, cut off from all that was going on in the Roman streets. Hugh also spent more and more time within the Vatican. Kappler had put a fulltime guard on the German College, so no escapees could be lodged there. But once in a while, Hugh defiantly went in and out, daring them to grab him.

The Rome Escape Line had acted fast. Mrs M was sent off to a farm outside the city. All of the apartments were shut down. But five of the Italian helpers were rounded up and some of our prisoners of war arrested.

And all everyone asked was "When will the Americans come? Where are the Allies?"

They were close but bogged down in the marshes and malarial swamps of Anzio, dying in their thousands, contained by the German forces. The Nazis were even boasting of "pushing the enemy back into the sea".

Ruby and Ethan were somewhere in another convent in the countryside. I ached to see her. And I ached for my mother to be safe.

We were stuck in limbo, in a half-life. I continued to sneak outside the Vatican, just to mooch around the Regina Coeli prison. I didn't dare sing anymore.

But Hugh caught me getting over the back wall.

"Boy, we'll figure out a way to get your mother out of there. God will find a way. But he moves in mysterious ways."

But I didn't believe in waiting for God. His ways were way too mysterious for me.

On one of my sneaky forays outside, I left a message for Roberto with Gianni at the café near the Jewish quarter. I said I would wait at the Vatican wall on the 22nd March near the gardens where no one would pass by. I would scale it if he came on Sunday at dawn. I reckoned no one would pay much attention then as they would all be at prayer. And the Swiss Guards took half an hour to patrol. We would have a few minutes.

That Sunday, I waited until the Palatine Guard unit had passed. On my way to the wall, I swung by the Vatican bakery. The baker had left a tray of rolls out to cool. So I swiped five of them, mussing up the other ones. He'd notice, but I was hoping he wouldn't care.

In the distance was the low rumble of heavy artillery,

perhaps twenty miles away. The Allies were getting closer. But not quickly enough.

To my great delight, when I scaled the wall, I looked over the other side to see a red cap ascending. Soon Roberto was sitting beside me. He looked older, leaner. But the same Roberto still gleamed from within when his face cracked a smile.

"Comrade!" he exclaimed, thumping me on the back. He held up his feet on which were gleaming jackboots. "Thanks to you all of us have the best shoes of any partisans in Italy."

"But they were Primo's boots," I said. "You had the brogues."

He looked down. "Primo is dead," he said sadly. "Killed in a bobjack attack. I walk in his shoes now. That is why we are now renamed the Primo Unit in his honour. We won't rest now until every German is gone from Italian soil. *Long live Italy!*"

I felt sad too, thinking of the kind bookish boy who had turned into a fighter, who would never be a professor now.

"But the good news is the Nazis are our best recruiters. We now have ten more resistance fighters, including four army deserters, a shepherd and a former soldier. And a couple of girls too who try to make Gigi comb her hair. The tide is turning," he told me. "They will be gone by the summer."

"We hear the guns getting closer," I said. "But they are bogged down. The Germans are giving the Allies a hard time of it. It's a real scrap."

"The Allies need to recruit some brave stubborn donkeys like Asinello, who keep trudging up the hill no matter what!" Roberto laughed, and I was glad Asinello was a proud partisan, playing his part in the resistance.

I reminded him about my mother in the prison and asked again if he would help me release her.

But he just smiled sadly. "It's too dangerous for us. We are too conspicuous, and we don't know the city well enough."

"Can you get me a gun?" I asked.

But he just laughed. "What about your hunchback friend?'

I told him how I was confined to the Vatican, among the priests and nuns. And the many Jews who had been given refuge.

To my own shame, I felt my bottom lip tremble. I started to cough to hide the tears spilling from my eyes. Roberto touched me lightly on the arm.

"As I told you before, you get her out of the city and we will escort her anywhere she needs to go. That's a promise to our 'quartermaster'. We are still at the hut, you know where. Get a message to Gianni. He will arrange an escort to us. It's so well hidden no one not in the know will ever find us."

I reminded him about Ada Gobetti, who might be able to arrange safe passage.

He whistled. "Since you told me about her I have learned what a legend she is! Runs the whole Turin operation, I've heard. Italian women are the best!"

I looked at my watch. We had just a few minutes before the Palatine guard reversed their circuit.

Roberto threw his arms around me in a rough embrace. "Look after yourself, little brother," he said. His voice was thick like he was choking back emotion.

I gave him the loaves from the Vatican bakery, still moist and marked with a cross.

"I'm sure these will agree with Gigi's stomach."

Roberto's eyes lit up. "Wonderful!" he said.

Then he bent in close and spoke urgently. "Tomorrow is the 23rd March, isn't it? It's the anniversary of Fascism in Italy, so they want to make a bit of a show. Stay away from the Via Rasella. I heard something might be going down. We had to deliver gelignite to someone. Now I'm off to paint the town red!"

He took something wrapped in brown paper and secured with rough twine out of his jacket and laid it on the top of the wall. He tapped it and said, "A little present."

Roberto then dropped out of sight. The Palatine Guard was nearly upon us. He had dropped the whole 15 feet and landed like a cat on all fours. For one heart-stopping moment I thought he'd hurt himself but then he sprang back upright and doffed his red cap to me, before running off, showing me the soles of his jackboots. He was carrying something else as well as the bread. It looked like a paintbrush and a tin of paint. Probably so he could pretend to be a painter.

I grabbed the packet and quickly found the toeholds and shimmied down the wall, making my way back by darting from bush to bush. I was curious about the packet and wondered if it was bobjacks.

As I flitted behind a group of trimmed trees and hid, I saw the Pope pass by, shimmering like a ghost in white, his Guards a respectful ten paces behind him luckily for me. He was at prayer, his eyes cast down. He looked even thinner than before as if he was vanishing.

As soon as they passed, I crouched down and peeked inside the packet, unable to contain my curiosity any further. Inside the paper, wrapped in some sacking was something cold and gleaming.

A gun!

I picked it up and held it briefly in my hand, in shock, feeling like I was committing a sin holding it in this holy place. Then I imagined holding it to the temple of my mortal enemy, Kappler.

"Die," I mumbled. "You miserable cur!"

I felt strong and powerful.

The sound of footsteps crunching on gravel gave me a start. It was two of the Palatine Guards making their rounds.

I was too nervous to carry the gun, so I resolved to bury it. There were lots of piles of soil and rubble in the Vatican garden. I knew where they came from – the secret excavations of the bones of Saint Peter.

I went near the overgrown thicket by the far wall and

found a big pile of rubble beside a thorn bush. I decided to bury the gun in the roots of the bush and cover it with debris. I was in luck. The gardener had left his spade. I was used to digging in the Vatican thanks to my spy-work burying records. I looked around to search for landmarks. I was in a direct line to the rose garden. I would find it easily again.

I left it safely buried and walked off. But, as I went my elation began to dim. It was what I wanted, to have a gun, to feel stronger. But it began to weigh on my conscience like a stone.

That evening, Hugh had some news for me. He wanted me to take a message to the Salesian Fathers out near the Ardeatine Caves on the Via Appia, just outside the city. The prisoners of war were still making their way to him but, with all the restriction inside Rome and the Vatican, it was safer to keep them in the countryside. He wanted Father Dominic, one of his helpers, to set up a few safe places. I was the safest courier to hand. Delia's chauffeur Franco would take me in the morning.

The next day was another B-17 day, cold but clear like crystal, a perfect day for bombs to fall from the sky. But frustrating because it was the anniversary of Mussolini establishing Fascism and there were "celebrations" all over the city organised by the Blackshirts and their Nazi friends. Several streets were blocked off.

I told Franco to avoid Via Rasella and he assured me that

he would pass nearby but would avoid it.

He shrugged his shoulders. "Partisans are always warning of this and that. But they don't stand a chance of getting so deep into the heart of Rome."

We crossed the Vittorio Emanuele Bridge and even we in the diplomatic car were waved away from Corso Emanuele. Franco had no choice but to take a roundabout route. He groaned. It was going to take three times longer than usual to get through the city.

It was around two o'clock and as we rounded a street not far from Via Rasella there was an almighty *BOOM!* So loud I was thrown back in my seat as if I'd been pushed or punched. People stuck their heads out of top-floor windows, women and men ran into the street.

Traffic came to a halt and Franco and I got out of the car.

"It came from Via Rasella," a woman said. "The column of soldiers going back to the barracks. They've been blown sky high!"

For a few minutes rumours flew up and down the street like scampering rats from a burning building. The Resistance had attacked. Bombs had been thrown. The Americans had finally arrived. Then people got frightened and scurried back indoors.

Franco saw a post-office worker that he knew. The man was breathless, his face scared and haunted. Franco took out a flask from the compartment in the dashboard and the man took a drink.

"It was carnage!" he said. "The Resistance bombed the

column of Nazi recruits going back from training. At least thirty are killed. High-ranking Nazis are stumbling about screaming for vengeance. I fled. They wanted to shoot everyone in the street. Then someone said there are going to be reprisals. Get as far away from here as you can!"

"Any Italians killed?" Franco asked.

The postman nodded his head. "I heard there was a couple. A thirteen-year-old boy and a middle-aged man. But the streets were deserted. It was siesta time. There was an explosion of dynamite that was hidden in a rubbish cart. Children followed the marchers but two of the partisans disguised as road cleaners chased them off by kicking away their football. Then *boom*! It was raining glass. It blew a big hole in a stone wall and a crater in the ground. The Germans shot frantically at the windows. But it was only a handful of partisans."

"And the partisans? Have they been captured?" I asked, worrying that Roberto might be caught up in it.

"They all got away," the postman shook his head. "I don't know how. But they will be hunted down like dogs." He coughed. "I saw them stacking the German dead in a row, fifty feet long. The street was full of groans and cries. A general was running around drunk shouting *'Rache!'* *Revenge!* like a stricken beast. They dragged people kicking and screaming from their houses. They lined up about two hundred at the Barberini Palace gates. They have all been arrested."

Franco leapt into the car and I followed. I thought of the

recruits I'd seen in the street, the Bozen police regiment in their rotten green uniforms singing *"Hupf, Mein Mädel!"*, their stupid song. *"Skip, my Lass!"* These Bozen were from South Tyrol. They even used to be Italians until Hitler took them over. Farmers mostly, older and younger than the average recruits now that Hitler was running out of troops. They were made to sing by their commander while marching, chests out, crowing like roosters. An innocent, cheerful little song poisoning the air when sung in time to marching jackboots. Singing other songs too. Happy tunes but not when sung by men with guns. Men forced to serve Hitler. They would sing it no more.

Now a mother or a wife somewhere in a mountain village would be getting a dreaded telegram, the postman huffing and puffing up the snowy driveway. And again that vision of my father suspended between heaven and earth hovered in my mind's eye. At least they would know either way.

Franco grasped the steering wheel, grim-faced. "Reprisals," he said. "It is only a question now of how much blood will flow."

An icy hand gripped my heart.

"Will they kill their prisoners?" I asked. Their faces in the Via Tasso crowded into my mind. Don Pietro. Stame the opera singer. Montezemolo the battered colonel.

My mother.

Franco shrugged. "We won't know until it happens. But there will be carnage in our 'open city'." He almost hurled the words.

As we passed by the Vittorio Emanuele II statue in all its stupid pomp and glory there was a big slogan daubed in red paint: "*Death to the Nazis! Death to the Fascists!*" Roberto, I thought. Painting the town red.

And the bomb – how did I feel about it? An act of violence in a violent city. It seemed as if the light had gone out of the city even when the sun shone. The SS and the Gestapo in their uniforms and the Fascist lackeys licking their boots, outdoing them in evil. There was a greyness, a sadness you could see in the very air. A Rome where you saw sad, gaunt people on the run. One half hiding the other half. And then a bomb blowing a hole and the invading army to pieces. I thought of the Jews herded off like cattle, the men swept away in round-ups, the children run over in the street by speeding German trucks. The Nazis didn't need a partisan bomb going off as an excuse to kill us in the "open city". They were already slaughtering us when they pleased. They did not need provoking. The guerrilla war had been going on for some time. The Nazis didn't want people to know they weren't as strong as they thought.

But they were people too, with mothers and sisters, children and pet dogs. Those young boys not much older than me in the back of the truck singing "*In die Heimat, in die Heimat, es wird besser gehen!*" – at home all will be better. Blown to pieces. They would never go home again.

Could I do it? I could throw a bobjack or help someone who planted a bomb. But could I pull a trigger? I didn't know. I was glad I was too young to find out if I was a coward or a killer. Maybe it was one thing to just kill your enemy or only kill the ones who were torturers and murderers. Another to just kill civilians because you could. Were the partisans different from their enemies? Yes, I thought. They didn't just kill innocent civilians. They were trying to push the Germans *out*. The Nazis on the other hand killed anyone who got in their way.

But you have a gun, Leo, a little voice, said. *What will you do with it?*

And yet my father dropped bombs that fell on small children, cows and pigs in the French countryside, as well as German ships and troops. My mother hid partisans and smuggled messages. Hugh would have nothing to do with guns but he'd do everything else in his power to save lives. All these questions boiled in my mind. But one fact was true. The Nazis weren't invited here. They weren't just fighting soldiers. All of us were the enemy. They would kill me, Leo the Unlucky, for being in their way or for just being half-Jewish.

Chapter 36

We finally reached the Via Appia in the south of the city. The original colossal cobblestones, rutted and chipped by time, still paved the way and it was like we'd travelled two thousand years into the past. Along the margins, villas peeped from behind hedgerows and burnt fields lay open to the sky. Aside from the occasional plane passing overhead, it felt like we were back in ancient Rome.

But the shadow of the war fell here as well. There were Nazi posters nailed onto trees, a swastika flag flew outside one of the villas where a sentry was posted. Must have been a headquarters.

At a crossroads just past the Catacombs of San Callisto, a sign pointed the way to the Ardeatine Caves. We followed a country lane sunk deep in birdsong and drew up at a wrought-iron gate in a high stone wall. Through the gate, beyond a lawn hemmed with flowerbeds, rose the high stone buttery-yellow building of the Salesian religious community, shrouded in silence.

We rang the bell and immediately a priest opened the gates. They had been expecting us. The building was deathly silent. I was curious to see these Ardeatine caves nearby where the lava cement came from, the stuff they mined to build Rome. But Franco said when he dropped me off that it was only a disused quarry – holes in the ground and a mound over the main cave entrance. I shouldn't go inside because they were dangerous. He told me the fathers here gave tours of the catacombs. But I didn't want to see any more old underground tombs. They also hid people there, I knew – partisans and Jews.

The priests and students didn't mind me. I wandered around and then when no one was looking, I scaled the wall so I could mooch around outside and have a look at the caves. It was mid-afternoon after three thirty. The dark mound of the cave entrance, beneath a grassy hillock, rose ahead of me. Franco was right. It wasn't much to write home about.

The clouds were heavy in the sky, there was an ominous feeling in the air. I felt suddenly frightened for no reason.

I saw an old lady gathering grass. But then I realised there was a German sentry outside the cave. He fired a warning shot. The woman fell and didn't move again.

I crouched in the grass.

"Come here, boy!" a shepherd called me urgently to a

copse of trees and low bushes.

I crawled towards him. He pulled me down behind the bushes. Peeping through the branches, I watched Nazi trucks pull up and turn around, then reverse into the mouth of the cave. Nazi soldiers got out of the trucks and formed a cordon and then some of the soldiers went up to patrol the grassy area above the cave. There was lots of shouting. I had a sick feeling and stopped looking. But I could hear more trucks pulling up. Loud shouting in German.

But all was silent in the countryside. And then muffled noises like far-off barking dogs. I followed the lead of the shepherd and crawled on my belly back in the direction of the Salesian Fathers' house.

I told the chief priest about the woman being shot and the activity at the cave. I shuddered, feeling ill. That trembling feeling I had at the Jewish ghetto when they came for everyone. He sent someone off to the cave to find out. I was sent to bed shivering and stayed there all of the next day.

Terrible nightmares made me toss and turn: of the mouth of a cave that was really the jaws of a snarling beast, the werewolf that Ruby talked of. It had flaming eyes and chomped on whole lorryloads and trucks of people, tossing off bones from its mouth. And then boiling lava issued from the jaws, scorching and burning the whole land. The werewolf got mixed up with the Nachzehrer the terrifying creature of Ethan's stories, chewing the bones of dead people. That could only be killed by putting a coin in its mouth and cutting off its head.

And then sometime in the night – explosions. Bombs going off. Far away. But my bed was a flaming coffin and I was lost in the abyss of my bad dreams about the mouth of that cave.

The next morning there was a newspaper on the refectory table. I thumbed through it, still feeling shaky but glad to be out of bed.

A priest looked at me with a shocked face. "Something terrible has happened in Rome," he said. He read out the notice on the front page of the Vatican newspaper. He was Dutch with excellent English and he summarised it for me.

"During the afternoon of March 23, 1944 criminal elements threw bombs at a German police column on Via Rasella . . . The German Command has given orders that for every German killed, ten enemies and criminals will be shot. The order has already been carried out."

The words sent a chill down my spine.

"They have already killed ten Italians for every German who died?" I asked.

The priest nodded his head.

I was feeling thick-headed. Slow. I couldn't take it all in, what I had nearly seen or not seen.

"Reprisals," the priest said. "They have killed over three hundred men."

A raging fire of anger gripped me.

The order has been carried out. Orders. Orders. The

Order has been carried out. Just following Orders. How I hate that word ORDERS! Write it small. Write it big. Whisper it or shout it. Following bad ORDERS is still a CRIME! The truth was Kappler wanted to do this. He was a demon, an agent of Satan, dripping in blood.

The next day, a dreadful smell wafted in on the breeze. A few of the priests went to look at the cave. These priests who gave guided tours and sold holy pictures and knickknacks. They came back in shock, their faces the colour of ashes. They had crept into the cave carrying candles. Inside were bodies heaped upon bodies. A massacre, the priests wept. A massacre! They sent word to the Vatican.

Then the Nazis came and dumped rubbish at the mouth of the caves to hide the smell. Soon after engineers came and blew up the mouth of the tunnel, sealing it into a tomb. Now it was a catacomb haunted by new ghosts.

I was desperate to get back to the Vatican, away from these killing fields of death. I wandered around the house like a ghost myself until one of the priests asked me kindly to help in the garden. I was glad to plunge my hands into the soil, planting vegetables. Digging up weeds. The priest gave me almonds and early plums from the garden. The juice ran down my face. The sun shone, the plums tasted sweet as life. The Nazis killed but we still breathed and ate.

Franco arrived two days later and I could tell by his grim

face that he knew about the massacre.

I left with him after a hurried goodbye to some of the priests.

"All over Rome people are looking for their loved ones who have been taken from the prisons. The streets are strange and silent." Franco gripped the wheel as he steered around a sharp bend. "Men from all walks of life are missing. From Colonel Montezemolo to a fifteen-year-old boy. Jews, southerners even some foreigners."

I shuddered. "No women?"

"No," he said. "Not so far."

I was desperate now to know if my mother was all right. So immediately we got back I jumped straight out of the car in a hurry to enter the German College to find Hugh. There was now a Nazi guard outside, but when he saw the diplomatic car and I waved my choirboy pass, he let me through.

Hugh was teeing up a golf ball, lost in thought. I knew by the look of him he was aware of the grim news.

He looked up and smiled then came to embrace me. "Before you ask – your mother is safe," he said. "The confessor to the prisoners at the Regina Coeli checked for me."

He told me what he knew. The confessor priest visiting the prison heard stories from the prisoners of other cellmates spirited away. One group of ten were even about to be released. But Kappler wanted to make up the numbers, ten men for every 33 of the German soldiers killed.

Hugh had pieced all the news together from his high-level sources. Hitler, disturbed in his Wolf's Lair, angry as a mad beast, ordered a massacre. The Germans in Rome, knowing they didn't have the resources to carry it out, bartered and struck a bargain. A deal. Not fifty but ten Italians for every one German killed. So 330. Hitler ordered that it had to take place within 24 hours – a policy of "night and fog". Confuse and surprise the enemy.

Kappler said he would only kill those who were due to be executed. But he didn't have enough. So they pulled the men at random from prisons and Via Tasso. They had to get the numbers right, exact their revenge ten times over, as if being organised and precise about it made it better.

Then all night Keppler and his dogs scurrying about drawing up lists. Turning themselves into gods. So they came for the Jews. They came for anyone they had. Old men and teenagers, partisans and priests.

There was no time to execute them in the normal way, tied to a chair or up against a wall with a firing squad. No. They had to find a killing chamber. The cave was ideal for their vile purpose. It could also become a burial chamber. They would cover up their crime.

Several nights in a row, Hugh got down and said the rosary – a decade for every soul. And wept. Five of our helpers were missing. Five brave souls. It was one of the few times I ever saw Hugh cry.

"You know, the Bozen regiment who were attacked refused to carry out the massacres at the caves. I take comfort from this. We must remember only our humanity," Hugh said. "There is good in us all."

But I was angry. Kappler had supervised the massacre. There were rumours he'd even carried out many of the executions himself.

"*They are evil!*" I shouted. "You don't mean to say you would help Kappler? I want to kill him!"

"They must be brought to justice but I hope I would have the strength from God to not do him harm," said Hugh. "God has no country. No boundaries or flags. We help all who suffer."

I shook my head. One thing I knew, I would never be a priest.

For the next few weeks rumours swirled as if Ruby's creatures of the whirlwind were carrying them around the land. Spring had come, poppies were in the hedgerows now and even trees blasted by bombs were trying to bud and flower. But for many families all over Italy grief had struck their homes. I wondered if Kappler had deliberately chosen his victims to make every village in Italy suffer.

I was desperate for news of Don Pietro. Franco drove out to Maria Teresa but she was frantic. A letter had arrived, a few weeks after the massacre – in German. She had it translated. Don Pietro had died at the Ardeatine caves. I was heartbroken.

But it seemed something went wrong too. Italian patriots tried to reckon the dead. And there were 335 men unaccounted for. Five extra. The Nazis weren't as organised as they thought.

I got word from Gobbo through Franco and I was overjoyed. There was going to be an attack on Regina Coeli. They would free my mother and smuggle her out.

But then disaster struck. Gobbo was on the run, rumoured to be dead or gone into hiding with his gang after he was accused of leading an attack that killed three German soldiers. In revenge Kappler rounded up half the men and boys in Quadraro, another partisan suburb where Gobbo also operated. A thousand souls sent to hell in workcamps.

And then more grim news. The lack of bread and food was at near-starvation levels in some quarters.

Mother Mary Saint Luke from the Vatican Information Bureau rang Hugh at the German College, warning him Rome was a powder keg.

On April 6th in front of a bakery in Tiburtino, a poor suburb, a guard killed a mother desperate for bread. The next day an inscription appeared on the sidewalk, dictated by a partisan poet:

Here the fascists murdered,
Caterina Martinella
A mother who could not stand
To hear the hungry cry
All together, of her seven children.

The next day in Ostiense, fascists and Nazis executed in cold blood ten women who stormed the flour mill that supplied the German army. The Nazis threw the mothers' bodies in the Tiber.

This killing of mothers was too much to bear. I waited for Hugh after Mass at 6 am in the sacristy of the German church.

"If nobody will help me rescue my mother, I will do it myself or die in the attempt," I said. "I'll go on the Vatican bicycle and throw a bomb at them." I knew even as I said it that it would be a futile gesture. But I wanted Hugh to know I was serious.

Hugh looked me in the eye and nodded. "I'll see what I can do. I'll see if Delia can help out."

Chapter 37

The brown wool material was very scratchy and the wimple made my head feel like it was in a vice but I did my best to look holy and keep my head bent beneath the veil, as we were waved in by the guards to Regina Coeli prison. We were once more carrying supplies in the drab brown habits of our German nuns. Hugh had insisted on accompanying me, even though I asked for Father Spike or one of the other priests. But he claimed that he was the last person they would be expecting, so we were safe. I had grown used to trusting Hugh, so I didn't question it.

On our way through the exercise yard, I did a double take. To my immense surprise I saw Joseph, Don Pietro's cellmate. He was pale and haunted-looking but also stood tall as he could. I tugged at Hugh's arm.

"That man! He was at Via Tasso with Don Pietro, in the

same cell – maybe he knows what happened to him."

Hugh spoke briefly with the guard, saying in his German-accented Italian that he knew the man, at the same time passing him a packet of Camel cigarettes and a box of matches. His eyes nearly fell out of his head. He went into a corner to smoke and we were granted a brief audience.

We gave Joseph some cigarettes too and he lit one up immediately. His eyes burned when he told me. "I was tied to the hand of the good father Don Pietro. He had bad dreams the night before, tossing and turning. He spent the morning in prayer and fasting. Then the dreaded words as the guards came for us: *Los, Los! Raus! Raus! Schnell! Schnell!* – Move it. Out! Quick! Don Pietro said 'Courage!' to me and blessed and embraced me."

He paused to take a drag on his cigarette, his hand shaking with the memory.

"We were crammed into the trucks, the ones they use to transport fresh meat. We could smell the remains of rotting flesh. 'Soon you will all be dung!' a guard jeered at us. But Don Pietro blessed him and laughed good-naturedly like the saint he is. Was." Joseph gulped and his voice broke into a sob. "When we got off the truck there was much confusion. We milled around, milling around in our fetters. Don Pietro began to pray and bless everyone. There was Simoni the old general. Colonel Montezemolo, battered from interrogation. Young and old partisans. Stame the opera singer. But others too, just picked up in round-ups. The best of men." He paused, staring into space for a moment. But went on with his story, his voice cracking with emotion.

"And the very best of all – Don Pietro, praying and blessing us in his strong voice. 'Addio!' he said to me. A final farewell. Then with superhuman strength he raised his arms and broke the rope. I was no longer attached. As everyone was drawn to him, holy magnet that he was, I made my escape onto a little grassy area above the cave. Then I broke through a gap in the cordon of guards around the cave. They were anxious, disorganised . . ." He paused again, his eyes staring into space as if he could see it all projected there. "I scaled a wall into a field. Then a guard caught me. I still had the rope around my hand."

I gasped, but Joseph held up his hand. I touched it. The last place touched by Don Pietro.

"The guard was from my old unit in Anzio, a fellow Austrian. It was a miracle. He knew me as the doctor and interpreter who had deserted. He grabbed me and put me on a truck making its way back to Via Tasso. I was beaten and starved. But I am still alive! They turned that labyrinth of caves into a human abattoir!"

I wept. But Hugh bid me dry my tears so we could continue the plan to rescue my mother.

"We must try to get you out," said Hugh to Joseph.

But Joseph shook his head. "It is safer for me here. Soon the Americans will come and if I am in prison they will know I was an enemy of the Nazis. If I get picked up outside I might be mistaken for one of them." He almost

344

sobbed the last word.

I embraced him. And he laughed to see a boy in a nun's habit.

"Promise me, Leo, you will live too. So you can tell all the stories."

I nodded my head.

"They can kill as much as they like, but they cannot kill the good in people," Joseph said simply. "I will survive and someday bear witness to all that happened. Until then, I will remain here, silent."

The guard came to take him back. I passed Joseph a bun, the only thing I had as a gift.

A friendly prison guard came to give us a message. Franco had arrived in Delia's car.

It was time for our plan. I bade Joseph goodbye, thankful that he had survived. Hopeful that someday he would tell the world what had happened. Grateful too, that circumstance had led me away from Via Tasso, the den of evil. Who knows, if I'd still been there, I might too have been slaughtered at the caves.

We went back into the medical wing. The plan was that my mother had finally succumbed to "Syndrome K". Word had been sent through the chaplain to the doctor. We were to don medical paper masks over our mouths and accompany her to Tiber Island for quarantine. Franco had already arranged a bribe for the Fascist guards not to pay too much attention when we left the prison. But in the car, my mother and I would change places. She would wear the habit and take on the identity of a nun. We had interceded with the prison governor. Also bribed the warders. All we had to do was get her out past the checkpoints.

My mother was laid out in the side room, already covered in a hessian sack. She had been given some injection to make it look like she was gravely ill.

My heart nearly stopped when I rolled back the sack to check it was she. She looked serene, cold as marble, not breathing at all. Hugh told me the doctor had given her something that slowed her breathing. Once safe they would administer another injection of adrenaline to start her heart going faster again.

The female prison warder who wanted Lucky Strikes was overjoyed with her two packets. She left us alone while we made our preparations. I'd asked her to tell the doctor to give my mother's "special" cake to someone else.

But the other friendly prison warder came back to tell us that there was a problem. The car had been forced to drive on and would have to come back. We would have to wait. Hugh took out a vial and broke it. The stench was overwhelming. Sulphur, so no one would question her rotting illness.

After half an hour of agony, sitting in the stench, the car arrived. We carried the stretcher through the prison, almost gagging from the nauseating odour.

But outside we were in for a shock. The Fascist guards Franco had bribed had been replaced by Nazis who insisted on examining our passes and my mother on the stretcher.

They peered into my face. One of them, an officer, spoke to me in German, a fat little man with a double chin and piggy eyes. Panic must have flashed through my eyes because he butted me roughly with his rifle. I couldn't understand his words, but he seemed to be asking me to pull down my mask.

But Hugh stood between us and spoke to him in German.

As his soldiers moved to examine my mother in the sacking, Hugh waved a certificate at them signed by the doctor.

"*Achtung!*" he shouted. "*Syndrom K!*"

They shrank back then, gagging at the stench of sulphur. The officer, recoiling from us, waved the certificate away.

"*Schnell!*" shouted the piggy-eyed officer.

We continued and reached the limousine. The back seats had been folded down and it was temporarily turned into an ambulance.

Franco drove off as quickly as he could towards the banks of the Tiber where the island lay.

A boatman awaited us. It was getting late now, the red sun falling towards the water.

Quickly, in the car, I took off the habit as Hugh unwrapped my mummified mother from the sacking.

She was pale as a winter dawn, bloodless like a statue.

Father Spike arrived to give her the injection. We rubbed her hands hoping to revive her.

But she wasn't breathing. Both Hugh and Spike began to pray.

347

"Mama!" I begged. "Please! Come back! For me, for Ruby."

I stroked her beautiful face, curiously unaged now. Mother, don't die, I pleaded inside.

I sang then. Our song from home. "If I Were a Blackbird", of course.

"If I was a blackbird, I'd whistle and sing ..."

Spike took up the song, his pure tenor voice swooping up to heaven. *"And I'd follow the ship that my true love sails in!"*

Franco kept a look-out.

The Tiber flowed on. The sun was setting as my mother lay dying. The clouds turned blood-red. It was beautiful but I sensed a scream passing through nature. It seemed to me that I heard that scream. The sky shrieked.

"Leo!" Hugh was holding me. "Stop screaming!"

I hadn't realised I was doing it for real. I broke into sobs and embraced my mother.

But something extraordinary happened. As my tears fell on her face, her chapped lips parted. Her eyes opened, those startling blue eyes like pieces of the sky.

"Leo," she breathed. "I dreamed I was dead and you woke me with a scream."

She sat bolt upright and smiled.

Hugh gave a little cheer. "You had us worried for a moment there, Eily," he said.

She looked puzzled then laughed. "It's a long time since anyone called me that."

Franco came down from the bridge. "You need to hurry. Patrols will come around soon."

Quickly, Spike gave her a drink and this seemed to give her some energy. We helped her into the habit. I couldn't help noticing that her legs were as thin as a bird's and her once strong arms withered to sticks.

Soon she was dressed, looking much better in the habit that I ever could. She took my face in her hands and kissed me lightly on the brow. Already in the warm air of Rome, the prison pallor was leaving her. As she was leaving me. How many times could my heart break in this damn war!

"Leo, my Lionheart. Soon this war will be over. We will be reunited."

A rush of feeling bubbled up inside me like a mountain spring.

"Look after Ruby for me."

"But what if . . ."

She put her finger to my lips. "Shush, my darling. God has brought us this far. After the war ends we will eat at the gelateria in Rome together. That's a promise."

"With Daddy too?"

She nodded but she didn't speak. She couldn't lie to me but she smiled at some distant memory. "Your daddy loved ice cream. Strawberry-flavoured."

"Can I have two ice creams?" I asked, licking my lips.

She smiled. "You can have ten!" She tenderly stroked my hair that was falling into my eyes, like she'd done since I was a little kid. Then she fumbled inside her pocket and produced a locket and pressed it into my hand. "I should have given you this long ago," she said. "Look under the photograph of your father."

There was a rumble in the distance. A patrol car was approaching.

She embraced me and then, accompanied by Father Spike, got into the boat. The plash of the oars. As the sun sunk on the red water, the dark V of the water's rush, as the boat cut into the Tiber. The boat disappeared under the bridge. The moon rose and the pinpricks of the stars pinned the darkness to the sky.

She was gone.

Back in the German College when all was quiet and Hugh fast asleep, I opened the locket by candlelight. Inside were two photographs, my father and mother looking young and carefree. Carefully with my nail I prised off the photo of my father. Inside was a tiny piece of flimsy tissue paper folded many times. I carefully unfurled it. There was tiny miniscule writing on it – like a fairy's – but I recognised it. My father's writing. Squinting by candlelight I read it.

Dear Leo,

If you are reading this then I am probably already gone. Maybe in some dogfight. Maybe shot down in a sullen sky. But Leo, my love, you must live on. It is not really a sacrifice because I have done it so you and Ruby will be free to live your lives in the sun. Take care of Mama and Ruby – they are the best, you already know that, Leo my beloved son. Live life to the full, my little lionheart.

And chin up, old boy! I know you will make me proud.
Your Dad

That night I dreamed of my father's plane suspended between heaven and earth over the sea. But this time it fell out of the sky and landed with a splash. A breeze ruffled the waves. And all trace of it disappeared.

Chapter 38

May 1944

It was May now, early summer. and everyone had sunk into despair. It felt like the Allies were never going to come to relieve us. We had a new enemy. Hunger. Stalking the street, gnawing at the stomachs of even the fine ladies in their mantillas.

There had been more food riots since the women were killed.

The bread ration was reduced to the weight of a single roll. It was not even bread. Some mixture of chickpeas, mulberry leaves, something powdery from an elm tree, a dash of flour. The first time I tasted it I spat it out.

And imagine this! The Pope tried to feed the poor but the convoys of trucks carrying flour were constantly bombed by the Allies because the Nazis joined the convoys hoping for cover. Sir D'Arcy Osborne tried to speak to the Allies about it. But word came back from Churchill that Rome was just another occupied city. It would have to wait like all the others.

The massacre in the Ardeatine Caves was like an open wound. By striking the capital, they had struck the whole country. By some evil wizardry the dead represented a perfect cross section of the Eternal City. Hugh said many Masses for them. But it was dangerous. In another church a student was hauled off to Via Tasso for shouting out prayers for the Ardeatine dead.

Major Sam and I found out all we could to compile a list of the dead for our records. It was our way of paying tribute, of saying you can't just erase people.

There were twenty-seven members of the armed forces – all patriots, all lionhearts. Montezemolo the aristocratic colonel, who had all his teeth and nails pulled out but still wouldn't speak. General Simoni, aged sixty-four who they tortured with a blowtorch, defiant till the end.

Southerners Northerners, Romans and a Sardinian.

Anarchists who didn't believe in leaders or government.

The Bandiera Rossa – the Red Flag – a workers' partisan group, lost more than sixty members. Like Orfeo Mucci, a man so proud and rebellious he would never doff a cap to a superior, so he just never wore a cap. He died with no man superior to his courage.

Armando Bussi, a republican who had lost his left eye in World War One.

Blacksmiths. Including Enrico Ferola, maker of bobjacks.

Housepainters.

Varnishers.

Carpenters.

Joiners.

Eighty-seven clerks.

Seventy-one merchants. Some pedlars, some big shop-owners.

Paulo Petrucci, a teacher from Trieste, acquitted of charges in a Nazi court. Yet killed like all the others because he had been in the wrong place at the wrong time.

Thirty-nine industrial workers.

Twenty-seven artisans.

Eleven lawyers.

And then Gio, friend of Don Pietro, activist, teacher, communist, political commissar of the GAP. I saw him still in my mind's eye, framed by the doorway, fist raised, saying goodbye.

Rendina, a colonel in the Resistance, who had passed me on the stairs.

Men from Emilia, Tuscany, Piedmont. A farmer, a farm hand, a wine-seller, a chauffeur.

A man from the Ukraine.

And Stame whose golden voice soothed prisoners in Via Tasso every night though his own body was broken.

And seventy-five Jews, ten of them born in Germany. The Jews were less than half of one per cent of the population of Rome, Hugh told me. But fifty per cent of the native Romans killed at the Fosse Ardeatine.

Six members of the Di Consiglio family aged seventeen to seventy-four.

Michele Di Veroli was only fifteen and died with his father. He was only three years older than me.

Imagine all those lives begun in the four corners of Italy and beyond to finish their lives in a dark cave. All the names. A whole alphabet of them. Imagine them trying to bury it under a rubbish dump.

But Ruby told me she had a strange dream. Ruby said their ghosts reached their skeletal hands up through the soil and though their mouths were full of mud, they still cried out for justice. Buried in that quarry from where the material that built Rome was taken. It was like striking into the heart of Italy.

And in Ruby's dream, the artisans, the soldiers, the teachers rose as a silent army. Ghosts silvery in the moonlight. They all pointed their fingers at Kappler in Rome. And they weren't shot or broken. They were whole. Because they had died as heroes brave and true.

Sometimes in Ruby's dream they all hummed together, a keening sound like a high wind. And sometimes they sang nonsense songs like in a nursery. But mostly they stood silently and pointed in the direction of Rome, silvery and transparent in the moonlight.

A secret army. They flew up and entered people's hearts. And if the Nazis had killed ten for every one of their own slain, then each of them had entered ten thousand hearts and made even more Italians part of the Resistance. Made them want freedom. And Ruby was right. Dead men do talk. Their souls rise like a plume of smoke and make us cry out for justice.

But one had survived. Joseph. Thanks to Don Pietro, magnificent to the last. And the bones were still there. Some days they would speak and tell their story.

"Someday the world will know and there will be a pilgrimage to the caves," Hugh said. "And in the meantime we will honour them by caring for the living."

Chapter 39

But it was getting harder to care for the living with hunger the new beast stalking Rome. It became a nightmare ensuring all the escapees were fed. Even the Vatican felt the pinch. Though the priests and nuns were so used to fasting, they were able to withstand it. But the Vatican trucks taking food to the capital were constantly bombed.

I found myself dreaming of food all the time. Spaghetti and potatoes, fish and sausages. Panettone, Christmas pudding. Even salt and sugar were in short supply. But the thoughts of food were painful as they made me remember. My mother's comforting Irish stew. The cakes and milky Galatine sweets Delia brought us the day my mother disappeared. Sister Boniface's steaming barley soup. The nutty-fruity bite of the special Jewish pizza from the ghetto. The apples from the orchard where Ruby and Ethan stayed, so crisp and clean. The pangiallo Christmas cake from the seminary as the Nazis raided. I could nearly taste the crumbs in my mouth.

There was so little food, I heard from Mother Mary Saint Luke that Lulu the well-brought-up kitten had killed a rat in her new home.

The gun in the Vatican gardens played on my mind. Just suppose they found it and blamed Hugh. I resolved to dispose of it.

I waited until the sun was low and crept outside. Hugh was due out of the Basilica at six. I had at least an hour. I went into the Vatican gardens and, grabbing a spade left by a gardener near the rose garden, quickly dug up the gun from its hiding place. It was like a miniature mummy, cold and damp and smelling of earth. I hid it in the big pocket inside my jacket.

I scaled the boundary wall at the back of the Vatican gardens, so the guards wouldn't question me at the main gate. But I spied a Nazi checkpoint to the south. So hugging the boundary path that went all around the Vatican City, I decided to go around by the north and cut through St. Peter's Square.

As I passed along the edge of the colonnade, where there were some administrative buildings near the Holy Office, some sixth sense made me look up as the sun broke through the clouds. I caught the shaft of something long and metallic through the window on the top floor. A rifle! I just knew. It was within shooting range of the place where Hugh habitually nipped through the colonnade on his way back to the German college.

I crept up to the side of the building. To my surprise, the door was unlocked, the building deserted. I went up the stairs to the top floor, unwrapping the gun as I went. I put it in my jacket pocket. Then I crept into the room where I guessed the rifle was in position.

To my horror Kappler was standing beside a rifle mounted on a tripod, looking down the barrel. It looked like he was planning to assassinate Hugh himself.

I pulled the gun from my jacket and, stepping across the room as if it was booby-trapped, I crept up on him.

The first he knew of my arrival was when I placed the cold gun against his temple.

He flinched. Flicked his eyes towards me, then raised his hands.

The gun was slipping in my greasy hands. My outstretched arm trembled with the effort. Seconds passed like hours.

I panicked and he sensed it. He tried to grab the gun. But I backed off, the gun wobbly in my hand. It was very heavy now. I thought I would drop it. But I held on tight.

"Why have you got a rifle trained on the square? Are you trying to kill Hugh?" My voice was as wobbly as my hand. The gun flailed all over the place. I was worried I would shoot my foot.

But Kappler just stared at me with his pale-blue eyes

almost popping out of his head.

"Stupid boy. Put that gun down."

He took a step closer to me, an arrogant look on his face. But I cocked the trigger and he stepped back. I was sweating now. It poured down my face into my eyes.

"You have nothing to gain by shooting me," he said in a reasonable voice. "You will be arrested by my Gestapo." Then he paused. "Assuming you know how to shoot."

I looked at his fish eyes. The scar on his left cheek. I hated the man with my whole being.

I lost my temper and pulled the trigger, aiming at his feet. He sprang back. The shot rang out like the crack of a whip and I recoiled from the blast, my ears ringing.

"You have made your point and done me a favour by alerting my men." His voice was icy, bloodless. But there were beads of sweat on his forehead. "If you let me go now, you will hear nothing more about it. In a few moments my officers will be here and you will be arrested anyway."

I stood, my arms rigid. "Why did you kill all those people in the cave?"

"This is a war. I was given a direct order to carry out. I am a soldier," he said.

I noticed how thin the lips were that the words came out of. His face bloodless.

"Did you know I have applied five times to fight at the front? But I was told to stay here to do my duty."

"And your duty included killing prisoners like Don Pietro in cold blood in a cave!" I was shouting now.

I saw a muscle twitch in his face.

"You don't know what you speak of, boy. Rome and the Vatican are nests of spies. It is kill or be killed." Then he looked up at me. "Go on, pull the trigger. You are no different from me."

"*You killed Don Pietro!*" I shouted again. "*And the general. And the wine-seller and Gio the teacher!*"

"Drop the gun," he said again. Taking a step forward.

I waved the gun wildly at him. "Stay where you are! Keep your hands up!"

He did as I asked.

There was a silence then. Nothing but the sound of our heavy breathing in the room. The air was still between us.

Sweat trickled into my eyes. Or was it tears?

"Perhaps you could explain to me then why this Monsignor Hugh O'Flaherty spies for the mortal enemy of the Irish. The British have oppressed his race for centuries. He is a traitor." He was talking to stop me doing anything.

"Hugh is not a traitor. He loves people. And is good and kind. Do you know, he said he would help even you!"

Kappler shook his head and laughed, a short barking sound. "Time will tell. But you aren't like him. Are you? You are no different from me. You will eliminate the enemies who stand in your way."

I looked at him down the barrel of the gun. This maniac. This demon who had lied and cheated and tortured and killed in Rome. No one in Rome would mourn him if I pulled the trigger.

Hugh would be crossing the steps soon.

"I will never be like you," I said.

"You don't have the courage," he sneered. "You will live the rest of your life in the knowledge you are a coward."

My whole body trembled now. I was in danger of dropping the gun.

Kappler took a step closer. A smile played on his lips.

"Go on, pull the trigger. You know you are no better than me."

"You don't make the rules anymore!" I shouted. *"Your day is over!"*

He took another step closer and put his hand out, his eyes taunting me.

I stiffened and tightened my trigger finger. But suddenly Hugh's words came back to me and I said: "You are the dark, Kappler. And the dark will never put out the dark. Only the light can put out the dark. It only takes one candle to illuminate the blackness and because of that you will never win."

Kappler looked at me with pure hatred. Or maybe it was fear.

But either way my fate was decided. I heard feet hammering like hooves coming up the stairs. Sweat dropping into my eyes.

I had maybe twenty seconds. I ordered him to stand in the corner of the room with his back to me. Then I hastily took the rifle down off the tripod, never taking my eyes off him. At least he couldn't shoot Hugh with it now.

The rifle was heavy and I wasn't going to fire it anyway. So I took out the bullets and threw them on the floor.

But I was too late. The doors burst open.

"Leo!"

It wasn't Kappler's Nazi henchmen. It was John May with the Swiss Guard in their plain uniforms.

"Drop your gun, Kappler! You are way out of order!" John shouted. *"Come 'ere, Leo!"*

It was Kappler's turn to look astonished.

"The Allies are less than a day away. The game's up, Kappler," John said.

Kappler surprised me by taking his gun out of his holster and dropping it to the floor. In my panic I hadn't considered that he could have pulled that gun on me.

"In that case I seek sanctuary in the Vatican." Kappler's voice was even, like it was an everyday request.

The guards looked at each other but John May shook his head. "Sorry, guvnor. No can do. Pope says on your orders we ain't allowed take any more refugees."

Kappler glared at him. "I have the right!"

"Pity for you then that you've asked the wrong bloke," said May.

Kappler stood up straight. "So arrest me."

"Can't do that either. You see, we might be on the wrong side of the line and don't have the powers," John May grinned. "We shouldn't really be here but seeing it was Leo and 'e's just a young fella we've bent the rules as the line runs too close to judge either way round 'ere. The boundaries aren't always clear Kappler. As you know only too well."

A breeze ruffled the curtain at the window. Kappler's stance had changed. He dropped his shoulders, he looked almost meek.

"You may not realise it," he said, "but I am much more reasonable than some of my compatriots who would happily bomb Rome into the ground. I can stop unnecessary force."

"So you is tryin' to say you might be the saviour of Rome now!" John May was incredulous. "Well, I think Leo should decide your fate."

I looked at the man before me, almost an object of pity now, standing before us in pretend humility. The man who had arrested my mother. The man who had ordered me and countless others to be tortured. Who had shot in cold blood innocent men in the Ardeatine Caves, maybe even Don Pietro. Who had become almost deranged in his attempts to kill our beloved Hugh.

I could see in Kappler's eyes he knew he was going to die.

I fired the gun. The bullet entered the plasterwork behind him, splintering the chalky walls. I had aimed above his head. I saw him wince, then stand there, dazed to be still alive.

"Go," I said. "We will not take you to the Vatican. You cannot cross the line. See, I am not like you at all. I don't kill for the sake of it. Some day I hope to see you answer for your crimes."

Kappler looked like he was going to burst a blood vessel.

May looked him up and down. "Clear orf now. We're giving you a sporting chance. It's more than your lot would ever do."

Kappler quickly glanced left and right. Then without any warning he plunged through the guards and out the door.

The Guards took the rifle away.

But Kappler's gun was still lying on the ground. May lifted it up and held it in his hand. It was a German luger pistol. Terrifying and sleek. He took out the bullets and handed it to me.

"Perhaps, Leo, you would like it as a souvenir."

I took it with a smile. "I have other plans for it. See you back at the Vatican."

I now had two guns to dispose of. I'd put my gun back in my pocket. I went out the door and ran with all my might towards the Tiber.

I stood for a moment, wanting to plunge into its waters, wanting to wash myself from this dirty war. But first I hurled the guns one after the other into its depths. The first one skittered over the waves. The second dropped like a stone. Let them sleep with the fishes for all eternity. I thought.

I waded in up to my waist. The water felt pure, bracing.

Then I swam with the current. I wasn't like Kappler. I couldn't kill a man in cold blood. Let him answer for his crimes to God, as Hugh said.

I dived deep with hammering heart, right into the pulse of the current. The rolling waves, the rush of the cold water, the thrill of the dive, setting me free.

Chapter 40

June 1944

On Sunday the 4th of June, a strange shower rained from the sky – leaflets from the Allies urging Romans to do everything in our power to prevent the destruction of the city. To leave free passages everywhere for military vehicles.

"Rome is yours! Your job is to save the city, ours is to destroy the enemy."

Were the Nazis really that close to leaving? The guns were getting nearer. Planes were fighting over the city and the roar of anti-aircraft guns alternated with the rat-tat-tat of machine guns.

But there were bigger gaps between the gunfire as the day wore on.

The Germans were escaping in disorder. No attempt at military formation, leaving in stolen cars, horse-drawn vehicles, even in carts belonging to the street-cleaning department. Some had rifles, others pistols in their hands. But no one interfered. They were leaving. They were frightened. There were some explosions as they blew up barracks and even the Fiat factory. But we let them leave.

Crowds stood on pavements, sat on the steps of churches, at the tables of cafés, watching them go, doing and saying nothing. The tide had turned for Rome. The Allies were creeping closer minute by minute. And now the Germans were fleeing. Fleeing like rats from a sinking ship.

One of the most pathetic sights was seeing Italian Blackshirts try hitching a lift, only to be kicked off a gun carriage by German soldiers. No honour among thieves and murderers.

We watched them from the roof of the Santa Maria Hospice, Sir D'Arcy Osborne drinking champagne, Hugh with a tumbler of whiskey, the sun glowing red in the sky.

The Germans were wild-eyed, unshaven, unkempt, on foot, in stolen cars, skulking out of the city like vermin. So different when they marched in triumphant in their jackboots. Somewhere in that teeming multitude was Kappler.

"Rome had little strategic value, and the Nazis are aware that it would have been a public relations disaster with Catholic Germans to wreck the Eternal City." Sir D'Arcy Osborne sipped his drink, calm as ever but with a lightness that was new to him.

Hugh clapped me on the back. "It's not every twelve-year-old who can say they've played a part in chasing out the Nazis."

I smiled but I felt like a hot-air balloon still tethered to the earth. I was happy but also thinking about all the fallen. Of the Jews in the ghetto, of Primo. Of the Ardeatine Caves and even of Ethan's cat flattened by a Nazi truck. And I thought of my father too who would never see the liberation he had fought for.

"May we live all the days of our lives." Hugh held his tumbler of whiskey aloft. "Those of us who are still living."

5th of June 1944

And then after all the waiting it was as though the Allies had crept in, the American tanks stealing in like shadows. I had been too excited to sleep. Hugh was the same. Our fitful slumber was interrupted by what sounded like outbreaks of cheering as the Allies moved towards the heart of Rome.

Straight after six o'clock Mass, Monsignor Hugh and I stood on the steps of Saint Peter's in the early dawn, the sky pink with the promise of sun. The square was almost deserted, except for several people walking about dazed as if wakened from a dream.

A jeep drove up, emblazoned with the Allied star, accompanied by several covered vehicles and gun carriages with the American white star. One might even have been a tank, it was hard to see under all the people standing on it and cheering.

They were followed by crowds of excited people, a lot of them children.

"General Mark Clark here," the head man in the jeep said.

There was a red-haired woman in the back seat of the car with him, dressed in a doctor's white coat, with a Red Cross armband. She said with a laugh that she had hitched a lift.

"Is it yourself, Molly O'Donovan?" Hugh exclaimed to her. "I thought you were in India!"

"It's a long story." She shook her head of red curls that glowed like fire. "But I'm here now to set up a field hospital with the general. 'Markus Clarkus' we call him – the new Conqueror of Rome!" She joshed the general lightly on the elbow. "Do you know what one of our guys said when he saw the Colosseum? 'My God, they bombed that too!'"

We all laughed, hysterical almost. It was the funniest thing on the happiest day.

"Is there anything I could do for you?" Hugh asked the general, beaming his widest smile.

"Why, Monsignor, I'd sure like to visit Capitoline Hill. I hear it's the most important of the Seven Hills. You can understand why I might like to have my photo taken at *Caput Mundi* – the capital of the world. Can you point me in the right direction?"

Hugh looked at me. "I can do better than that. This lad here will lead you there, the same route as Caesar's victorious legions," he paused, "on his bicycle."

I was only short of jumping for joy.

"It will be an honour, sir," I said.

The general beamed with pride.

Then Hugh looked down at his feet and over to the white line at the entrance.

"Now if you'd like to follow me, I'll show you the way and there's something I have to do at the entrance."

"Hop on board, Padre," the General said.

So Hugh and I hopped on the side of the open jeep. The crowd cheered wildly as we drove through. A blur of laughing, joyous faces.

As we got to the line that stretched across the cobblestones from one colonnade to the other, the jeep slowed down and Hugh jumped out.

He bounded up to the line as the jeep pulled up beside him.

Then Hugh leapt in the air and danced a little Irish jig, jumping right across the line.

"I've been waiting a year to do that!" he joked.

We all gave him a round of applause.

I looked at his feet. The soles were flapping against the rest of the shoe like gaping mouths. I shook my head. Not only had he saved so many people, avoided the Nazis so many times. He did it in a pair of shoes that were falling apart.

A Swiss Guard brought me my bicycle and so we set off. Me at the front – pedalling for all I was worth in a right royal progress. Up past the tunnel where the *popolini* took refuge, now all out cheering and dancing. Workmen tossed their caps into the air. Women threw flowers in streets narrow and wide. But the crowds parted respectfully like they must have done for Caesar's victorious troops. Rome was finally an open city. The first hour of the first day of our liberation. Free.

I reached the top of the hill, followed by the General. He went off to do the pomp stuff that generals do, followed by cameras and newspaper reporters.

I stood a little way off, surveying the Eternal City I had come to love. How wonderful it was to stand in the light and not look over my shoulder. And I thought of all the people who had fought and died in this city in the shadows. So I could stand here. Free.

As I stood, a charm of goldfinches, their plumage blazing, flew down near where my hand rested on the wall. I thought of Ruby and Ethan. I thought of my mother, hoping she had reached Switzerland.

But most of all I thought of all the people we had lost. Don Pietro and all those brave men in the cave. My father, lying with the fishes somewhere in the English Channel. I thought of how Hugh had risked his life time and time again. If only Ruby could be with me to celebrate, that would make the day more perfect.

Well, what do you know, I turned round only to see coming up the path a crown of russet hair flaming in the morning sun. It was Ruby in the arms of Hugh, Ethan by his side. In a moment we would all be together, joined in a hug on this most happy of days. In that heartbeat, I knew I was Leo the Lucky. Lucky to have such family and friends. Lucky to be alive. And even in that space before they joined me, I knew that it was one of the most blessed moments of my life.

And I still don't know if I believe in God or the Pope and all that stuff. Or angels and saints. Or even Ruby's fairies and spirits.

But I do know one thing. In the very worst of war, you see the best in people.

And I sure believe in Monsignor Hugh O'Flaherty.

Authors's note

During the Nazi occupation, Rome was a hotbed of intrigue, a tinderbox, a place of spies and shadows and brutal murders alongside astonishing heroism. A place where over seven thousand people perished during the Nazi occupation and one half of the population was hiding the other half. This is a fictional re-imagining but I hope true to the incredible spirit of the people who fought oppression. I have tried to be as faithful as possible to the events of the time while simplifying the narrative. And while I relied heavily on many wonderful first-hand narratives and historical accounts, in places my imagination has filled the gap where details are sketchy. The Monsignor's secret tunnel route in and out of the Vatican, for example, may or may not exist. All errors and mistakes are my own.

Monsignor Hugh O'Flaherty and the leading figures of the Rome Escape Line, John May, Sir Darcy Osborne, Henrietta Chevalier (Mrs M), Delia Murphy, Major Sam Derry and countless others were very much real flesh-and-blood heroes. I have also stitched in the story of another great hero Don Pietro Pappagallo who perished in the Ardeatine Caves along with five of Hugh's helpers. There isn't much evidence that they knew each other, but it's entirely possible as they played for the same team as it were, and Hugh knew everybody.

The Nazi Commandant, Kappler, the Fascist torturer Koch, and Caruso were all too real. Koch and Caruso were executed. Kappler was imprisoned for war crimes, where his only regular visitor was Monsignor Hugh O'Flaherty. Not only did Hugh forgive his enemy but he received him into the Catholic Church.

Leo, Ruby and his family are conjured out of my imagination, but they are woven from the stuff of reality. There were brave boys running messages, little girls fleeing from danger, Jewish children hiding in convents, teenage deserters fighting with the partisans.

Children are often invisible in the grand narratives, or portrayed as victims. But they can also be agents of history and show astonishing courage and initiative. I hope the characters I have invented and the portrayal of the real people I have stitched into the unfolding of historical events are a testament to the bravery and resilience of all those who lived through those traumatic times.

Acknowledgements

I first encountered Monsignor Hugh O'Flaherty at my nephew Senan's confirmation in Killarney when his headmaster Colm O'Súilleabháin at Muire na Mainistreach, "The Mon", pointed to a mural of the Monsignor on the wall and said, "Behold the subject of your new book." Colm, you were right, and I can't thank you enough for pointing me in the right direction.

With thanks to publisher Paula Campbell at Poolbeg who has been a real cheerleader for this book and is doing so much to bring a love of history to a young audience. To all at Poolbeg, Kieran Devlin, Caroline Maloney, and the team who work tirelessly behind the scenes to bring the book to print.

To David Prendergast who shows great fortitude and patience during the production. It's much appreciated.

Blessings and bouquets to Gaye Shortland my editor who

goes to great lengths to ensure historical accuracy. Always calm under fire, her wit and humour enlivens the process!

To Derry Dillon, an illustrator who goes the extra mile to bring the front cover alive.

I owe an enormous debt to Marianna Salvalaio who advised me on native Italian turns of phrase. Thanks also to Joel Lazarus for sharing with me the story of his Jewish grandparents' life in London during the 1930's and 40's.

Thanks to my niece Aoife O'Leary who helped me with research. Also to my husband Marc and daughter Rosa for their good-humoured support.

I owe a lot to my first readers, Daniel Cassidy, William Murphy, Patrick Collinson, Audrey and Tim O'Leary (the Kerry consultant), Stephen, Neil, Karen and Kenneth Murphy. All gave me invaluable feedback on early drafts.

And last but not least, to Monsignor Hugh O'Flaherty himself. The more I learned about him – champion golfer, scholar, linguist, humanitarian – the more I admired him. I hope he can forgive me for any liberties I have taken with the story or if I have misrepresented him. I am fully confident that he would. But even though all the governments of Italy, the United Kingdom, the United States and Israel showered this modest man with awards in his lifetime, and he was even played by Gregory Peck in a 1983 TV film, "The Scarlet and the Black", I would really like his immense contribution to be honoured down the generations. I'm not an expert in these matters, but if anyone deserves to be considered for sainthood, surely it's him.

Historical Characters – World War II in Rome

The German Occupiers
Lieutenant Colonel Herbert Kappler, Chief of the Gestapo in Rome

Captain Erich Priebke, Kappler's aide and torturer

Baron Ernst von Weizsäcker, German Ambassador to the Pope

Prince Otto Von Bismarck, Nazi envoy to Rome, grandson of the "Iron Chancellor"

Adolf Hitler, German Fürher (leader)

The Italian Fascists (Blackshirts)
Benito Mussolini – Il Duce, dictator of Italy, head of a puppet regime dominated by Hitler

Pietro Caruso, Rome's Fascist Chief of Police

Pietro Koch, head of the "Koch Gang" Fascist Secret Police, torturer

The Vatican and Clergy
Pope Pius XII, Roman born

Monsignor Hugh O'Flaherty, Irish priest and head of the Rome Escape Line, known as "The Pimpernel of the Vatican"

Mother Mary Saint Luke, American nun working in the Vatican Information Bureau

Don Pietro Pappagallo, chaplain to the Sisters of the Child Jesus, Italian anti-fascist who supplied forged documents for those persecuted by the Fascists

Father Palazzini, assistant Vice-Rector at the Roman Seminary who hid Jews and partisans

Don Perosi, composer and Perpetual Director of the Sistine Choir

The Rome Escape Line
Monsignor Hugh O'Flaherty, senior official at the Vatican, born in Killarney Ireland, who led the Rome Escape Line that protected 6,500 Allied prisoners, Jewish people and partisans during the Nazi occupation in Rome

Sir D'Arcy Osborne, British Special Envoy to the Pope and one of the Council of Three who led the Rome Escape Line

Count Sarsfield Salazar, Swiss Diplomat and one of the Council of Three who led Rome Escape Line

Prince Filippo Doria Pamphilj, anti-Fascist and supporter of the Rome Escape Line

John May, Butler to Sir D'Arcy Osborne and black-market expert

Delia Murphy, renowned singer and wife of the Irish Envoy to the Vatican

Blon Kiernan, Delia's 19-year-old daughter, a medical student who worked with the Rome Escape line.

Dr. Thomas J. Kiernan, husband of Delia and Irish Minister to the Pope

Henrietta Chevalier, known as Mrs. M, Maltese widow and mother of seven children who sheltered prisoners of war

Major Sam Derry, escaped British prisoner of war, who became a leading organiser of the Rome Escape Line

Bill Simpson and John Furman, British escaped prisoners of war, active in the Escape Line

Allies and Resistance

Ada Gobetti, prominent anti-fascist in Turin and leader of the Italian Resistance. Kept a famous diary all through the war

General Mark J. Clark, American General who led the Allies into Rome

Il Gobbo del Quarticciolo, seventeen-year-old Giuseppe Albano, nicknamed "The Hunchback of Quarticciolo". Head of a group of boy partisan/ bandits who robbed from the Nazis to give to the poor

TIMELINE OF KEY EVENTS WORLD WAR II IN ITALY

1943

9 July–17 August: Allies invade Sicily.

8 September: Italians surrender to Allies. Germans quickly occupy Italy.

9 September: Allied landings at Salerno and Taranto, mainland Italy.

11 September: Germans occupy Rome.

12 September: Germans rescue Mussolini from prison.

14 September: Allied landings in Sardinia; Heavy fighting at Salerno.

23 September: Mussolini re-establishes Fascist government in northern Italy as a puppet regime of Hitler.

1 October: Allies enter Naples.

13 October: Liberated Southern Italy declares war on Germany.

5 November: bombing of Vatican by plane presumed to be German or Italian Fascist.

1 December: German line on the Sangro River broken.

18 Dec: German soldiers killed at a trattoria in the Prati District in Rome. Start of series of Partisan attacks against the Germans in the heart of Rome.

19 Dec: assault on the heavily guarded Hotel Flora, headquarters of the German High Command. Death toll kept secret. A few days later there was an attack on German guard post at Regina Coeli. Death toll kept secret but dozen of guards fell dead or wounded. As a result of attacks curfew brought back to 7pm. Use of bicycles prohibited after 5pm.

21 December: Fascist Koch gang invade and round up Jewish and partisan refugees in hiding at the Roman Seminary beside the Basilica of San Giovanni. More than 18 people arrested. Similar raids carried out on other Vatican properties.

1944

17 January: U.S. 5th Army offensive along the Gustav line begins. First attack towards Cassino.

22 January: Allied landing at Anzio, behind the German lines at Cassino. By 12 midnight, some 45,000 Allied troops and 3,000 vehicles are on the beaches.

3 February: First counter-attack by Germans at Anzio.

3 February: Koch's gang raid a papal basilica, St Paul Outside-the-Walls. 66 people were arrested, including nine Jews.

15–18 February: In an effort to destroy what they believed were German defensive positions at the historic Benedictine monastery of the top of Monte Cassino, Allied bombers lay waste to the monastery, killing over 230 men women and children who had taken refuge there.

16 February: Second German counter-attack at Anzio.

19 Feb–30th March: The Italian winter makes its arrival and postpones any further Allied offensives for the next month.

23 March: Partisan bomb on Via Rassella kills 33 members of the Nazi Bozen regiment. Two civilians also killed. Death toll eventually rises to 42.

24 March: In reprisal for the attack, the Nazis under the direct command of Kappler execute 335 prisoners at the Ardeatine Caves, them blow up the entrances to the caves. The massacre and subsequent cover-up causes international revulsion.

17 April: Kappler orders the round-up of nearly 1,000 men in the Quadraro district after Il Gobbo, the hunchback partisan and bandit, is accused of killing 3 German soldiers.

11–12 May: Allied forces open new offensive against

Gustav line in Italy.

18 May: Polish troops capture Cassino.

5 June: Allies led by American General Mark Clark enter Rome.

6 June: D-Day landings in France

16 July: Allies capture Arezzo.

17 July: Allies cross the Arno River.

1945

1 April: Allied offensive in Northern Italy

28 April: Mussolini is captured and hanged by Italian partisans; Allies take Venice.

29 April: U.S. 7th Army liberates Dachau Concentration Camp

30 April: Adolf Hitler commits suicide.

2 May: German troops in Italy surrender.

7 May: Unconditional surrender of all German forces to Allies.

8 May: V-E (Victory in Europe) Day.

Reading List

Biographies

There are several good biographies on Monsignor Hugh O'Flaherty.

For children: *Hugh O'Flaherty, His Wartime Adventures* by Alison Walsh, Collins Press 2010

For adults: *Hide and Seek, The Irish Priest in the Vatican who Defied the Nazi Command* by Stephen Walker, Lyons Press 2012

The Vatican Pimpernel by Brian Fleming, The Collins Press 2014

Scarlet Pimpernel of the Vatican by J. P. Gallagher, Ignatius Press 2009 – the book that inspired the film *The Scarlet and the Black*

Publications

Diaries and Memoirs

Inside Rome with the Germans by Jane Scrivener, The Macmillan Company 1949 (out of print but available on Kindle) – a lively detailed diary written under an alias by Mother Mary Saint Luke who worked in the Vatican Information Bureau.

Partisan Diaries by Ada Gobetti, OUP (USA) 2014 – a wonderful classic by an astonishing woman, tireless organiser, mother and partisan, one of the inventors of the Italian resistance

The Rome Escape Line by Sam L. Derry, published by Harrap 1960 (out of print) – a stirring account by British Major escaped POW who was one of the principal organisers of the Escape Line

A Vatican Lifeline '44 by William Simpson, published by Leo Cooper 1995 – an engaging account of being part of the

Rome Escape Line by a British escapee and key organiser

O Roma Felix: Practical Guide for Walks in Rome by Monsignor Hugh O'Flaherty and John Smit, Enrico Verdesi publishers Rome 1959 – now out of print but a great way to get a flavor of the Monsignor's boundless energy.

I'll Live Till I Die, The Story of Delia Murphy by Aidan O'Hara, Drumlin 1997 – a warm and affectionate portrait of a real character and pioneer of Irish folk music

A British Boy in Fascist Italy by Peter Ghiringhelli 2010 – a remarkable and unique memoir of life under Mussolini.

World War II in Italy

The Order Has Been Carried Out by Alessandro Portelli, Palgrave Macmillan 2003 – a masterpiece of oral history, stitching together first person narratives, family history and official sources of the partisan attack on Via Rassella and the massacre at the Ardeatine Caves.

October 16, 1943, Eight Jews by Giacomo Debenedetti, Notre Dame 2001 – a searing masterpiece based on eyewitness accounts of the round-up in the Jewish ghetto

A Civil War, A History of the Italian Resistance by Claudio Pavone, Verso 2013 – a monumental work on the politics and ideology of fascism and resistance.

The Battle for Rome by Robert Katz. Simon & Schuster 2003 – a lively account written like a thriller of the intrigue surrounding the Nazi occupation. Not much on the Rome Escape Line but a vivid retelling of the Partisans campaign and the controversy surrounding the role of Pope Pius XII

Novels

History by Elsa Morante, and Penguin Modern Classics 2002 – a sprawling, poignant epic of the war from the point of view of the victims

The Path to the *Nest* of *Spiders, and Penguin Modern Classics 2009* by the Italian writer Italo Calvino – a classic novel about partisans

Films and Documentaries

The Scarlet and The Black DVD 2003 – an atmospheric 1983 film for television starring Gregory Peck as the Monsignor focusing on his duel with Kappler played by Christopher Plummer. PG Cert but may be frightening for younger children.

The Pimpernel of the Vatican, TG4 DVD 2008– an excellent documentary with amazing photographs and footage, including newsreel of Monsignor Hugh O'Flaherty chatting to General Mark Clark in Saint Peter's Square as Rome is liberated by the Allies.

Rome, Open City by Roberto Rossellini, DVD 2005 – an iconic masterpiece filmed shortly as the Nazis departed Rome. The portrayal of the saintly priest is based on Don Pietro Pappagallo.

God Has No Country – a critically acclaimed one-man show written and directed by Killarney-born actor/playwright Donal Courtney.
https://www.godhasnocountry.com

Website

www.hughoflaherty.com is the website of the Hugh O'Flaherty Memorial Society and a source of invaluable information.

As seen on the RTÉ Toy Show

Now that you're hooked why not try

The Easter Rising 1916

Molly's Diary

PATRICIA MURPHY

also published by Poolbeg.

The number one bestseller
30,000 copies sold

HANDS ON HISTORY

Here's a sneak preview . . .

*E*aster 1916. The Great War rages in Europe with two hundred thousand Irishmen fighting in the British Army. But a small group of Irish nationalists refuse to fight for Britain and strike a blow for Irish freedom. Caught up in the action in Dublin is twelve-year-old Molly O'Donovan. This is her diary.

Molly's Diary

📖   📖   📖

9 o'clock, Saturday morning, 22nd April 1916 – MY BIRTHDAY!
My bedroom, 9 Sackville Street, Dublin, Ireland, Second City of the British Empire.

My name is Molly O'Donovan and I am twelve years old today. Hurray! My father is Chief Technical Officer at the General Post Office (GPO for short) and makes sure everyone gets their telegraphs and telephone calls. My mother is called Bessie. She is a Quaker from Enniskillen in the North of Ireland. We live opposite the GPO in Sackville Street, Dublin, the widest street in Europe, in a tall thin house above a tailor's shop.

My brother Jack is two years older than me – and teases me something rotten!

I had hoped to fill my new diary with elegant words and clever thoughts but all I've had are constant interruptions. I only had to pick up my new fountain pen earlier at breakfast for Jack to make fun of me.

"Why on earth would a boring girl need a diary!" he jeered. "Dear Diary, today I broke a comb in my awful red hair, I played nurses with my silly dolls. Blah, blah, blah!"

Jack tried to swipe the diary from me but I held it out of reach.

"Die, Imperial Enemy! God save Ireland!" he cried and the eejit tried to bayonet my diary with his fork.

"Shush! I'm writing down EVERYTHING that happens. So you'd better stop jumping off roofs and marching with rebels!" I made a face at him but he made a worse one back and stabbed again at my lovely diary. "Hands off! It's the best present ever!"

It's true. It's vellum and hand-bound in leather with my name carved on the front. It has a little lock and all. Mother's friend, Addy, who works in Eason Stationers, made it.

Then our char Nancy Maguire chimed in. "Janey Mac! Would yeh ever stop actin' the maggot, young Jack," she scolded. She is quite old and crinkly and her face is sooty from cleaning the grate.

Jack mimed shooting at me with a rifle, the dangerous galoot.

"At least your sister's not hangin' outside old Fenian bomber's tobacco shops like you and our Anto," said Nancy.

Anto is Nancy's fifteen-year-old son, a messenger boy with buck teeth and sticky-out ears. Jack thinks the sun shines out of his scrawny backside.

"Nancy, who are the Fenians?" I asked.

"A shower of no-account troublemakers from way back who want to bomb us all into bein' an Irish Republic," she said, shaking her brush. "I'll give them the tail-end of this if they come too close."

Jack was going to rugby-tackle me so I jumped up on my chair to hold the diary out of arm's reach.

In all the rough and tumble we hadn't noticed that my father had walked into the room and heard what we'd been saying.

"What's this about Fenians?" he asked sharply.

"If I catch our Anto with dem bowsies marchin' around like tin soldiers," said Nancy, "I'll box his ears and theirs too."

My father suppressed a smile. He thinks Nancy is very funny.

"Lookin' for an Ireland Republic while my poor aul' husband Mossy and Jemsie me firstborn are fightin' the Germans," continued Nancy.

Both are soldiers with the Dublin Fusiliers in Flanders. So Nancy is one of the 'Separation Women' who wait to get money every week from the Post Office because their husbands are off fighting the Germans.

The Kaiser in Germany started the war. It's a long story. A madman in Serbia shot a duke and now everyone is fighting everybody. It all gets very confusing because some of the Irish, and not just the old Fenians that Nancy wants to wallop with her brush, won't fight for England against Germany and want an independent Ireland. Friends of Jack, I'll have you know.

"'We serve neither King nor Kaiser but Ireland!'" said Jack defiantly. He'd told me he saw this slogan on a big banner outside Liberty Hall down on Burgh Quay. It's the headquarters of the Trade Unionists who want the employers to give their workers more money and rights. They are yet another group who have their own army. There are so many armies marching about it's surprising they don't all bump into each other.

"I'm amazed you could even read that banner on Liberty Hall," I said to Jack. This was unkind and I immediately felt bad. Jack has problems with reading.

"If I ever see that Kaiser, I'll make him sit on his big pointy helmet – that'll put some manners on him," said Nancy.

"Nancy should be the Prime Minister," I giggled.

"And that fella Tom Clarke in the tobacco shop around the corner," she went on. "What that aul' Fenian bomb-maker says is more dangerous than the matches he sells. As for yer one, Countess Marzipan!"

"Countess Markievicz. Her husband is a Polish Count, though she herself is Anglo-Irish," corrected my father who is a stickler for accuracy.

"Whatever she's called, she's a bit of a consequence with her smokin' and trousers and big hats," said Nancy. "Turnin' all those young boys to devilment!"

"Isn't Anto in the Countess's Scouts –" I began, but Jack pinched me hard and looked daggers at me, so I bit my tongue. Luckily Nancy didn't hear me and was going on about how the Countess should stick to making soup for the poor.

"At the Post Office we maintain a neutral stance," said my father sternly to Jack. "I suggest you do the same, young man."

Jack kicked the chair leg. "I'll do as I please," he mumbled.

"Not when you're in my house," said Father. "Go to your room."

Jack skulked upstairs. My father hurried out. I was left standing on the chair, holding my Dear Diary, like a scarecrow. And my father hadn't even noticed!

I heard my father in the hall, taking his hat and umbrella from the hallstand, and then his exclamation of "Good God!"

He rushed back into the room and I thought I was in for it.

"Molly, I nearly forgot to wish you Happy Birthday!"

I jumped down and embraced him, for I love my daddy dearly and wish I could spend more time with him – but he is always so busy keeping the General Post Office going and says it is the most important building in Ireland. Not a telegram would be received nor a telephone call put through without my daddy looking after all the wires.

We heard a clatter at the front door. It was my mother arriving back with the delivery boy from the Dublin Bread Company, known as the DBC. As it's Holy Saturday it's closed for the rest of the day. The stout little boy was juggling several packages, including my birthday cake! His name is Tommy Keenan and he looks like he eats most of the cakes. He was wearing a little tricolour badge, the green, white and orange flag of the Republicans, so I think he is a Fenian too!

"Where's our wee Jack?" Mother asked anxiously in her soft Northern Irish accent. (Jack is heading towards six foot and is not at all wee!)

My father pointed up towards the ceiling, with an expression that indicated he had been sent to his room in disgrace. He kissed my mother on the cheek.

"The telegraph wires are always humming, holiday or no holiday," he said, heading for the door. This made me think of busy bees humming in a hive.

"Don't forget we're taking Molly to Bewley's Café when we come back from Howth Head," said my mother.

My father brightened up. "Make sure Jack goes to the sea. The fresh air will blow those silly notions out of his head."

"I'll write it all down in my diary!" I said excitedly.

"We better all watch our pee's and poo's so," proclaimed Nancy.

We all laughed. Nancy, of course, meant P's and Q's. Though I confess that doesn't make much sense either.

My mother gave her a bundle of old baby clothes and I helped her carry them to the door. I can't think why she needs baby clothes. Nancy is an old woman with lots of wobbly teeth and more like a grandmother – though I know she doesn't have grandchildren.

As she left Nancy whispered to me, "My Anto and Jack are good boys really. If Mossy were here, he'd tan Anto's hide to knock some sense into him."

"My mother won't let Father hit Jack," I said. It's because she's a Quaker and they are against war and violence, but Father would not like to do it anyhow.

"Yer da is as daecent as any man who ever wore a hat, and yer ma is a saint," said Nancy.

That is true for sure. Mother is always giving loaves of bread and stuff to old people in the slums, like in Moore Street.

Everything quietened down for a while after that but

Jack is wrong about my life being boring so, Dear Diary, together we are going to show him! I know one or two secrets about him and presently I may reveal them if he isn't nice to me!

But let me tell you more about myself and my family. I was christened Margaret but everyone calls me Molly. I am tall for my age with reddish hair and a dusting of freckles. My mother says my hair is "Titian" like the women in the pre-Raphaelite paintings. Jack says my hair is like rusty old springs and I look like I have the measles – that I am so ugly no one will want to marry me. But I don't care. There IS someone who wants to marry me – even if it's only Anto. Though I don't want to marry him. So Jack is wrong!

Jack is also wrong about me playing nurses with my dolls. I'm practising being a doctor like my grandfather, a Surgeon Major in the Army in India who died before we could meet him. Or my mother's friend, Dr Ella Webb, who lives in Hatch Street. She even has a husband and four children. So I hope to be a doctor like her.

My father tells Jack he won't amount to much. But even if he is not one for book learning and gets his words all jumbled up, Jack is very clever. He knows how to fix watches and bicycles. He repaired my music box when no one else could. It belonged to my grandmother in India and plays "The Last Rose of Summer" by Thomas Moore. Father told me that the music reminded her of home when she felt lonely.

Jack can also climb anything. He scales the roofs all over Dublin (this is a secret!). His friends call him "Jack the Cat" for he would make a great cat burglar and can land on his feet from any height.

We play this game where I dare Jack to put one of his tin soldiers in a difficult place. You should see where those soldiers get to! The chimney of the Provost's House, Trinity College. On the shoulder of the statue of Daniel O'Connell. Even the roof of the GPO between the statues of Fidelity and Hibernia!

Jack is golden. His hair is an unusual amber-gold that glows in the light, a prettier shade than mine, his skin is tanned and he has brown eyes. Lots of girls like him. Like Hyacinth O'Hare who lives a few houses down who is thirteen and has fat sausage curls like a spaniel. I've looked out the window just now and, yes, she is standing outside on the pavement hoping to see him on her way to her dancing class. How pathetic! She's supposed to be my friend but she's always mooning over Jack, making googly eyes at him.

My father's job at the General Post Office was specially created for him, as he knows so much about telephones and telegraphs. He has even been to America to visit Mr Edison who invented them. They have been rebuilding the Dublin Post Office and my father made sure they had all the best equipment in the world. It opened six weeks ago and Mr Norway, the head of the Post Office, and the Lord Lieutenant gave a special thanks to my father. We were all very proud.

We even have our own telephone that stands on its own table in the sitting room like a statue to be adored. It is like a big brass candlestick with a mouthpiece on top with a listening device attached by a wire. Truth be told, it is almost never used as the only people we know with telephones are mother's friend Dr Ella Webb and Great-aunt Bessie in Belfast. Father is usually at work so makes all his calls from the GPO. And the higher-ups and staff always send a messenger to fetch him if there is an emergency, which is often – too often, says my mother. But my, when that telephone rings it's like the bell of a ship and we all jump to attention!

How I love to look out our window at the General Post Office! You see, Dublin is the second city of the British Empire which is so mighty the sun never sets on it. That makes our GPO the second most important, after London, in the whole world!

As I said, Sackville Street is the widest street in Europe. It hums like a hive with shoeblacks outside calling out to polish shoes, the flower-sellers around Nelson's Pillar singing, "Get your daffs – a penny a bunch!" and the paper-sellers shouting out the news: "Battle of Verdun still raging on the Western Front!" The telegram boys skitter past on foot or whizz by on their bikes and all day long the deep-red mail cars come and go with the royal insignia, GR for Georgius Rex (King George), on the side. They carry sackfuls of letters, postcards and parcels destined for all over. It's the very navel of the world!

I have to stop writing now as Miss Nosy Nugent is coming for half an hour to teach English grammar and stuff. *Groan.* I don't go to school because we have moved around so much. We have lived in London, Manchester, Belfast, Birmingham and Dublin. But I love Dublin best.

My mother wants me to learn Latin and improve my Mathematics so I can sit the scholarship exams for Alexandra College for Girls in Sandymount and the Dominican Convent in Eccles Street. Those schools believe in educating girls to be the same as men. My father says my mother should not be encouraging me in such notions. But Mother will bring him round. She believes in votes for women.

Miss Nugent says I will fail every exam on account of being so lazy. I don't care because school is probably full of very stuck-up young ladies – and I am not exactly a young lady. (This is a secret. Sometimes I pick my nose when no one is looking. And Jack and I have "passing wind" competitions. This is something we both excel in. Shame it is not a proper subject. We would be professors! But now that I am twelve I won't do those babyish things any more.)

I've peeked in his room and Jack has already sneaked out his window. I bet as I've been writing he has scrambled over the rooftops and is laughing at the people in bathrobes visiting the Hamman Turkish Baths, or he's larking around the Pagoda roof of the Dublin Bread Company and stealing a bun.

Or maybe something worse! When we were on holiday in the Lake District he learned how to climb with ropes and grappling irons, and now he practises all over Dublin's parapets. The rascal is planning to scale bridges next. He secretly plots dangerous forays. I found maps and drawings in his room of different routes around Dublin by rooftop. There are sketches of bridges: the Loopline Railway Bridge, a viaduct crossing the Liffey by the Customs House, Butt Bridge over to Tara Street, O'Connell Bridge, the Ha'penny footbridge and so on up to the Bridge at Knightsbridge Station on the way to the Phoenix Park. Miss Nugent would be amazed how carefully he plots his escapades! I told you he was clever.

My parents fear he has taken to drinking and gambling, sneaking out at all hours, and that that's why he's always hanging around Tom Clarke's tobacco shop in Little Britain Street. But, Dear Diary, as promised it's time for me to tell you a big secret . . . the truth is he really has joined Countess Markievicz's Boy Scouts . . . and as Tom Clarke is not just a tobacconist with a long droopy mustache like a walrus but, as Nancy says, a Fenian bomber who spent fifteen years in jail, well, all I can say is the sparks would be flying if my parents put two and two together!

Once I ran into Mr Clarke's shop for a dare. It is quite a fancy shop on the outside with big gold lettering and a swinging sign for "Titbits" magazine. It has a hugely high counter and leaning on it was a portly young gentleman in an overcoat. He was talking to Mr Clarke's wife, who is a sharp little woman and a bit scary, and he didn't see me come in.

I recognised him as Mr Pearse, the schoolmaster who wants everyone to talk Irish and writes poems. His first name is Patrick but lots of people call him by the Irish version of it which is Pádraig. My mother went to see him about Jack going to his school, Saint Enda's in Rathfarmham, when he was thrown out of Belvedere College. They would have taken him and she thought Mr Pearse has some very good ideas about education. But he was too romantic about ideas of blood sacrifice, she said. I thought this meant Jack would have to kill a goat or something, like Abraham in the bible, but my mother explained it meant dying for your country in a fight. Mr Pearse wants Ireland to be free of English rule even if we all have to die. But who will live in the country then, asks Nancy.

When Mother heard from Nancy that even some of the Irish nationalists had taken their children from the school, that put paid to that scheme.

Pearse looked very solemn and a bit squinty-eyed that day in the shop.

"It is a sacred duty," he was saying to Mr Clarke's wife. "The wives and dependents will be in good hands with you."

Mrs Clarke looked a bit sad when he said this, so perhaps she has a lot of things to worry about.

He then noticed that I was standing there like a gobdaw, so he smiled at me, bade Mrs Clarke good day and left.

Mrs Clarke was arranging the little tricolour badges she sells for a penny that the bakery boy, Tommy, was wearing this morning.

"Can I help you?" she said smartly.

"I-I-I was looking for my brother Jack," I stammered.

She visibly relaxed. "You're in the wrong place."

I didn't dare ever go back in again.

Anto swears all the Clarkes are able to shoot guns, including the children. And they even have a secret hidey-hole in the back of their privy. Anto talks such arrant nonsense, I'm amazed his nose isn't as long as Pinnochio's!

I am sworn not to tell my parents about Jack. Miss Nugent doesn't know how to control him – or me!

Dear Diary, I confess I sometimes join him – hitching up my skirts to shimmy up drainpipes and scramble on the roof of the Pillar Café and the Imperial Hotel. It is a bit scary but great fun. I am not as nimble or courageous as Jack and wouldn't dare do it without him, but now that I am twelve I will try to be braver.

My mother says I am too devoted to my brother and that I am like his shadow, that if he put his hand in the fire I would too. Alas, that is no longer true. Now he only wants to be with Anto and I am very sad.

But, in truth, Jack is as important to me as my own heartbeat. If anything ever happened to him, I fear I would pine so much I would die. I think I would do anything for him. I know it is silly but sometimes I dream he gets into trouble, and that only I can save him.

Miss Nugent has just come in downstairs. She has a face like a fish, bulging eyes, no chin and a mouth clamped shut in disapproval of everything. She has just come back from being a governess in India. That's why my father employed her – to give her a start, he said. Her real aim, Nancy says, is to trap someone into marrying her. She met some horrid old colonel on the boat who is staying in the same hotel as she is and she is laying siege to him.

"I would rather teach all the heathens in Asia than even one O'Donovan in this filthy godforsaken backwater," she says a thousand times a day.

I'd better go. Miss Nugent is calling me. But I only have to stand her for half an hour for an English lesson.

HANDS ON HISTORY

The Irish Civil War 1922-23

Ava's Diary

Life sucks for twelve-year-old Irish-American Ava when she is dragged back to Dublin by her mother after her parents' messy divorce. She is bullied at her new school and her only friend is moody teenage neighbour Mal, who has secrets of his own.

But when Ava finds a sliver of an emerald and a bundle of old letters in the attic, she is plunged into a historical mystery linking the missing crown jewels of Tsarist Russia to the heart of Ireland's bloody civil war in 1922.

As a newly independent Ireland split over supporting the new Free State or fighting on for a Republic, danger lurked around every corner and friends became foes. Who was the author of the letters, young medical student Molly O'Donovan? Why did her brother Jack the Cat smuggle the jewels from the United States and end up on the run from both sides? And did her football mad cousin Dan survive running messages through the crossfire?

Through the eyes of Molly, Ava encounters the death of Michael Collins, deadly ambushes in Kerry and the tragic fate of former comrades.

As Ava learns about the bitter civil war, she is forced to confront the conflict in her own life. Can the journey into the past help her to learn the importance of reconciliation and new beginnings?

ISBN 978-1-78199-8823

Patricia Murphy